An
American
In Paris

BOOKS BY SIOBHAN CURHAM

FICTION
Sweet FA
Frankie Says Relapse
The Scene Stealers

NON-FICTION
Antenatal & Postnatal Depression
Dare to Dream
Dare to Write a Novel
Something More: A Spiritual Misfit's Search for Meaning

AN
AMERICAN
IN PARIS

SIOBHAN CURHAM

Bookouture

Published by Bookouture in 2021

An imprint of Storyfire Ltd.
Carmelite House
50 Victoria Embankment
London EC4Y 0DZ

www.bookouture.com

ISBN: 978-1-80019-011-5
eBook ISBN: 978-1-80019-010-8

This novel is dedicated to my mum, Anne Cumming, and to the memory of my grandma, Florence Thomson.

'Day by day and night by night we were together – all else has long been forgotten by me.'

Walt Whitman

FLORENCE

June 1937, New York

As the ship's horn let out an almighty blast, I turned away from the crowds of people lining the harbour – the men raising their hats, the women waving their handkerchiefs – and tilted my face to the sun. My beloved Walt Whitman once said: 'Keep your face always towards the sunshine, and the shadows will fall behind you.' As the June warmth kissed my skin I pictured the shadows of my former life falling behind me. Joe Fraser and his bloodshot eyes and stale whisky breath. The manager of the Nylon Club and my ex-boss, Roxy, refusing to believe my account of what happened. Or rather, *choosing* not to believe me. There's an important difference. Then I pictured a shadow that was formed of sorrow rather than anger: my daddy, on his farm in Arkansas, surrounded by the chucks, horses and cattle. When I wrote him I was joining a dance troupe in Paris, he wrote back: 'So even New York City wasn't able to break you in, then.' My daddy was a man of few words. So few, in fact, I could pretty much write them all on a cigarette card:

Mornin'.
I'll be off to milk the cows, then.
Evenin'.

I took my cigarettes from my purse. The card inside was from a series of crazy predictions about the future, titled: *The Age of*

Power and Wonder. I looked to see what today's prediction would be. My previous favourite had been a card prophesying that one day, television presenters would be able to broadcast live from the seabed. I gazed over the railings at the widening expanse of water between the ship and the harbour. While I loved the notion of being able to journey to the seabed and film whatever weird and wonderful critters might be down there, now I was about to be afloat on the ocean for at least six days, I wasn't so sure I wanted to know what might be lurking under the waves. Leastways, not until I was back on dry land.

I looked back at the card. 'A time is coming when men will no longer need to employ men to do menial work,' it read, next to a picture of a goggly-eyed figure made from metal, kind of how I imagined the Tin Woodman from the book *The Wonderful Wizard of Oz* to look. 'Many experiments have been made in providing domestic mechanical servants,' the card went on. *Hmm.* Didn't men have that already, in the shape of women? I lit my cigarette and glanced around. Some of the passengers were starting to head inside the ship, no doubt to become acquainted with their cabins. But I was enjoying the salt air and sunshine too much — and boy, did I need it.

I moved along the deck towards the rear of the ship. I was pretty sure there had to be a technical term for the rear, just like left and right were port and starboard. I decided to make it my mission to learn all I could about seafaring from this trip. I never liked to pass up the opportunity for a little self-education. I found a spot by the railings and drank in the view. The sea stretched out like a fresh grey slate in front of me, which felt kind of symbolic. The further out we got, the more the breeze picked up, whipping around my neck and waking me from the daze I'd been in ever since Fraser attacked me, or tried to attack me. He hadn't figured on my acrobatic skills coming in just as useful for self-defence as they did for dancing. I thought of my high kick cracking into his chin and finally I was able to smile at the memory – now I knew he wouldn't be able to dispatch one of his hoodlums to deal with me. A thick black plume of smoke billowed from the ship's funnel and there was another loud honk of the horn, as if the captain, or whoever the hell blows the horn on a ship, was celebrating the fact that my daring dream was coming true.

When I'd told my old school pal Rosalie I was going to France, her jaw had fallen open and she'd stared at me like I'd told her I was setting sail for Timbuktu.

'You can't spend your whole life running away from things, Florence,' she'd said with a dramatic sigh. Dramatic sighs were Rosalie's speciality, and she seemed to reserve the most dramatic for me. But what she didn't understand was that I was never running *from* things, I was always running *to* them. To something better, brighter, more filled with adventure. It was why I'd left Arkansas for New York, and it was why I was leaving New York for Paris. I believed with every fibre of my being that life was far too precious to waste a single moment someplace that wasn't making me happy. Or, as my beloved Walt would say: 'Dismiss whatever insults your own soul; and your very flesh shall be a great poem.' I wanted my life to be a great poem – or a great song and dance at least! And if I couldn't make that happen in Gay Paree then, quite frankly, there was no hope for me.

SAGE

March 2018, London

As Sage struggled to open her make-up-clogged eyes, she glimpsed a blurred trail on the bedroom floor. Adidas trainers... heeled boots... camisole top... crumpled T-shirt... skinny jeans... much larger jeans... boxer shorts, fraying at the waist... bra... men's socks... thong... empty condom wrapper. As she searched through the fog of her hangover for the story behind the trail, she heard the ragged breath of someone in the bed beside her and tequila-flavoured bile burned in her throat. Only a week ago she'd written a post about how the first moments upon waking were critical in determining how your day would pan out.

'Starting your day with nourishment, gratitude and joy sets you up for an awesome day to come,' she'd written. 'Write a gratitude list. Drink lemon water. Move your body.' She'd posted a heavily filtered photo of herself holding a gratitude journal alongside the caption, with a hipster-style jam jar of lemon water artfully positioned at the front of the shot. Sage was all too aware that if she moved her body right now, she would more than likely vomit. So she lay, corpse-like, and tried to recollect the chain of events from the night before that had led her to here. She had a flashback of pounding music and lightning strobes. The chink of glasses. The downing of 'Shot! Shot! Shot!'s. A man pulling her towards him on the dancefloor. His arms around her. Her head resting briefly on his shoulder. The sweet sensation of being held.

Cut to club toilet. Snorting a line between the welt-like cigarette burns on top of the cistern. Picking up her phone.

Sage frowned as she tried to recall what had happened next. The fog of her hangover was too thick to penetrate and dread began budding inside her. She gingerly leaned over the edge of the bed and scanned the floor for any sign of her phone. The man lying beside her grunted. Why had she brought him back here? She never brought hook-ups back to her place, for obvious reasons. Another fragment from last night drifted back to her: 'I've missed the last train out of London. An Uber back to Brighton will cost at least a ton. Be a sweetheart…'

She sat up and it was as if the whole world had tilted on its axis. Fighting the urge to retch, she looked around the room. Her bag was lying on its side by the doors to the balcony. Somehow, she managed to stumble her way over to it. But all that was inside was her purse, a pack of cigarette papers, some gum and her emergency tampon. Then she had another flashback, this time of leaning against the toilet wall, talking into her phone. Maybe she'd called someone? Or had she made a video? Had she *posted* a video? Her head started pounding. The man in her bed rolled over, belched and opened his eyes.

Another of Sage's posts came back to haunt her, one she'd written on Valentine's Day. 'If you don't love yourself, you'll never be able to truly love another #selflove #selfloverules.' She'd posted it along with the photo of a spray-painted heart she'd found on a wall in Brick Lane. She didn't really get the statement to be honest, but it was something she'd seen a million times online and in magazines, so she knew it would garner a lot of likes. And it had. Forty-five thousand, six hundred and seventy-one to be precise. But surely what had happened between her and Tom was living proof that the statement was complete crap. She'd had no trouble loving him during their three-year relationship, in spite of his cheating and her subsequent self-loathing.

'Morning, sexy,' last night's man said, shifting into a semi-upright position. It wasn't until he lustfully eyed her up and down that she realised she was naked.

'Morning.' Her voice came out dry and raspy. 'Have you seen my phone?'

The man shook his head and reached for his own phone on the nightstand beside him. His arms were covered in tattoos, a mismatching collage of a serpent, anchor, Celtic cross and what looked like a football club emblem. As he started scrolling, rage bubbled inside of Sage. In her list of what not to do when waking up in bed with another human, scrolling through your phone was right at the top.

'You're going to have to go,' she said coldly.

He looked up. 'What, don't I even get a cup of tea?'

'I don't do bed and breakfast,' she replied, looking on top of her dressing table. There was still no sign of her phone. *Damn.* Had she left it in the club?

'Don't be like that,' the man wheedled. God, she hated wheedling voices, especially when she had a clanging headache.

'Like what?'

'So uptight.'

'I'm not uptight,' she snapped.

'Yeah, well you certainly weren't last night,' he said, with a chortle that made her already clammy skin crawl. Then he frowned. 'Have we met before – before last night, I mean? You look kind of familiar.'

Her stomach churned. 'I very much doubt it.' She turned away and pulled a T-shirt and some joggers from her wardrobe. *Please, please, please, just get up and leave*, she silently willed as she quickly got dressed.

'Nice place you've got here,' he said, picking his jeans up from the floor.

'Thanks.'

'Must have cost a fair bit, being in Primrose Hill. Isn't this where all the celebrities live?'

She remained silent.

He put on his T-shirt. It said: '*SPACE IBIZA*' on the front. That figured. He had the craggy face, floppy hair and gold Cuban neck chain that screamed raver. *Elderly* raver. Last night in the dim lighting of the club he'd seemed boyish and fun, but now... Now he looked as if he was well into his forties, which meant that technically he could be old enough to be her father. Sage had another awkward flashback, of her hands pulling at that T-shirt, tugging it over his head. She swallowed hard. Why had she done this again? Why had she had another soulless one-night stand? She knew they always left her feeling hollow.

The man hoiked up his jeans and put his phone in his back pocket. 'All right then, love, I'll be off.'

I'm not your love, Sage thought. Cue another flashback, of her on top of him, his hands cupping her breasts. The comfort of feeling him inside her. The power of hearing him moan. The rush of her orgasm. That was why she did it. These days, it was the only time she actually felt something. But however powerful the wave of ecstasy, it left as quickly as it rushed in, sucking her will to live out with it. She stood rooted to the spot as the man walked past her. *Don't go. I'm not really a bitch. Please, could you just hold me again?* She snapped to her senses and followed him out of the bedroom in time to see him glancing at the framed YouTube awards on the wall in the hallway.

'This way,' she said, guiding him to the door. 'The lift's just outside on the left.'

'OK, thanks.' He looked at her curiously again.

'Bye,' she said, practically pushing him out of the door.

Once he'd gone and she'd heard the reassuring ping of the lift doors opening, she leaned against the wall and breathed a sigh of relief. Then she headed for the kitchen and put some coffee on to brew.

'This kitchen's wasted on you,' her mum, Elizabeth, had said, laughing, the day she came to visit for the first time. And it was true. The kitchen was larger than the entire studio apartment Sage had been living in before. With its acres of black marble counter space, huge stove and American-sized fridge and freezer, it was the kind of kitchen built for a family or someone who loved to cook. Sage was neither of those things.

'Yeah well, the fridge will come in handy for all my leftover takeaways,' she'd joked back. 'And you know you're welcome to come any time and cook me dinner.'

They'd both laughed at this. Elizabeth was as reluctant a cook as her daughter, or rather, she had been. Sage felt a sharp stab of pain as she mentally corrected her mum's tense from present to past. It was coming up on a year since Elizabeth had died and Sage still hadn't got her head around the fact that she was really gone. She searched the loaded dishwasher for the least dirty cup and gave it a rinse. Then she opened her laptop and went straight to her YouTube page to check she hadn't posted anything there last night.

Thankfully, the page was exactly as she'd left it the morning before, with a video extolling the virtues of clean eating. She'd posted it while licking the fat from her fingers following a bacon and sausage ciabatta. The number '213' hovered in red over the notification bell, a sign that always used to give her a heady dopamine hit, but now it elicited nothing. She opened another window and clicked on her Instagram page. As soon as it opened, she saw a sight that made her mouth go even drier. The most recent post was an image of her, with black make-up smears beneath bloodshot eyes and her top half falling off her shoulder. Then she saw the little 'play' icon that made her realise it wasn't a photo, it was a video. She clicked on the post and read the first of the 498 comments.

'What a state! #trainwreck'

'Isn't it time Sage Segal got cancelled? #loser'

'I can't believe she said that!!! ⊗'

With trembling fingers, Sage pressed 'play'.

FLORENCE

June 1937, Paris

I arrived in France having learned two things: number one, the rear of the boat was called the stern. Number two, tragically, I did not possess sea legs, which was hugely ironic considering what my legs were able to do and how far they'd gotten me. I was so grateful to get back on dry land, I felt like throwing myself onto the harbour floor and wailing a thousand thank yous. But I really didn't want my French adventure to get off on the wrong foot, and besides, I was too weak from hunger for any kind of prostrating. Pretty much the only thing I'd been able to stomach the entire trip was water and dry crackers. As I held my case close to me and hurried to the station, I vowed that if I ever did return to America, it would be by plane. After all, if it was good enough for Charles Lindbergh, it was good enough for me. I smiled as I thought of my eleven-year-old self, huddled by the radio in the kitchen, listening breathless to the news that Lindbergh's *Spirit of St. Louis* had touched down in France safely. Once I'd done my chores, I spent the whole of the next day racing around the farm with my arms outstretched like the wings of a plane.

After an unfortunate mix-up at the station, which saw me mistaking the gentlemen's bathroom for the powder room, I found my way to my train carriage and hoisted my case onto the shelf above my seat. I used to be self-conscious about my height, just as I was self-conscious about my lack of curves – I used to hate it as a kid when Daddy called me his 'string bean'; oh, how I longed to be called something soft and voluptuous, like 'peach' – but by the time I'd turned twenty-one I wasn't all that bothered. I guess I'd come to see the advantage of having legs like a pair of stilts and how they were a ticket to a life of high-kicking adventure.

Once my case was safely housed, I sat down and began my favourite sport of observing my fellow passengers without it appearing as if I was observing them. Pretending to read provides a magnificent cover for this pastime. So I took my battered copy of Walt Whitman poems from my purse and opened it on a random page. Well, I say random, but due to chronic over-reading, it automatically fell open at the start of my favourite, 'Song of Myself'. I glanced over the top of the book at the woman sitting opposite me. Instantly, my heart sank. She was so perfect, she looked more like a china doll than a flesh-and-blood human being. Her hat was tilted so that it cut a sharp angle across her forehead, and tumbling out from beneath were the most perfectly styled black curls I had ever seen. She was wearing an immaculately tailored dress, the colour of claret, nipped in at the waist to accentuate her hourglass hips. And her lips were as plump and glossy as a juicy ripe strawberry. I'd chosen to wear my favourite grey trouser suit with a rose-pink fedora for my arrival in Paris but, seen through the prism of this mannequin of perfection, I felt *très* dreary and awkward. This must have been what Bessie meant in the postscript to her last letter: 'PS: The women here are so chic they make you want to be just like them AND stab their eyes out with envy.'

The doll woman shifted her gaze from the window to me. I quickly looked down at my book and read the first line to boost my flagging spirits: 'I celebrate myself and sing myself.' I closed my eyes and imagined Walt with his bushy white hair and long white beard actually uttering those words to me. I'd first started pretending that Walt Whitman was my long-lost grandfather when I was about thirteen. With no mom, and a father who preferred talking to cattle than humans, it had seemed like the most enterprising option. If I couldn't have a family member to confide my greatest hopes and deepest fears in, then dang it, I'd invent one!

A sharp-suited man entered the carriage and sat down next to doll-woman. I spied him glancing sideways at her legs. Then he said something to her in French. For a moment, I was mesmerised. Is there any language more beautiful than French? For all I knew he could have been saying, 'I like to feast on slugs and rotting eggs,' but it still would have sounded divine.

Doll-woman said something in response, her voice as soft and melodic as a lullaby. Bessie used to say that my Southern drawl was the sexiest thing she'd ever heard, but obviously that was before she moved to Paris, when she'd only had the nasal twang of New Yorkers to compare it to. I gazed blankly at my book and let their voices wash over me. I only knew a few words of French at that point, but it was my greatest ambition to become fluent before I left Paris. If only I'd known then that by the time I left Paris, I would be fluent in so much more.

The train's whistle blew, followed by a loud hiss of steam, and we slowly started chugging from the station. I gazed out of the window as the drab grey stone brightened into the vivid green of fields. Oh boy, was I happy to see grass and trees. There had been times at sea, usually when I was hunched over the toilet in my cabin, retching, that I'd started giving up hope I'd ever be reunited with terra firma again.

The man's voice grew louder and even though I couldn't understand what he was saying, I could definitely detect an undercurrent of innuendo. It was something I'd become an expert at fending off in the four years I'd been dancing. Usually, the sharpness of my tongue was enough to defuse it. Or, in Joe

Fraser's case, the deftness of a well-aimed kick. I gazed back at
the trees, comforting myself with the fact that I was now a whole
continent away from Fraser and his warped fantasies.

Doll-woman said something with a new sharpness to her tone.
I glanced over just in time to see the man look away, red-faced.
I couldn't help feeling a little disappointed that the first French
man I'd encountered had turned out to be a sleaze. I had been
hoping that once I was in the country that had invented romance,
I'd finally meet a man who didn't have his brain located in his
pants. A man who would talk to me for hours about music, life
and poetry. A man who would woo me with imaginative gestures
that would inflame my very spirit. Surely a man like this had to
exist? Knowing my lousy luck, my perfect soul mate did exist,
but was living in an igloo in outer Antarctica, or somewhere
equally unreachable. I looked back at my book. I didn't need a
man, I reminded myself. I was more than capable of making a
song of myself.

Five hours later, as I hauled my suitcase along what felt like a
never-ending road to nowhere in the heart of Paris, I felt like
less of a song and more of a funeral dirge. I'd decided against
taking the Métro to Montmartre and chose to walk from Gare
Saint-Lazare instead, reasoning that a gal can only take so many
new adventures in one day. I thought I'd be safer walking, less
likely to get lost. Bessie had said in her letter that it should take
no more than half an hour to get to my new lodgings – 'Twenty
minutes on your long legs.' But I must have made a wrong turning
somewhere. To make matters worse, the sun was like a furnace.
The deodorant I was wearing was supposed to 'Turn armpits into
charmpits', according to the advertisement, but I feared the smell
that was now emanating from them was more akin to a cesspit.
I paused to wipe my brow and take a breath. Automobiles raced

past like shiny black beetles scuttling. Everyone who passed me on the sidewalk seemed so carefree and gay – and so certain of where they were going! I have to say that by that point, the French language was beginning to lose its charm for me. The thought of being lost and alone someplace no one could understand me was more than slightly alarming. I took a right down a side street, as much to get some shade from the tall buildings as anything, and I spied an elderly man in a flat cap and shirtsleeves, sweeping the path outside his shop. I headed over to him.

'*Excusez-moi?*'

'*Oui?*'

So far, so good. I held out Bessie's letter with the address of my lodgings on it. 'Could you tell me how to get to Montmartre, to this address please, I mean, *s'il vous plaît?*'

The man frowned at me, then looked back at the page. He chattered something in French, which I had no hope of understanding, pointed along the street, then gestured right.

'Thank you. *Merci!*' I exclaimed and carried on my way.

I walked until I saw a turning on my right, and there, looming above the narrow street was a sight that made my heart sing with relief. Could it be…? I looked back at Bessie's letter. 'Look out for the church on top of the hill that resembles three huge white breasts,' she'd written. Bessie was obsessed with the human anatomy, especially when it came to pleasure. 'The church is called Sacré-Coeur. Climb to the top of the hill and you will be in Montmartre!' I was so happy to see the church, I found a sudden burst of energy, which lasted approximately three minutes – the time it took to reach the foot of the hill and be presented with the tallest, steepest set of stone steps I had ever encountered. The thought of dragging my case up this man-made mountain was too much to bear. So I opened my case and took out the bottle of soda I'd bought at a kiosk outside the station. It was warm and sickly, but in that moment, it was like drinking nectar from heaven. I downed about half the bottle, then put it back in my case and began my ascent. But after about five steps, calamity struck. I obviously hadn't shut my case properly, because all of a sudden it flew open and all of the contents scattered in a wide arc around me.

'Darn it!' I yelped as I crouched down and started to retrieve them as fast as I could. All the while, I was aware of feet hurrying by me. Feet no doubt belonging to the effortlessly chic and carefree French, the polar opposite to me, with my frazzled hair, cesspit armpits and burning cheeks.

I heard a man say something in French right behind me and then a hand appeared, holding a pair of my nylons. *Oh, Lord have mercy!*

'Thank you!' I said, grabbing them without daring to look at the hand's owner.

'Aha, you are English,' the voice said. I was so overjoyed to hear my native tongue, I spun around.

The owner of the voice was tall and wiry and about my age, with floppy brown hair and big brown eyes as a soulful as a puppy dog's. But it was his smile that I noticed more than anything. It was so relaxed, a smile that conjured words in my mind like 'lolling', 'ambling' and 'meandering'.

'Actually, I'm American,' I said, when I'd finally composed myself enough to speak.

'How do you do?' He held out his hand. The formality of his address was in sharp contrast with his appearance. His shirt was half-untucked with sleeves rolled up, and his trousers were baggy with a patch on the knee.

I had no option but to shake his hand, still crouching there on the steps, surrounded by my undergarments. 'I guess I didn't shut it properly,' I said by way of explanation as I repacked my case, then shut it and checked the catches twice over.

'An easy mistake.' He treated me to that sleepy grin again. 'Hey, did you forget this?' He handed me my book of Walt Whitman poetry.

'Oh, yes, thank you.'

'May I compliment you on your taste?'

I frowned at him. Was this guy a chancer, or was he genuinely a fan of Walt?

'Are you familiar with his poems?' I asked.

'Of course.'

I still wasn't sure if he was feeding me a line. I realised I was hardly a prime catch, what with my frizzy hair and sweaty armpits and all, but some men truly weren't fussy. 'So, which is your favourite poem of his?'

'"I Saw in Louisiana a Live-Oak Growing",' he replied instantly.

Hmm. I still wasn't convinced. At the ripe old age of twenty-one, I'd become pretty cynical when it came to men. 'Do you have a favourite line from the poem?'

He nodded. '"It grew there uttering joyous leaves of dark green."' He gazed off dreamily to some trees on the hill. 'I love how Whitman saw leaves as joyful exclamations. I have never looked at a tree in the same way since reading that poem.'

I stared at him, fighting the urge to grin. I loved that line too. Every spring when the leaves grew back on the trees on our farm, it felt as if they were joyfully uttering: *We're here! We're back again!*

'Would you like some help?' he asked, looking back at me. 'With your case?'

Ordinarily I would never have admitted defeat. But it was so hot and I was feeling so weak by that point, I had no choice but to nod numbly.

'Which is your favourite poem of his?' he asked, taking the case from me.

'"Song of Myself".'

'That isn't a poem, that is a bible!'

'What do you mean?'

His cheeks flushed. 'I mean it is something to live by, no?'

By this point I'd started to wonder if I was having some weird kind of heat-induced hallucination. Ever since I'd first read 'Song of Myself', I had tried to live my life by it. I'd never thought of it as a bible, though, and I had to admit, I kind of liked the idea. I sure found a lot more inspiration in the Gospel According to Walt than I did in the gospels I'd studied in Bible lessons at school.

'Where are you headed?' he asked as we made our way up the steps.

'To my new lodgings.' A shiver of excitement ran up my spine as I uttered those words.

'You are living here, in Paris?' His eyes widened.

I nodded. 'How about you?'

'I am just visiting – this time. I plan to move here for good next year.' He gave a wistful smile. 'I am Otto. Otto Weiss, from Austria.'

'Nice to meet you, Otto Weiss, from Austria. I'm Florence. Florence Thornton from Arkansas.'

'Ah, you are named after the most beautiful place in all of Italy.'

'You've been?'

'Yes, as a child. My parents and I went there on holiday.'

As we climbed the steps, Otto told me all about Florence, which I have to say was a wonderful distraction from the heat. Finally, we reached the summit and the three white breasts of the church loomed over us.

'Wow!' I exclaimed. It looked even more spectacular up close.

'It is quite something, no?' Otto grinned. 'And it is even more beautiful inside. Although I'm not sure I'm supposed to enjoy a Catholic church quite so much, being Jewish.'

I laughed. 'I like to imagine that God doesn't mind where you choose to meet with him.'

Otto nodded. 'I like that idea. So, where is it you have to go?'

'I'm not exactly sure. I mean, I know the address but I don't know how to get there.' I took Bessie's letter from my pocket. 'Place du Tertre.'

Otto gave me the kind of goofy grin you'd expect to see on a jackpot winner. 'You are going to be living in the Place du Tertre?' he exclaimed.

'I guess so, yes.'

He clapped his hand to his heart. 'That is where Picasso once lived. And Renoir, he lived just around the corner.'

'Swell.' Much as it was interesting to discover these facts, I was a little too hot and bothered to share Otto's ecstasy.

'I'm sorry. I am an artist. Or at least, I dream to be. They are my heroes.'

'Aha.' That explained a lot. Otto's scruffy demeanour might have looked a little out of place amongst the chic Parisians, but I knew straight away that he'd look right at home behind an easel.

'Oh boy – as you Americans would say.' He smiled at me. 'You are in for a treat.'

I couldn't help feeling encouraged by his enthusiasm, in spite of my exhaustion.

'This way,' he said, leading me along a cobbled street to the left of the church.

'Oh, you don't have to take me right there. Pointing me in the right direction would be just fine,' I called after him. But he was already charging on ahead.

I heard and smelled Place du Tertre before I saw it. The lilting accordion music, the sweet aroma of what I would soon come to learn were freshly made crêpes. We turned a corner and I stood, transfixed, by the prettiest, liveliest place I'd ever seen. A square lined with cafés and restaurants and trees, and dotted everywhere in between were artists, painting away at their easels. I saw instantly why Otto was so crazy about it.

'Isn't it magnificent?' he said.

I nodded, speechless. Groups of people were sitting at tables outside the cafés and restaurants, chatting animatedly, their chairs arranged so they were all facing out. I wasn't sure whether this was in order to see or to be seen. They all looked so colourful. So interesting. And for the first time in my life, I saw black and white people eating and drinking together openly. It was a sight that made every cell in my body sing.

'What number building do you need?' Otto asked.

Instantly, my New York City street smarts kicked in. Although he seemed like a real nice guy, I wasn't so sure I wanted a man knowing my new address before I'd even moved in.

Otto must have read this in my expression because he quickly handed me my case. 'Here. I'm sorry. I should leave you now. You are bound to find it yourself.'

'Thank you.' I took the case from him and as our fingers brushed, I felt the strangest sensation. Like a spark of static. I guess he must have felt it too, from the way he was looking at me.

'I was wondering...' he said.

'Yes?'

'Tomorrow, it is my last day in Paris and, if you are free, would you like to come to the Musée du Louvre with me?'

'The Louvre museum?' I recognised the name from the list of places I'd made, titled: 'Places I have to see before I die – Paris edition'.

He nodded. 'I realise that we have only just met, but I am like Whitman in the poem. I do not know how a live-oak can be so happy on its own, without a friend near. It would be wonderful to have a companion to admire the art with.'

I would tell Otto later that this was the line that clinched it for me. I couldn't help thinking it was a sign from Walt himself. 'I would like that, yes.'

'So, what do you say we meet outside Sacré-Coeur, the church, at eleven?'

Bessie had told me in her letter that I wouldn't have to start rehearsals for a couple of days after my arrival, so I knew I was free. 'Sure.'

He grinned, then shook my hand again. 'It was so very nice to meet you, Florence.'

'You too, Otto.'

He strode off the way we'd come and I set off around the square, my hand still tingling from where his had brushed it.

SAGE

March 2018

'Hey guys!' Sage slurred on the video. 'I think it's time for a reality check.'

Even though she'd spent most of the last four years watching herself on video, nothing could have prepared Sage for the dread she was now feeling, as she viewed her latest Instagram post.

'Cos when you think about it, nothing in this social media world is really real, is it?' Video-Sage continued, giving a loud sniff and wiping her nose with the back of her hand. *Shit.* It was so obvious she was high. Hopefully the viewers wouldn't realise. 'Like, I tell you how to live every single day. How to be successful. How to be happy. How to find love.' At this point, Video-Sage snorted with laughter. 'Hashtag irony! And you suck it all up like a load of dumb – what's that word? What's that thing, that like, jumps mindlessly off a cliff?' Video-Sage swayed slightly. 'Lemmings, that's it. You're all like lemmings, the way you follow people like me. Why can't you make your own mind up about things? Why do you need my opinion on everything? Can't you see that it's all fake? That we're all just trying to make money out of you?' At this point, Video-Sage erupted into laughter again. 'I can't believe how much money I get paid just to tell you guys that I bought a scented candle that smells like frickin' Christmas, or that you should drink green juice out of a jam jar. And don't even get me started on the avocados! What's wrong with you people?'

Sage shuddered. All of the deepest, darkest thoughts she'd been bottling up for the past few months were being laid bare for all to see.

Video-Sage sniffed again. 'Stop being such dumb little followers and start thinking for yourselves.'

Oh God, please let this be the end, Sage silently pleaded, as Video-Sage swayed to one side. In the background, there was the sound of a door opening, bringing with it a wave of pulsing music.

'Better go, cos I've got a man waiting for me and I'm going to take him home and guess what?' Video-Sage loomed so close to the camera, the screen was filled with the image of the locket around her neck. 'We're going to have sex and I don't even know his name.' There was one more burst of laughter and then finally, the video ended.

'Shit, shit, shit, shit, shit!' Sage mumbled, looking back at the comments.

'What a slag'

'OMG! I can't believe she's so two-faced'

'Unfollowed!'

On and on and on they went. Finally, Sage snapped out of her shocked daze. She had to delete the video. It had only been up for – she checked the time – ten hours. She pressed 'delete', leaned back in her chair and took a breath to try and ground herself. She wondered if her manager, Danny, had seen the video. Someone at the talent agency was bound to have seen it and alerted him. She had to find her phone. He'd probably been trying to get hold of her. She poured herself a cup of coffee and headed for the bathroom. And there, on the side of the sink, was her phone, the screen filled with notifications. Sage perched on the side of the bath and began to read. Five missed calls from Danny. *Shit.* It was OK though, at least she'd taken down the video. She pressed redial and started mentally practising her excuses.

It was late. I was drunk. Someone must have spiked my drink.

And then, 'Sage! What the hell?'

'Danny, I'm so sorry. I had too much to drink. It had been a really bad day. But don't worry, I've deleted the video.'

'It's too late. It's already been on *The Late Show* in America, and now it's all over Twitter.'

'*The Late Show?*' Sage slid onto the floor.

'Yes, the host did quite the routine about it. You're going to have to come into the office and we'll brainstorm ideas for an apology video. In the meantime, I'll issue a release saying that you weren't in your right mind. Is there anything we can use as an excuse? Something other than you'd had a skin-full?'

Sage smarted. She knew she'd messed up but did he really have to be so harsh?

'Hang on a minute, isn't it coming up to the anniversary of your mum's death?'

'Yes, but…'

'Excellent. We'll use that. See you later.' The line went dead.

Danny's chosen excuse was actually painfully close to the mark. Sage *had* been struggling as the anniversary of Elizabeth's death grew closer, but there was no way she was going to use her mother to get some kind of sympathy vote. As an older mother – she had had Sage when she was forty-six – and a bookish university professor, Elizabeth had never got the whole social media thing, and Sage had kept her out of all her online postings.

'You really made all the money for this place by making videos?' Elizabeth had asked, wide-eyed, on that first visit to the flat.

'And writing posts,' Sage had answered defensively. Back then, she'd still felt excited by her new-found fame and fortune; she'd even felt proud of it. She loved the writing side of what she did. She'd even dreamed of one day writing a self-help book – oh, the irony.

'But I don't understand,' Elizabeth had said, stepping onto the balcony and gazing out at Primrose Hill. 'How does that make you so much money?'

'It's all about marketing reach,' Sage had informed her. 'Mine's huge because I have so many people following me, so I get paid loads for ads and product endorsements.'

Elizabeth had smiled and shook her head. 'Well, as long as you're happy, *ma princesse…*' Elizabeth had left her native France at the age of twenty, but she'd always retained her accent and her fondness for French terms of endearment.

And Sage *had* been happy then. Or at least, she'd thought so. She'd just bought her dream apartment. She'd met Tom, her supposed dream boyfriend. Everywhere she'd gone, teenage girls had giggled and gazed at her adoringly, and young women had wanted to be her friend. The happiness hadn't lasted, though. Maybe it had never been real. Maybe she'd only ever been viewing things through a rose-tinted filter.

She hauled herself up off the floor and got into the shower, scrubbing and scrubbing at her skin until it was red raw. But she still felt numb. Even in the middle of what she knew was a crisis, she found it hard to really care. She turned the water off, wrapped herself in a towel and went back to her bedroom to stare at her reflection in the wardrobe mirror. Her long legs were thinner than ever and her face looked hollowed out. Instinctively, she felt for her locket. Her mother had worn the locket every day of her life. It had been found around her neck when she was discovered as a newborn baby, abandoned in a Paris church. As Sage clutched it, she felt an instant rush of relief. There were two birds engraved on the silver oval disc, hooked together by their talons, and the words *'We were together'* around the edge. There was a tiny hinge on the side of the locket that indicated half of it was missing, but it had always been this way. Even though she'd never liked talking about her history, Elizabeth had treasured the locket as the only thing connecting her to her birth mother. Now, it was doing the same for Sage.

'I miss you,' she whispered. Then she sat down at her dressing table and began making up her face with the focus of an artist at their easel. Sage had never really been that into make-up, but as soon as she'd signed with Danny's Spark Agency, he'd hammered home to her that make-over videos were the way forward if she wanted to grow her AdSense revenue. He hadn't been wrong, and so Sage had become a somewhat reluctant beauty vlogger.

After twenty minutes of toning, shading, highlighting and plucking, Sage was transformed, her eyes made wide and bright and her cheeks glowing. She filled her take-out cup with coffee, picked up her phone and car keys and took the lift down to the basement car park. It was only when she was pulling out that she noticed that a small crowd had gathered at the front of the building.

'There she is!' she heard someone yell, and the figures came swarming like wasps up the narrow side street towards her. Without looking back, she put her foot down and roared away.

Sage emerged into the open-plan office of the Spark Agency and looked around. Danny was standing by the water cooler dressed in his usual uniform of skinny jeans, polo shirt and Converse; an outfit that would look cool on a skater boy but looked slightly questionable on a balding man of fifty with the beginnings of a paunch. He took one look at her and came hurrying over.

'Sage. Oh wow, what a shitstorm.'

'I'm sorry.' She looked down at the floor. She'd never had a father-figure in her life, so, as her manager, Danny was the closest she'd come to one. It did not feel good to lose his approval.

Thankfully, his expression softened. 'Don't worry. Today's news is tomorrow's chip paper, as my old man used to say. Right, we need to get you out of that make-up.'

'What?'

'You look too polished. It's probably best if you go make-up free for the video. And, not that I'm telling you what to do or anything, but if you feel the urge to cry, you know, don't fight it.'

'But—'

'I've sent out the release. Mentioned your mum dying of cancer, etc, etc. Hopefully that will win people back over.'

'Oh hey, Sage.' Danny's assistant Allison came hurrying over. 'Danny, I've just had Green Goddess Smoothies on the phone. They're pulling the endorsement deal.'

'Shit.' Danny frowned. 'That's the third we've lost today.'

'Seriously?' Sage's heart began thudding.

'Go and take off your make-up and let's get that video shot and online ASAP. But let me see it first before you post it, OK?'

'OK.' Sage looked at Allison. 'Do you have any make-up remover?'

'Yes, we've got some of the samples from your range for Boots.'

'Which has also been put on hold,' Danny interjected.

'Oh.'

Sage trudged through to the toilets with a bottle of her Sage Says Cleanse cleanser, which was now likely to become a collector's item. Not that anyone would want to collect it, by the sounds of things. Against her better judgement, she took out her phone and checked Twitter. Her notifications were through the roof. People declaring that they were unfollowing her. People calling her names. People demanding that other people unfollow her. Even though she'd deleted it from her Instagram, the clips from her video that had been featured on *The Late Show* had gone viral. Someone had even turned one of the parts where she sniffed into a GIF with the caption 'DON'T DO DRUGS, KIDS.' She dabbed some cleanser onto a piece of toilet tissue and started rubbing at her face, harder and harder, until all of the carefully applied make-up had gone and her eyes stung.

'Stupid, stupid, stupid!' she said to her reflection. Why had she made that video? What had she been thinking? She ruffled her hair and went back into the office.

'That's more like it,' Danny said, nodding appraisingly. 'OK, we need it to look like you've shot this at home, with no staging. Beth's set something up for you in her office.'

Beth was the publicity manager at Spark, all bleached teeth and hair extensions, with a fake tan to match her personality.

'Hey, babe,' she said, with faux warmth, as Sage walked through the door. 'Are you ready to do your video?'

Sage nodded. She had the weirdest feeling of disconnect, as if she were viewing her life the way she would watch a movie, rather than directly participating in it.

'So, we need you to say you're like, really sorry. What with your mum's anniversary coming up, you weren't thinking straight and you had too much to drink, and obviously you didn't mean any of it.'

But I did, Sage thought, with a sickening realisation. *I meant every word.*

'I'm going to close the blinds to make the lighting as dull as possible,' Beth said, going over to the window. 'And obviously don't use any filters – apart from Gingham, maybe, as that's quite a good one for washing the colour out.'

'Right.'

'And maybe you could start to cry at some point?'

Sage nodded numbly. It seemed as if everyone wanted her to cry, but the truth was, she hadn't properly cried since her mother's funeral. She'd been scared that if she started, she'd never stop.

Beth tapped her long, baby pink nails on the desk. 'Do you want me to stay with you, babe, or would you rather do it on your own?'

'On my own, please.'

'OK, cool. If you could do it against that plain bit of wall, that would be great.' Beth gestured to the one bit of wall space that wasn't covered with framed prints of inspirational quotes like 'LIVE, LOVE, LAUGH' and 'DANCE LIKE NO ONE'S WATCHING'. 'Then you can make out you've filmed it at home.'

Sage watched as Beth left the room. She didn't know what to say. She felt wrung out with hunger and exhaustion. But then, finally, a thought cut through the numbness in her brain. *This is all total bullshit.* She held out her phone and turned the camera on.

FLORENCE

June 1937

According to Bessie, my new lodgings were above a restaurant named La Crémaillère. I walked around the square, scanning each restaurant front, trying to appear nonchalant, as if strolling around Parisian squares was all a part of my daily routine. As I passed a couple of the artists, they called out to me. I kept my head held high and turned away, as if I was far too busy knowing exactly where I was going to notice them.

The restaurant turned out to be on the opposite side of the square from the corner I'd entered. I can't tell you how relieved I was when I saw the dark green façade and the elegant gold lettering. I took a moment to dab at the sweat on my brow with my handkerchief before entering. It was everything I'd imagined a Parisian restaurant to be, and then some. The walls were the colour of caramel, with intricately carved wooden covings. Large mirrors in gilt frames hung at regular intervals, making the place seem double its size, and circular fans on the ceiling hummed, bringing a welcome relief from the heat. It was late afternoon, so most of the tables were empty, set with dazzling glasses and gleaming cutlery, ready for the evening service. I hurried over to the bar, with Bessie's letter in hand. A stocky man of about thirty was standing behind the bar, polishing glasses.

'*Bonjour. Je m'appelle* Florence. I am a friend of Bessie's. Bessie,' I said again, for emphasis.

'Aha! Bessie!' His face lit up. Clearly, my pal had made her mark on Paris the same way she'd done in New York.

'I am François.' He reached beneath the counter and pulled out a set of keys on a piece of red string. 'You will follow me,' he said, coming out from behind the bar.

He led me back out into the square, to a nondescript door at the side of the restaurant. He unlocked the door and I followed him into a dark and mercifully cool passageway, leading to some stairs. This guy wasn't quite as gallant as Otto and charged on ahead, leaving me to haul my case. But I was so excited to have finally found my new home, I wasn't bothered. At least, I wasn't until we kept going, up and up and up the twisting, turning staircase. Every time we approached a door I hoped it would be mine, but it wasn't to be. My door was literally the last and the highest in the building.

François said something in French, then seeing my blank expression, he said, 'For you.' He pointed at the door, then unlocked it and handed me the keys.

'Thank you. *Merci.*' For an awkward moment I thought he was going to follow me inside, but he turned and went.

I stepped inside and locked the door behind me. I could pretty much see the entire apartment from where I was standing. A small kitchenette area with a table opened out into a room containing a closet and divan bed. At the far end of the room there were three shuttered windows, reaching from floor to ceiling. There was a door to my right, which I guessed led to the bathroom. I put down my case and hurried over to the windows. I'd gotten so disoriented from all the twisting and turning on the staircase, I had no idea which way they would be facing. *Please, please, face the square,* I silently prayed before opening one of the shutters. What I saw took my breath away. Not only did my room overlook the square, but from up there it looked even more stunning, because it was seen through the lacy branches of a tree. And to cap it all, the largest snowy white dome of Sacré-Coeur was visible too. As I looked at bright green leaves bobbing in front of me, I thought of Otto and couldn't help smiling. It had only been a few minutes since we'd said goodbye, but already our encounter had taken on a dream-like quality.

Enough mooning about like a love-struck kid, I scolded myself. I had to go find Bessie. I freshened up in the closet-sized bathroom, then put on clean nylons and a primrose yellow dress with puff sleeves and a drop waist. I powdered my face, applied a coat of rose-pink lipstick and a spritz of Blue Grass. Now, I was ready to go meet Bessie and properly greet Paris.

According to Bessie, the club was only a ten-minute walk from my room – '*Five minutes on your long legs!*' I memorised the directions before leaving, so that I could walk through the square with at least some degree of purpose. Dusk was falling and the birds in the tree outside my room were beginning their bed-time chorus. I fought the urge to stay a while and listen, exiting the square onto a cobbled street and setting off down the hill.

With its quaint cafés and pretty houses painted in pastel shades of yellow, blue and pink, Montmartre was like a village within the city and I fell in love with her instantly. This time, Bessie's directions were easy to follow and I soon found the avenue her music hall was located on. It was a bit of a heartland for bars and clubs, by the looks of things. The neon signs and bursts of music drifting from the doors reminded me of Harlem. It was edgy and vibrant and full of possibility and I drank it all in. Bessie's music hall, Le Flamant Rose, was midway along the avenue. Again, it was easy to find, due to the bright pink flamingo sign hanging over the door. A couple of guys dressed in sharp suits and shiny spats and carrying instrument cases were about to enter the club, so I hurried in behind them. I found myself in a small foyer with a plush black carpet and hot pink walls. A heavily made-up cloakroom attendant was sitting behind a desk, filing her nails. She smiled at the guys, then frowned at me.

'We are not open yet,' she said to me in French – or at least that's what I assumed she was saying, from the way she was shaking her head.

'I'm here to see Bessie,' I said quickly.

'You are Bessie's friend from New York?' one of the musicians said to me in English with a strong French accent.

'Yes.' I was so relieved he could speak English, I wanted to hug him.

The other musician, an older black guy with greying hair, broke into a grin. 'Hey, I'm Charlie,' he said, offering me his huge paw of a hand in greeting. My relief grew as I heard his American accent. 'This is Pierre, and you must be the infamous Florence?'

'Oh, I'm not so sure I'm infamous. I—'

'Who are you trying to kid, honey?' came a throaty drawl from the other side of a curtained doorway. And then Bessie appeared in all of her buxom, auburn-haired glory, clad in an emerald velvet dress.

'Florence! Dear heart!' she exclaimed.

'Bessie! Doll face!' I replied, and we fell around laughing before she grabbed me in an embrace.

My first thought was that she'd grown larger, softer. Clearly, I made the opposite impression.

'Look at you, all skin and bone,' she said, holding me at arm's length and giving me the once-over.

'I got really sick on the boat,' I explained.

'Ha! Well, do not fret, *ma chérie*. A few days of French cuisine will put some curves back on you.'

The two musicians nodded enthusiastically.

'What are you guys gawping at?' Bessie scolded with a twinkly-eyed grin. 'Ain't you got warm-ups to do?'

They tipped their hats to me and hurried off through the curtains.

'Speaking of food,' Bessie continued, 'have you eaten?'

I shook my head. 'I'm famished.'

'All righty then, let's get you fed.' She tucked her arm in mine and led me into the club.

'Gee whiz!' I exclaimed as I took it all in. The place was far bigger than it appeared from the outside. Gleaming round tables lit by flickering lamps were arranged in a horseshoe around a polished dancefloor. Beyond that was the stage. I felt another shiver of excitement as I pictured myself up there, dancing in front of an audience of Parisians.

'What do you reckon?' Bessie asked, and in spite of her wisecracking broad from the Bronx front, I could tell she really wanted me to like it.

'I reckon you should be really proud. It's incredible.'

Relief flooded her face. 'Isn't it? And you and I are going to have the best adventures here. Roxy's ain't a patch on this place.'

As I followed her to her private office at the back of the club, I felt full to the brim with gratitude for Bessie. She'd been my fairy godmother when I'd first shown up in New York at seventeen with barely a dime to my name, and now she was waving her magic wand all over my life again, in Paris.

The next few hours were a blur of talking nine to the dozen, stopping only to drink red wine and eat steak fried in garlic butter, all topped off with a silver platter of exquisite little cookies called macarons. Bessie filled me in on all she'd been up to since arriving in Paris two years previously. By all accounts she hadn't just arrived on the French scene, she'd conquered it. Using the incredible imagination that had made her queen of the New York dance hall scene, she'd conjured up shows with the most spectacular routines and costumes, attracting the crème de la crème of French society like moths to a flame.

'I'm so glad we've been reunited in Paris, dear heart,' Bessie said breathlessly, before I left. 'This place is like nowhere else on earth. Here we have the freedom to do and be anything!'

It breaks my heart recalling these words now, when I think of what was to come.

As I made my way back up the hill to the Place du Tertre, the flickering glow of the street lights only added to the feeling that my life had become a magical fairy tale. 'Good evening, Mister Tree,' I whispered when I reached La Crémaillère, gazing up into its spindly branches. The square was quieter now, but the air still echoed with the chatter and laughter of the last of the diners, and a couple of artists were still sitting at their easels painting. I made my way up to my room, slipped out of my clothes and into the bed, leaving the shutters and windows wide open. It was so blissful to be back in a bed on dry land, instead of that pesky ship's bunk, lurching from side to side. I gazed at the stars, glinting like diamonds between the branches, until my eyelids became heavy and I slipped into the welcome velvety darkness of sleep.

The next morning I was woken by the gentle cooing and chirping of the dawn chorus. The sky was streaked pale pink and the air smelled fresh and sweet. Memories from the previous day began forming in my mind and then I remembered Otto. When I'd told Bessie about our encounter on the steps, she'd shrieked with laughter.

'European men are so much more sophisticated than the guys back home,' she'd told me. 'You have to meet up with him. Besides, he's already seen your undergarments, so what have you got to lose?'

That was one major difference between Bessie and me – she focused way more on the physical when it came to her desires, whereas I focused far more on the emotional. The thing that intrigued me most about Otto wasn't his puppy dog eyes or his lazy grin – although those definitely held appeal – it was his ability to quote Walt Whitman's poetry. I didn't tell Bessie that, though, as she would have just hooted with laughter. Another thing in favour of me meeting Otto was that it was his last day in Paris. If he turned out to be a cad, it wouldn't matter because I'd never have to see him again. So, it was with that slightly pessimistic logic that I set off to meet the man who would come to mean everything to me.

SAGE

March 2018

'So, here I am at my management company,' Sage said into the camera on her phone. 'They've called me here to make a video apologising for the video I made last night. They've asked me to blame it all on my mother's death, to say that grief made me do it. Oh, and I'm supposed to pretend that I'm on my own at home and this is all coming from me – that I'm being totally authentic. But as you can see, that's total bullshit.' She panned the camera around the office before bringing it back on her. 'So, I'm not going to apologise, because the truth is, even though I was really drunk, I stand by what I said last night. This *is* all a money-making exercise. My management company are only freaking out because if I lose my sponsorship deals and endorsements, they lose their percentage. But it was never meant to be about making money. When I first started making my "Sage Says" posts and videos four years ago, I genuinely wanted to make a positive difference. I wanted to write about things that really mattered, in the hope that I might be able to help someone going through similar things. And it worked. So many people started following me. But somehow, I lost sight of my original goal and I lost sight of me, and I got swayed by the money, so I ended up writing about drinking out of jam jars and eating frickin' avocados. I don't even like avocados!' She gave a dry laugh. 'So, I'm sorry if what I said offended you, but really, if you strip out the drunkenness, can't you see that what I said in my video is true? That this whole culture is toxic and fake? Anyway, I've had enough. So you can put down your pitchforks and call off the lynching. I'm going.' She stopped recording and took a deep breath. Then she brought her locket up to her lips and kissed it. 'Thanks, Mum,' she whispered. Then she stood up and walked out of the office. Beth and Danny were hovering close to the door.

'Ah, there she is!' Danny said warmly. 'Let's have a look, then.'

Sage shook her head. 'I need to go.'

Danny's smile vanished. 'What? Where? Why?'

Sage ignored him and kept walking.

'Sage?' he called after her.

She kept walking. Out of the office and down the stairs. Into the car park and into her car. She put on her seatbelt and put her key in the ignition. Then she pressed 'upload' on the video and started driving home.

She lasted the entire drive without checking her phone. Thankfully, no one was hovering by the entrance to the car park at her apartment building, so she was able to slip in unseen. When she got into her flat, she stripped the sheets from the bed and stuffed them in the washing machine. Then she sat down at the kitchen counter, feeling dizzy and light-headed. It was only at this point that she realised she hadn't eaten all day. She looked in the fridge. It was empty, apart from the bottle of champagne Danny had sent her after she'd passed a million Instagram followers, and a tomato so over-ripe it had burst its skin.

Sage went online and ordered a pizza and then finally, her resolve wavered. She clicked on Twitter and the first thing she saw – apart from her notifications being off the scale again – was a tweet from the *Huff Post* titled: *'INFLUENCER EXPOSES ALL'.* The accompanying thumbnail was a still from her second video.

Sage clicked on the article. 'Is this the beginning of the end for the influencer culture?' the article began. 'It certainly seems to be the end of the road for Sage Segal.' It went on to chart her meteoric rise and 'spectacular drunken fall from grace'.

Over the past four years, Sage had become used to other people talking about her online, and it wasn't as if she hadn't had any previous detractors. One particularly stinging evening, an author she'd really respected had written a tweet calling her 'vacuous and shallow', so that had been a low point. Overall, though, Sage had been something of a global sweetheart. But now… Sage scanned the comments beneath the article. They were all, without exception, negative. People were either hurt that she'd been 'scamming' them, or had been aware the whole time that it was a scam and were now revelling in her downfall.

On and on she scrolled, until the words swam before her eyes and the one image everyone seemed to be using, of her bleary-eyed and drunk in the club toilet, became seared into her mind. She was wrenched from her spiral of doom by the buzz of the intercom.

'Pizza,' a man's voice barked as she picked up the receiver. When she opened the door, he gave her a knowing smirk. She grabbed the box and slammed the door, her appetite instantly gone. She felt raw and exposed and completely alone.

When Sage woke the next morning, there were a couple of seconds of ignorant bliss before the events of the previous day came slamming back into her. *But today's a new day,* she told herself as she sat up. What was that thing Danny had said about chip paper? Danny. She shuddered as she tried to imagine the effect her second video would have had upon the team at Spark. But she'd had to bring the whole charade to an end.

Sage got up and went through to the kitchen to take last night's untouched pizza from the fridge. She put on some coffee and tucked into a slice. She could practically hear her mother laughing. 'I told you that fridge would come in handy for my takeaways,' she murmured.

Once she was sufficiently fortified with pizza and caffeine, she plucked up the courage to turn on her phone. There were five voicemail messages from Danny, but she couldn't bring herself to listen to them yet so she checked her Instagram instead. The video she'd shared yesterday had got some likes, but nowhere near the level she was used to. There were plenty of comments, though. She scrolled through them, her eyes drawn to the words guaranteed to hurt the most.

'Phoney'... 'bitch'... 'greedy'... 'fake'... 'unfollow'... 'unfollow'... 'cancelled'... 'unfollow'... 'hope you die'... 'die bitch'

Sage felt the cold pizza churning in her stomach. What if some angry stalker decided to try and hurt her? Thanks to the paparazzi, her address was pretty much common knowledge, and anyone who didn't already know could easily find out via a quick search on Google. She went into the living room at the front of the apartment. The street below was glistening in the early spring sunshine, the trees starting to blossom, and the sky eggshell-blue. Then she noticed a group of teenage girls on the corner. Were they there for her? To yell abuse at her? To try and harm her? Sage stepped back from the window and put on the TV, creating some background noise to make her feel less alone. Then she went back into the kitchen and opened Twitter on her laptop. Right at the top of the list of trending topics was '#sageromp'. Her heart began to thud as she clicked on the hashtag. Up popped an image of a man who looked vaguely familiar next to the headline: *SAGE SEGAL'S ONE-NIGHT ROMP*.

'No!' Sage took a deep breath and clicked on the link to a tabloid newspaper. What followed was a lurid account from the man she'd slept with – whose name, it turned out, was Billy Yates – about their night together. As well as 'romp', other excruciating words used included 'lusty', 'horny' and 'frisky'.

'I'd say I wasn't the first fella she treated like that,' Billy mused at the end of the piece. 'She wouldn't even give me a cup of tea in the morning. I felt so used.'

'Oh for God's sake!' Sage clicked on the comments below the article.

> 'What a disgrace!'

> 'My daughter looks up to her!'

> 'What an appalling role model!'

> 'Ought to be ashamed!'

> 'Sage Segal is officially cancelled'

As Sage drowned in the hatred, she heard her name coming from the living room. She hurried through to see the host of *Good Morning Britain* gazing grave-faced into the camera. 'Is this really the kind of behaviour we want from our teenage girls' role models?' she asked, before turning to another middle-aged woman, who, the caption on the screen informed Sage, was a tabloid columnist.

'It's disgusting,' the woman spat, her thin lips pursed into a knot of indignation. 'Someone in her position shouldn't behave like this. She ought to be ashamed.'

Sage slumped down on the sofa, feeling herself shrinking away to nothing as two complete strangers pulled her apart on national television. Then they showed a clip from her first video, of Sage slurring and sniffing. Her own voice echoed out at her from the screen:

'Stop being such dumb little followers and start thinking for yourselves.'

'So ungrateful,' the tabloid columnist said.

'We ought to point out that we did reach out to Sage's management company for comment,' the host added. 'But there was no response.'

Sage wondered what that meant. Danny and the team at Spark had taken care of all of her business interests ever since she'd signed with them three years ago – ever since she'd started making serious money. Panic rose inside of her. She clasped her locket and closed her eyes. 'What should I do, Mum?'

But of course, Elizabeth wasn't there. She'd never be there again. Sage had no choice but to take care of things herself. She went back into the kitchen and listened to Danny's messages. The first two were conciliatory. 'Please call back. I'm sure we can still sort this out…' But by the third his tone had changed, and by the fifth it was icy. 'I take it you no longer require our representation, and given what you said about us in your video, I really think our working relationship is now untenable. I've emailed over a termination of contract document.'

Sage numbly clicked into her emails. There were a whole bunch from different newspapers and magazines. And there, sure enough, was one from Danny. She was about to open it, when an email just below it caught her eye. The subject read: *'I THINK I MIGHT HAVE THE OTHER HALF OF YOUR LOCKET.'*

FLORENCE

June 1937

I didn't notice Otto when I first got to the church, as the steps were humming with people bustling about and sitting in the sunshine. Then I heard him call my name. Much as I was trying to play it cool, the moment I saw him, I couldn't help grinning. He'd clearly made more of an effort with his appearance, wearing a crisp green shirt and patch-free trousers. A silk scarf the colour of the ocean was knotted around his neck, and his hair was freshly combed. I have to confess, I'd made something of an effort too, wearing a dark green dress with a nipped-in waist and butterfly sleeves, and a lilac headscarf wrapped around my hair in a turban, pinned in place with my favourite pearl brooch.

'You look like a flower,' was the first thing he said to me, as I walked up the steps to greet him.

'Thank you!' My smile grew. It was truly the highest compliment he could have paid me, and so unlike the cheesy lines I'd become accustomed to.

'Do you want to see inside the church before we go?' Otto asked. 'The nuns are about to begin their singing.'

'Sure.'

I have to confess that at that point, I hadn't set foot in a church since I was five, for my momma's funeral. My daddy pretty much lost his faith after her death and I have to say, as I got older and learned more about how she'd died, it was hard for me to believe in any kind of loving God. But as I walked through the large wooden doors with Otto, the sight that greeted me took my breath away. If the Sacré-Coeur was stunning on the outside, it was even more magnificent inside. The walls were lined with towering white stone archways leading to small alcoves, all set beneath three domed ceilings. Rows of gleaming wooden pews had been set up in the centre of the church, in front of a magnificent altar beneath the largest dome. A fresco of Jesus and Mary was painted on the ceiling in soothing shades of white, gold and cornflower blue. The golden heart painted on Jesus's chest glinted in the morning sunlight streaming in through the stained-glass windows.

'What do you think?' Otto whispered.

'It's really something,' I gasped.

'Come, let's sit.' He led me over to the wooden pews. As we sat down, a line of nuns in blue robes filed into the area behind the altar. They started singing what I guessed was a hymn in French. There were a handful of other people sitting on the pews. Most of them had their heads bowed in prayer. I closed my eyes and let the music drift over me. It was so different to the frenetic jazz I normally listened and danced to. Maybe it was the setting, but it felt as if there was something other-worldly about it. It wasn't just drifting over me; it felt as if it was drifting *into* me.

'They sing like this every day,' Otto whispered.

I thought of him coming here, sitting here, listening to the nuns, even though he was Jewish, and suddenly he seemed like the most intriguing man on God's green earth. Once the singing was over, we stepped back out into the sunshine and made our way down the hill to the nearest station. Everything about Paris seemed so effortlessly chic, even the Art Nouveau signs for the Métro. Otto bought the tickets and held the train door open for me like a perfect gent. He also made me laugh my head off, whispering a running commentary in English about our various fellow passengers. We nearly came unstuck when he told me in his commentator voice that a large bearded guy who'd just boarded was King Henry the Eighth, fresh from killing one of his wives. The guy turned and glowered at us and shook his head. It turned out some Parisians could speak English after all.

Situated on the Right Bank of the River Seine, the Musée du Louvre was one of the most magnificent buildings I had ever seen, which I realised was starting to become quite a theme.

'I can't believe I'm actually here,' I said to Otto as we made our way into the grand entrance hall of the museum. 'It all feels like a dream.'

'That is how I felt, the first time I visited it,' he replied.

'When was that?'

'Three days ago. This is my first time in Paris,' he explained. 'But I have dreamed of coming to Paris forever.'

'Me too! Or at least, I've dreamed of coming here ever since my dancing hero Josephine Baker came here, back when I was ten.'

'You like dancing?' Otto asked.

I nodded. For a brief moment, I considered not telling him I was a dancer. I knew that certain people made certain judgements about dancers. But then I reminded myself that I didn't give a hoot what people thought of me. And if Otto was one of those people, then it was just as well he was only here for one more day. Although if I was honest, I'd already gotten to the point where I really didn't want him to be one of those people.

'I am a dancer,' I said.

Otto stopped and stared at me. 'You are an enigma,' he said, with that grin.

'What makes you say that?' I enquired nonchalantly – although I have to tell you, the idea of being seen as a woman of mystery did appeal.

'Every time I think I understand who you might be, you surprise me.'

I nodded. 'Well, I could say exactly the same about you.'

'Really?' His eyes widened.

'Yeah. It's not every day I meet a guy who can quote Walt Whitman at me.'

'That is why I liked you the moment I saw you! When I saw you had his book.' He instantly blushed, as if embarrassed he'd said too much.

'Oh, you did, huh?'

'Yes.'

His honesty was disarming. I wasn't used to it. The guys we got in the clubs in New York tended to be full to the fedora with wisecracks and swagger. This guy was a breath of fresh air.

'So, you will be dancing in one of the Paris clubs?' Otto asked as we walked into the first chamber of the museum.

'Uh-huh. My friend Bessie is hostess at a music hall in Montmartre. She asked me to come dance for her.'

He smiled. 'I would like to see you dance.'

And again, there was nothing sleazy about the way he said it.

'Yeah well, maybe if you do come back to Paris next year, you can come see me,' I said breezily – but I already liked the idea of this very much.

'I would love to do that.'

'How come you can't come back for a year?' I asked as we drew level with the first painting. It was of the Virgin Mary holding the baby Jesus.

'I have to finish my studies.'

'Art?'

He shook his head. 'Accountancy.'

'Say what?' I stared at him, stunned. 'OK, you truly are an enigma.'

'It is for my father, to keep him happy. I said I would get my qualification so that if it doesn't work out for me as an artist, I will be able to make a living.' He grimaced. 'Although

I'd rather die a pauper than count up numbers for the rest of my days.'

I laughed, relieved. 'Yeah, my daddy tried to persuade me to become a teacher, but I couldn't bear the thought of being stuck in a musty old classroom talking about things for the rest of my days, instead of actually doing them.'

He looked at me and grinned, then took hold of my arm. 'Come, I want to show you a painting I think you will love.'

The painting was by Otto's hero, Renoir, and was called *Bal du Moulin de la Galette*. 'The Moulin de la Galette is a place where Parisians would go to eat and drink and dance in Montmartre back in the nineteenth century,' Otto explained.

The painting showed clusters of people sitting at tables and dancing in a tree-lined courtyard. The men were in suits and straw boaters, the women in Victorian-style dress. They all looked as if they were having a gay old time.

'*Moulin*,' I said, reading from the card beside the painting. 'Does that mean "windmill"?' I'd heard all about the Moulin Rouge, and the notion of having a music hall at a windmill really tickled me.

'Yes,' Otto replied. 'And the *galette* refers to the type of bread they would eat with their wine, made from the flour ground by the windmill.'

The thought of eating freshly baked bread and drinking wine and dancing sounded heavenly to me. 'Is it still open?'

He shook his head. 'No, but the Moulin Rouge – another windmill just down the street from it – is.'

'Ah yes, that's on my list of places to visit.'

The rest of our museum trip passed by in a blur. Otto turned out to be the perfect guide, sharing his vast knowledge of artwork in the most interesting and entertaining ways. Apparently, Picasso's full name was made up of twenty-three words and Salvador Dalí believed he was the reincarnation of his dead brother.

But my favourite of the anecdotes Otto shared was about Renoir, and how he'd been an apprentice in a Paris porcelain factory as a young man and would visit the Louvre on his lunchbreaks.

'He taught himself how to draw by coming and studying the works hanging here,' Otto told me, his brown eyes gleaming. 'And now, his own works hang here!'

I loved the idea of a young Renoir walking these same halls with a head full of dreams, and I had a hunch Otto shared similar ambitions. I hoped with all I had that he'd make it one day too, and not only because it would mean he'd be back in Paris.

After we'd explored every inch of the museum, we emerged into the afternoon sunshine and made our way back to the river. This time, I didn't feel intimidated by all of the chic Parisians bustling by. Walking with Otto, I felt part of the merry flow.

'Now we have seen my favourite place in Paris, I would like to take you somewhere I feel could become a favourite for you, if I may?' Otto announced.

'You may indeed. I'm intrigued.' My first thought was that he was going to take me to a music hall, but it was still too early for the clubs to be open.

'Come,' he said, leading me down a warren of narrow cobbled streets. Finally, we reached one named rue de l'Odéon. '*Et voilà!*' he announced triumphantly, gesturing at a store midway down the street. The gold lettering above the dark shopfront said 'SHAKESPEARE AND COMPANY' and the windows were filled with a slightly chaotic display of books. I felt my pulse quicken. 'It's a bookstore,' Otto explained. 'Well, I guess that much is obvious. But it is a bookstore with a difference – in Paris, at least. An American woman named Sylvia Beach owns it and all the books are in English.'

Now he was speaking my language – literally. Otto held the door open and I hurried inside. It's not often that I'm lost for words, but as I gazed around the store and breathed in the magical aroma of aging paper, words really did fail me. Unlike other bookstores I'd frequented – and there had been a few – all of the shelves were consigned to the walls, leaving the central space free for a desk and a couple of armchairs. Any spaces on the walls were crammed with framed, signed photographs of authors – I spied Hemingway instantly – and the floor was covered in rugs with mosaic-style patterns in ruby, emerald and cream. The overall effect was less bookstore and more cosy living room. Otto had been right, it became one of my favourite places in Paris instantly. Somehow, in spite of only having met me the day before, he seemed to know exactly what made me tick.

A woman with short brown hair and an intense stare stood behind the desk in the centre of the store. In front of her were more piles of books and a pair of brass weighing scales, a throwback to the days when books used to be sold by the pound.

'Bonjour,' she said, but although she was speaking French, I could detect an American accent. Could this be the owner of the store herself?

'Hello,' I said, with a beaming grin.

'American?' she asked.

'Yes. I'm Florence Thornton, I just arrived in Paris from New York.'

'Well, what do you know? I'm Sylvia Beach. Welcome to a little slice of home.' She gestured around the shop. 'Please do make yourself acquainted with the books.'

I didn't need a second invitation. I browsed around until I found the poetry section upstairs. After a few moments, Otto came to join me.

'I would like, if it is OK, to buy you a gift,' he said haltingly.

'Oh.' I watched as he took a book from the shelf. It was a collection of Henry David Thoreau's poems.

'I think if you like Walt Whitman, you will love these,' he said.

'Thank you,' was all I could manage to say. In that one moment, he'd shown me more thoughtfulness than a man had ever bestowed upon me before.

We went back downstairs to pay.

'Are you here on vacation?' Sylvia asked.

I shook my head. 'I'm here to work.'

'She's a dancer,' Otto said.

'Is that so? Where do you dance?'

'My friend Bessie's place. Le Flamant Rose.'

'Oh, I love that place!' she exclaimed. 'No doubt I shall see you again then.'

'Oh, you will,' I replied. 'If not there, then definitely here. I love it.'

Otto paid for the book and Sylvia put it in a brown paper bag and handed it to me. I left the store with my heart ablaze. My new life in Paris had truly begun.

'Are you hungry?' Otto asked.

I nodded. 'Starving.'

We found a little restaurant tucked away in the shadow of Notre-Dame and feasted on a dish called bouillon – a tasty broth of beef and vegetables. It was the perfect dish after my seasickness: hearty and full of much-needed nutrients.

'I do not want this day to end,' Otto said afterwards, as we meandered back through the city. We'd decided to walk back to Montmartre in order to drink in as much of Paris as possible.

'Me too,' I said. And even though I was so excited for my Parisian adventure to begin, part of me wanted to remain frozen there forever with him.

'We have so little time left, and there is so much I still want to know,' he declared.

'About what?' I asked.

'About you.'

'I feel the same! I know, how about we ask each other questions, like in an interview?' One of my many childhood aspirations had been to be a newspaper reporter.

'I like this idea,' he replied, with a twinkle in his eye. 'But no boring questions. We need to skip all that, go straight away to the good stuff.'

'Absolutely.'

'May I?' He offered me his arm.

'You may.' I linked my arm through his, and for a moment I thought I might faint from the intensity of feeling his skin upon mine.

'Would you like to go first?' he offered.

'OK.' I thought for a moment. 'What made you want to be an artist?'

He smiled dreamily. 'I see everything in colours – even feelings. It is what comes the most naturally to me.'

'How can you see feelings as colours?'

'Hey, it is my turn for the question!' he chuckled.

'OK.'

'What is your greatest dream?'

'To live a life of adventure,' I answered instantly.

'Yes, I thought as much.' His eyes twinkled. 'OK, now it is your turn.'

'How do you see feelings as colours?'

'I don't know, I just do. It is like a coloured lens comes over my eyes. When I am happy, everything is yellow. When I am scared, everything goes black.' There was something about the way he said this, and the way his face fell, that made me certain he'd felt scared quite recently.

'What are you scared of?' I asked softly.

'No! You cheat again with your two questions! It is my turn.' He looked thoughtful for a moment. 'If you were to be turned into a bird, which would you choose?'

'Oh, I like this question!' I replied. 'I would be a bald eagle!'

Otto burst out laughing. 'I did not expect you to say that.'

'Why not?' The tips of my cheeks began to burn. I'd loved bald eagles for so long, it had been my automatic response.

'I thought maybe you would say something more – how do you say? – feminine, like a dove.'

Now it was my turn to laugh. 'Who wants to be a dove? All they do is sit around all day and coo, which is very soothing and all, but it's hardly exciting.'

'And a bald eagle is exciting?'

'Of course.'

'How?'

'Well, for a start they have amazing eyesight. They can detect prey from two miles away.'

'Wow.' I was heartened to see that Otto looked genuinely impressed.

'And they have a wingspan of at least six feet.'

'That is huge. How do you know these things?'

'My daddy taught me. Every winter, we get bald eagles come nest in the trees on our farm. They feed from the fish in our lake.'

'Your farm sounds beautiful.'

'It is.' I felt a wistful pang as a memory of my daddy and I fishing on the lake filled my mind. 'When bald eagles are courting, they have this crazy ritual.'

Otto raised his eyebrows. 'What do they do?'

'They soar up real high, then they lock talons and start swirling and tumbling down to the ground like a cartwheel.' I grinned as I remembered the first time I'd ever seen this happen.

'But how do they land if they've locked talons?' Otto asked. Again, I was pleased to see that he looked genuinely concerned.

'That's what I thought the first time I saw it happen. I could hardly bear to watch! But they unlock talons just in time. My daddy said it's their way of testing out a potential mate. If they survive the death spiral, then they've got what it takes.' Then I added, as an afterthought, 'They mate for life.'

'I like that idea,' Otto said quietly.

'Me too,' I replied, not daring to look at him. 'Anyhow, you just had about three extra questions. Now it's my turn. What are you scared of?'

'Hitler,' he replied, without missing a beat.

'The German leader?'

He nodded. All of the joy had drained from his expression, and for a moment it was as if I could see the black lens of his fear too.

'Because you are Jewish?' I asked gently, and I'll never forget his answer.

'No, because I am human.' He looked down at the ground.

'But you are safe from Hitler, in Austria?' It was more of a question than a statement. Back then, my political knowledge was woeful. I knew that Hitler had been persecuting the Jews in his own country, but I didn't see him as any real threat to the rest of the world.

Otto shrugged. 'Germany has already forbidden Jews from working in our film industry, so who knows what will be next. But I only have another year before I can move here.'

I tightened my grip on his arm. 'Yes. And then you know you'll be safe. There's no way Hitler would be able to tell the French what to do!'

Otto laughed. 'And definitely not the Parisians!'

We carried on walking in companionable silence, and I imagined my feeling of joy shimmering all around us in a dazzling shade of gold, chasing any fear of Hitler away.

When we arrived back in Montmartre, I felt a sudden dread at the fact that my time with Otto was coming to an end. Night had fallen and the restaurants were buzzing.

'I guess you'll be wanting to get back to your hotel,' I said, hoping like crazy that I was wrong.

He shook his head. 'I was actually thinking we could have a picnic.'

'A picnic? But it's almost ten o'clock at night!'

'Which is the very best time to have a picnic, by moonlight.' His eyes sparkled.

I looked up at the sky. There was no sign of a moon. I didn't say that, though. The thought of a late-night picnic with Otto was the most magical thing I could imagine. 'But we don't have any food.'

'Yet. We don't have any food *yet*. Come with me.' He took my hand and led me down a narrow street to a café with stripy red and white awnings. Otto sweet-talked the matronly-looking owner into selling us a bottle of wine and some slices of cheese, along with a long, thin stick of bread called a baguette. Then we set off for the wide white steps in front of Sacré-Coeur. He unknotted the scarf around his neck and laid it on the ground. '*Et voilà*, a picnic blanket,' he laughed.

We talked for hours, there on those steps. Long after the wine had gone and all that was left of the bread were a few crumbs. And with every second that passed, I felt the strangest double-edged sensation – a deepening connection to Otto and a growing panic that he would soon be leaving.

'What are you thinking?' he asked softly when we fell silent.

'That I don't want you to leave.' I'd never been so honest with a man before, but truthfully, I'd never felt like this about a man before. I'd always kept them at arm's length – not because I feared them, but because I'd never met anyone I wanted to invite in.

'I don't want to leave either,' he said. He moved closer to me and placed his hand over mine on the stone step. It felt so warm, and safe and strong.

'Maybe we…' I broke off, too scared to voice my wish, in case he might judge me.

'Maybe we?' he asked.

'Could spend the night together. What's left of it, I mean.' My heart began thudding. Would he think me loose?

'I would like that very much,' he said softly. He stood up and held his hand out to me.

We walked in silence to the Place du Tertre, past my tree and in through the door next to the restaurant and up the stairs.

'Welcome to my humble abode,' I said, letting him into my room. I went over to the kitchen table and lit the lamp.

Just as I had done the day before, Otto headed straight for the windows. 'What a view! What a tree!' he exclaimed. I remember looking at him silhouetted against the window and thinking, *Finally, I have met my kindred spirit.* Then he turned to look back at me. 'I am afraid I am not so experienced,' he said, glancing from me to the bed.

'I'm not either,' I said, relief washing through me. The extent of my sexual experience back then amounted to nothing more than some light necking.

'Really?' He looked at me hopefully.

I nodded. 'I've never, you know, been with a man before.' I was worried that the magic of the evening might be ruined by the awkwardness of this exchange, but Otto strode over to me and cupped my face in his hands. 'All I want is to hold you.'

'That's all I want, too.'

And then in a hazy dance of kissing and stroking and shedding clothes, we ended up in each other's arms in bed beneath the covers.

'Tell me what you would like me to do,' he whispered, tracing his fingertips over my skin.

'Everything,' I whispered back, my body dissolving into pulses of pleasure.

*

Otto's train back to Austria left first thing the next morning, so we got up as soon as the dawn chorus began outside the window. As I watched him get dressed, my joy began curdling into a sorrow so sharp I could barely breathe. What if I never saw him again? What if he stayed in Austria and followed a career in accountancy and married the kind of woman who'd make the perfect accountant's wife, the kind of woman who never laddered her nylons and made embroidered tapestries of sayings like, 'There's no place like home'. What if…?

'I don't expect you to wait for me,' he said, coming back over to the bed. 'But I will return next year. And I will want to find you, if you will still want to find me.'

'I will,' I said firmly, and then I had an idea that lifted me slightly from my gloom. 'How about if we do want to find each other again, we meet in Montmartre, outside the church, one year from yesterday?'

'Yes!' he exclaimed. 'At eleven in the morning. What was yesterday's date?'

'The fourteenth of June.'

'It is a deal.' His gaze fell upon my book of Walt Whitman poems beside the bed. He picked it up and started leafing through the pages. 'I will write the date down in here so that you do not forget it.' He stopped leafing and wrote on the page. 'Now I must go.'

Our final embrace seemed to last forever, yet was over in an instant. And then, all of a sudden, he was gone. I stood by the window and waited for the sound of the heavy door below slamming shut. *If he's your kindred spirit, he'll look up,* I said to myself, a variation on a game I'd played with fate ever since I was a kid. I held my breath as Otto came into sight and began walking away. He wasn't going to turn around. We were doomed. This would be the last I would see of him. But then… Then he stopped, and oh so slowly, he turned. And when he saw me watching him, he broke into that grin, and he started blowing kisses up at me like crazy. I watched him until he disappeared, my eyes swimming with tears. Then I sat back down and picked up the book.

'*Meet me in Montmartre on June 14th*', he'd written boldly, above one of the poems. I noticed that he'd underlined one of the lines in the poem.

> '*Once I pass'd through a populous city imprinting my brain for future use with its shows, architecture, customs, traditions,*
> *Yet now, of all that city I remember only a woman I casually met there who detain'd me for love of me,*
> *Day by day and night by night <u>we were together – all else has long been forgotten by me.</u>*'

I held the poem to my chest and gazed out into the tree, praying to the spirit of Walt Whitman that Otto would one day return to me.

If I had known then what the answer to my prayer would mean, would I have changed my plea? The honest answer is that even after all this time, and all this pain, I still would have wished for him to come back to me.

SAGE

March 2018

Sage clicked on the email and began to read:

'Howdy!

I sure hope you don't mind me getting in touch out of the blue like this, but I saw the hullaballoo about you on the television last night and I recognised your locket. What I mean to say is, I think I might have the other half to your locket. May I ask if the writing on your half says "We were together"? My eyes aren't as good as they used to be and it was impossible to make out on the screen. I recognised the eagles doing their spiral, though. I know this is a long shot and I'm guessing you have quite a lot to deal with these days, but if you have a moment to reply to this I'd surely appreciate it. Please don't think I'm some kind of crank. Lord knows there's a lot of them about! But if you're interested in finding out where your locket came from, I think I can help you. Especially if you have a connection to Paris.

As my granddaddy used to say, take it easy, and if you can't take it easy, just take it!

Samuel T. Clancy'

Sage blinked hard at the screen to make sure she hadn't been seeing things. Then she looked at her locket, tracing her finger over the words 'We were together'. Who was this Samuel T. Clancy person? And how did he know the back half of her locket was missing? And how did he know about her connection to Paris? Could he be legit? And if he was for real, did he know why her mum had been abandoned in Paris as a baby?

Sage had always been intrigued by her mother's mysterious past. Could she finally be about to discover what had happened? If nothing else, it was nice to have a distraction from the online storm. She got herself a fresh cup of coffee and pressed 'reply', deciding to be overly cautious, just in case it was some kind of trick.

> 'Could you tell me a bit more about the locket and how you came to get your half of it?'

She checked what she'd written over and over to make sure that if Samuel T. Clancy was actually a journalist on a fishing expedition, she hadn't given them anything incriminating, and then she pressed 'send'. Slightly emboldened by this development, she went and had a shower and got dressed. Then she made an online order for some food shopping. Going to the supermarket had been hard enough before, when she was constantly being asked for selfies in the salad aisle, but there was no way she could go out now. Dealing with the online abuse was hard enough, but in the flesh it would just about finish her.

Every so often, she checked her emails for a reply from the mysterious Samuel, but there was nothing, only more messages from media outlets requesting interviews, and more hate mail via the 'Contact' page on her website. Her food arrived and Sage made herself an omelette – the one dish she could cook to perfection. It wasn't until the sun was beginning to dip low and gold over the London skyline outside, that she finally got a response to her email.

> *'Well howdy, Sage, it sure was exciting to hear back from you. I have what I think is the other half of your locket because it once belonged to my mother. My half has the same eagle design and the words "I forget the rest". It's inspired by a line from a poem. It's kind of awkward to discuss over this here email, but long story short, my momma had a baby in Paris back in 1946. March 1946, to be precise. But she wasn't able to take care of the baby, so she ended up leaving her someplace safe before returning to America, where she was from originally. She left the baby with one half of the locket and kept the other. I'm not sure how you've gotten hold of the locket – you could have come across it in a thrift store for all I know, so this might mean nothing to you. But if you know or knew someone who was born in Paris, then that person might be my momma's daughter – and my half-sister. I'm getting on a bit now and I'm not too good with this new-fangled technology, but I got someone who works here on my farm to take a photo of my half of the locket and apparently he has attached it to this missive, so you should be able to see it. I hope this message finds you well, Sage, or as well as can be expected given all the hogwash being written about you.*
>
> *Hang on in there, girl!*
> *Sam'*

Sage clicked on the attached image. And sure enough, there was what undeniably appeared to be the matching half of her locket. She took a moment to re-read the email and tried to compute what Sam, as he now referred to himself, had written.

If what he was saying was true, then he was her mum's brother – and Sage's uncle.

If what he was saying was true, then maybe Sage wasn't all alone in the world after all.

FLORENCE

June 1938

That first year in Paris passed in a blur. It was only when I thought of Otto that time seemed to drag. Otherwise, I had more than enough to occupy me. For starters, there was Bessie's show. She hadn't been kidding when she'd wrote me that she'd made 'spectacular' her motto. Every six months, she put on a new show at Le Flamant Rose, and with every show, she pushed the boundaries both visually and physically. By the time I'd been there a year, I was about to start my third show for her, this one on the theme of Greek goddesses. I'd been cast as a high-kicking Athena, complete with helmet and spear, and a very short robe. The fourteenth of June 1938 happened to be the first night of the show, so I woke that morning with a stomach frothing with nervous excitement.

'Good morning, Mister Tree,' I said, grinning at the branches outside the window bobbing in the breeze. 'Good morning, birds.'

The birds tweeted back at me, hopping and weaving through the leaves. I thought of the last time I'd seen Otto, one year previously, and I picked up my Walt Whitman book, turned to the dog-eared page and traced my finger over the words he'd written. Every time caution started telling me he wouldn't show and he'd probably forgotten all about me, another, deeper knowing took hold. It was crazy, but I felt so certain we would be reunited.

I took my time getting ready, employing all the skills I'd learned about make-up and hair from my year in Paris. Then I put on my slip and a new purchase, a cream crêpe dress, dotted with forget-me-nots. I'd chosen the pattern deliberately, willing Otto not to have forgotten about me.

Once I was ready, I made my way downstairs and out onto the square. I stopped off at my favourite café for a breakfast of black coffee and a freshly baked croissant. As I sat outside and watched the world go by, I reflected on how much had changed since I'd last seen Otto. Although I wasn't yet as fluent in French as the natives, I was able to hold my own in most conversations and I was teaching myself to read using French newspapers. I was enjoying dancing at Le Flamant Rose, and Montmartre now felt like home. The jigsaw pieces of a damned near perfect life had all fallen into place, there was just one piece missing. An image of Otto appeared in my mind, of how I'd last seen him, grinning and blowing kisses up at my window. I could be moments from seeing that smile again, from feeling those arms around me. Unable to sit still a second longer, I put some money on the table and made my way across the square.

The day wasn't as warm as it had been the year before, and a blank white sky was draped over the city like a sheet. I scanned the steps in front of the church, but there was no sign of that floppy hair or twinkly-eyed grin. I was early, though. I paced up and down for a couple of minutes. An old man was playing an accordion halfway up the steps. The music sounded so joyful, the perfect soundtrack for our reunion. I prepared to hear Otto's voice calling my name and I mentally rehearsed my response. The truth was, I'd been mentally rehearsing my response for a year. I would turn, feign surprise, as if I'd been miles away and not even thinking of him, and then I'd casually stroll towards him and he would sweep me into his arms and… I broke from my reverie and scanned the steps. Where was he? The church bells struck eleven and with every thunderous clang of the bell, I felt my heart sink. Otto hadn't struck me as the kind of guy to be late, especially not to an occasion as momentous as this. If he was going to come at all, surely he would have been early?

As more time passed, I felt increasingly ridiculous. My father's words from some eleven years previously suddenly came back to haunt me. 'You need to keep your feet on the ground, Florence.' The first ever talkie, *The Jazz Singer*, had just come out in movie theatres and all I'd been able to think of was becoming a star of the silver screen.

'I want to be a movie star when I grow up,' I'd announced when I got home from school, where *The Jazz Singer* had been all anyone could talk about at recess. 'I'm going to sing and dance and tell jokes, and audiences are going to be able to hear me!' I'd then burst into an impromptu tap dance routine on the stone kitchen floor.

'Folks like us don't become movie stars,' my daddy had said, with that gentle, humouring grin he always gave me, along with a slight shake of his head.

Folks like us don't have wild, passionate affairs with kindred spirits, I imagined him saying now, shaking his head as he took in the pitiful sight of me stranded alone outside the church.

I found myself in a true moral dilemma. Part of me was worried that something bad had happened to Otto. In March, the German army had moved into Austria and annexed the country, and I'd heard talk of Austrian Jews having their property stolen by the Nazis. Otto probably had more important things on his mind than coming to meet me. But he had been planning on moving to Paris. Surely the German occupation of Austria would have made him even more intent on coming here? Then a horrible thought occurred to me. What if he was in Paris already, but he just didn't want to see me? I took one last look around the steps and hurried home.

*

That night, I channelled all of my disappointment into my first performance as Athena. One of the most show-stopping moments of the revue was when I burst through a backdrop of Zeus' forehead – which was how Athena was supposed to have been born – and launched into a blistering, tribal-style routine, using my spear as a baton. I danced harder and faster than I'd ever done in my life before, trying to get all of my sadness about Otto out of my body. I wasn't conscious of the band or the audience or the chorus line; it was just me and the dance under that dazzling spotlight.

'Honey, you were on fire up there!' Bessie exclaimed as she burst into my dressing room after the show. She was wearing her lucky first night dress: a cleavage-enhancing number in ruby red, designed by Coco Chanel. It was deemed lucky because Pierre, the sax player in the house band, had bought it for her. The fact that Pierre was married and showed no sign of fulfilling his promise to leave his wife for Bessie had conveniently been overlooked. 'Come have a drink. A lot of people want to see you.'

Yes, but not Otto, I couldn't help thinking bitterly. I've never been one for drinking a lot, not even back then, but that night I said yes to every drink I was offered, and as the toast of the show, I was offered a lot. Midway through the night, Sylvia Beach, with whom I'd become firm friends due to my chronic book addiction, brought a man over to my table. He was heavy-set with a square jaw and Brylcreemed hair, but despite his gangster-like appearance, his smile was warm.

'Florence, I want you to meet my dear friend, Harry Bergman. Harry's just been made editor of the *New York Tribune*.'

Bergman extended his hand. 'How do you do?' He nodded to the stage. 'That was really quite something.'

'Thank you.' I have to admit, his admiration went a small way to salving the hurt I'd felt from Otto not showing. A small, childish part of me wanted to stamp my feet and say, 'There, see, some people appreciate me.'

'I've been telling Harry all about you,' Sylvia said, as they sat down at my table.

I took a cigarette from my case and quick as a flash, Harry produced a silver lighter from his waistcoat pocket and lit it for me. 'Oh really, how so?' I enquired, inhaling deeply. My first smoke after a performance always went down as smooth as silk.

'Harry's looking for a correspondent,' Sylvia said.

'A columnist,' he corrected.

'A columnist,' she echoed.

'Folks back home are just crazy to know what's going on over here,' Harry said, clicking his fingers to summon a waitress. 'I'm looking for someone to give them a taste of the show business life in Gay Paree. Someone with a flair for description.'

'I told him you'd be ideal,' Sylvia said with a grin. 'The way you recount the goings-on at Le Flamant Rose is so entertaining.'

Coming from the woman who had published James Joyce's *Ulysses*, I couldn't help but be flattered. A waitress came over and Harry ordered us all a round of champagne cocktails. And so it was that, dressed like a Greek goddess but with a heart still smarting, my newspaper column, 'An American in Paris', was born. Otto might not have shown up at the church, but it sure felt as if I was being offered a wonderful consolation prize.

SAGE

March 2018

As the plane hurtled along the runway, Sage experienced the usual rush she felt upon take-off, accompanied by a surge of relief. She was familiar with the saying, 'Wherever you go, there you are' – she'd even written a post inspired by it once, all about the importance of facing up to your problems instead of running away from them. But as Heathrow Airport shrank to toy-sized through the plane window, it felt pretty damn good to be leaving the UK and all of her problems behind her.

In the couple of weeks since she'd made her videos, the one thing that had kept her going was her communication with Sam. After the first couple of days, they'd graduated from email to a phone call and then to a video call, once he'd got 'a young whipper-snapper named Hunter' who worked on his farm to show him how to do it. Sage had told Sam how she'd come to be in possession of the locket, and he'd told her about his 'momma', a woman named Florence, who, it seemed, had been Elizabeth's birth mother and Sage's grandmother. According to Sam, Sage bore a striking likeness to Florence, too, which was what had prompted him to reach out after seeing her and the locket on *The Late Show*. Sage had begged him to tell her how Elizabeth had come to be abandoned in Paris, but Sam had annoyingly dodged this question, replying enigmatically that he'd 'rather Florence told her'. Whatever that was supposed to mean. Florence had died over ten years previously, so Sage wasn't sure how she'd be able to tell her anything, but apparently all would be revealed once she got to Sam's.

As a flight attendant delivered her auto-spiel about the in-flight entertainment, Sage settled back in her seat and allowed herself the faintest of smiles. After her mother had died and Tom had left, she'd felt so alone, but now it would appear she had a long-lost family, or a long-lost uncle at least. Sam had never married or had kids. When he'd invited her to come and visit him in a place called Arkansas, she'd jumped at the opportunity. If nothing else, it would help her escape the increasing stress and paranoia of living under siege.

After a nine-hour flight to Atlanta, a three-hour stopover, and a ninety-minute flight to Arkansas, Sage was feeling slightly less positive. As she queued for the terrifying prospect that was US Customs, she felt her anxiety start to build. What had she been thinking, coming halfway around the world to a place she couldn't even pronounce properly – how was she to know they said the final 's' in Arkansas as a 'w'?! – to stay with a random man she'd never met before? Sam had given a really convincing performance that he was for real – but what if he wasn't? What if he was some kind of axe murderer? Admittedly, if he was, he'd gone to enormously elaborate lengths to entice her into his lair, but still… As a gun-toting Customs official waved her through with a snarl and a grunt, Sage made the sobering realisation that she'd still rather be going to visit a potential serial killer than returning to the tsunami of hate back at home.

After retrieving her luggage, she made her way into the Arrivals lounge. Sam had said he'd be there to meet her, so she scanned the crowd for a weather-beaten man with silver hair. Finding no one matching Sam's appearance, she started looking at the name cards some of the people were holding. As her gaze fell upon a card saying, 'SAGE SEAGULL', she did a double-take. The guy holding it was young, or a lot younger than Sam anyway, appearing to be in his thirties and wearing a black T-shirt, jeans and a camo baseball cap. With closely cropped sandy hair and well-defined muscles, he looked like Action Man made human. Surely he couldn't be there for her – but could there really be someone named Sage Seagull on the same flight as her? She decided to approach him and find out.

'Hello?' she asked.

He looked at her, startled, as if he'd been miles away. 'Hey. Are you Sage?' His voice was deep, with a heavy Southern drawl.

She nodded. 'I was expecting someone else to meet me, though. And my surname isn't Seagull.'

'It's not?'

'No.'

He scratched his head. 'Could have sworn that's what Sam said. Did strike me as kind of strange.'

'So Sam sent you?'

'Uh-huh. I'm Hunter. I work on his farm. He was up to his elbows birthing a calf so he asked if I'd come get you.'

Trying to ignore the slightly disturbing image of Sam up to his elbows in a cow, Sage breathed a sigh of relief. Sam had mentioned Hunter several times in their emails and calls. He was the person who'd helped set up their video chats.

'All righty then, let's go,' Hunter said briskly, heading off across the concourse.

Running to catch up with his stride, Sage followed him over to an elevator, which they took to the fourth floor in total silence. As they emerged into the car park, Sage was greeted by a thick wall of humidity, and the enormity of what she'd done hit her all over again. She was now thousands of miles away from home and completely at the mercy of this hulk of a man who looked as if he was able to bench press a house.

'Here, let me take that,' Hunter said, gesturing at her case.

'It's fine. I'm strong. I do martial arts,' she said, instantly flushing. She'd meant it as some kind of warning shot not to try anything on, but it made her sound deranged.

'Is that so?' He gave her an amused grin. 'I wasn't aware martial arts involved the lifting of cases.'

'It doesn't. I just meant to say that I'm strong enough to carry my own.'

'I'm sure you are, but this here's my truck.' He gestured at a large black pickup beside them. 'I was just going to put it in the trunk for you.'

'Oh. I see. It's OK, I can do it.'

'Suit yourself.' He opened the boot and she hefted the case in, trying not to wince from the effort.

It turned out Hunter was a man of few words, which suited Sage just fine. Once they'd got onto the highway and the truck's air conditioning kicked in, she settled back and took in the scenery. She'd only been to America twice before, once to New York and once to LA, but with its dense forests and majestic mountain ranges, Arkansas was like a whole other country. The vivid blue sky seemed so much bigger here too, dotted with thick white clouds so beautiful it was as if they'd been painted on with an artist's brush. The only thing spoiling it was the music Hunter was playing on the stereo, a mash-up of rock and country, with lyrics that seemed to be limited to three key themes: death, heartbreak and Jesus.

After about an hour they exited the highway and started along a narrow road surrounded by fields.

'Almost there now,' Hunter announced, causing Sage to jump, as it was pretty much the first thing he'd said since leaving the airport.

She felt for the locket around her neck and thought of Elizabeth. *I wish you could be here, too.* Hunter took a right down a bumpy dirt track, and for a moment Sage thought her worst nightmare was about to come true and he was going to kill her – or worse. But then they came to a sun-bleached sign saying 'THORNTON FARM AND HORSES FOR HEROES'.

'Horses for Heroes?' Sage murmured questioningly.

Hunter nodded. 'That's what I do here.'

'I see.' Sage nodded, although he'd really only confused her further. But she couldn't think about that now. All she could think was that she was about to meet Elizabeth's long-lost brother and her own long-lost uncle.

Hunter pulled the truck up in front of a large white house with a sloping red roof. A wide porch ran the length of the house, containing a table and chairs and a couple of swing seats. A faded American flag fluttered from a pole by the front steps. As Sage got out of the truck and looked around, she felt the strangest sensation of familiarity. She wasn't sure why; she'd never been anywhere like this before. Maybe it was that she was meant to be there. Or maybe it was just the heat getting to her.

'Yo, Sam!' Hunter hollered, causing her to jump.

Sage's heart began thudding and her mouth went dry. The front door of the house flew open and a man with silvery cropped hair came half-running, half-striding down the porch steps and across the front yard towards them. He was tall and lean and wearing a red and blue chequered shirt and baggy faded jeans, held up with old-style braces.

'Well, I declare!' he exclaimed, in a drawl even stronger than Hunter's. 'If you aren't just the spit of her.' As he drew level with Sage, she could see that his eyes were shiny with tears, and in that moment, all of her doubts and fears disappeared.

'Hi, I'm Sage,' she said, holding out her hand, slightly awkwardly.

'I'm so sorry,' he said, grabbing her hand and shaking it heartily. 'Where are my manners? It's just that y'all look so like her. The green eyes. The heart-shaped face. The dimple. It feels a little like I'm seeing a ghost.'

In spite of the heat, Sage shivered.

'I'll be off then, go check on the horses,' Hunter said.

'Sure. Thanks for picking her up,' Sam said.

'Yes, thank you,' Sage added, but as Hunter strode off, she couldn't stop looking at Sam. Now that he was right in front of her, she could see that he had exactly the same nose and jawline as her mum. The effect was both comforting and disconcerting. He wasn't the only one seeing a ghost.

'Lord have mercy,' Sam chuckled, shaking his head. 'I can't believe you're here.'

'Me too.' Sage smiled. Unlike Hunter, who seemed so guarded, there was a natural warmth to Sam that instantly put her at ease.

'You must be hungry. And thirsty. Let me fix you some iced tea.' Sam grabbed her case. 'Follow me.'

He led her up the steps onto the porch and into the house. The front door opened into a large hallway. Off to one side, a beautiful grandfather clock ticked loudly, and ahead of them a wide staircase swept up and to the right. 'I'll show you to your room first and then we can have some tea.'

Sage followed him up the scuffed wooden stairs. Large fans like helicopter propellers hummed on the ceilings, providing a welcome relief from the heat. Sage's first impression was that it was like stepping inside the old-fashioned dolls' house her mother had bought her as a kid. And although its elegance was faded, it was undeniably homely.

'This was my momma's bedroom when she was a girl,' Sam said, taking Sage into a room at the back of the house. 'I thought you might like to stay here.'

'Your mum lived here?' Sage asked, glancing around the primrose-painted room. The wardrobe, dressing table and bed were all made from the same dark wood, and the bedspread and curtains were a riot of colour in mismatching floral prints. It was so different to Sage's apartment back at home, with its muted grey and white tones, but she instantly liked it. There was something cheering about all the colour.

'Uh-huh. She spent most of her life here, minus the years she was off on her adventures, of course. This place belonged to her daddy, my granddaddy. She inherited it when he passed, and I inherited it when she passed.'

'And when was that again?'

'About eleven years ago, just after she turned ninety-one.'

Sage felt a pang of sorrow. If only this had all happened sooner. If only Elizabeth had been able to meet her birth mother and her brother. She'd always been so closed off about what had happened, hurt by what she'd seen as her birth mother's rejection. But Sam was so warm and lovely; surely there had to be more to what had happened?

'There's a bathroom for you through there.' Sam nodded to a door beside the wardrobe. 'How about you take a minute to freshen up and I'll go fix us some iced tea?'

'That would be great. Thank you.'

He chuckled. 'Man, I love your accent. Y'all sound just like the queen.'

Sage suppressed a grin. With her South London twang, she definitely did not sound like royalty, but perhaps all Brits sounded the same to the American ear. She spotted a framed black and white photo of a young woman on the nightstand beside the bed. 'Is that... Is that her?'

'Sure is. Now, you tell me there's no likeness.'

Sage went over and picked up the photo. 'Wow.' With their thick wavy hair and bold eyebrows, there was no denying the striking resemblance between herself and Florence. They even shared the same dimple in the middle of their chins, that Sage had been teased about in school but Elizabeth had reassured her was a sign of great beauty. Sure enough, once Sage had become famous, her dimple had been the object of affection in many an Instagram comment, usually accompanied with the hashtag '#dimplegoals'.

'We really do look alike.'

'For sure. I'd say you have her same spirit, too.'

'Really?' Sage looked back at the photo. With her twinkly-eyed yet defiant grin, Florence certainly looked spirited.

'Yes, ma'am. I picked up on that in those videos of yours, where you're calling all of that internet stuff out for being phoney.'

Sage looked at him hopefully. It was so nice to hear a positive take on her meltdown, especially coming from someone who was actually her family.

'I have to admit, I didn't really understand a whole lot of what you were saying,' Sam continued. 'But it was the way you said it. It reminded me of my momma and how she'd get so fired up about things. But you'll find that out for yourself soon enough.'

'I will?' she asked, confused.

'Uh-huh. But first, let's have some tea.'

Once Sage had freshened up, she went back downstairs and found Sam out on the porch, setting a jug and some glasses down on the table.

'You ever had iced tea before?' he asked, gesturing at the jug. It was full of a golden liquid, with ice cubes and lemon slices bobbing on the surface.

Sage shook her head and sat down.

'Well, you better get used to it. We drink it like water down here in the South.' He poured her a glass and Sage took a sip. It was sweet and refreshing.

'I like it.'

'Just you wait till you try our barbeque. Boy, are you in for a treat. Here, I figured you'd want to see this.' Sam fumbled in his pocket and pulled something out, passing it to her. Sage's pulse quickened as she realised it was the other half of the locket. She held it up to her half, and sure enough, it was the perfect fit.

'I feel like Cinderella,' she joked.

'Can you imagine if y'all had come all this way and it didn't fit!' Sam chuckled.

'Hmm, it would have been a slight anticlimax.'

He smiled. 'We can take the locket into town tomorrow and have it fixed for you, if you like?'

'But don't you want to keep your half?'

'Nah. I have enough memories of my momma up here.' He tapped the side of his head. 'She would have wanted you to have it. Besides, I don't really think it would suit me.'

Sage giggled. 'Good point.' She looked at the writing on both halves of the locket. 'Did this quote have a special meaning? Did Florence have the locket made especially for my mother, so they'd always have a memento of each other?'

Sam shook his head. 'That's certainly why she left the locket with her. But she didn't have it made specially. She'd already owned it a few years by the time your mom was born. It was the thing that meant the most in the world to her, so it was quite a big deal for her to leave half of it with her, but you'll find out all about that.'

Sage couldn't wait. The more time she spent with Sam, the more her head filled with questions.

Sam poured himself a glass of iced tea and took a sip. 'So, how are you doing? It must have been a hell of a time, having to deal with all that fuss and bother without your momma there to support you.'

Sage nodded. 'It was. I'm so glad to be here,' she said quietly.

'Well, it sure is good to have you here.' He laughed. 'Ain't life a doozy? There I was thinking I was all alone in the world, and then up you pop, my very own niece!'

'That's exactly how I was feeling,' Sage exclaimed. 'I can't believe I've got an uncle.'

'And a grandma.' He grinned. 'I know she isn't here any more, but she left you something that I think you'll find real helpful.'

'She did?' Sage's heart began to pound.

'Uh-huh. Wait here and I'll go get it.'

As Sam went back inside, Sage surveyed the landscape. The house was surrounded by a patchwork of green, brown and yellow fields, dotted with a couple of barns, beyond which was a wooded area. In the distance, containing it all, was a rugged mountain range. It felt strange to be surrounded by so much open space. Strange but freeing. Over in the distance, she saw a figure she guessed was Hunter with a couple of horses. It all felt so peaceful, like living inside a landscape painting.

Sam returned with a vintage hard shell suitcase. It was the kind Sage had used in photo shoots for Instagram when she wanted to capture a classic retro feel. But while the cases she'd used had been brand new replicas in pretty pastel shades of pink and blue, this one was the real deal, dented and scuffed and brown.

'There's a whole bunch of your grandma's stuff in here,' Sam said, placing the case on the table and clicking the latches open. 'But I'm guessing you should start with her story.'

'She wrote her story?'

'Well, she never had it published or anything. She wrote it when she was about to turn eighty. You'll see why once you've read it.'

He reached inside the case and handed Sage a yellowing manuscript. 'Why don't you make a start on this while I fix us some dinner?'

'That sounds great.'

Sage turned to the first page and began to read, her skin tingling with excitement.

FLORENCE

June 1939

I almost didn't go looking for Otto the following year. And when I did, I was far less hopeful and open-hearted than the first time. After two years of dancing in Paris and one year as a columnist, I'd toughened up quite a bit. On the outside at least. The truth was, my love affair with Paris was beginning to fade. Writing 'An American in Paris' was in many ways to blame. Although I was able to get away with the occasional bit of pithy social commentary, Harry was far more interested in salacious gossip, and so my mind became trained to seek out and write about the trivial, beneath headlines like, *Aristocrat a Lowdown Love Rat!* and *The Dame to Blame in Wedding Day Shame!* The worst thing was, the more salacious the column became, the more people seemed to lap it up. Thankfully, I had the cover of anonymity. The identity of the writer of 'An American in Paris' was never revealed, which I guess added to its intrigue. Instead of a photo of me at the top of the column, there was the darkened silhouette of a woman's head, with sharply bobbed hair, and a cigarette-holder perched between her lips.

Don't get me wrong, I'd enjoyed it at first. I loved playing with words and swapping them around to find the perfect fit. I bought myself a typewriter and set it up on the table in my kitchen, and boy did I love the clickety-clack of the keys when the ideas came flowing. But by the summer of 1939, I was beginning to tire of

flimflammery and tittle-tattle. If I'd known then what was right
around the corner, of the things I'd soon be writing about, maybe
I would have had more appreciation for a time when my readers'
worlds were rocked by the revelation that their favourite singer
wore a wig.

But anyway, on the fourteenth of June 1939, I breezed past
Sacré-Coeur at eleven o'clock exactly, not a second early, scanned
the steps, then breezed my way back as soon as I realised there
was no sign of Otto. As I returned to my room, the certainty I'd
felt about us one day being reunited had the same quality as a
dream upon wakening. The harder I tried to cling on to it, the
more it faded from view. But of course, I still had one tangible
thing to cling to: his writing in my book. When I got back that
day, I looked at the line he'd underlined in the poem and frowned.
The words, 'All else has long been forgotten by me' now seemed
to taunt me. Clearly, I had been long forgotten by Otto.

Or had I? I was still using newspapers to teach myself French,
and every so often I would come across a story about the worsen-
ing plight of the Austrian Jews. What if something terrible had
happened to him? This thought always sent a shiver of dread
through me. But regardless, he hadn't shown up again, so I had
to let all romantic notions of him go.

Thankfully, that day I had an important soirée to get to.
A British aristocrat named Lady Hamilton-Jones was having
her summer ball, and the cream of French society would be in
attendance. Lady Hamilton-Jones, or Lady Rattling-Bones, as
Bessie and I referred to her, due to her skeletal appearance, was
known for having the most extravagant parties in all of Paris.
Rumour was, she'd even imported some tigers from India for this
shindig. Bessie had told me that Wallis Simpson was going to be
in attendance, and one of the Mitford sisters. Hopefully, I'd be
able to get at least four columns' worth of material. And if one
of the tigers escaped and ended up devouring a guest, I could

have my very first front-page scoop! But as I got changed into a Chanel gown, a knotted strand of pearls and a brand new pair of silver Mary Janes, I couldn't help wishing I was getting ready for an afternoon of wandering around Paris with Otto, talking art and music and poetry instead.

As so often happened when it came to my column, the party inspired two responses in me – the things I burned to write about, and the things I knew would actually get published. The day was oppressively hot, which didn't help, and by the time I'd had two Jack Roses – a cocktail made from applejack, vermouth and gin, as featured in Hemingway's *The Sun Also Rises* – the disappointment I'd been trying not to feel at Otto's no-show was morphing into a silent despair. Maybe it was the fierceness of the afternoon sun, but the women with their gaudy hats and garish gowns seemed too bright and shiny, their braying laughter too loud. The dripping opulence felt tasteless, somehow. Even the new dance floor that Lady Rattling-Bones had had installed in her garden, with glass walls and a super-duper sprung floor, didn't elicit the slightest thrill in me. I didn't understand how these people could all be so blasé about what was happening elsewhere in Europe. There was plenty of talk about the Germans at the party, but more in the way you'd talk about an irritating gnat that needed swatting away.

'We're just fine, we have the Maginot Line' seemed to be the theme of the day. But would these fortifications be enough to keep the Nazis at bay? I remembered the fear I'd seen in Otto's eyes, two years previously, when he'd talked about Hitler. And the contrast between his concern and the indifference of my fellow party guests made my stomach churn.

'Dear heart, are you OK?' Bessie asked, when she found me languishing beneath a willow tree by the champagne bar.

'I'm feeling a little woozy,' I replied. 'Must be the heat.'

She clasped hold of my arm. 'Say, you aren't in the family way?'

'No! Of course not.' Since my night with Otto, the furthest I'd gotten with a guy was on the night of my twenty-third birthday, when I'd engaged in some smooching purely to console myself that I wasn't all alone and unloved. As I reflected on this now, I couldn't help feeling slightly pitiful. Whether I cared to admit it or not, I'd been saving myself for someone who clearly wasn't ever coming back to me. This realisation, combined with the braying laughter of the party guests and the sweltering heat, made me feel sick.

'Wallis Simpson is here,' Bessie said, breathlessly. 'The king – I mean, the duke – isn't though.' Bessie might have been a tough broad from the Bronx, but when it came to British royalty, she turned into a gushing kid.

'That's great,' I lied. I knew I ought to go and hunt Simpson down, tail her for a bit, to see if I could hook myself some gossip for the column, but I'd far rather have stayed in the shade of the willow tree.

'Are you coming to dance?' Bessie asked.

'I will in a moment. I think I just need to stand in the shade for a bit.'

'Hang on a second,' Bessie said with a frown. 'What date is it?'

'Fourteenth of June,' I replied glumly. It was a date I'd come to see as a curse.

'Wasn't that the date you were supposed to meet that fellow?' she said softly.

'What fellow?' I asked, silently cursing. I hadn't told Bessie I was going looking for Otto this year after last year's humiliation.

'The Austrian fellow. Your kindred spirit.'

My glum expression must have given the game away.

'You did! Don't tell me, he didn't show up again.'

I shook my head. 'I really don't care, though. I just took a stroll past the church on the off-chance.'

'Oh, honey.' Bessie grabbed me in one of her all-encompassing embraces. She was always able to see through any pretence I tried to make.

'It was a dumb idea,' I muttered. 'It's been two years. He's obviously forgotten all about me.'

Bessie frowned and shook her head. 'If he has, he needs his head examining.' She lowered her voice an octave and adopted the throaty drawl we always used when messing around. 'You, my dear, are a dame among dames!'

'Thank you.'

'Come and dance,' she implored. 'Let's show these crusty Brits how the Lindy Hop is really done.'

'Sure, just give me a few more minutes,' I replied.

'OK, sweet cheeks.'

I watched Bessie sashay her way back up the lawn, and not for the first time, I wished that some of her chutzpah would rub off on me. It wasn't that Bessie didn't feel things. She was still madly in love with Pierre, who still hadn't left his wife for her. But Bessie didn't mope around, pining. She threw herself into other flings. The night before, she'd told me that her goal for Lady Hamilton-Jones' ball was to neck with at least three different people – men or women. I was willing to bet my bottom dollar she'd double that score.

I looked at one of the tigers Lady Hamilton-Jones had imported from India, pacing up and down inside its gilded cage. It felt like the perfect metaphor for the party, all of us trapped inside a glittering prison that shone so bright, most of us were too dazzled to see the bars. This was the column I burned to write, but I knew Harry would have my guts for garters if I filed it. As I leaned against the trunk of the tree I saw a well-known French actress slipping off behind the summer house, hand-in-hand with an equally well-known and very married American diplomat. The headline *'Ooh la la – Adultery by the Champagne Bar'* popped into my head, making me want to stab myself. Unable to take it any longer, I slunk off across the lawn and out through the gates, desperate to be home.

I took the Métro halfway, then decided to walk the rest to try and clear my head. Much as I hated to admit it, I was starting to feel the way I'd done in New York before I'd left, and before that in Arkansas. A familiar burning sensation of boredom and frustration, a craving for there to be more to life than this. But what? Why did I always end up so dissatisfied with my lot? And why did others not? As I made my way up the steps to Montmartre, a thought of my mother randomly popped into my head.

'The trouble with you is you have your momma's restless spirit,' my daddy once said to me when I was ten, and I had announced that I wanted to run away and join the circus and please could he help me in my endeavours by erecting a tightrope in the hayloft, so I'd have a cushioned fall when I practised.

'What do you mean?' I asked. He hardly ever spoke of my momma, so I couldn't resist this opportunity to find out more.

'She was never able to stay still. She always had to take risks.'

'Like what?'

'Like the day she died,' he said, his deep voice cracking.

All I knew by that point was that my mom had died after falling from a horse.

'How had she taken a risk?' I was sure I must have used up my quota of questions, but to my surprise he replied, his eyes ablaze with fury and grief.

'Riding without a saddle. Riding like the wind.'

This was the image of my mom that came to me that evening on the steps. Riding like the wind, with her long hair streaming out behind her, fuelled by the same fire I felt burning in my belly, the same desperation to be free. I sighed and looked up at the church. That was why I'd liked Otto so much. I'd recognised that same spirit in him. 'Where are you?' I whispered up into the air. And I pictured my question lifting like a wisp of smoke, being carried higher and higher, all the way to Austria, until it somehow reached his ears.

My new shoes were really starting to hurt now, tearing into the backs of my heels, so I sat down at the top of the steps and removed them. I could walk the rest of the way in stockinged feet. I looked at the twinkling lights of Paris spread out beneath me. The mountainous climb was always made worth it by this view.

'Florence?' A man's voice broke my reverie.

At first I thought I had to be imagining things. But then I heard him say my name again. Louder, and coming from right behind me.

'Florence? Is it you?'

I turned slowly, not wanting to be wrong. But I wasn't. It was him. Thinner than before, and scruffier, but it was Otto, standing on the steps behind me.

'You – you came!' I stammered, getting to my feet.

He reached out his hand to help me.

'I was late this morning. Only by two minutes and when you weren't here… I decided to stay, just in case.'

'You've been here all day?'

He nodded.

I laughed and shook my head. 'I was here, too. At eleven, I mean. But after you hadn't turned up last year, I thought you'd forgotten about me, so I didn't wait.'

'I would never forget about you.' And then finally, that grin returned to his face, although I couldn't help noticing a sadness in his eyes. '"We were together. All else has long been forgotten by me."'

'You remembered,' was all I was able to say in response.

He nodded. 'I'm so sorry I wasn't able to come last year. Things, they were very difficult. I thought about you, though.'

'I thought about you, too.'

He shook his head. 'You must have hated me for not showing.'

'No.' I smiled. 'Well, only a bit.'

'So...' he asked quietly.

'So...?'

I don't think I've ever felt a more powerful compulsion to hold someone, to touch them, to kiss them. It took every muscle in my body just to stay still.

'Oh, Florence, it is so good to see you!' He took a step closer, so that we were toe to toe. His chin was covered in stubble and there were dark rings beneath his eyes. He was like a faded version of the Otto in my memories. Not that it mattered. All that mattered was he hadn't forgotten. He was here. I felt his fingertips reaching for mine. It was the most delicate touch, and yet it sent a powerful charge through me.

'I didn't know...' he whispered. 'Do you... have you... are you taken?'

'Taken?'

'By someone else.'

'No!'

And now his grin was back in all its glory, this time reaching his eyes. 'I was so sure you would be married by now.'

'What? No!'

'But you are so...' He broke off. 'Magnificent!'

At this point I started to laugh. 'I don't feel magnificent.'

'Why? Are you OK?' He instantly looked concerned.

'I wasn't, but then...'

'Then?'

'You appeared like an answer to my prayers.'

And at that, he leaned forward and kissed me, tentatively at first, then with an intensity that made my body feel as if it had dissolved into shimmering moonlight.

'Come on, let's go,' I said, tugging on Otto's hand.

'Wait a moment, don't you need these?' he asked, picking up my shoes.

I giggled. I was so giddy from excitement, I'd completely forgotten I'd taken them off.

'I am always picking up your clothes from these steps,' he joked.

I laughed as I remembered that day of our first meeting, and how he'd found me surrounded by my underwear. It felt like another lifetime ago, and judging by Otto's changed appearance, it had been the same for him too.

'It is so good to finally be back!' Otto exclaimed, as we made our way into the Place du Tertre. Handfuls of diners were sitting outside the restaurants, making the most of the balmy evening. A bereted artist called over to us from behind his easel. But we both ignored him. I didn't want to dilute my time with Otto with anyone. François, the manager of La Crémaillère, was out wiping tables when we reached the restaurant.

'*Bonsoir*, Florence,' he greeted me, then looked at Otto curiously.

'*Bonsoir,*' I said. 'This is my friend, Otto.'

Otto mumbled a greeting and stared at the floor. He seemed shyer than I remembered him. I unlocked the heavy door and we slipped inside. As always, the dark stairwell was mercifully cool. I practically skipped up the stairs in my stockinged feet, all too aware of Otto right behind me. The deadness I'd been feeling for the past few months had gone, and I'd been brought back to life by his presence. Finally, we reached my room and my fingers trembled as I unlocked the door. When I thought of the crushing disappointment I'd been wrestling with the last time I'd been here, just hours before, and how convinced I'd been that I'd never see Otto again, I had to pinch myself to make sure I hadn't become lost in a daydream.

'It is just as I remember it,' Otto murmured as he followed me into the room. 'The kitchen, the chair, the table, the windows.'

'You have a good memory,' I joked.

'I made myself remember it – and you – every day since we last met. Even on the very worst days…' He tapered off and his smile faded. 'I kept rereading you like a book, inside here.' He tapped the side of his head.

For the first time in a year, since the first time I went to meet him on the steps and he wasn't there, I was able to stop pretending that it was no big deal, that he was no big deal, that what we had shared meant nothing. Now Otto was standing in front of me again, I was able to confess to myself that he meant everything. The enormity of that realisation was overwhelming.

'I've thought of you every day, too,' I whispered. And it was true. Even on those days when I'd cursed myself for thinking about him, he had still been in my thoughts.

'I would imagine you, looking out at this tree,' he said, going over to the window.

'Well, that would be accurate. I do spend a crazy amount of time gazing into those branches,' I joked.

'I used to imagine that if I was thinking of you looking at the tree while you were actually looking at it, you'd somehow receive the message.' He laughed. 'It is silly.'

I thought of the moment on the steps earlier, when I'd pictured sending a message to him in Austria. 'It isn't silly. Would you like something to drink?'

'Oh, yes please!' His eagerness made me wonder how long it had been since he'd eaten.

'Are you hungry? I could fix us something.' I lit the lamp on the kitchen table.

'If you're sure?'

'Of course.'

Otto came to join me in the kitchenette. As he took off his jacket I noticed that, just like his face, his arms were definitely thinner than before.

'So, what have you been doing?' I asked breezily as I took a baton of bread from the cupboard and a bottle of wine from the shelf.

'Trying to escape Hitler,' he said with a bitter laugh. 'Everything changed when the Anschluss happened.' He sat down at the table.

'The Anschluss?'

'When the Germans annexed Austria last year. The persecution of the Jews in Germany might have been a gradual thing, but not this – overnight, we were declared second-class citizens. I had to leave my college. My parents had to declare all of their assets. We lost just about everything.'

'I'm so sorry.' I sat down beside him and poured us some wine.

'Thank you.' He raised his glass. 'To being together again.'

'To being together.' I cut the bread into thick slices and took the lid off the china butter dish. The butter was soft as cream in the heat. 'So, you weren't able to come to Paris last summer?'

He shook his head. 'I didn't want to leave my parents. It was becoming so dangerous. We tried to get visas to move to another country, but too many people were having the same idea, it was impossible to get them.' He took a large bite of his bread.

'Then what happened?'

'Then vom Rath was assassinated.'

'Vom Rath?' The name rang a bell. I knew I'd seen it in a newspaper but couldn't remember when or why or who he was.

'He was a Nazi who had been posted to the German embassy in Paris,' Otto explained. 'A Polish Jew came to the embassy and shot him. When he died, the Germans used it as an excuse to launch Kristallnacht – the Night of Broken Glass.'

'I remember now – I read about the assassination,' I exclaimed. 'But what was the Night of Broken Glass?' The phrase sent a shiver through me.

'The Nazis went on a rampage, setting fire to our synagogues, arresting Jews, beating them, murdering them.'

I looked at Otto in the flickering light of the lamp, at the lines fanning his eyes and the hollows beneath his cheekbones. Whatever he'd witnessed seemed to have etched itself into his being.

'What did you do? How did you end up in France?'

'My parents insisted I leave.'

'Without them?'

He nodded and his eyes became shiny with tears. 'They thought they'd be safer staying there, being older. They thought that the Nazis wouldn't want anything from them. I only hope they're right. I went to Belgium at first. My father's childhood friend Ernst and his family live in Brussels, so I went there as a refugee in January. I helped Ernst in his jewellery store to earn my keep.'

'I can't believe how much has happened,' I said, taking a sip of my drink. And I had a feeling he was only telling me the very tip of the iceberg.

'Enough about me.' He blinked away his tears. 'How about you? How have you found Paris? Tell me all about your adventures.'

After hearing what Otto and his family had been through, my 'adventures' seemed silly and frivolous and I felt too embarrassed to go into too much detail. 'Nothing much to report really. I'm still dancing at my friend's music hall.'

'And you've been writing?' he asked, nodding at the typewriter.

'Oh, yes. I write a column for a New York paper. It's nothing much, a silly thing…'

'What?' He looked at me, stunned. 'How can you say it is silly? This is an amazing achievement.'

'Trust me, it really isn't.'

He cocked his head to one side and frowned. 'How so?'

'My editor only wants me to write gossip.'

'Gossip?'

'Yes, things I pick up in the club. Which famous person's having an affair, which glamorous singer wears a wig, that kind of thing. It's stupid.'

Otto grinned. 'It sounds kind of fun to me. Which glamorous singer wears a wig?'

I laughed. 'Now, that would be telling. When did you come to France?' I asked, eager to shift the spotlight.

'Today.'

'Today?'

'Yes, that was why I was a bit late this morning. My train was delayed. I didn't want to miss another opportunity to see you. Even though I thought you'd probably given up on me. I had to come and see.'

I laughed and shook my head. 'I still can't believe you were there.'

'I still can't believe *you* were there.'

The energy in the room shifted, all of the gloom evaporating with the intensifying heat between us.

'How long are you here for? Where are you staying?'

He shrugged. 'I guess I am here for good.'

'In Paris?'

He nodded and studied my face as if worried he might detect displeasure in my expression. 'I cannot go home. I no longer have a home. And here in France, I am safe from the Nazis. And here in France…'

'Yes?'

'There is you.'

We shifted closer in our seats.

'You look as majestic as an eagle,' he whispered, giving my ball gown an appraising look.

'You remembered,' I whispered back.

'Of course.' He took my hand in his. 'How could I forget?'

As our fingers entwined, I pictured us as eagles soaring, our talons locking.

And then suddenly we were spiralling our way to the bed, and my gown was slipping to the floor and he was pulling his shirt up and over his head. I ran my fingers over his chest, tracing the contours of his ribs protruding through his skin. I pressed my face into the light nest of hair on his chest and inhaled him in, holding him tighter and tighter, to convince myself again that I wasn't dreaming.

'Oh, Florence,' he sighed in my ear, before pulling me onto the bed.

Afterwards, we lay wrapped up in each other, the shadow of the tree casting a lattice-like pattern upon our skin.

'You still have the book,' he said, noticing my Walt Whitman collection on the bedside cabinet.

'Of course.'

He leaned over and began flicking through until he reached the page he'd written on.

'I always had a feeling you'd come back,' I whispered. 'Even when you weren't there last year. It was the strangest thing.'

'I do not think it is strange,' he replied. 'Kindred spirits, we know these things.'

And then, just when I thought it was impossible for me to experience any more joy, he got out of bed and fetched something from his jacket pocket.

'I made this for you,' he said, handing me a small package. 'When I was working for Ernst at his jeweller's store.'

I took the package and opened it. Inside was a silver locket on a chain. A pair of birds had been carved on both sides, cartwheeling through the air together, talons locked.

'The bald eagles,' I whispered.

'Us,' he replied.

Some words had been engraved around each side of the locket. I held it up to the lamplight so I was able to read.

'*We were together,*' one side said. '*I forget the rest*' was etched into the other.

'From the poem,' I murmured.

Otto undid the clasp and gently put the locket around my neck. Then I sank back into his arms.

That night, I lay awake long after Otto had fallen asleep. The frustration I'd been feeling just hours before had gone completely, as had the desire to run away. All I wanted was to stay like this, in Otto's arms, with Walt Whitman's words of love pressed against my heart, forever.

SAGE

March 2018

'How are you getting on?'

Sage looked up from the manuscript to see Sam standing in the front doorway. He was wearing an old white apron splattered with stains over his shirt and jeans.

'It's amazing. I can't believe she did all of that.'

'Where are y'all up to?'

'The bit where Otto comes back to Paris and gives her the locket.' Instinctively, Sage felt for the locket around her neck. All this time she'd thought of it as a memento of her mother, but now she could feel the essence of Otto and Florence etched into the silver too, making it all the more magical.

'Ha! You still haven't read the half of it!' Sam said with a grin. 'But can I tear you away long enough to get something to eat?'

'Of course.' Sage followed him into the house, clutching the manuscript. Now she finally had her mysterious grandmother's story in her grasp, she didn't want to lose sight of it.

Sam brought her through to a large kitchen at the back of the house. Just like the other rooms, it was rustic and homely, with a huge old-fashioned stove, a wooden dresser lined with colourful plates and bowls, and a round table in the centre, covered in a red and white gingham tablecloth. Whatever he'd been cooking smelled delicious.

'Take a seat,' he said, gesturing to the table.

She sat down and watched as he plated up what looked like fried fillets of fish. Then he took a loaf of freshly baked bread from a cooling rack and brought it over to the table.

'Catfish and cornbread,' he announced. 'And I made us some slaw, too. Don't be shy, dig in.'

Sage buttered a slice of the warm yellow bread and took a bite. 'This is delicious!' she exclaimed.

'Why, thank you. I learned how to bake it from my grand-daddy – your great granddaddy.'

'Florence's dad, the one who lived on this farm?'

'Uh-huh. He was a fine man. Didn't say much, but when he did, it really counted.'

'Did he teach you about farming too?'

'A little. He died when I was fifteen though, so I learned most of it from my mom.'

'Oh!' Sage couldn't hide her shock. From what she'd read so far, Florence hadn't seemed the greatest fan of farm life.

'Do you guys get catfish back home?' Sam asked, offering her the dish of coleslaw.

'Only the TV show,' Sage joked.

Sam looked at her blankly. She guessed he wasn't much of a fan of reality TV.

'It's one of our staple dishes.'

Sage took a bite. The crispy breadcrumb coating gave way to tender, flaky white fish. 'This is great.' For the first time in years, Sage wolfed down her food without thinking about its calorific content or how much exercise she'd have to put her body through to burn it off. That had been another downside of living her life so publicly. She'd opened her body up to constant scrutiny, and somewhere along the line she'd become her own fiercest critic. It was only when she'd taken her last bite that she realised Sam was staring at her.

'Well, I'll be darned if you don't eat just like her too,' he said softly.

Sage felt a warm glow inside. Now she'd begun reading about Florence, it felt like a real compliment to be compared to her. 'It's funny, but even though she was in her twenties so long ago, I feel like we have quite a lot in common.'

'Oh yeah?'

'The writing thing, I mean. I could really relate to what she said about having to write about things she didn't really want to.'

Sam topped up her iced water. 'How's that?'

'Well, when I first started posting online I really wanted to write about things that mattered, but those kind of posts didn't get me endorsement deals.'

He looked at her blankly.

'They didn't make me any money. So I ended up writing about make-up and stuff, so I could get companies to pay me.'

'Is that why you got so fed up with it all, why you made that video?'

'Kind of, yeah. That and the fact that my life had become a total disaster area. I was sick of pretending everything was perfect.'

'Hmm, I'm pretty sure perfect doesn't exist.'

Sage nodded, and all of a sudden she was hit by a wave of exhaustion so strong she couldn't help yawning.

'You must be pooped. What time is it back in Britain?'

It was only when Sage took her phone from her pocket that she realised she hadn't checked it since arriving at the airport. 'Just gone one in the morning,' she replied, trying to ignore the row of notifications across the screen.

'Shoot.' Sam started clearing away the plates. 'Do you want to head on up to bed and we can start afresh in the morning?'

'That would be great.' She stood up. 'Is it OK if I take Florence's story with me?'

'Of course, and you sleep for as long as you need, you hear?'

'I will. Thank you.'

Sage went upstairs and into her room – *Florence's* room. Now she'd read some of her grandmother's story, this fact bore way more significance for her. She pictured a young Florence lying on the bed, dreaming of a life of adventure as a dancer in New York. She went over to the window and looked out. The air was filled with a high-pitched whirring that sounded like crickets. Whatever it was, she found it really soothing. To the left of the farmhouse there was an old oak tree she hadn't really noticed before, but now, like everything else, it was imbued with a deeper meaning. She pictured Florence leaning out of the window, talking to the tree, excitedly greeting the arrival of its new leaves each spring. Then she thought of Otto. Sage had never met a man who could recite poetry by heart, or who called her magnificent, or who she could imagine turning up two years after they first met because he hadn't stopped thinking about her. Tom had been her only long-term partner and he'd sucked all the love from her, leaving nothing but an empty husk. The men she'd met since had all been sleazeballs, especially the guy who'd sold the story of their night together to the press. She shuddered at the recollection. But hadn't it been the same for Florence, before she'd arrived in Paris? She hurried over to the manuscript and skimmed back through the pages she'd read. Yes, there was the guy called Joe Fraser, who sounded like a really nasty piece of work, and she'd complained about the men she met in the clubs where she danced.

Sage sat on the bed and thought back to the night she'd first met Tom at a party in a converted warehouse in Shoreditch. 'You look a lot hotter in real life,' was the first thing he'd said to her. At first, she'd like the fact that he didn't kiss her butt. At least he wasn't fake. But he'd turned out to be the biggest faker of them all, cheating on her with a so-called friend. Bitterness grew sharp inside of her, and now that her thoughts had been sent spiralling back to her former life, she felt the compulsion to check her phone.

There was yet more abuse on Twitter, and although she'd turned off the comments on her most recent Instagram posts, it hadn't deterred the haters. They'd simply scrolled back and started posting their vitriol on older posts. *'It's the Sage Segal is over party #cancelled'*, a user called @clarebearmummy had written. Sage clicked on her profile. 'Clarebearmummy' appeared to be the mother of two young kids, who lived in Surrey and had a penchant for taking selfies on the school run. Why did this person think she had the right to cancel anyone? What did it even mean to cancel someone? Did this grown woman and complete stranger wish that Sage no longer existed? Did she want her dead?

Sage flung her phone down. It landed on top of Florence's manuscript. She wondered what her grandmother would have made of it all. She had a feeling Florence wouldn't have stood for it, but what else could Sage do? She'd tried posting an honest, heartfelt – and non-drunken – video, and that had only seemed to make people hate her more. She opened her case and pulled out her pyjamas. As she slipped beneath the rose-patterned quilt, her eyes were stinging from exhaustion, but she didn't want the poisonous words from her socials to be the last thing she read before going to sleep. She picked up the manuscript and continued to read.

FLORENCE

1939

The day after my reunion with Otto, I took him to meet Bessie at the club. She was pretty much dumbstruck when I introduced him – and Bessie being struck dumb was rarer than an eclipse of the sun.

'Otto? But… but… isn't he your fourteenth of June guy?' she spluttered.

'He sure is. He just turned up a little later than planned,' I laughed, causing Otto to blush.

'Well, I'll be damned!' Once she'd gotten over her initial shock, Bessie showed Otto the same warmth she'd shown me when I'd turned up in New York City with next to nothing. She put out a few feelers, and within a week she'd found a guy who could provide him with false papers and got him a job as a packer at La Samaritaine department store. I'd worried that Otto would find it tiresome to work such a dead-end job, given that his dream was to be an artist, but when he met me in the club the night after his first shift, his eyes were gleaming with excitement.

'The store is only a two-minute walk from the Musée du Louvre!' he exclaimed. 'I can go there on my lunchbreak just like Renoir did!' That night, he sat at a table in the corner of Le Flamant Rose with a new sketchpad on the table in front of him, drawing away. Much as I hated to admit it, I'd been worried things might get kind of awkward between us, once Otto saw me dance. My Venus costume left very little to the imagination, and my routine involved high kicks and ass wiggles that left even less to be imagined. But Otto was completely unfazed. When I went over to his table at the end of the night, he handed me a piece of paper. On it was a drawing of me in my Venus regalia with a huge pair of wings.

'This was how I saw you tonight,' he told me. 'Like an eagle dancing.'

It was the first time I'd seen one of his drawings and it took my breath away. There was an energy to his artwork, a rawness, that was captivating. I felt a burst of anger at Hitler for almost having thwarted Otto's artistic dreams. But he was in Paris now, finally. And I hoped that, just like Renoir, his dreams would soon start coming true.

When Bessie saw the picture, she commissioned Otto to do a painting of Le Flamant Rose on the spot. That night he and I lay in each other's arms, chattering away until the dawn chorus, all aglow with possibility.

It wasn't until August that our bubble well and truly burst. The threat of war with Germany, which I'd been trying so hard to avoid since Otto's return, was becoming impossible to ignore. Trenches had been dug around the city for bomb shelters and we'd all been issued with gas masks. There was still great faith in the invincibility of the Maginot Line, but having learned from Otto what the Nazis had done in Austria, I wasn't so sure. I think we were both trying to stay strong and happy for each other, but then one night at the end of August, Otto came to see me in my dressing room at the club, looking distraught.

'I had to go to the Louvre today,' he told me.

'On your lunchbreak?' I asked, applying some rouge to my cheeks.

'No, for work. The curators at the museum have been called back from their vacation and they needed our help.'

I stared at his reflection in the mirror. 'What do you mean?' Most Parisians left the city during the month of August for their summer vacation; it was highly unusual for them to return for anything.

'They are worried about a German invasion,' Otto said gravely. 'So they have taken the major works of art into hiding in the country.'

'Oh no!' My stomach churned. Surely the museum wouldn't go to all that trouble unless they really believed that war, and a possible German invasion, was imminent? 'But why did they need your help?'

'Packing the artwork into crates.' He looked heartbroken. 'I had to help pack the *Mona Lisa*. And today, I touched a Renoir.'

'Oh, Otto.' I stood up and threw my arms around him.

'All these years, I have longed to see these paintings, to be close to them,' he murmured. 'And today, I got closer than I've ever been and all I wanted to do was cry. All of those empty frames left lying on the floor, like abandoned corpses.'

'But frames are replaceable,' I said, taking his face in my hands. 'The paintings are still alive and you helped save them.'

He shook his head. 'The Nazis will find them. They will destroy them. They destroy everything.'

The bitterness in his voice was so out of character, it sent a shudder through me. I hated seeing him so low. A memory of my daddy came back to me, from foaling season when I'd been about twelve years old. One of my favourite horses, Blossom, had been having real trouble birthing. She'd kept making this horrible keening noise and thrashing her head from side to side. I'd been terrified and I could tell my daddy was, too. 'We mustn't show her we are afraid,' he'd told me. 'Even if we are. She needs to feel our strength.' And so we sang to Blossom, my daddy and I, for half the night. We sang her lullabies and 'The Star-Spangled Banner' and told her jokes and recounted stories, and somehow, deep in the night, Blossom quit panicking and gave birth to a beautiful foal we named Hope.

I sensed that just like Blossom, Otto needed my strength right then, even if I had to fake it.

'Listen, there's no way Hitler's going to conquer the French,' I said, taking hold of his hands. 'We have the British army on our side, and the Maginot Line. The worst they will do is bomb Paris, and now they'll never be able to bomb the paintings. You will go down as a hero in art history. In years to come, when those paintings are all back in their rightful place, you'll be able to go to the Louvre and tell people, "I saved the *Mona Lisa*!"'

A faint smile appeared on Otto's face. 'I suppose this is true.'

'Of course it is.' I kissed him on the cheek, leaving a bright red lipstick print.

Four days later Germany invaded Poland, and France and Britain entered the war.

It's hard to describe the atmosphere in Paris during the next few months. I might do better to try and describe my own personal feelings, as they were surely a microcosm of all that was happening outside on the streets. My emotions seemed to swing like a pendulum. I would have days when I felt as if I could take on the world – days when my faith in the French and British armies was strong – and other days when hope deserted me and I could barely breathe for the sense of foreboding. And even though the Germans were still miles away geographically, their presence was felt all too keenly on the streets of Paris.

Thousands of men aged between eighteen and thirty-five were conscripted and dispatched to the front. Bessie was heartbroken when Pierre was drafted. She was even more heartbroken when the clubs were forced to shut due to the blackout and the midnight curfew. As the French men left, a tide of refugees swept in on their wake. The sidewalks were crowded with people trudging along with the weight of the world on their shoulders and all of their worldly goods crammed into battered cases. It broke my heart to see the fear in their eyes, and it made my blood boil that one man should be responsible for so much pain. I stopped reading the papers to teach myself French as I couldn't bear to see the name *Hitler, Hitler, Hitler* all over the pages. Of course, my hatred was personal as well as political, as I was becoming increasingly scared for Otto's safety. He'd travelled so far to escape the Nazis – but what if it wasn't far enough?

The only slight silver lining came in the form of a request from Harry. He wanted my column to switch its focus away from tittle-tattle to look at how Parisian women were coping with the war. Apparently, the folks back home were just dying to know. The day I tried to write my first more serious column, Otto came home from work to find me hunched over the typewriter, surrounded by a pile of magazines, crumpled-up balls of paper littering the floor.

'Can I ask your advice about something?' I said, as he leaned down to kiss the top of my head.

'You may.' He took a stick of bread and a small parcel wrapped in greaseproof paper from his bag. 'I have fresh sardines,' he announced proudly.

'Oh, you doll!' I exclaimed. Food was already getting harder to come by, especially fish.

'I bought it from François downstairs.' He went and lit the stove. 'What advice do you need?'

'I'm trying to write my first column about the war for the *Tribune* and I'm getting so frustrated.'

'Why?'

'Harry wants to know how the women in Paris are dealing with the war, but writing about it is making me mad. Listen to this.' I turned to an advertisement for Helena Rubenstein make-up in

Vogue magazine. '"These days it is the duty of everyone, especially women, to communicate to those one loves, the optimism which results in confidence in oneself." So what they're saying is, all us gals need to do is put on lipstick, and we'll all be just swell. Or look at this one.' I shoved a copy of *Le Jardin des Modes* under Otto's nose. 'It says here that French women must stay exactly how their men fighting at the front want them – "not ugly"!' I started pacing up and down the small kitchenette. 'I mean, is that all we are good for – not looking ugly? Is that really how us women must defeat the Nazis? By wearing lipstick!'

Otto smiled. 'Of course not.'

I sighed. 'I'm sorry, it's just driving me crazy, all this sitting around waiting. I want to do something!'

'You can do something,' he said softly.

I looked at him blankly.

'You are being asked to write about what it is like here, for the American readers, yes?'

I nodded.

'Then don't write about lipstick and looking pretty, write about the reality – beneath the make-up. You can tell America what is really happening. Write about the hardship and the fear. Maybe if they know the truth, America might join with us in fighting Germany.' His eyes gleamed with hope. 'Then surely Hitler wouldn't stand a chance.'

'You're right!' I planted a kiss on his lips, sat back down at my typewriter, and started to write as if Otto's life – and indeed mine – depended on it.

SAGE

March 2018

The next morning, Sage woke to the sound of paper scrunching. She opened her eyes, taking in the floral symphony that was the bedspread and curtains. She had absolutely no idea where she was. Then it all came flooding back. She sat bolt upright and rubbed her eyes. Florence's manuscript lay beside her on the pillow, where she'd fallen asleep reading it. Somewhere outside, a cockerel crowed. Sage went over to the window and opened the curtains. The sun was just rising over the mountains in the distance, painting the sky pink, purple and gold.

'Good morning, Mister Tree,' she whispered to the oak, smiling as she thought of Florence doing exactly the same all those years before. Just as she was wondering if Sam was up yet, she spotted him over by the chicken coop, throwing handfuls of feed on the ground for the chickens, who were clucking and bustling around him. He was wearing a faded red T-shirt, denim dungarees and a Stetson hat. Sage had never seen a man dressed like this in real life before. The entire scene through her window was like something from a Western movie. She found it weirdly comforting, maybe because it was the polar opposite of her life back home.

She went through to the bathroom and stepped into the shower. While she was washing, she thought back to the part of Florence's story she'd read before falling asleep. She couldn't begin to imagine what it must have been like for Florence and Otto in Paris, waiting for the German army to arrive. It had been almost ten years since Sage had studied history in school, but from what she could remember, the Nazis had occupied Paris for almost all of the Second World War. What had happened to Florence and Otto once they'd arrived?

The war had always seemed so far removed from Sage before, something terrible that had happened to other people, another lifetime ago. The thought of her own grandmother being so directly affected sent a shiver down her spine. Sage finished showering and put on a T-shirt and jeans, then she made the bed and placed Florence's manuscript neatly on the pillow.

'I'll be back soon,' she whispered, before leaving the room.

Sam took her to a local diner called the Wagon Wheel for breakfast, although his idea of 'local' was actually a twenty-minute drive away.

'This was your grandma's favourite place,' he told her, as they pulled into the small parking lot outside. The sign at the front of the diner was made from a customised wagon wheel placed on top of a post. 'WELCOME TO THE WAGON WHEEL: HEARTY FOOD FOR ALL THE FAMILY', it read. 'It's been here since she was a kid. Still run by the same family.'

As Sage followed Sam inside, she experienced the same frisson of excitement she always used to feel when she travelled somewhere new as a kid – back before her life had begun to be experienced through the dulling lens of social media and constantly having to seek out content for vlogs, photos and posts. With its diner-style booths, rustic decor and life-sized cut-outs of Elvis and Dolly Parton by the counter, the Wagon Wheel was so different to anything Sage had seen before, she felt as if she was in a whole other world.

'Why, Samuel Clancy, who do we have here?' a woman cried from behind an old-style cash register. She was about Sam's age, with greying auburn hair piled on top of her head in a wispy bun.

'This here's the young lady I was telling you about: my niece, Sage, all the way from London, England,' Sam replied proudly. 'Sage, this is Marybelle Delaney, the proprietor of this fine establishment.'

'Hi,' Sage said awkwardly.

'Lordy, if she isn't the spitting image of Florence!' Marybelle came out from behind the counter, bringing with her a comforting scent of roses and vanilla. She clasped Sage's hands. 'Your grandmother was a remarkable woman.'

'So I hear.' Sage couldn't help feeling proud.

'Well, would you listen to that accent! Isn't she the cutest thing?' Sam nodded and Sage's warm glow grew.

'Y'all sit yourselves down and I'll bring you over some coffee.'

Marybelle bustled back behind the counter and Sam led Sage over to a booth in the window. The red Formica table had been laid with a pair of Elvis salt and pepper shakers and a plastic ketchup bottle in the shape of a tomato.

'Here you go,' Sam said, handing Sage a menu. 'Get whatever you fancy.'

Sage scanned the list. There were about fifty variations on pancakes, all sounding equally delicious. Then she saw something that made her stop in her tracks.

'Er, what are biscuits and gravy?'

'Another fine Southern staple,' Sam replied with a grin.

'But isn't that…' She was about to say 'gross', but she didn't want to appear rude.

'It's great with the sausage,' Sam added.

'But aren't biscuits a bit too sweet to have with gravy – and sausage?' Her stomach churned at the thought.

'Nah, they're just right, you should give 'em a try.'

Marybelle came over, holding a pot of coffee. 'Are you guys ready to order?'

Sam looked at Sage.

'Could I have the blueberry pancakes please?'

Marybelle clasped her hand to her heart. 'Your accent is so cute. You sound just like the queen.'

'That's what I said,' Sam chuckled.

'Have y'all ever seen the queen?' Marybelle asked. 'I just love your royal family.'

'No, but I once met Prince William at a charity event.' Sage felt a wistful pang at the memory. The event had been a fundraiser for homeless teens, back when her star had still been on the rise and she'd believed she could make some kind of positive difference as an influencer.

Marybelle's eyes widened. 'Oh, bless your heart.' She turned to Sam. 'So, what'll it be?'

'I'll have the biscuits and gravy and sausage please, MB.'

'No problem. Y'all enjoy your coffee.' She took the menus and went back behind the counter.

'This place is great,' Sage said, taking a good look around.

'Yeah, I like it. It's my home from home to be honest. I don't always fancy cooking for myself, and it's good to get out and get a little company.'

'Yeah.' Sage thought of how long it had been since she'd been able to go out to a restaurant or café and feel comforted by the presence of others, instead of threatened or paranoid. Even before the internet crap-storm, going out had become increasingly stressful. On the odd occasion when she didn't get complete strangers talking to her like they knew her, or asking for selfies – or even worse, taking photos of her without her permission – the fear that it might happen was just as stressful. The truth was, she hadn't felt as relaxed as she did in the Wagon Wheel since she'd hung out in cafés with her friends at uni.

'So, did you get to read any more of your grandma's story?' Sam asked.

'A bit, but then I fell asleep. I'm up to the part where they're waiting for the Germans to arrive in Paris.'

He nodded gravely. 'It was a terrible business. You know, I used to wonder how Hitler was able to do what he did, how he got so many people to go along with him, but now I'm not so sure.'

Sage shivered. Surely there would never be another movement as evil as the Nazis? 'Do you really think it could happen again?'

'If the circumstances were right, I think so, yes. People can be very easy to manipulate, Sage, especially if they haven't got enough dollars in the bank or food in their belly.'

Sage frowned. 'But surely it's different now. We all know a lot more now that we've got the internet. Wouldn't we be harder to manipulate?'

He shrugged. 'Well, I don't know. From what I've seen of the internet lately, I'd say it makes it even easier to get people to hate each other for no good reason.'

Sage took a sip of her coffee and pondered what he'd just said. The fact was, every single person who'd posted hateful comments about her didn't actually know her. She'd been so quick to believe that she somehow deserved their vitriol, but was it really justified?

'I think you're going to get a lot from your grandma's story,' Sam continued.

Sage nodded. 'I already am.'

It turned out that American 'biscuits' were completely different to their UK counterparts – more like light and fluffy savoury scones, making the whole pairing with gravy and sausage a far more appetising prospect. When Sage explained the communication breakdown to Sam, he hooted with laughter. 'Hey, Marybelle, in England they call cookies "biscuits".'

'What?' Marybelle looked astounded.

'Did y'all think I was going to get chocolate chips with my sausage and gravy?' Sam chortled.

'Yes! It was very traumatic!'

After filling up on the most delicious stack of pancakes Sage had ever eaten, they left, with promises to Marybelle that they'd come back soon for dinner on the house. Then they paid a visit to the general store, for something called grits, which Sage really hoped was more appetising than it sounded. When they got back to the farm, Hunter was just getting out of his truck in the front yard. He was wearing a white T-shirt and jeans and a brown leather Stetson.

'Morning,' he greeted them gruffly with a tip of his hat.

'Morning,' Sage replied, with a cheery zest born of the Wagon Wheel's bottomless coffee.

'My first client just cancelled, so I think I'm gonna go for a ride,' Hunter said to Sam.

Sam's face lit up. 'Hey, Sage, you ever ridden a horse before?'

'I had lessons as a kid, but I haven't ridden since I went to uni. It's been about seven years,' she added, to underline her desire to nip the prospect of going riding with Hunter right in the bud.

'It's just like riding a bike,' Sam said. 'You never forget. What say you go for a ride with Hunter while I see to the cows?'

Hunter looked about as enthused as Sage at this idea, scuffing the toe of his boot on the dusty ground.

'I think you'd love it,' Sam said, clearly the only one enamoured with the idea.

'But won't I get in the way?' Sage looked at Hunter, hoping he'd take the escape route she was offering.

'No, it's OK,' he mumbled.

'That's great!' Sam exclaimed.

'I don't have any riding gear.'

'No problem. Hunter has a bunch down at the stables for his clients to use.'

'Right.' Who the hell were these clients of Hunter's? Sage wondered. And why would anyone want to pay for his monosyllabic, unfriendly service?

'See you later, have fun!' Sam called over his shoulder as he strode back to the house.

Without saying a word, Hunter began marching off towards the stables. Sage ran to catch up with him.

'So, what is it that you do exactly, here on the farm?' she asked, as they reached a shed beside the stables and Hunter unlocked the door.

'I help veterans.'

She waited for him to expand, but he remained silent. 'What? Army veterans?'

'Yup. What size feet are you?'

'Oh – uh – six. But that's UK sizing.'

'Right. Can I have one of your sneakers?'

'What?'

'So I can figure out the correct size.'

'Oh, yes, of course.' She took off one of her trainers and handed it to him.

He disappeared into the shed. Feeling awkward and embarrassed, Sage instinctively reached for her phone and clicked on Instagram. She had over two hundred message requests. Stupidly, she clicked on the top one, from a user named @bigboytrev_99: *'you can suck my dick any time sexy'*

She shuddered. The thought of some random man going to the effort of finding her profile, looking through her pictures and typing those words to her, made her skin crawl. She clicked on another of the message requests. This one was from a woman: *'who do u think u r u stupid slag?'* Even though her heart was now racing and she'd broken into a cold sweat, she kept looking at the messages.

'I hope you die'

'Suck my dick'

'Stupid bitch'

'I'm gonna come to your house and rape you'

The words spiralled before her eyes like a kaleidoscope of hate. Sage leaned on the side of the shed to steady herself, but her panic kept growing. At some point she'd have to go back to the UK and face this. She couldn't hide away here forever. But what if the men who were sending her these messages found out where she lived? What if one of them actually broke into her apartment and raped her? What if they were there now, waiting for her? Her throat tightened and she struggled to breathe; it was as if the temperature had soared by about ten degrees. She sank onto the floor and put her head in her hands.

'You OK?'

She jumped at the sound of Hunter's voice and opened her eyes to see his feet on the ground in front of her. 'Yeah. I just…' But it was no good. Much as she didn't want to make a fool of herself in front of him, she was too far gone. 'I… just… need… a… moment,' she gasped through shallow breaths.

'Do you want me to go get Sam?'

She shook her head.

'Here. Have some water.' He crouched down, offering her a bottle of water.

'Thanks.' She managed a sip, and another, and slowly her heart rate returned to something close to normal.

'What happened?' Hunter sat down beside her.

'I just saw something that made me… It panicked me.'

'What? Out here?' He looked around.

'No, on the internet.'

'Ah.' He nodded. And Sage had the horrible realisation that he'd probably seen her video on *The Late Show*. Sam was bound to have said something about it. Again, she felt violated. But it was all her own doing. If she hadn't made that drunken video, if she hadn't boasted about having sex with that man, it wouldn't have encouraged every lowlife to crawl out from beneath their rocks to attack her.

'So, you ready to go meet the horses?' Hunter asked, handing her a pair of boots.

'Oh, yes, OK.' For once she was grateful for his brusqueness and lack of interest.

Once she'd put on her boots and riding hat, they went down to a paddock where about ten horses were grazing.

'All righty then,' Hunter said, opening the gate and ushering her in.

It had been so long since she'd been around horses, she felt nervous at first. They all seemed so much bigger than she remembered them.

'I want you to take a stroll around, so your horse can find you,' Hunter instructed.

'Oh, OK.' This was certainly different to how things had been done at her riding school in the UK, where she'd been assigned a horse by the riding instructor. She strolled around the edge of the paddock, watching as some of the horses went over to Hunter, whinnying happy greetings. Sage had a horrible thought – what if none of them wanted to be hers? What if they hated her, like everyone else did? Then she heard a nickering sound and turned to see a huge chestnut horse right behind her.

'Hello,' Sage said, tentatively.

The horse nodded its head, as if in greeting.

'Who are you?' Sage asked, stroking the horse's nose.

'That's Whisky,' Hunter called over. 'I had a feeling he might like you.'

Sage felt a wave of relief. Someone – or rather something – liked her. As she continued stroking the horse, he put his head around Sage and gently pressed her to his sleek body. Sage relaxed into the embrace and felt her breathing slow to match Whisky's. And there beneath the boundless sky, for just a moment, Sage felt complete and utter peace.

FLORENCE

June 1940

The morning of the fourteenth of June 1940 was eerily quiet. There wasn't even a dawn chorus. The week before, the city's petrol reserves had been set alight to stop the Germans from getting their hands on them. The resulting impenetrable black cloud of smoke had choked Paris for days, driving all the birds from the city, or killing them stone dead. It felt as if a part of my soul had died along with them. After invading Belgium in May, the Germans had broken through the supposedly impenetrable Maginot Line and begun their march on Paris. For two long days, Otto and I had stayed in our room and waited, while many other Parisians fled, loading as many possessions as they could into cars, taxicabs or even infants' prams. As artillery fire lit up the sky like shooting stars on the night of the thirteenth, word was that the Germans had reached Paris and were amassing just outside the city gates.

'Maybe it is better this way,' I said to Otto as soon as he woke, continuing the conversation we'd been having the night before, as if we'd never stopped for sleep. 'Maybe it is better that the French capitulated. At least this way there won't be any fighting in Paris. At least the city won't be destroyed.' But my words hung empty and meaningless in the air between us. The truth was, I was hopping mad at what I saw as the weakness of the French and the British, and at Roosevelt and my home country for not coming to their aid. I was also terrified for Otto's safety.

Otto frowned. 'There are many ways to destroy a city – not just with bombs.'

'I hate Hitler,' I said for the umpteenth time. 'And now he has stolen our anniversary from us.'

'What do you mean?'

'June the fourteenth.' I felt a flush of embarrassment. How could I have expected Otto to remember our anniversary in the light of all that was happening?

'He hasn't stolen it from us, we won't let him,' Otto declared. He got out of bed and went over to his case in the corner. 'I have something for you.' He opened the case and took out a sheet of paper. It was a watercolour painting of the Place du Tertre, as seen from our window at night. I feasted my eyes on the golden splashes of light coming from the restaurant windows and the white dome of Sacré-Coeur glowing against an inky blue sky. Otto had populated the square with artists at their easels and elegantly dressed figures passing through. The whole thing was framed with a delicate green fringe of leaves from our tree. He hadn't just captured a likeness of the square; he'd captured its magic. A magic that had vanished in recent weeks, with most of the restaurants bringing down their shutters in expectation of the German invasion. Even the artists had gone. But now I had this beautiful, vibrant snapshot to remind me of how it used to be.

'I love it,' I whispered, feeling too choked to say anything more.

'We are in it, too,' Otto said with a grin. 'Can you see?'

I studied the painting and spotted a thin figure with tousled brown hair standing at an easel, paintbrush aloft. 'Is that you?' I asked, pointing at the figure.

'Yes, and can you see you?'

It took a moment, but then I saw her – me – in the far corner of the square, beneath the milky white glow of the basilica, clad in an emerald green ball gown, one hand pressed against my heart, the other aloft as if I was dancing.

Completely unexpectedly, I burst into tears.

'What is it? Do you not like it?' Otto looked so concerned, it only made my pathetic blubbing worse.

I shook my head. 'No, I love it. It's just so long since I have felt like that, so carefree. But I love that I have this to remind me of how we used to be.'

Otto frowned. 'This painting isn't of our past; it is of our future.'

I gulped my tears down. 'Really?'

'Yes,' he replied firmly. 'It is strange, all this time I have been running from the Germans I have felt so helpless, but now they are here, I don't want to run any more. I want to stay and fight – for this.' He pointed at the painting. 'For us.' He wrapped his arms around me.

'But how can we fight? What can we do?' I murmured into his chest.

'We will find ways,' he replied.

I felt his determination seeping into me, like some weird kind of osmosis. 'Yes, we will. I got you a gift too.' I leaned over and reached under the bed. I'd got him a leather-bound copy of *Walden* by Henry David Thoreau. Otto had mentioned wanting to read it a few months previously, so I'd filed a request with Sylvia at Shakespeare and Company, which she'd eagerly fulfilled.

'This is perfect!' Otto exclaimed, opening the book and inhaling its pages. I took this as yet another sign that he was indeed my kindred spirit – is there any aroma sweeter than the unique musty scent of a book?

By late morning, my stomach was growling with hunger and I was feeling restless. Otto's pep talk about fighting back had done the trick and I felt a strange urge to confront the enemy we had spent so long dreading.

'Shall we go out, see what's happening?' I suggested. 'See if any of the *boulangeries* are open to get some bread?'

Walking through Montmartre that morning was like the eerie calm right before a storm. The roads were deserted, not an automobile in sight, and although there were a few other people on the sidewalks, we all hurried by each other, without a word of greeting or even making eye contact. Otto and I carried on walking deeper into the city, the silence between us thickening like humidity. I'm not sure what was going through Otto's mind that morning as we kept marching towards the enemy he'd spent so long running from, but if he was scared, he didn't show it. And his courage emboldened me. As we reached the heart of Paris, the sidewalks become more populated.

'They are here,' a young boy cried as he cycled past. 'They are on the Champs-Élysées.'

We carried on walking, arm in arm, and then finally, we saw them. Columns and columns of soldiers, spreading through the streets like a toxic grey vapour. Quite a crowd had gathered on the sidewalks, watching in numb silence. A couple of the soldiers had broken ranks and were approaching the crowds, offering candy and bananas to the kids present. I have to admit, this took me by surprise. As did the soldiers' beaming grins. They didn't look like evil killers. They looked just like the kind of guys who came to the club, or a blonder version at least. A little girl a few feet away from us took a banana she'd been offered and began peeling it excitedly.

'*Non, non, non!*' another, older child exclaimed, knocking the banana from her grasp and onto the street. 'Maman told you not to take anything from them. It might be poisoned!'

The little girl's bottom lip began to quiver as she looked mournfully at the banana, now being trampled beneath the marching feet. I glanced at the solider who had given it to her and saw that his beaming smile had gone. His face was now a mask of cold indifference. A chill went through me, right to the bone.

'Shall we go?' I whispered to Otto and he nodded.

'You must write about this,' he muttered, as we made our way back home, through the comparative safety of the narrow backstreets. 'For your column. You must write about the day freedom left Paris.'

And that's exactly what I did, as soon as we got home. Even if I wasn't sure if I'd be able to get my columns to Harry any more, I wrote all about the day of the toxic grey vapour and the poisoned banana. Then Otto and I went to bed, and we made love with an urgency I'd never experienced before, turning our bodies into a desperate prayer for love and hope.

The French called the nine months between the declaration of war and the German occupation *'la drôle de guerre'* – the phoney war – but for me, the real phoney war came in the months after the occupation, when the Germans tried to pretend they were our best buddies. The candy-giving routine continued, and posters started going up around town, emblazoned with the words: *'Populations abandonnées faites confiance au soldat allemand!'*, urging the 'abandoned population' to have faith in the German soldiers. The poster featured a picture of a dashing soldier with a French child in his arms, while another two kids looked on adoringly. It made my stomach heave.

Another thing that made my stomach turn was how quickly the German soldiers came flocking to Montmartre to feast on the nightlife.

'How can you let them in?' I hissed to Bessie, the first night the grey uniforms, peaked caps and jack boots started appearing at Le Flamant Rose.

'How can I not?' she hissed back.

'But think of what they've done to Pierre.'

There had been no word of what had happened to Pierre, but the French had suffered huge losses at the front, and those who hadn't died had been captured by the Germans and interned in prison camps.

'Trust me, I'm thinking of nothing else,' Bessie replied, her voice breaking. For the first time since I'd known her, I saw a chink in her tough broad façade.

'I'm sorry,' I whispered. 'I just hate this so much.'

'Me too, but it's dog-eat-dog, now, Florence. We've all gotta do whatever we need to to get by.'

That night, when I came home to Otto I felt a new despair. 'I don't want to dance for them, they make me sick!' I whispered – the fact that I couldn't yell in case I was somehow overheard making me all the more frustrated.

'I think you should,' he replied.

'Say what?' This was the very last thing I was expecting.

'Perhaps you dancing for them will be useful.'

'What do you mean?'

Otto looked at me, eyes gleaming. 'The resistance is already beginning. Today, at work, my friend Emil told me that the Polish Jews in Paris are organising something. He asked if I wanted to be a part of it.'

'What kind of something?'

'I don't know yet. Some kind of resistance. Maybe you can do the same, at the club. You might hear the soldiers saying things that could be useful, especially if they don't know that you understand German.'

I nodded slowly as I processed this idea. For the past year, Otto had been teaching me his native tongue, German, and I had been helping him with his French. This could definitely put me at some kind of advantage. What if, instead of being a plaything for the Germans, I could use my position as a dancer to help thwart them? I have to say the idea appealed to me, and it stopped me from feeling so powerless. 'But what would I do with any information I got?'

'I don't know – yet. But there will be something,' Otto replied, smiling confidently. 'Come sit, I want to tell you a story.'

I sat down beside him on the bed. 'What kind of story?'

'A Jewish story about how the world came to be. Actually, it is more a story of *why* the world came to be.'

'Go on.' I took off my shoes and rubbed my aching feet.

'It is the story of *tikkun olam*,' he continued. '*Tikkun* is Hebrew for repairing something.'

'OK.'

'The story is that God deliberately created a world that was supposed to fall apart.'

'Ha! Well, he did a mighty fine job!' I exclaimed.

'Shh.' Otto smiled and put his finger to his lips. 'The world was supposed to fall apart so that we humans would be given a purpose.'

I looked at him questioningly.

'It is our job to put the pieces back together. Within each piece, there is a spark of light, a spark of the divine. We need to seek out that light.'

I frowned. 'But how is there any light in what the Nazis are doing?'

'We find the light by resisting them.' His eyes shone with hope. 'Don't you see? Each thing we do to counter their hate will bring a spark of light back to the world and help put it back together.'

'I guess so.' I laughed. 'How do you always manage to make things seem better?'

He grinned. 'I look for the light in things.'

*

I found my own glimmer of light just a couple of weeks later at the club. I was putting on my make-up, ready for curtain up, when there was a knock on my dressing room door and Bessie appeared with guy I'd never seen before. He was a tall, thin streak of a man, with eyes made bulbous through the thick glass of his spectacles.

'This is Charles Pennington,' she told me. 'He says he'd like to speak with you. Says it's urgent.' She raised her eyebrows as if to say, *Whaddaya gonna do?*

I frowned at them both in the mirror. I was in no mood for entertaining strange men in my dressing room. Bessie should have known better. Bessie promptly disappeared. Charles Pennington shifted from one foot to the other, glancing around nervously. I'm guessing he hadn't been that close to a semi-naked woman dressed as a peacock before – Bessie's latest extravaganza was titled 'The Dance of the Birds', and had turned Le Flamant Rose into a glorified aviary.

'I understand from our mutual friend, Sylvia, that you write for the *New York Tribune*,' he said, in a clipped British accent.

'You know Sylvia?' Now he had my full attention.

'Yes. And she conveyed to me that you... you might want to... to do your bit.'

'My bit?'

'Yes' – he lowered his voice to a whisper – 'for the war effort.'

So that was the reason for the ants in his pants routine. He wasn't nervous about my near-nudity; he was nervous because he was risking everything to come see me. My indifference transformed into something close to excitement. 'Go on.'

'We feel that your column could be of a lot of use,' he continued.

'We?' I enquired.

'Myself and certain friends in Britain.'

Now he really had my attention. 'How so?'

'There is certain information that will come in very useful in Britain. Information about life here in Paris, under the occupation.'

'What kind of information?'

'Things like the new ration cards and the curfew and German checkpoints. Things that only a genuine Parisian – or an American living in Paris – would know.'

'OK.' I had no clue how this information would help anyone. Surely it would only make them morbidly depressed?

'There are certain people to whom this information will prove invaluable.'

'Really?'

'Yes.' His huge eyes met mine in the mirror and I could tell that he was deadly serious. 'So, what do you say?'

'Sure. I'd be happy to help.'

'Excellent. I'll let my contacts know and I'll notify Harry Bergman.' He turned to leave. 'Obviously, you need to keep to the writing style for which you've become known. See the information as planting seeds. Subtlety is key. What you are doing mustn't appear obvious.'

Hmm, I thought to myself. There was little danger of that. I wasn't even sure what I was supposed to be doing, or who I was supposed to be helping. But the knowledge that I would be helping made such a difference. When I took to the stage that night and paraded in front of the sea of grey, I felt empowered for the first time in the four months since they'd arrived.

Later, when I returned home I was excited to share my news with Otto. I found him sitting in the dark on the floor beside the bed.

'I have news,' I announced, taking off my coat and shoes. 'Are you OK?'

'I have news too,' he replied glumly.

'What is it?' My heart began to thud as I went over to join him.

'The government have passed a statute against the Jewish.'

'Which government?'

'The French government.'

'But I don't understand.'

'French Jews are now only allowed to work in menial jobs, and foreign Jews are to be interned in prison camps.'

'Foreign Jews? But that's…'

'Me.' He looked completely defeated.

'But you have your false papers and identity card. You'll be OK.'

'But why should I have to deny that I am Jewish? And what about all the other Jews who aren't able to? How will I be able to look them in the eye? I went to the Jewish Centre today and they said that it would be safest for me to either leave Paris or go into hiding.'

'Leave Paris?'

'I'm not leaving Paris. I'm not leaving you. I can hide here if I need to, can't I?' He looked at me anxiously.

'Of course.' I managed to force a smile, but the thought of Otto having to hide away in our room like some kind of fugitive criminal made my blood boil. He held out his hand. I took it and slumped against him.

'I hate Hitler,' I muttered. 'And I hate Pétain.' As far as I was concerned the new French leader was the lowest of the low, selling out his country and the Jewish people to the Nazis.

'Yes, well, I love you,' Otto said, with his uncanny knack of switching from a negative to a positive. 'So, what is your news?'

'Oh, a guy came to see me at the club tonight – a British guy. Apparently Sylvia sent him. He asked me if I would put lots of everyday details about life in Paris into my columns, as a way of letting the Brits know what's going on here.'

Otto's face lit up. 'This is wonderful.'

'You think?'

'Of course. This is how you fight back.'

'That's what I figured. It sure feels like a weird way of fighting back, though. I can't really see how it will help.' I rested my head

on his shoulder and we sat in silence, all of the exuberance I'd
been feeling since Charles Pennington's visit shrinking beneath
the weight of my fear for Otto.

For the next month, I spent my nights dancing at the club and my
days hunched over my typewriter, composing columns peppered
with what I hoped would be useful details. I enjoyed the challenge of composing a column that could be read on two levels. A
piece about Coco Chanel shutting up shop and moving into the
Hotel Ritz also mentioned in passing that this was the preferred
residence of the high brass German officers. Instead of picturing
an American woman reading my column and writing to her, I
started picturing Winston Churchill sitting on the other side of
the table as I typed, puffing on his cigar as I fed him titbits that
might come in useful. I imagined him giving one of his rousing
speeches at the end of the war when the Germans were finally
defeated. 'We fought on the beaches, we fought on the landing
grounds, we fought in the fields and in the streets, and we fought
in the newspaper columns,' and thanking me personally for the
invaluable intelligence I was able to smuggle out under a cover
of beauty tips and gossip. It felt so good to actually be doing
something, and it helped keep Otto's spirits buoyed too.

Then, one day in November, something truly exciting happened. I'd gone into town to see Sylvia, and as I was making my
way back home I heard a commotion.

'What's going on?' I asked a young man who was running
the opposite way.

'They are protesting about Bonsergent,' he replied.

Jacques Bonsergent had been in the news recently, when he'd
been arrested for allegedly punching a German soldier. He'd
been coming home from a wedding with some friends when the
altercation had supposedly happened outside Gare Saint-Lazare

station. He continued to protest his innocence but the Germans wouldn't release him.

I hurried along the street. Sure enough, the road was filled with young people. So many young people. All protesting against the Germans. It was a sight that brought tears to my eyes and made my heart sing. Finally, the Parisians were waking from their stunned daze and fighting back. This was the *tikkun* that Otto had spoken about in action, and I saw immediately that it would make wonderful material for my column. I pictured Churchill himself cheering at the news.

That night, I wrote a column about how hard it was getting for a gal to find nylons in Paris, with the following seemingly inconsequential aside: 'Imagine my dismay when I attempted to take a short cut past the Arc de Triomphe, only to find it filled with thousands of Parisians all protesting the arrest of one of their fellow countrymen, Jacques Bonsergent for allegedly punching a German soldier.' Once I'd written it, Otto and I drank glasses of watery wine and waltzed around the room in our bare feet, humming 'La Marseillaise'.

It feels kind of naïve now, but back then I truly believed the tide was turning, and that the French would rise up and overthrow their occupiers. Harsh reality was to slap me on the face only a few weeks later. It was the day before Christmas Eve, and I'd gone to collect my weekly ration of meat. I was standing in the endless queue for the butcher's, when I saw two German soldiers putting up a poster on a café wall. Straight away I noticed Jacques Bonsergent's name in huge letters at the top. Then my blood ran cold. The poster was announcing his execution. The soldiers had stuck it next to a poster advertising the fun to be had in Gay Paree. I'll never forget that awful juxtaposition.

I was worried Otto would be devastated by the news – to the point where I almost considered not telling him – but the

Germans were putting the posters up all over the place; there was no way I'd be able to shield him from it. When I got home and told him, his face was expressionless. He spent the rest of the day hunched over his sketchpad while I sat at my typewriter, trying and failing to write a column about Christmas fashion that casually dropped in the execution of Paris's first hope of resistance.

Needless to say, Christmas 1940 was a strange affair. As some kind of perverse gesture of goodwill, the Germans extended the normal curfew of 11 p.m. to 3 a.m. and clubs were allowed to stay open until 2.30. Bessie decided to put on a Christmas-themed revue, asking me to perform a particularly acrobatic display to a jazzed-up version of 'Silent Night'. There was a strange atmosphere in the club that night – a tangible seam of sadness running through the forced jollity. Bessie was drinking Scotch neat, which she only ever did when she was in crisis, the band kept dropping notes and playing out of key, and I found one of the girls from the chorus weeping in the restroom during the interval. Her sweetheart had been killed fighting at the front, and the enormity of her loss was really hitting home. 'I can't believe I won't have another Christmas with him,' she wept on my shoulder. As I hugged her tightly, I thought of Otto waiting for me in our room. What if we didn't have another Christmas together after this? The fact that our very existence now seemed to hang by a thread was terrifying.

As soon as the show ended, I got changed and slipped out of the club by the side door. All I wanted was to get home to Otto. But as I emerged into the cold night air, I heard a strange muffled gasp from behind me. I turned to see a German in a heavy greatcoat leaning against the wall, his head in his hands, his shoulders quivering. At first I thought he was laughing but then the sound came again and I realised he was crying. I prepared to sneak off along the passageway, but a sudden icy breeze caused the door to slam behind me. The soldier removed his hands from his face and our eyes met in the darkness.

'*Bonsoir,*' he said, taking a handkerchief from his coat pocket and wiping his eyes.

'*Bonsoir.*'

He must have detected my American accent because he then started speaking in English.

'I enjoyed your dance this evening.'

'Thank you.'

'You must excuse me.' He wiped his eyes again.

'It's OK. It's Christmas. It's an emotional time of year.' I immediately berated myself for being too friendly. But what could I do? He had all the power. Although he didn't exactly look all that powerful in that moment, as he blew his nose into his handkerchief. He felt in his pocket again and brought out a pack of cigarettes. 'Smoke?' he asked, offering them to me.

This instantly placed me in a moral dilemma. I was really in no mood for fraternising with the enemy, but what if this was an opportunity? What if I discovered something from him that I could use in my column? So I took a cigarette.

'Thanks.'

As he leaned towards me, I could smell the booze on his breath. 'Have you ever lost anyone close to you?' he asked quietly as he lit my cigarette.

I was momentarily dumbstruck. Up until this point I'd seen the Germans as a grey, uniformed mass, devoid of all feeling and emotion. I wasn't sure how to deal with this seemingly all-too-human being in front of me.

'Yeah, I lost my mom when I was a kid,' I replied.

His eyes widened. 'Oh, I am sorry. That is a terrible loss.'

What about the terrible losses you've been inflicting on people? I wanted to say, but obviously I remained silent.

'I lost my best friend this year,' he murmured, before taking a long drag on his cigarette. His fingers were long and thin, elegant almost. I remember thinking that they looked out of place on someone who was part of such a brutal force. 'I saw him die, right in front of me.' He scuffed the ground in front of him with the toe of his shoe, as if his friend had died right there, beside Le Flamant Rose. 'I wasn't able to save him.'

I stared at him. Why was he telling me this? And more importantly, how was I supposed to react? I took a moment to try and figure things out. He was clearly drunk and that was why he was being so indiscreet. But on the other hand, he'd hardly see me as any kind of threat. As far as he was concerned, I was just a woman, a dancer, and as an American, I wasn't even officially an enemy of Germany. I imagined an apparition of Churchill hovering in the darkness behind him. *Earn his trust,* I pictured him saying. *Get the blighter to confide in you.*

'I'm sorry,' I said softly.

'I can't get it from my mind. The blood, his screams.' He looked at me then, really looked at me, and for a split second, his identity faded away and all I could see was the anguish in his eyes. I was so confused by this, I felt the overwhelming desire to leave.

'I should go,' I said. 'Thanks for the smoke and – I hope you find peace.' And although this is hard to admit, in that moment, part of me truly meant it.

'Thank you.' He cleared his throat. 'Happy Christmas.'

'And you.'

I hurried off up the hill, my heart pounding and my thoughts tangled in confusion. I didn't want to see the Germans as humans, with friends and feelings. I had to see them as the enemy. They *were* the enemy. I got home to find Otto sitting at the table, with two plates of bread and cheese laid out in front of him.

'Happy Christmas,' he said, with his trademark lopsided grin. The fact that these were the last words I'd heard from the German soldier made me feel slightly sick. So what if the soldier had seen his friend die? He was a Nazi. He'd doubtless killed many people in battle. I couldn't believe I'd felt an iota of sympathy for him, and decided to never, ever tell Otto what had happened.

'Happy Christmas.' I bent down to kiss him and kicked off my shoes.

'How was work?'

I shrugged. 'A Christmas farce. Still, at least I'm off now for two days.'

'Yes.' He took my hand and pulled me onto his lap. 'I had an idea.'

'Oh yeah?'

'What if for two days, we forget all about the Germans?'

'How?' I poured myself a glass of wine.

'By the power of our imaginations.'

This was a challenge I was only too happy to accept. I snuggled into him. 'Tell me more.'

'Well, with our imaginations we can pretend we are anywhere.'

'This is true.'

'So why don't we take it in turns to conjure up places we can travel to?'

'I love this idea. And I love you.' I planted a kiss full on his lips.

And so it was that we spent what was left of Christmas Eve pretending to feast on freshly caught catfish and freshly baked corn bread back in my hometown in Arkansas.

Early on Christmas Day morning, we decided to venture out for a walk. The plan had been to go to the steps in front of Sacré-Coeur and use our imaginations to transport us back to the time we first met, when Paris, and we, were still free. But even our vivid imaginations weren't able to erase the sight of the swastikas taunting us from the flags fluttering from buildings in the breeze.

Then I saw something that made me catch my breath. Someone had placed a bouquet of flowers by the railings at the side of the hilltop, beneath one of the posters announcing Jacques Bonsergent's execution.

'Look!' I gasped, pointing to the flowers. 'Do you think someone put them there in his memory?'

Otto looked just as amazed as I felt. 'I think so, yes.'

We carried on walking until we found another poster and beneath it, more flowers, and this time, a candle.

'This is wonderful,' Otto whispered.

Suddenly, our imaginary game was forgotten. We walked arm in arm through Montmartre, looking for more posters and finding more shrines. It was the best Christmas present I could possibly have been given – the thought of all those Parisians sneaking out on Christmas Eve, planting flowers like kisses all over the city.

'Come, we must make our own tribute,' Otto said.

We walked along one of the narrow streets snaking down the side of the hill until we found a garden with bright yellow jasmine clambering the wall. I checked the coast was clear and Otto broke off a sprig. Then we carried on walking until we found another of the Germans' hateful posters, and we turned it into our own act of love and remembrance.

We spent the rest of Christmas Day in bed – more for warmth than anything else, as coal was becoming as hard to come by in Paris as food. Otto brought his hometown of Vienna alive to me through countless stories and sketches. It was magical. But as the minutes ticked by, and daylight faded to dusk and then to dark, the happiness I felt became diluted with dread. No matter how powerful our imaginations, Otto and I weren't able to magic away the enemy lurking just beyond the door. Who knew what evil they would inflict upon us next.

SAGE

March 2018

Sage stopped reading and wiped the tears from her eyes. She'd been hoping that Florence and Otto would have somehow escaped Paris and the Nazis to safety. The notion that they had stayed to try and fight back took her breath away. They had been so brave. She thought of her panic attack by the stables earlier and felt slightly embarrassed. She'd spent so long living her life online that it had come to feel like reality. But it wasn't real, was it? Twitter and Instagram were like rooms where everyone went to yell about themselves and at each other, but they were rooms you could leave. She wasn't like Florence and Otto, trapped in an occupied city. She didn't have to be online, letting complete strangers vilify her. She could have a real life in the real world, with people who actually knew her.

Sage put down the manuscript and picked up her phone. She opened Twitter and, ignoring all the new notifications, she went straight to her settings and pressed 'delete account'.

'Are you sure?' a message popped up.

'Oh yes,' she replied under her breath. It felt as if she were channelling Florence and Otto's fighting spirit. Next, she went to Instagram. This was a lot harder. She'd put so much work into her Instagram page, posted so many photos, written so many captions. She didn't want to do anything too hasty. So she temporarily took her account offline instead. On a roll, she went to her website and took that offline, too. She felt a beautiful weightless sense of freedom. She'd slammed the door in the face of the haters, and it had only taken a couple of seconds.

Sage got off the bed and went over to the window. The afternoon sun was high in the sky and the birds were singing. She thought of what Florence had written about the birds in Paris dying from the burning petrol fumes. She wasn't sure why, but of all the horrifying details in Florence's account of the Germans' arrival in Paris, this was the one that had got to her the most. It seemed so symbolic. She glanced back around the bedroom, thinking of her grandmother. The more she read her words, the more Florence was becoming real in her mind, like one of those old-style Polaroid images developing. She imagined a teenage Florence practising dance routines in front of the wardrobe mirror.

Her gaze fell upon a framed painting on the wall. She hadn't paid it much attention before, but now she spied a majestic white dome that seemed oddly familiar. She hurried over to take a closer look. There were the golden splashes of light coming from the restaurant windows, there was the green fringe of leaves framing the top of the painting. And there was the figure in the corner of the square, beneath the church, wearing a green dress and dancing for joy. Sage traced her finger over the glass, above the depiction of Florence, and she imagined Otto all those years ago, infusing his brushstrokes with his love. What must it be like, to experience such love?

She felt a strange compulsion to touch the painting itself and took it from the wall, fumbling with the clasps at the back of the frame. As she carefully removed it, she thought of Florence and Otto's fingers touching this same piece of paper. Then she turned it over and saw a message handwritten in pencil, so faded it was barely visible. She took it over to the window and held it up to the sunlight.

'*To my darling Florence, with all my love, Otto*
"*We were together, I forget the rest*"
14ᵗʰ June 1940'

A lump formed in Sage's throat. And then she had a thought that sent her heart racing: she knew that Florence was her grandmother, but what if Otto was her grandfather?

FLORENCE

1941

I'm not the kind of person to believe in omens, but it was impossible not to take what happened on New Year's Day 1941 as a sign of something terrible to come. It had snowed heavily on New Year's Eve and I woke up shivering, despite being fully clothed and in Otto's arms. A sliver of pale light was creeping in through a crack in the shutters, but instead of the dawn chorus, all I could hear was a dull, repetitive thud. Ever since the air raids in June, I'd become a much lighter sleeper, waking with a start at the slightest sound. So my first thought was that it could be distant artillery fire. But as I came to, I realised that the noise was much closer. I sat up with a start and pulled the shutter open, causing Otto to roll over, but not to wake. I wiped the condensation from the icy glass and peered out. All seemed to be normal at first – or the new normal, at least. A couple of German soldiers were patrolling through the square, disappearing off in the direction of Sacré-Coeur. The owner of the café opposite was brushing snow from the tables outside. Then I heard the thudding sound again, coming from right beneath the window. I looked down and gasped in shock.

'What is it?' Otto murmured.

'Someone's chopping down our tree!' I exclaimed, leaping from the bed.

'What?' Otto frowned and rubbed his eyes. 'Where are you going?'

'To stop him, of course.'

'Florence!'

But it was too late, I was already pulling on my coat and shoes and heading to the door.

I flew down the stairs and outside, over to the murderous fiend brandishing the axe. He was bundled up so tightly in his coat, hat and scarf that I didn't realise that it was François until I was right up close.

'What – what are you doing?' I spluttered.

'Oh, good morning, Florence.' He lowered his axe and smiled at me.

I looked at my beloved tree. He'd already made quite a dent in the trunk, but all was not lost. It was still standing.

'Why are you trying to chop down the tree?'

'For firewood. It is so cold. We are scared the baby will catch a chill.'

'But…' I broke off. François's wife had just had a baby. How could I deny them heat?

'Would you like some?' he asked.

I shook my head. 'It's OK.'

It probably sounds ridiculous, in light of all the horrors to come, that I should have got so upset, but in my mind it wasn't just a tree. It was a symbol of how life had used to be. And the fact that it needed to be chopped down for firewood was a bitter reminder of how the Nazis were plundering everything they could get their hands on, while we starved and shivered.

'Happy New Year,' François called after me as I headed back inside. The words stung like a taunt.

When I got back to our room, I climbed into bed and pulled the blankets over my head, completely inconsolable, in spite of Otto's attempts to cheer me. And when I heard the terrible creak and crash signalling my tree's demise, I sobbed bitterly into the pillow. I couldn't even bring myself to say, 'I hate Hitler.' I was beyond hate, mired in a terrible swamp of despondency. At some point, I drifted off to sleep.

I woke later, experiencing the strange sensation of warmth. I opened my eyes to see a fire crackling away in the grate. Otto was crouched in front of it, head bent, deep in concentration.

'Is that… is that wood from our tree?'

He turned and nodded. 'François brought some up, while you were asleep. He gave us some bread and pâté from the restaurant, too.' Otto came over and stroked my hair. 'I know how much you loved the tree, but think of this as its final gift to you, bringing you heat.'

I looked at the flames crackling away merrily, and I had to admit, it was a beautiful sight to see. It was also wonderful to feel warmth soaking into my skin.

'There will be other trees,' Otto whispered as I came to join him in front of the fire.

'I know, it just feels so sad to see it go.'

'Not all of it.' Otto grinned. 'I carved you this to keep.' He handed me a small wooden bird.

'From the tree?'

He nodded.

'I love you so much!' I exclaimed, flinging my arms around him. 'How do you always know exactly what to do to make me happy?'

He felt for the locket around my neck. 'Because you are my kindred eagle spirit.'

'I am!' My eyes filled with tears. I don't think I'd ever felt anything as acutely as I felt my love for Otto in that moment.

As the bitterly cold winter dragged on and food and fuel grew increasingly scarce, relations between the French and their occupiers became icier, too. The Germans had not taken too kindly to their posters about Bonsergent's execution being turned into shrines, and they had now declared the defacing of posters an act of sabotage punishable by death.

As a dancer and an American, I was slightly cushioned from the hardship all around me. The Germans clearly saw Montmartre as their playground and so the clubs and bars continued to thrive. Every time I felt guilty about this fact, I consoled myself with the knowledge that I was helping the Allies via my column – not that I'd picked up anything useful from the Germans in the club. Unlike Bessie, I couldn't bring myself to drink with them, and would always hurry home to Otto as soon as the show was over. But I kept peppering my copy with details I thought might come in useful, like the new ration cards and their hideous cardboard wallets, and the *très chic* gas mask holder designed by Jeanne Lanvin for any Parisian woman lucky enough to have 180 francs to burn. I was particularly proud of the column I wrote about the growing fad for elegant turbans to hide greasy hair (due to the lack of warm water and soap), where I managed to weave in the fact that British citizens living in France were now being arrested by the Germans, and even their French wives weren't safe. The imaginary Churchill in my head loved this one and even lit a celebratory cigar as he bellowed, 'Thank you kindly, my dear!' Every time I wired my copy over to Harry via Western Union, I felt a small stab of pride. I was desperate to do more though, a desperation that was fuelled in large part by Otto's declining spirits.

A rumour had been sweeping the city that the Germans were going to ask all French men aged between eighteen and forty-three to register with them. According to his false papers, Otto was a French man of twenty-three, but any official registration process could very well show the papers to be forged. Deciding that it was no longer safe for him to go to work – the Germans

were doing more and more spot checks at the Métro stations
– Otto quit his job at the store and decided to hide out in our
room. At first I'd felt hugely relieved by this. At least I'd now be
spared the terror of never knowing if he'd make it home safely
each day. But I was soon to learn that keeping someone physically
safe doesn't guarantee their mental well-being.

The cracks started to show after Otto had been house-bound
for a couple of weeks. Instead of waiting up for me, like he used
to, I'd come home to find him asleep. And in the mornings,
instead of bounding from bed to make breakfast, he'd be quiet
and listless. One night, I came home from the club to find he'd
left his sketchpad open on the table. I leafed through to see what
he'd been doing and was shocked at the transformation in his
drawings. They were so much darker. Where his scenes of Paris
used to be populated with lively, smiling faces, now spectres and
monsters lurked in shadows. And his country landscapes were
unforgiving and bleak. On one page, towards the back of the
pad, he'd written a list:

'Florence
Mother and Father
Painting
Renoir
Paris
Vienna
Apfelstrudel'

I wasn't going to ask him about it, as I didn't want him to
think I'd been snooping, but then curiosity got the better of me.

'I had a look at your drawings last night,' I told him, as we
sat down to a grim breakfast of dry bread and chicory coffee.
Real coffee was another thing that had been plundered by the
Nazis – another crime that was unforgivable in my book.

'Oh yes?' Otto sighed. 'They aren't very good, I'm afraid. I feel as if my muse has abandoned me.' He gave a tight little laugh. 'Maybe she, too, has been captured by the Nazis.'

'Don't say that. They were great. I... uh... I saw a list... at the back of the pad.'

For a moment he looked blank, then his face flushed. 'Oh that.'

'What's it for? I saw I was at the top,' I chuckled, trying to make light of it.

'It is a list of reasons,' he replied.

'Reasons for what?'

'Reasons not to give up.'

His answer was like a sucker punch to my stomach. I gripped hold of his hands. 'What do you mean?'

'Just to remind me.'

'But why do you need reminding? Otto?'

He stared towards the shuttered windows. 'Sometimes, even though I try to find the light, I feel this darkness.'

I gulped and nodded. I felt the darkness too. But at least I was still able to go outside, to breathe in the fresh air and sunlight. At least I was still able to walk around freely and dance every evening. At least I wasn't being hunted simply because of my religion.

'It's ironic, isn't it? That I should have dreamed for so long to live in Paris.' He sighed. 'Never in my wildest dreams did I imagine it being like this. Me, a prisoner in the very square I dreamed of working on as an artist, but unable to do a thing, unable to contact my parents, even, unable to know if they are still living.'

'Don't say that!'

'Why?' His eyes filled with anguish. 'It's been two months now with no letter from them. I don't even know if they're dead or living.'

'Of course they're still living!' I leapt up and came around to stand beside him. 'Stand up.'

'Why?' He slowly got to his feet.

'So I can give you this.' I pulled him to me and hugged him tightly. 'We will beat them,' I whispered. 'You mustn't give up hope.'

'Thank you.' His body sank into mine and he gripped me so tight I thought he might never let me go.

When I walked to work that night, I felt rigid with worry. I'd never seen Otto so low and I didn't know what I could do to help. As I went down the hill, I passed two uniformed German women on the sidewalk. They were laughing and chatting as if they didn't have a care in the world, the same way Bessie and I used to gad about back on the streets of New York. Their jollity caused a fury to rise up inside of me. I wanted to rip at their ugly plain uniforms and spit in their faces. To them, being posted in Paris was some kind of holiday, as they greedily helped themselves to all it had to offer. How could they not care about the suffering they caused? How could they laugh so gaily, when so many around them were crying in pain?

I marched into the club and along the corridor leading to the dressing rooms. I couldn't wait to get up onto that stage and high kick the rage out of my body. As I passed Bessie's office, I heard her throaty laugh. Then I heard a man's voice – a man's voice with a thick German accent. I stopped dead. The door burst open and Bessie wafted out on a cloud of Chanel No. 5. She was clad in a scarlet satin dress that was cleavage-enhancing even by her standards. Behind her loomed a soldier. A high-ranking soldier, judging by the stripes on his collar. He had slicked-back hair so fair it was almost white, and pale blue eyes set a little too close together, giving him a slightly piggy appearance.

'Here's Florence!' Bessie exclaimed. 'She's one of my finest dancers; you'll just love her.'

The soldier looked me up and down.

Somehow, I forced myself to smile.

'Officer von Fritsch has just been stationed here in Paris,' Bessie said, grinning at me. 'I told him we'd show him a swell time, give him a little taste of the Big Apple.'

'Big Apple?' The officer looked at her questioningly.

'It's a nickname for New York, honey!' Bessie gave a tinkling, girly laugh I'd never heard her use before. Its shrillness set my teeth on edge.

I looked at her, trying to convey the sentiment, *What the hell's gotten into you?* with just the power of my gaze. Judging by her dreamy grin, it didn't appear to work.

'I always wanted to go to New York,' the officer said, wistfully.

'Well, tonight you'll get the next best thing,' Bessie replied. 'We've got jazz straight out of Harlem, and Florence was the queen of the New York scene.'

I gave her another hard stare. Yes, folks back home enjoyed my acrobatics, but I'd hardly have referred to myself as the queen of any scene.

Bessie patted the soldier on the arm. 'Trust me, honey, here at Le Flamant Rose we've got dancing to die for.'

Now he was the one giving her a piercing stare.

'Oh, good Lord, I didn't mean literally!' Bessie exclaimed, clutching her hands to her bosom.

The sight of her fawning all over him caused my stomach to churn.

'That is good,' he replied in clipped tones. 'I look forward to the show.'

'Let me escort you to your table,' Bessie said, guiding him off along the corridor without a backward glance.

I stared after them, dumbfounded. I understood that Bessie needed to keep the Germans sweet in order to keep Le Flamant Rose in business, but was it really necessary to have private soirées with officers? A horrible thought occurred to me. What if the pressure of the war had gotten too much for her? What if she'd sold out to the enemy? What if I could no longer trust her?

And then I had the worst thought of all. Bessie knew about Otto. She knew he was Jewish.

SAGE

March 2018

'Sage, lunch is ready!' Sam called up the stairs.

Sage reluctantly put the manuscript down. There was no way she wanted to stop reading now. What if Bessie betrayed Florence and Otto to the Nazis? But she could hardly tell Sam she didn't want any lunch, not after he'd gone to the trouble of cooking for her. And whatever he'd been cooking smelled delicious: a spicy seafood aroma was wafting up from the kitchen.

'I thought we could have lunch in here,' Sam said as Sage came downstairs, ushering her through to a room at the front of the house. With chintzy curtains, a polished wooden table and beautifully upholstered chairs, it was a lot smarter than the rest of the house. There was a lovely old rocking chair in the window, looking out over the fields and mountains.

'My momma loved this room,' he said, following her gaze to the chair. 'It was where she'd come to read. She wrote her story right here at this table too.'

'Really?' As Sage sat down, she pictured Florence sitting across from her, typing away, blissfully unaware that one day her own granddaughter would be reading her words at that very same table. The thought made her skin tingle.

'I made us some shrimp and grits,' Sam said, handing her a plate of prawns nestled on a bed of something yellow, which Sage assumed had to be the infamous grits. 'There's some smoked ham and peppers in there too, just to spice things up a bit.' He sat down opposite her and they began to eat.

'This is delicious!' Sage exclaimed, as the carnival of flavours dissolved on her tongue.

'Why, thank you!' Sam poured her a glass of iced water from a jug on the table. 'So how did y'all get on with the horses?'

'It was great. I found a horse I loved – or rather, he found me.'

Sam chuckled. 'Ah yes, Hunter's all about letting the horse choose.'

'He said they're able to read us and pick up on our emotions.'

'Sure can. They're very sensitive creatures. So you enjoyed it, then?'

Sage nodded. 'I'd been feeling a little stressed, you know, about everything going on back home, but when I rode Whisky it was as if all my problems disappeared.'

Sam smiled. 'They're great stress-relievers. Hunter's gotten some great results helping traumatised veterans.'

'He helps veterans with trauma?'

'Uh-huh. Some of them are shook up real bad, too. They've seen their friends killed, or they've been badly injured in action, or in a lot of cases, both. But once they've been working with Hunter and his horses for a while, they're like new men – and women.'

Sage thought of the German man in Florence's story who'd seen his best friend die. Like Florence, she'd always thought the Nazis must have been evil and devoid of emotion to have been able to do what they did. She sighed. 'Why does life have to be so complicated?'

Sam laughed. 'Some folks say complicated, others might call it interesting.'

Sage continued eating. It turned out that being outside with the horses for most of the morning had given her a huge appetite.

'Was Hunter in the army too?'

'Uh-huh. He had a pretty bad experience on a tour in Afghanistan. He saw half his squad killed in a rocket attack. He was just a kid of eighteen.'

'That's horrible.'

'Sure was. He came to work on the farm when he got discharged from the army, and that's when he discovered his love of horses.' Sam chuckled. 'And their love for him!'

'It's so great that he helps other people who've been through similar things.'

'For sure.'

As they carried on eating, Sage thought of Hunter. She'd put his brusqueness down to arrogance before, but now she saw him in a whole new light and she realised she'd been no better than her online tormentors, quickly forming a judgement without even knowing, or bothering to know, the full picture. She looked at the rocking chair.

'What was Florence like, as a mum?'

Sam looked down at the table. 'She was great. But there was a sadness about her that she was never able to shake… War's a terrible thing.'

Sage nodded. And even though she had no direct experience, she felt she was really starting to understand how painful and long-reaching the tentacles of war could be.

FLORENCE

1941

When I danced that night, I was so distracted. All I could see was Bessie at the main table, right in front of the stage, with her officer friend and a bunch of other grey uniforms. During the can-can, I imagined a row of German soldiers standing in front of me and aimed my kicks straight at their heads. It didn't help. At the end of the number they were all still sitting there, laughing and drinking, and my supposed best friend – a shining red rose in the sea of grey – was giggling away without a care in the world. I couldn't get off that stage and back into the dressing room fast enough.

I was just about to take off my costume when Bessie burst through the door.

'Don't get changed!' she cried. 'I want you to come have a drink with us.'

Us. The tiny word struck me with the force of a bullet. Bessie and the Nazis were now 'us'.

'I don't want to drink with you,' I muttered, pulling off my diamanté headpiece.

'Florence!' Bessie shut the door behind her and glared at me in the mirror. 'What's gotten into you?'

'What's gotten into *me?*' I stared at her incredulously. *Calm down*, a voice in my head said. A soothing voice remarkably similar to Otto's. *You need this job; you can't afford to blow your top*. I thought of Otto hidden away in our room, unable to work. I owed it to him to keep it together. I bit down on my lip.

'Yes! Why are you being so moody?'

I stared back at her reflection and took a deep breath to try and compose myself. 'I'm just surprised to see you acting so pally with those Germans,' I muttered.

'Those Germans are paying our wages,' Bessie replied sharply. 'They can help us in other ways, too. Officer von Fritsch says he can get us all the nylons and cigarettes and candy we need.'

'Great,' I replied flatly, horrified that Bessie could be so easily bought.

She came over and grabbed me by the arms. I could smell the Scotch on her breath, mingled with her perfume. 'What is it? What's wrong?'

I tried so hard to make myself lie, to tell her that nothing was wrong, and her drinking with Nazis was all fine and dandy, but I couldn't. 'So what if Officer Fritsch is the Nazi Santa Claus, with his nylons and candy?' I hissed. 'Think of what they're doing to France, what they're doing to the Jews. How can you not care?'

'Oh, I care,' she replied, her expression hardening. 'I care about not dying.'

So that was it. She'd rather save her own skin than stand up for what was right. It was a horrible feeling, standing in front of someone you thought you knew as well as yourself, and realising you never knew them at all.

'And if you care about not dying, you'll come out front and you'll have a drink and you'll laugh at their jokes and smile sweetly.' Her gaze was now filled with her trademark steel.

What could I do? She might not have been my friend any more, but she was still my boss, and I still needed my job. For Otto.

'OK.'

'Good.' She stood there, waiting, arms folded, while I brushed my hair and reapplied my lipstick. It felt as if she was the jailor waiting to accompany me to my execution.

We walked along the corridor back to the bar in total silence. The German soldiers were still sitting at their tables, with some of the chorus girls now in attendance, hovering around them like glittering hummingbirds. As we walked past one of the tables, I heard a couple of men speaking in German. Thanks to Otto's lessons, I was able to tell that they were talking about a train coming in at a certain time. My apprehension morphed into a weird kind of excitement as I remembered what Otto had said about maybe overhearing something useful in the club. The key was to not let the Germans know that I understood them. Thankfully, I had a great poker face, although I had told turncoat Bessie about my German lessons. Hopefully she'd have forgotten.

Think of it like playing a role, I told myself, as we headed over to von Fritsch's table. I might not be up on the stage any more, but I was still performing. I took a deep breath and got into character before treating von Fritsch and the rest of his cronies to a slightly bashful smile.

'Here she is, the star of the show!' Bessie declared as we reached the table.

One of the men leapt up and pulled out a chair for me. He was the only one not dressed in military attire, wearing a smart black suit instead. It was only as we were sitting down that I realised he was the guy I'd seen on Christmas Eve, crying by the side door of the club.

'Thank you,' I said, realising it was probably best not to acknowledge we'd already met, given the circumstances.

'You are very welcome.' He smiled. 'My name is Klaus. Can I get you a drink?'

Again, my stomach lurched, as the enormity of what I was doing hit me. All I could think of was Otto, waiting for me at home in our room, in our bed. What would he think if he could see me now? *You're just performing*, I reminded myself. *You could find out something that might help the people fighting the Germans.*

'Thank you, I'll have a vodka martini,' I replied, feeling sick.

'Good call,' Bessie exclaimed, grinning at me as if our dressing room altercation had never happened and we were still best buddies.

Thankfully, she then proceeded to chat enough for the both of us. I was able to sit back, sipping my drink. Officer von Fritsch clearly had the hots for her – or his icy, piggy-eyed version of the hots at least – emitting a tight little laugh after every one of her jokes and blatantly staring at her chest. Bessie handled him the way I'd seen her handle hundreds of men before – at least, before she'd met Pierre. Treating him to coquettish smiles and fluttering eyelashes. The whole song and dance made me sick. The three other men at the table weren't saying anything of any interest, either. Klaus sat there drinking and smoking and barely saying a word, while the other two got involved in an endless discussion about Wagner. I was trying to figure out how to make my excuses and leave when, finally, Klaus spoke.

'So tell me, how long have you been dancing?'

Remember, this is a performance, I told myself, forcing my mouth into a smile. 'Ever since I was a kid. I always loved acrobatics. My real dream was to run away and join the circus.'

'So she ran away and joined me instead!' Bessie exclaimed, with yet another simpering giggle.

Klaus raised his eyebrows questioningly.

'I moved to New York when I was seventeen and starting dancing in Bessie's club there.'

'I see.' He smiled, but the smile didn't quite reach his eyes, which still seemed tinged with sadness. 'I used to dream of joining the circus too.'

'You did?' My curiosity trumped my desire not to appear too friendly.

'Yes. I always wanted to walk the – the rope, you know?'

'The tightrope?'

'Yes.' His smile grew. 'It is funny, isn't it, to think of what we dreamed of as kids.'

Yeah, real funny, especially when you end up going from circus performer to Nazi, I felt like saying. I swallowed it down and nodded.

'I enjoy watching you dance.' He gave me another warm smile.

Instantly, my skin prickled. What would I do if he started coming on to me? I couldn't even rely on Bessie for a way out, as she'd probably encourage it.

'You have a real fire – in here.' He tapped his hand on his chest. 'A real passion.'

Von Fritsch barked something at him in German. I was able to translate the words 'stupid' and 'fool'. The other men at the table burst out laughing. Klaus' cheeks flushed and he looked down at his lap. I kept my face poker straight as I processed these latest developments. My instant appraisal was that although they were all Nazi assholes, Klaus might not be as much of an asshole as the others.

'I am sorry,' he said to me, putting out his cigarette in one of the flamingo-embossed ashtrays. 'I am very tired. I think I shall go now.'

'Oh. OK.' For the second time since I met him, I was in the weird position of feeling slightly sorry for him. *Don't feel sorry for him; he's the enemy*, I quickly reminded myself.

Klaus said something to von Fritsch in German, too quickly for me to understand, then he tipped his hat to me and headed for the door.

I finished my drink, then stood up too. 'I ought to get home. It was very nice to meet you,' I said, looking directly at von Fritsch. Boy, was I warming to my performance. I glanced at

Bessie, dreading that she might shake her head and insist I stay, but to my relief, she nodded.

'See you tomorrow, dear heart.'

'See you tomorrow.' I couldn't bring myself to use my usual term of endearment. The men at the table all stood as I left. I couldn't help finding their chivalry hugely ironic, but forced myself to smile through gritted teeth.

Outside, a bitter wind swept down the hill, causing my eyes to water. Off in the distance I heard a sound that had become all too familiar, the sharp, clean click of soldiers' boots. I pulled my coat tighter around me and hurried along the pitch-black street. Then, from out of the shadows, someone grabbed my arm. It took everything I had not to scream. I spun round and saw Otto lurking in a darkened shop doorway.

'Otto! What are you doing? Why are you out?' I quickly scanned the street. Thankfully it was deserted. But it was way past curfew. As a dancer, I had special paperwork allowing me out later – but Otto didn't. If he got caught by the Germans, he could end up in all kinds of trouble.

'You were late. I was worried,' he whispered.

'Come on, quick.' I linked arms with him and we hurried up the hill.

'Why were you late?' he whispered.

'I'll tell you when we get back,' I hissed in response.

All the way home, in between jumping out of my skin at the slightest noise, I tried to compose an excuse to Otto in my head that wouldn't involve me telling him I'd been drinking with German soldiers. I'd been so convinced he'd be asleep when I arrived home, I'd assumed I'd never have to tell him.

I don't think I'd ever been so relieved to get back to the Place du Tertre. As soon as the heavy exterior door closed behind us and we were in the darkness of the stairwell, my legs almost buckled from relief.

'Well?' Otto said, as soon as we got up to our room and I'd locked the door behind us.

It's funny. I'd never had a problem telling a white lie before, especially if it was to save the other person's feelings, but with Otto, lying just didn't seem to be an option. I felt as if he could see right through me.

'Bessie asked me to have a drink with some Germans after the show,' I said quietly.

'What? German soldiers?' His face crumpled with shock and pain.

'I had no choice. Bessie insisted I do it.' I was aware how pitiful I sounded, like a kid blaming another to try and wriggle out of trouble.

Otto started pacing up and down the room. 'Why would she do that? Why would she make you do that?'

'She says she needs to keep the Germans happy to keep the club open. I wanted to refuse. I wanted to walk out, but if I lose my job, what will we do? And then I remembered what you said, about my knowing some German coming in useful. So I tried to see it as an opportunity to... to spy on them.'

'And did you hear anything useful?' Otto stopped pacing and looked at me.

I shook my head.

'So, what *did* you hear? What did they say?' Even in the darkness I could tell he was getting frantic.

'Nothing much. I heard a couple of them talking about a train time, but I'm not sure what it was to do with and then they started talking about Wagner.'

'Wagner?'

'Yes.'

Otto looked so crushed by this disclosure I decided not to tell him about Klaus' dream of joining the circus. 'They sit around talking music while they... while they...' He broke off. I'd never seen him look so furious.

'I left as soon as I could, and if you want me to quit my job, I will. I can look for something else. Maybe Sylvia needs help in the bookstore.' But I knew there was slim hope of this. I knew she was struggling to make ends meet, like everyone else.

'No, no, you have to keep your job.' Otto came back over to me. 'It's just the thought of them talking to you, drinking with you.'

'I know. It made me sick too. I'll go in early tomorrow and see Bessie. See if I can talk some sense into her.'

Otto took my hands in his. 'I'm sorry I got so upset. I was worried when you didn't come home on time.'

'You shouldn't have gone out after curfew, you fool,' I replied, hugging him to me.

'You know me, I always like to break the rules.' He gave me a sheepish grin.

'Yes, but still, it's too risky.'

'I thought you were a bald eagle. I thought you were capable of spinning through the air in a death-defying spiral,' he teased.

'I am.'

'Oh yes?' He held me at arm's length and stared at me. There was such longing in his eyes, it triggered a jolt of yearning deep in the pit of my stomach. I took off my hat and kicked off my shoes.

'I love you,' he whispered.

'I love you, too.'

And then we were tearing at each other's clothes, he was lifting me onto the table, and his hands and mouth were exploring every inch of my skin. It felt as if he was reclaiming me. And boy, did I need him to.

The next day, Otto was fidgety and restless. He reminded me of one of the tigers Lady Hamilton-Jones had imported from India for her summer ball, trapped in its glitzy cage, what felt like another lifetime ago.

'Are you sure you want me to go?' I asked him for about the millionth time. 'I could always call Bessie from the phone in the restaurant and tell her I'm sick.'

'No, no, you have to go,' he said, but all of the colour and expression seemed to have drained from his face.

'All righty then. But I'm going to call and ask if I can come in early to have a chat.'

My sorrow at leaving Otto in such a dejected state turned to anxiety as soon as I'd called Bessie and began making my way down the hill to the club. I wasn't entirely sure what I was going to say to Bessie, but I had to say something. I couldn't stand the thought of a repeat of yesterday. I got to Le Flamant Rose so early that, apart from a couple of cleaning staff mopping the dancefloor, the place was deserted. I headed straight for Bessie's office.

Please, please, please, don't let Officer Piggy be in there, I willed as I knocked on the door.

'Come in,' Bessie called.

Thankfully, she was on her own, sitting at her desk poring over a leather-bound ledger.

'Florence!' she cried, smiling as if our heated words from the night before had never happened. 'So, you wanted to have a word?'

I nodded.

'Can we talk down in the cellar? I need to check some stock and I could do with some help.'

I followed her along the corridor to a door at the very back of the club, and down the steep flight of stone steps to the cellar. As Bessie lit a lamp and opened the cellar door, a smell of damp seeped out to greet us. I followed her inside and looked around. I'd only been in the cellar once before, when I'd first arrived in Paris and Bessie had insisted on giving me a guided tour of the entire club. It had given me the creeps back then, and nothing had changed. The place was lined with wooden shelves housing barrels of beer and bottles of wine, behind which, who knew what might be lurking. The flickering lamplight made it seem all the more sinister, not helped by the faint drip of water coming from the far corner.

'So, what do you need me to do?' I asked, eager to get this whole stock check over with as quickly as possible.

'What did you want to talk to me about?' Bessie whispered, shutting the door behind her.

'Oh, uh, about what happened last night,' I whispered back, although I wasn't entirely sure why we needed to lower our voices. Surely the only things that could hear us down here were the rats? I shuddered at the thought.

'What about last night?' She came closer, the lamp casting weird, flickering patterns upon her face.

'I don't feel comfortable drinking with the Germans.'

'Why not?'

Was she kidding? Did I really have to spell it out? 'Look, I know America isn't at war with Germany – yet, at least – but don't you feel any loyalty to the French?'

'A lot of French people seem to like the Germans,' she replied glibly.

'Well, they're either traitors or stupid.' I could feel my blood begin to boil again, and I wasn't able to stop it. 'Don't you care about what they're doing to the Jews? And what about Pierre? Have you forgotten him already?' I sighed and looked away. I'd blown it. I waited for her to give me my marching orders.

'What do you reckon?' Bessie said, looking at a cupboard beside me. 'Does she pass the test?'

'What test? What are you talking about? And why are you talking to a cupboard?' I stared at her, confused.

'I think she has passed the test admirably,' a clipped British voice replied from inside the cupboard, causing me to jump out of my skin.

Bessie let out a hoot of laughter then clapped her hand to her mouth. 'Your face!' she whispered. 'You look like you've seen a ghost!'

'What's going on? Who is that?' I gasped as a figure emerged from the cupboard. A tall, thin figure, wearing thick glasses. 'Mr Pennington? What… Why are you here?'

'He's here to see if you'll help,' Bessie replied, her eyes glinting with excitement in the lamplight.

'Help with what?' I whispered.

'Help beat Hitler.'

'But… but I thought… last night, when you were drinking with them. I thought you liked Officer von Fritsch…' I stammered.

'I hate Officer von Fritsch,' Bessie hissed.

'You mean… you don't… you're not…' I spluttered, desperately trying to make sense of these dramatic developments.

'Bessie has very kindly offered to help us in our fight against the Germans,' Pennington whispered from the shadows.

'And we want you to help, too.' Bessie beamed at me like she'd just invited me to go to the state fair, and as much as it was great to realise that my old friend was still my old friend, I needed a moment for this strange new reality to sink in. Bessie wasn't a turncoat after all; she was working against the Germans!

'I had to test you, just to make sure,' Bessie said.

'Test me?'

'Uh-huh. Last night. All that tosh about nylons and candy. All that sucking up to the Germans. Making you come for a drink.' Bessie gave a quietened-down version of her trademark snigger.

'You rotter!' I exclaimed. 'I hated you. I thought you'd become a traitor.'

'And that's exactly why you passed the test,' Pennington said.

I frowned. What was he still doing here in Paris? 'Is it safe for you to be here?' I asked.

'It's not safe at all,' Bessie whispered theatrically. 'He's here undercover as part of the resistance.'

'Yes, well, the less said about that the better,' Pennington said, giving her a stern look.

'Oh yes, sorry.' Bessie looked at me and grinned. 'So, whaddaya say? Are you in?'

'Of course I am. But what do you want me to do?'

'Your newspaper columns have come in very useful,' Pennington said, making my heart swell. Maybe my Churchill fantasies hadn't been fantasies after all. Maybe…

'We would like to utilise the fact that you're an American journalist,' Pennington continued, interrupting my reverie.

'I am?' It was a little hard for me to see my tittle-tattle as journalism.

'Of course you are,' Bessie said, giving me a nudge in the ribs.

I looked at her and shook my head, still unable to believe her act of deception – and that I'd fallen for it! 'How would you like to use it?' An incredible thought occurred to me. Did the British want me to start writing serious articles? Was I finally going to be asked to write something of substance?

'As an American journalist, you're able to travel freely in France,' Pennington replied. 'Or at least, a lot more freely than many of us. And as a woman, you're even less likely to arouse suspicion.'

'Uh-huh.' I nodded. Now that I'd gotten over my initial shock, I very much liked the way this conversation was going. I pictured myself, notebook and pen in hand, traversing the land in search of gripping war tales.

'We need a courier,' Pennington continued. 'Someone to transport important papers and messages.'

'Oh.' I had not seen this coming. 'What kind of messages?'

'I'm afraid I can't divulge that kind of information, as much for your own safety as anyone else's. But you can rest assured you would be playing a vital role in the war effort. Churchill himself has requested it.'

'Churchill asked for me?' My eyes widened.

'Well, uh, no, not you personally,' Pennington replied. 'But he has requested that we set up a secret army to set Europe ablaze.'

'Wow!' After months of feeling totally at the mercy of the Nazis, I couldn't help feeling stirred by this rousing rhetoric – even if delivering messages felt slightly less exciting than the daring journalistic escapades I'd been imagining. Maybe if I performed well as a courier, they'd consider making me a more serious foreign correspondent, writing about things that really mattered.

'I'm in. I'll do it,' I said.

'Atta girl!' Bessie whispered, giving me a hug.

'Excellent.' Pennington straightened his tie and cleared his throat. 'You'll receive your instructions here, at the club.'

'Isn't that a bit risky?' I asked. 'I mean, most nights the place is hopping with Germans.'

'That's what's so genius about it,' Bessie said with a grin. 'They're not going to suspect we'd be up to anything right under their noses.'

'Quite,' Pennington agreed. 'All right. I must go before the club opens.' He turned to me and shook my hand. 'We'll be in touch again very soon.'

'OK. Thank you.' I wasn't sure what else to say. In the space of a few minutes, my world had turned on its head.

Pennington slipped out of the cellar and I followed Bessie to her office.

'I don't know about you, but I need a drink,' she said, taking a bottle of Scotch from the cabinet in the corner.

'Sure.' I sat down in one of the leather armchairs by the fireplace. 'I can't believe what just happened.'

She put her finger to her lips. 'We need to be real careful,' she said quietly as she brought me my drink. 'From now on, you have to operate as if you can't trust anyone.'

I shivered. I'd been so caught up in the notion of helping Churchill defeat the cursed Nazis, I hadn't really contemplated how much I'd be risking. And then I thought of Otto. What would he make of this latest development? I was pretty sure he'd be happy that Bessie wasn't in cahoots with the enemy, but would my more active role make his confinement to our room all the more frustrating?

'What is it? You look worried,' Bessie asked, perching on the arm of my chair. 'Are you having second thoughts?'

'No, it's Otto. I'm worried about him.' I told her all about my concerns for Otto, now he was no longer able to work, and how I thought that being trapped in our room was starting to drive him crazy.

'Hmm.' Bessie pursed her brightly painted lips. 'What if I was to commission him to do some artwork? I need some new posters advertising the club.'

'Seriously? That would be great.' I grinned. 'I sure am glad you're not a Nazi collaborator!'

She laughed and shook her head. 'I can't believe you would think that of me.'

'What was I supposed to think? You were so convincing.'

'Good, cos I'm gonna need to be.' Her smile faded. 'We both are.' We sat in silence for a moment, then she chinked her glass against mine. 'Here's to our best show yet.'

I nodded and took a drink, the Scotch burning a comfortingly warm trail down my throat as I contemplated the life-threatening performance ahead of us.

'I have good news,' I announced – quietly of course – as I arrived back in our room later that evening. Otto was lying on the bed awake, staring up at the ceiling.

'What is it?' He propped himself onto his elbow.

'Bessie isn't a traitor after all.' I came and sat down beside him. 'She's working with the British.'

'What?' For the first time in ages, Otto looked genuinely excited. He sat up straight.

'When I went to see her tonight, she took me down to the cellar. She told me she needed help checking some stock, but when we got down there, this English guy was in the cupboard and he asked me if I'd help them, too.'

'What English guy? Who was he? Why was he in a cupboard?'

'Shhh!' I whispered. 'We have to be really careful.'

'I'm sorry,' he whispered back. 'Who was he? What did he say?'

Bessie had warned me not to give Otto too many details. 'Just in case he ever got captured and tortured,' she added, sending a chill right through me. I had to tell him something, though, to cheer him up and give him hope.

'He said he was working for the British government.'

'And Bessie is working with him?'

'Yes. She's using the club to get closer to the Germans to try and get information on them. All of that stuff last night was all a big act, and a way of testing me.'

Otto looked confused.

'She wanted to see if I hated the Germans too, enough to fight against them.'

Otto laughed and shook his head. 'That is incredible.' Then his smile faded. 'But what is it they want you to do?'

'Oh, nothing too serious,' I replied as nonchalantly as I could. 'Just take messages to people. I can travel around quite easily because I'm American and a journalist.'

'This is… it is such a surprise.' Otto looked as amazed as I had felt earlier in the cellar.

'I know. And I have some good news for you, too. Bessie's asked if you'll design some posters for the club. I've got all the details here.' I took a piece of paper from my coat pocket and handed it to him. 'Obviously she'll pay you.' I looked at him, hoping to see a smile.

He studied the piece of paper and nodded. 'OK.'

I hugged him tightly. 'It's all going to be OK,' I murmured into his chest. 'I reckon we'll have those Nazis out of France by the end of the year.'

If I'd known then that it would be another four years before we finally defeated Hitler, I'm not sure I would have embarked upon my new mission with quite such vigour. But on balance, I think I'm glad that we don't know our future. If nothing else, it enables us to move forward with hope in our hearts instead of despair.

SAGE

March 2018

Sage placed the manuscript beside her on the porch swing and gazed out across the fields. It was late afternoon and the sun was beginning its descent over the mountains, turning the peaks crimson. Down in the paddock, Hunter was working with one of his clients and Sam had gone to town to get some feed. Sage had turned down the invitation to go with him, eager to get back to Florence's story.

She took a moment to absorb everything she'd just read. Bessie hadn't been a traitor after all; she'd been a hero and a true friend. Sage thought wistfully of her best friend in university, a fellow English literature student called Hannah, who had a predisposition to vintage clothes, Oscar Wilde and calling everyone 'chook' as a term of endearment. From the moment they'd met at a spoken word event at the student union, they'd bonded over a shared love of poetry and hatred of the braying rugby lads and their stupid drinking games. But then they'd graduated, and Sage had moved back home to London and Hannah to Blackpool. They'd made the effort to go and visit each other at first, but as Sage's online presence had grown, their friendship had faded. In her last text to Sage, Hannah had written: *'I don't suppose you'll want to know me now that you're famous ☺ .'* The '☺' had felt weighted and Sage meant to reply straight away, but she'd been at a content creator convention in LA and by the time she'd remembered, almost a month had gone by. In spite of her profuse apologies, Hannah had never messaged again. By then, Sage had felt that maybe her friendship with Hannah had come to a natural end.

Reading about Florence and Bessie, though, made Sage realise that she'd never shared that same closeness with any of her influencer friends. If anything, those friendships had seemed to come with a slightly competitive subtext and a sense that it was all part of the online performance, designed to prove they were all members of the cool clique. Tellingly, none of them had reached out to see how Sage was doing since the online storm – although to be fair, her videos had been attacking the industry that had made them all rich.

Then she had a horrible thought: what if her online friends had joined in with the hate? Like an addict dying for a fix, she felt the sickening urge to check her phone. *Don't do it; you know it never ends well,* a voice in her head pleaded. *But don't you want to see what they might have said?* another, slyer, voice asked.

Sage took her phone from her pocket and searched for the profile of Kitty Klein – an Instagrammer who specialised in 'intuitive eating'. Of all her online friends, Kitty was the one Sage felt closest too. They'd bonded one night in the ladies' toilets at an awards ceremony, when Kitty had confided in Sage that, despite being known as an expert on food, she'd been struggling with bulimia for years. Kitty was also managed by Danny and the Spark Agency, and Danny had frequently arranged for her and Sage to do collabs – supposedly candid photos or videos of them hanging out together in clothes they'd been paid to wear, and/or eating food they'd been paid to consume.

As she scrolled through Kitty's latest images, Sage was relieved to see they were all the standard beautifully shot photos of Kitty eating a salad or drinking a smoothie. Then she got to a selfie of Kitty gazing earnestly into the lens. Sage tried to read the caption, but Instagram wouldn't allow it as she wasn't logged into an account. She told herself to put down her phone. But again, the compulsion to check was too strong. So, feeling hot with shame at her lack of willpower, she brought her own account back online and clicked onto Kitty's page. *'MY PERSONAL RESPONSE TO SAGE SEGAL'*, the caption began:

> *'Hey guys, I just wanted to say a few words about Sage Segal and her recent videos. Clearly Sage has some serious issues to deal with right now and she wasn't in her right mind, or sober, when she made those videos but I just want you to know that there's no way I support what Sage said. I love you guys so much and I'm so grateful for all of your support, especially during what has been a really stressful few days in the aftermath of those videos. I pray that Sage gets the help she so badly needs but I have to distance myself from her now for the sake of my own mental health. Thank you so much for your understanding. You guys are the best. If you'd like to know more about how this whole nightmare has affected me sign up to my members-only subscription service via Patreon. Link and payment details in bio. Love you guys! Xxxxx #blessed #gratitude #addict #addictions'*

Sage stared at her phone, trying to comprehend what she'd just read. *I told you, you shouldn't have looked,* her inner voice taunted. But she had looked, and now she couldn't un-see Kitty's words. Why had she said that Sage was drunk in both videos? Surely it was obvious she was sober in the second one. And why had she used the 'addict' and 'addiction' hashtags? As the horrible truth dawned, Sage felt physically sick. Kitty was trying to portray her as a drink- and drug-addled unstable person, and in her sickly-sweet way she was stoking up more hate. Just a glance at the comments from her followers, all declaring their love for Kitty and hatred for Sage, confirmed that. Then Sage had an even more horrible thought: what if Danny was behind the post, using one of his clients to try and rectify the damage caused by another?

Sage heard a man's voice calling in the distance and looked across the field to see Hunter and his client galloping off into the woods. She'd felt so good earlier when they'd taken the horses for a trot around the field. But now everything was pressing back in on her again, making her want to fade away to nothing. She put down her phone and picked up Florence's manuscript, desperate to escape the pit of self-loathing opening up inside of her, threatening to swallow her whole.

FLORENCE

1941

I received my first assignment as a courier for the resistance the following week.

'Check your locker,' Bessie told me, when I arrived at the club one night and bumped into her in the foyer. 'I've left the music you asked me for there.'

I was about to say, 'What music?' when I noticed her pointed stare. 'OK. Thank you,' I replied breezily.

I went into my dressing room and opened my locker, skin tingling; I had no idea what would be awaiting me. I half-expected to see Charles Pennington all squashed up inside, peering out at me through his thick glasses. Instead, there was a folder containing a piece of sheet music. What the hell? For a moment, I wondered if I was experiencing some kind of amnesia. Had I asked Bessie for some music and forgotten all about it? Then I saw something written in pencil at the top of the sheet: *'Piano lesson'*, next to an address, tomorrow's date and the time 11 a.m. The name of the street wasn't one I recognised, but I had a map of Paris at home so I figured I'd easily find it.

For the rest of the night, I was so excited. *I know something you don't know*, I silently sang to those grey-clad creeps with every shimmy and kick of my performance. *We aren't just your playthings; we're the resistance!*

However, my new-found fervour was instantly tested when I received a message in my dressing room after the show, telling me that Bessie would like me to join her for a drink. I found her at her table with Officer von Fritsch and two men I hadn't seen before. There was no sign of Klaus. I couldn't help feeling slightly disappointed. Not because I liked him – he was a Nazi, so to like him would be a physical impossibility – but because he was the only German I'd met so far who didn't give me the heebie-jeebies. I fixed a grin to my face and took a seat.

'Great show, Florence,' Bessie said, raising her glass to me.

'Yes, very good,' von Fritsch muttered, raising his glass too.

'Thank you,' I said. *And to hell with you*, I added in my mind.

The other men at the table started looking at me and speaking in German. Although I could only make out a few words, I could tell from their gaze that what they were saying wasn't exactly chivalrous. It gave me a flashback to the day I'd arrived in France, and the sleazy man I'd seen on the train. The men downed their drinks, then refilled their glasses from a bottle of brandy on the table.

'So, where you live?' one of them asked me, in pidgin French.

'She lives with me,' Bessie replied, quick as a flash.

I tried to ignore the dread building inside of me. Bessie and I had had our share of run-ins with hoodlums back in our Harlem days, but back then, we'd always had plenty of other guys around to protect us. Now we were totally on our own, not to mention outnumbered. I glanced around the club at some of the chorus girls drinking at the other soldiers' tables. Then I spied Klaus, drinking on his own at the bar.

'You have very nice legs,' Officer Sleazebag continued.

All the better for kicking you with, I wanted to reply. Instead, I kept smiling sweetly. 'I'm just going to use the restroom,' I said to Bessie.

'Sure thing.'

As I left the bar, I was faced with a real dilemma. If I slipped off home to safety, I'd be leaving Bessie alone with those men. But surely no one would mess with her while she was in von Fritsch's favour? Apart from, of course, von Fritsch. I shuddered at the thought and hurried off to the dressing room. Not wanting to waste time getting changed, I put my hat and coat on over my costume. Then I tucked the sheet music into my bag and quickly slipped into the corridor and out the side door.

I was just approaching the end of the passageway when I heard a sound behind me. I turned and saw two figures silhouetted against the light from inside. Then the door closed and they were absorbed into the darkness.

'Where are you going?' one of them called after me.

My stomach flipped. It was the men from Bessie's table. I hurried on, pretending not to hear them, and I heard the sharp click of their boots on the ground as they ran after me.

'Halt!' One of them grabbed me by the arm and pinned me against the wall.

Back when I was thirteen and began growing breasts – a development that, at the time, disgusted me – my daddy took me out into the yard and taught me some basic self-defence moves. Thanks to him, I knew that right now I had a couple of options open to me – I could bring my knee up into his groin, or punch him just beneath the nose. Both would incapacitate him, for a few moments at least. But something told me neither of these would be the best option against a couple of Nazis.

'I wasn't feeling so good,' I replied softly instead. 'I feel sick.' This much was definitely true.

The other man muttered something in German and I recognised the word 'whore'.

Keep calm, my inner voice of Otto urged me. *Don't let him make you lose your cool; don't let them know you understand German.*

The man holding me loosened his grip and traced his finger across my cheek. His breath smelled of a sour mix of stale booze and cigarettes.

I hate you, I thought, while looking back at him and forcing myself to smile.

The other guy, who was shorter and stockier, leered at me, muttering something under his breath. I saw the gleam of his pistol strapped beneath his arm, and for a moment, I was paralysed. Then an instinct for self-preservation kicked in.

'Let's go back inside, have another drink,' I said breezily, trying to make my way back down the passageway.

'*Nein!*' the taller man barked, grabbing my arm again. He said something to his pal and they started laughing. Then the stocky one pulled at my coat, ripping it open. A couple of the buttons burst off and onto the floor.

'Hey!' I yelled.

'Shut up, American bitch,' the taller man muttered in English. Then I heard the clink of a belt being unbuckled.

'No!' I yelled and shoved him away.

There was a terrible silence, then the stocky one reached for his gun.

The next moment, the club door opened, and a beam of light swept along the passageway. I heard the sound of feet marching towards us and my heart sank. What if it was another German? I realised I was faced with a terrible choice – I could either be raped by a bunch of Nazi pigs, or die fighting them off. But as the figure drew closer, the soldiers stepped away from me, as if suddenly scared. I drew a breath, and saw that the other man was Klaus. He barked something in German and the soldiers clicked their heels and gave a salute, then scuttled off and away down the street.

'Are you OK?' Klaus asked, looking at my torn-open coat.

'Yes.' The relief surging through my body caused my eyes to fill with tears, much to my annoyance. As I tried to wipe them away with my hand, Klaus produced a handkerchief from his coat pocket.

'Here,' he said softly, holding it out to me.

'I'm sorry. I'm OK,' I replied, trying to stop my voice from trembling.

'It is OK. First it was my turn to cry out here, now it is yours,' he said, gesturing at the passageway and smiling.

'I guess so.' I dabbed at my eyes.

'I am very sorry. They are a disgrace to their uniform.'

Are you kidding? I thought. *You're all a disgrace.*

'Come, I shall walk you home.'

'Oh, no, it's OK. You really don't have to.'

'I just want to make sure you are safe. I would like to think another man would do the same for my wife.'

'You're married?'

'Yes.' The sadness returned to his eyes. 'She is in Berlin, with our children.'

An image formed in my mind of Klaus sitting on a sofa with a blonde German woman and a couple of blonde kids bouncing on his lap. He seemed so different to the others, it was unnerving. But at least I felt relatively safe with him. I pictured the other two lurking in the shadows somewhere, waiting to pounce on me.

'Maybe you could walk me up the hill?'

He nodded. 'It would be my pleasure.'

I did up my coat with the buttons that were left, and we walked out onto the street. I couldn't help being struck by the irony that here I was, with a message in my bag for the resistance, being escorted home by a German. I appreciated the fact that Klaus didn't try and make small talk. When we got to the top of the hill, he came to a halt.

'Will you be OK here?'

'Yes,' I replied. 'Thank you.'

'You are welcome, and again, I'm sorry for what happened. They will be punished for their behaviour.'

'OK. Good.' I nodded and continued on my way, my heart still pounding and my palms still clammy.

It was only when I reached the Place du Tertre and reached into my pocket for my keys that I realised I still had his handkerchief.

I had been hoping to crawl straight into bed and Otto's arms, but I came in to find him slumped at the table in front of his sketchpad, balls of crumpled paper surrounding him on the floor.

'What's with the balls of paper? Been working on your juggling routine?' I wisecracked, desperately hoping things weren't as bad as they appeared and that there was a harmless explanation for this scene of despair.

'I can't do it,' he said, slumping forward with his head in his hands.

'Can't do what?'

'The poster for Bessie. I've spent all night trying to come up with designs but when I think of what it's for, I just... I lose all inspiration.'

'But it's for the club.' I came and sat beside him.

'It's for the Nazis. To try and get them to come to the club.' He sighed. 'It feels wrong to do what I love for them.'

'But you're doing it for Bessie and she doesn't want to help them,' I reminded him.

'I know, but still. I'd rather be using my art against them.'

I nodded. 'I know what you mean. It still makes me sick to my stomach, having to dance for them.'

'What happened to your coat?' He looked at the missing buttons and frowned.

'Oh, I was taking it off in a hurry and they came off.' There was no way I could tell him what had really happened, not with the mood he was in. I felt a pang of bitterness. I hated how the Nazis were coming between us, making me create secrets from Otto I had no wish to keep. 'Should I tell Bessie you don't want to do the job, then?'

Otto sighed. 'I should do it. We need the money. I just wish there was something else I could do.'

He stayed up drawing – or trying to draw – late into the night. I lay in bed, listening to the scratch of his pencil and the sound of his sighs, wishing with all my might that he would find his way back to hope.

SAGE

March 2018

Sage stopped reading and took a breath. She'd been clenching her fists so tightly, there were crescent-shaped grooves in her palms from her nails. Reading about Florence's experiences had once again given her a welcome shift in perspective when it came to her own problems and made them fade in comparison. So what if Kitty had turned on her? She'd clearly never been a real friend. She heard the sound of men's voices and looked up to see Hunter and his client walking across the front yard. As they drew closer, she saw that one side of the man's face was shiny and mottled red, as if it had been badly burned.

'She's really starting to relax around me now,' Sage heard the man say.

'That's because she can feel you relaxing,' Hunter replied. 'Being around a horse is just like taking a look in the mirror.'

They reached a battered-looking car parked next to Hunter's truck.

'Thanks, dude,' the man said.

'No problem,' Hunter replied. 'Thank you for all your hard work.'

Pretending to read the manuscript, Sage watched as the two men hugged. She smiled as she realised she was doing exactly what Florence used to do: reading to hide the fact she was people-watching. The man got in his car and drove away. Hunter looked over at Sage.

'Howdy,' he called, raising his hat.

'Oh hey,' Sage replied, as if she'd only just spotted him. Then she thought about what Sam had told her over lunch and resolved to make an effort to be friendlier. 'Would you like some iced tea?'

'Oh… well… OK.' He strode up the porch steps and sat down on the swing seat opposite hers.

'How did your session with your client go?' Sage asked, pouring him a glass.

'Awesome. He made some real progress today.'

'That's great.' Sage handed him his drink.

'What are you reading?' Hunter asked, looking at the manuscript.

'It's something my grandma – Sam's mum – wrote, about her life.'

'I bet it's a good read. She was a fine woman. She helped me out a lot when I first came to work here.'

'Why? What did she—' Sage broke off at the sound of tyres scrunching on the gravel. She turned to see Sam pulling up in front of the house.

'Hey, kids,' he called, getting down from his truck. 'How's it going?'

'Not bad,' Hunter replied. He downed his tea and got to his feet. 'I'd better get back.' He put on his hat and gazed out over the fields. 'I was wonderin'… Would you like to help me get the horses ready in the morning?'

'She's our guest,' Sam said, as he joined them on the porch. 'And she's on vacation. You can't ask her to muck out like a farm hand.'

'Well, if it's too much hard work for you…?' Hunter looked at Sage with what she thought might actually be the beginnings of a grin.

'Of course it isn't,' she retorted.

'Awesome. I'll see you in the morning, then. We start at five.'
'Five?'

'I did try to save you,' Sam chuckled.

'Five is fine,' Sage said quickly. 'I was expecting it to be earlier, actually.'

'Yeah, yeah.' Hunter set off down the porch steps. 'I'll be seein' ya, then.'

'Yep, see you.'

Sam sat on the porch swing and helped himself to some iced tea. 'So, how's it going?' he asked, nodding at the manuscript.

'It's getting pretty intense. I just read the bit where she thought she was going to be attacked by the German soldiers outside the club.'

Sam grimaced. 'I hated that part.'

'It was interesting that Klaus helped her, though.'

'Uh-huh. Reading about Klaus gave me hope for humanity.' Sam took off his baseball cap and wiped the sweat from his brow. 'So, are y'all hungry yet? I thought I'd take you out for some barbecue.'

'That would be great.' Sage looked out over the fields. The cicadas had started their whirring evening chorus and the setting sun was causing the grass to glow gold. 'Thank you so much.'

'What for?'

'This. Being so nice to me. Everything.'

Sam cleared his throat, looking slightly embarrassed. 'Honey, you are welcome. That's what family's for. Takin' care of each other. Now, let's go get fed.'

As Sage picked up the manuscript and followed him inside, the emptiness she'd been feeling began filling with gratitude.

FLORENCE

1941

The next morning I woke bright and early, my body crackling with nerves at the prospect of my first mission as a courier for the resistance. I'd decided against telling Otto for two reasons. One, I didn't want him feeling even worse about not being able to do anything, and two, I remembered what Bessie had said about the less being said about our work, the better. I told him instead that I was going to see Sylvia at Shakespeare and Company. Remembering what Charles Pennington had said about women being the perfect couriers as they aroused no suspicion, I dressed in a figure-hugging black number from Chanel, deciding to play the role of a pretty little thing, far too concerned with my appearance to possibly be working for the resistance. Otto looked me up and down as I came out of the bathroom.

'You look beautiful.'

I instantly felt vile that I couldn't tell him the real reason for my chic appearance. 'Thank you, *mon cher*,' I replied, kissing him on top of the head. Now it felt as if I was playing a role for Otto too, and this didn't sit well with me at all. I checked my lipstick and took a jacket from the closet. 'I shouldn't be long.' Then I realised I had no clue how long my mission might take. 'Unless Sylvia needs help in the store.'

'Of course,' Otto replied. His innocent, trusting smile only made my guilt grow.

*

The address I'd been sent to was in the twentieth arrondissement, right by Père-Lachaise cemetery. I tried not to take this as some kind of sign. The Métro was crawling with German soldiers, and although they weren't doing a formal check of papers, their eyes felt like searchlights as they swept over my body. It made me realise that dressing so chicly might not have been the greatest idea. Next time, if there was a next time, I'd wear something a little more drab and dreary. I was just breathing a sigh of relief that I'd gotten to my destination safely, when the flow of passengers out of Père-Lachaise station came to a halt.

'What is it? What's going on?' a young guy next to me kept asking as we all queued by the steps to the exit. He kept looking around anxiously and sweat was beading above his lip. With his chestnut hair and brown eyes, he kind of reminded me of Otto. His anxiety reminded me of him, too.

'Why aren't we moving?' the guy said again, louder this time, causing people to turn and stare at him. I wanted to take him to one side and tell him to cool it, that he wasn't doing himself any favours by doing such a convincing impression of a startled rabbit, but I thought of the sheet music in my bag, and the secret message it must contain. I hadn't been able to figure it out, but what if the Germans did? I couldn't afford to bring any attention to myself by association. So, as the young man began cursing under his breath, I kept my gaze fixed straight ahead. Then I heard a kerfuffle behind me. Two German soldiers had appeared from out of nowhere and grabbed the young man by the collar.

'What are you so nervous about?' one of them asked him in French.

I suppressed a shudder. Had this all been a deliberate ploy? Had they planted soldiers at the back of the queue to see who panicked at the thought of going through a checkpoint? They'd caught us like rats in a trap. In spite of my growing panic, I kept looking ahead and focused on my breathing. Inhaling and exhaling, slow and steady.

'Identity card and papers!' one of the soldiers barked.

The young man fumbled in his pocket and pulled out a card.

'Jewish!' the other soldier spat.

My heart sank.

The young man began pleading with them in French. He had a wife at home and a newborn baby, he said. He needed to get back to them.

There was a loud cracking sound as one of the soldiers hit him hard across the face. The young man staggered into me. I wanted to hug him, hold him, protect him, but I couldn't, and that feeling of impotence enraged me. Once again, I stared straight ahead and started mentally reciting Walt Whitman to try and stay calm. 'Apart from the pulling and hauling stands what I am ... amused, complacent, compassionating, idle, unitary...' What came next? I wracked my brains... 'Both in and out of the game.' I kept reciting those lines over and over to try and drown out the cries of the young man as he was dragged away. And I kept reciting them as I approached the checkpoint and showed my papers to the soldiers waiting there.

'What is your business in Père-Lachaise?' one of them barked at me.

'I have a music lesson,' I replied, my heart thudding. But that seemed to be enough for them and they waved me on my way.

When I finally emerged from the Métro, the sunshine felt too joyful and bright a backdrop to what I'd just witnessed. As far as I was concerned, Paris should be covered in a grey shroud of cloud until the Nazis had been driven out. I'd memorised the route to my destination from the station so as not to draw attention to myself by looking at a map. Thankfully, I remembered it, and within five minutes I'd arrived at a nondescript apartment building with white walls and shuttered windows, the kind you saw on almost every block in Paris. I entered the cool, stone-floored entrance and went up four flights of stairs. When I reached the apartment, I took a breath and checked my watch. It was one minute to eleven. I waited until it was eleven exactly and knocked on the door. For a while, nothing happened and I wondered if I'd been sent on a wild goose chase, or even worse, I'd come to the wrong address. I was just about to pull the music from my bag to check, when I heard the sound of a bolt sliding and the door slowly opened. A middle-aged woman wearing an apron peered out at me.

'*Oui?*' she enquired.

'I'm Antoinette,' I said, in French, remembering my code name at the very last moment.

She looked at me blankly and for a horrible moment I thought it was some kind of trap.

'Why have you come here?'

'I have your music.'

Thankfully, she gave a nod of recognition. I took the sheet from my bag and passed it to her.

'*Merci,*' she said before closing the door.

I stared at the shut door for a moment, feeling a tremendous sense of anticlimax. I wasn't sure what I'd been expecting from my mission, but it was definitely more than this.

When I got home, our room was empty. I scanned it, looking for any clues as to where Otto might have gone, but there was nothing. I sat on the bed and gazed out at the space where the tree used to be. I picked up the bird Otto had carved me and whispered, 'I miss you, Mister Tree.' I thought back to how happy and carefree I'd felt the day I first arrived in Montmartre. It was almost impossible to comprehend how much had changed since then, and how such evil had been able to triumph. But not for much longer, I tried to reassure myself. I looked around the room again. Where the hell was Otto?

He still wasn't home by the time I had to leave for work. I'd started going out of my mind with anxiety. I kept thinking of the young man I'd seen at the Métro station. Had the same terrible fate befallen Otto? I should have done something to help the man at the station, I thought. I should have pretended I was with him. If anything bad had happened to Otto, it would be my fault for not helping the other guy – some kind of karmic retribution. But if I had helped him, I would have probably gotten myself arrested too, and then I'd have been no good to anyone. On and on, my anxiety multiplied.

I wanted to stay home and wait for Otto, but I didn't want to let Bessie down, especially after disappearing on her the night before. I needed to explain what had happened. So I freshened up and got changed, then I went through to the kitchenette. Otto's sketchpad was on the table, so I opened it to a blank page and wrote: *'Gone to work. Worried about you!!!'* Then I picked up my coat from where I'd left it the night before on the back of a chair. Seeing the missing buttons sent a shudder through me. What if the men who'd harassed me were back in the club tonight? As I tried to push the thought from my mind, I saw something that almost made my heart stop beating. There, on the table, was Klaus's handkerchief. I picked it up and saw the initials 'KS' embroidered in red silk in the corner. How had it gotten from my coat pocket to the table? My thoughts started racing. I knew I hadn't taken it out, which meant it must have been Otto. That wasn't such a big deal though, was it? I could have gotten the handkerchief from someone who worked at the club – like one of the musicians. I stuffed it back in my pocket and left.

When I got to Le Flamant Rose, I found Bessie waiting for me in my dressing room, sorting through my costume rail. I was so pleased to see her after the tension of the day, it took everything I had not to collapse into her arms.

'Dear heart, are you OK?' she asked. 'Where'd you get to last night?'

'I was trying to get away from those sleazeballs at our table,' I whispered, 'but they followed me out of the club.'

Bessie frowned. 'I thought something was up when they got up to leave right after you said you were going to the restroom. I went and checked everything was OK, but when you weren't there, I figured you'd gone home. Are you all right?' She gripped my arms. 'Did those monsters hurt you?'

I shook my head. 'That Klaus guy came out and scared them off.'

Bessie breathed a sigh of relief. 'And how about today? Did you... you know... go to your music lesson?'

'Yes.' I sat down in front of the mirror.

Bessie stood behind me and looked at my reflection. 'You OK? You look kind of pale.'

'Otto's disappeared,' I whispered.

'What?'

'When I got back from my... my music lesson... he wasn't in our room, and he still wasn't back when I left to come here.'

'Maybe he went to see a friend.'

'I don't think so. He hasn't been going out at all since the Germans and the police started clamping down on the Jews. I've got a really bad feeling.'

'Dang.' Bessie placed her hands on my shoulders and gave them a squeeze. 'Do you want the night off, to go look for him?'

'I'm not sure. I wouldn't know where to start looking.'

'Oh, honey. Try not to worry.' Bessie planted a kiss on top of my head. 'Take the night off and go look for him, or wait for him at home at least. And if there's no sign of him by curfew, go down to the restaurant and call me at the club.'

'Are you sure?'

'Sure I'm sure. Now scram.'

I stood up and gave her a hug. 'Thanks, doll face, I owe ya.'

I got home to find the room still empty. And now that night had fallen, Otto's absence took on even more sinister connotations. To make matters worse, I didn't even have my tree to confide in any more, so I talked to my little wooden bird instead.

'Where's he gone? What's happened to him? Please let him be all right.' But of course, the bird just stared back at me dumbly through its carved eyes.

In my desperation, I started ransacking the place for any clue as to where Otto might have gone. Having found nothing in the closets, or his pockets, I tipped the contents of the bin onto the kitchen table. In amongst the turnip and potato peelings were the crumpled balls of paper from his failed attempts at designing Bessie's poster. I lit the lamp and smoothed one of them out. He'd sketched the outline of a row of flamingos doing the can-can, which made me smile – until I saw that each of the flamingo's eyes were tiny swastikas. Dread swept through me. Is that how he saw me, as a Nazi sympathiser? Is that why he'd left? Even though he'd said he didn't mind me mixing with German soldiers at the club, had the discovery of the handkerchief in my pocket been the final straw? Had he correctly guessed it belonged to one of them? If only I'd told him the truth this morning, that I was going on a mission for the resistance, he might not have doubted me.

I was jolted from my panicked thoughts by a loud thudding at the door. I stood, frozen at the table. Ever since the Germans had started rounding up Jews and Otto had gone into hiding, I'd lived in fear of a loud knock on the door. I pictured a group of soldiers out there, waiting to charge in. What if they were the soldiers from last night who'd almost attacked me? Then I came to my senses, leapt to my feet and grabbed the sharpest knife from the drawer. Those Nazi bastards were going to get more than they bargained for.

I crept into the tiny bathroom and hid behind the door. I heard another thud from outside and then the clink of a key in the lock. What the hell? How did they have a key? Maybe they'd gone into the restaurant and François had given them the spare. Maybe François had denounced us. Maybe he'd told them Otto was Jewish. I remained as still as stone as the door crashed open and someone came into the room. I hardly dared breathe as I heard the door close again and footsteps go right past me. It sounded as if there was only one person, though. But who? Then I heard a low whistling. I frowned. Whoever it was, they were whistling 'La Marseillaise'. But it could still be a trap. I heard the footsteps coming back towards the bathroom. As the door opened, I raised the knife, ready to attack.

'Florence! What on earth?' Otto stared at me, horrified.

'Otto!' I dropped the knife and it clattered onto the linoleum floor.

'Why were you holding a knife? And where have you been?'

'What do you mean, where have I been? Where have *you* been?' My fear turned into a weird mixture of frustration and relief. 'I thought the Nazis had got you, you fool.' I pummelled his chest with my fists.

'Hey.' He grabbed my hands and pulled me to him. 'It is OK. I am OK. After you left, I was feeling so bored cooped up here, so I decided to go and meet you at Shakespeare and Company,' he explained.

I kept my face pressed to his chest and held my breath.

'But you weren't there, and Sylvia told me you hadn't arranged to see her today at all.' He let go of me and took a step back, staring at me in the darkness.

'I can explain. Shall we get a drink?'

He nodded, grim-faced.

I stepped out of the bathroom to find a bike leaning against the wall. Clearly, this was what had caused all the thudding. 'What the hell? Where did this come from?'

'I got it today, from Emil.'

'You saw Emil?'

He nodded. 'So, where were you today?'

I filled the kettle and lit the stove. 'I had to take a message somewhere,' I whispered.

'For the resistance?' he whispered back.

I nodded. 'I'm not supposed to tell you anything, in case… in case…'

'I understand.' He sighed and sat down at the table. 'God, I hate how the Germans… how they get inside here.' He tapped the side of his head.

'What do you mean?' My pulse quickened.

'How they make you suspicious of everything.'

I felt sick. Had he been suspicious of me? Unable to bear the thought of any mistrust between us, I sat down next to him. 'I have to tell you something, but you have to promise me you won't go crazy.'

'OK.' He looked at me anxiously.

'Something happened, last night, after work, at the club.'

'What?'

'Two German soldiers followed me outside and they… well, they started hassling me.'

'Hassling?'

I nodded. 'Coming on to me.'

Otto's expression turned to thunder.

'I tried to fight them off, but—'

'What did those bastards do?' his voice rose.

'Shhh! It was OK. Another German guy came out and he sent them packing.'

Otto ran his hand through his hair, the way he always did when he was anxious. 'And then what happened?'

'Nothing much. The guy gave me his handkerchief because, well, I started to cry.' My cheeks began to burn from the shame of having to admit this to Otto. 'They didn't hurt me, though; I was just shaken up.'

Otto nodded. 'And then what?'

'Then he walked me to the top of the hill.'

Otto looked horrified. 'He walked you home?'

'Just to the top of the hill. He said that he hoped another man would do the same for his wife.'

I watched as Otto stood up, sat down, then stood up again, praying that the fact that Klaus was married would be enough to placate him.

'I should be the one walking you home,' he whispered frantically. 'I should be the one protecting you.'

'I know, but you can't. You have to stay here and stay safe.'

He shook his head. 'Not any more. I have to do something.' He frowned. 'Is that why the buttons had come off your coat?'

'Yes.'

Otto said something in German. It was a word he hadn't taught me yet, but from the way he said it, I was pretty sure he was cussing. 'Are you sure they didn't hurt you?'

'Yes.'

'Why didn't you tell me?'

'You were so down last night. I didn't want to make you feel worse.'

'But I did feel worse – all today, when I found out that you'd lied about where you were going, and then...' He broke off, looking sheepish.

'What?'

'This morning I was looking in your pocket for some matches and I found his handkerchief, and...'

I felt sick at the thought of Otto not trusting me, but by the same token, how could I blame him? I had lied to him about where I was going. The kettle began its shrill whistle, adding to the tension gathering like a storm in my head. I got up and removed it from the stove.

'I would never, ever betray you,' I said softly, keeping my back to him so he wouldn't see the tears forming in my eyes.

And then, mercifully, I heard him get up and I felt him right behind me. I leaned into him and closed my eyes.

'I know, and I am sorry,' he whispered, wrapping his arms around me. 'All of this time in this room, just going over and over things, it is starting to send me crazy.'

'No, I should have told you what happened last night and I should have told you what I was doing this morning.' I turned to face him.

'No more secrets?' he whispered.

'No more secrets.'

He kissed me softly and all of the tension ebbed from my body.

'How did it go this morning?'

'OK, I think.'

'That's good.' He smiled. 'I have some good news too.'

'Oh yeah?'

'Yes. As I said, when you weren't at the store with Sylvia I decided to go and see Emil, and you will never guess what happened.'

'What?'

'He is working for the resistance, too. And he wants me to help him.' Otto's smile grew.

'How?'

'He is going to produce a pamphlet to let people know what they can do to fight back against the Germans.'

Goosebumps erupted on my skin. 'That's great. But how is he going to produce it?'

'He knows someone who works at the Musée du Louvre who has access to a printing press and has said he'll help us. Emil asked if I will draw some anti-Nazi cartoons and help distribute the pamphlets, hence...' He nodded at the bicycle. 'And he wants to know if you'll write for us.'

'What kind of thing would you like me to write?' I was so excited by this point, I think my goosebumps had goosebumps.

'Articles that will inspire people to fight back. So, what do you say?'

'Yes. I say yes!' I cried.

It seems almost perverse to say this, given the tension and hardship growing all around us, but for the next few months I felt more alive than I've ever done before or since. Now Otto and I had a shared mission and purpose, it deepened our bond and strengthened our love. It turned out that my first assignment to deliver the sheet music was just a test, a dummy run, to see if I had what it took to deliver the goods, both literally and figuratively. Apparently, I passed with flying colours and subsequently I received new 'cargo' to transport across Paris on a weekly basis. It would usually show up in the form of some kind of document in my locker at the club, then Bessie would slip me a separate piece of paper with an address, time and date, which I had to destroy as soon as I'd memorised it.

Then, one day in early June, I received an altogether different kind of cargo. Bessie had called me into the club early, supposedly for a rehearsal, but when I got there she presented me with a brown leather suitcase and told me that I needed to take it to a suburb east of Paris.

'I need you to take this to my friend Marcel,' she said loudly, for the benefit of anyone who might be eavesdropping.

'Gee whizz, what's in it?' I exclaimed. The case was heavy.

'Theatre props,' she said pointedly. Then she hugged me to her. 'Be careful,' she whispered in my ear.

Well, that obviously set my imagination into overdrive. What was in the case? A bomb? Weapons? A dead body?! It certainly felt heavy enough.

'When do I need to go?' I asked.

'Now,' she replied, handing me a cigarette paper. It contained an address written in tiny writing. 'Once you've memorised it, eat it,' she said, nodding at the paper.

Seeing Bessie this serious was a sobering experience. I put down the case and hugged her tightly. 'See you later, doll face,' I quipped, trying to lighten the mood.

'See you later, dear heart,' she replied, but without her trademark grin.

I took the Métro to the main line station. Thankfully, the trains were running on time for once and I made it on board without any fuss. Worried I wouldn't be able to lift the case onto the shelf above my seat, I tucked it in beside me and took a book from my bag to pretend to read. My people-watching on trains had taken on a more serious edge now, as I was constantly on the lookout for anyone who might be following me. There was very little of note going on in my carriage though, other than a stern-faced elderly woman staring out of the window and a thin bespectacled man reading the newspaper, *Pariser Zeitung*. Although it was a barefaced lie to call this a newspaper, as it had been created by the Nazis to spread their propaganda. Seeing the man reading it made me feel glad all over again for the part I was playing in trying to counter the Nazi lies, and so proud of Otto for the pamphlet he was helping to create. Even though it terrified me to contemplate what would happen to him if he ever got caught, it was worth it to see the return of his spirit and creativity.

Just as the train's whistle blew and we started chugging out of the station, the door to our compartment opened. I glanced up and it took everything I'd got not to do a cartoon-style double-take. It was Klaus. I'd only seen him a couple of times at the club since the incident with the two soldiers in the passageway. He didn't notice me at first, as he was too busy putting his case on the shelf above the seat opposite me. As usual, he was wearing a crisply pressed black suit and fedora. It crossed my mind to lift my book right up so it was covering my face, but that would have been ridiculous, as I could hardly keep it there for the whole journey. So I kept reading, pretending I hadn't seen him, counting in my head to try and stay calm. *One... two...*

'Florence. How nice to see you!'

I looked up and feigned surprise. 'Klaus! What a surprise!'

The elderly woman glared at me.

'What are you doing here? Where are you going?' Normally, when a Nazi asked you these questions, it was with a menace that put fear into your bones, but Klaus asked with the warmth of an old friend.

'I'm taking some props to a friend,' I replied. 'For a play he's directing.'

'That is great. What play is it?' Again, he asked with a smile.

'*The Merchant of Venice*,' I replied, without missing a beat. It came into my mind because Otto had mentioned it just the night before. I'd never read or seen the play before, but according to Otto it portrayed the Jews unfavourably and the Nazis had broadcast it shortly after the Night of Broken Glass as propaganda to support their cause. Klaus nodded his head approvingly, making me remember all too keenly that for all of his mild-mannered, gentlemanly ways, he was still a Nazi.

'I would like to see that play.'

'I'll let you know as soon as they're done rehearsing.' I'd gotten so into my story by now, I was actually starting to picture my imaginary friend Marcel directing his cast using the contents of my case. But thinking of the case instantly caused me to shiver. It was literally a couple of feet away from Klaus. And then paranoia started to kick in. What the hell was he doing on the same train as me? In the same compartment? *Poker face*, I reminded myself. Whatever happened, I couldn't show Klaus that I was rattled.

'So, where have you been?' I asked. 'Haven't seen you at the club in a while.'

'I had to go away,' he replied. He looked tired. There were bags beneath his eyes and the wrinkles in his brow looked more pronounced. 'How are things at the club?'

'Good. We're starting a new revue next week, with an Ancient Egyptian theme.'

'Ancient Egypt is one of my favourite subjects,' Klaus said, removing his hat and placing it on his lap. Then, as if realising his exuberance was not quite in keeping with the intimidating image the Germans seemed so intent on conveying, he cleared his throat and sat up straight. 'I mean, it was when I was a child. I was fascinated by the tomb of Tutankhamun.'

'Me too!' I actually wasn't lying. I'd had a major fascination with Tutankhamun and his spooky tomb back when I was a kid.

The elderly woman by the window coughed loudly and gave me a look that could only be described as disgust. Shame burned through me, but then I remembered why I was really there on that train, making small talk with a Nazi. *I'm risking everything for you and your country*, I wanted to hiss at her, but instead I smiled sweetly.

'I remember when Carter discovered the tomb,' Klaus continued. 'For a long time after that, I wanted to be an archaeologist.'

'It put an end to your circus dream then?'

He laughed. 'Yes indeed. Did you know that the tomb had been robbed, right after Tutankhamun's death and before his burial?'

'I did not, no.'

'Yes, when Carter excavated it he found that two of the inner doors had been broken and certain objects were missing.' Klaus's face lit up at the memory. 'I loved the idea of discovering a crime thousands of years after it had been committed.'

I nodded enthusiastically. But then I thought of all the treasures the Germans had plundered since their occupation of France. They were no different to whoever had raided Tutankhamun's tomb.

'Maybe that is why I joined the police,' Klaus continued, with a grin, 'because it made me fascinated with the idea of solving crimes.'

This revelation tested my poker face to the limit. Did this mean that Klaus was a member of Hitler's secret police force – the dreaded Gestapo? It would explain why he was never in a military uniform. As my mind whirred and my palms went clammy, I kept on smiling.

'Say, did you hear about the curse of Tutankhamun?' I asked breezily.

'I did,' he chuckled. 'And that was the end of my archaeologist dream.'

For the rest of the journey, Klaus and I talked all things Ancient Egypt. When the train pulled into my station, I felt a wave of panic. What if he was getting off here too? I'd deliberately avoided telling him where I was going in case he was following me.

'Well, this is me,' I said, leaving it to the very last minute, relieved he'd shown no signs of preparing to disembark. My heart sank as he stood up.

'It has been very nice to see you again.'

'Yes, you too.' Did this mean he was saying goodbye and staying on the train? I picked up my case, trying not to wince at its weight.

Klaus put his hat on. 'Would you like my help with your case?'

I wanted to yell, *No!* but I knew that to refuse him would definitely arouse suspicion. 'That would be very kind of you,' I replied.

As he took it from me, I had a sudden flashback to the day I'd met Otto, when my case had burst open on the steps. What if the same thing happened now, and whatever was inside the case spilled all over the platform? *Stay calm, stay calm, stay calm,* I silently chanted as I followed Klaus off the train. Thankfully, the case remained intact. Klaus placed it on the platform and reboarded the train, lifting his hat to me in farewell.

'See you soon, at the club,' he called.

'Yes, see you!' I replied gaily.

I noticed several French people giving me angry stares as they walked by. But now was not the time for winning a popularity contest. I comforted myself with the thought that if they knew what I was really doing, they would cheer me.

As I approached the ticket barrier, the elderly woman from my carriage drew level with me.

'*Sale pute,*' she hissed under her breath.

Dirty whore. The words stung like iodine. Even though I knew the truth, even though I was risking my life to try and defeat the Germans, and even though I felt as if I'd just endured the most high-stakes poker game of my life, I couldn't stop my cheeks from flushing. I showed my ticket and identity card to the man on duty and hauled my case through the barrier.

The sun was beating down outside and my skin prickled with sweat. I took a moment to compose myself. I'd emerged onto a tree-lined street comprising of a couple of houses and a row of shops – a café, a bookstore and a *boulangerie*. The air was filled with birdsong, but the beauty of the place was tainted by the old woman's bitter words, still ringing in my ears. It was only when I got to the end of the street that I realised I hadn't checked to see if I was being followed. I stopped by the bookstore and gave myself a telling off. I couldn't allow myself to get rattled like this. It wasn't just my life at stake if I got captured. I looked in the shop window, pretending to be inspecting the books, which to be honest, were a pathetic affair compared to Sylvia's exuberant window displays. I'd chosen to look in a side window, as it was at just the right angle to reflect the rest of the street. I could see that there were only a couple of people behind me – two women, carrying string shopping bags. I breathed a sigh of relief and carried on my way.

I'd memorised the turnings I needed to take – left, right, left, left – and after about ten minutes, which felt more like ten hours carrying the heavy case in the heat, I arrived at my destination. It turned out to be a small house in a terraced row. As I drew close, I noticed that one of the neighbours opposite was sitting on his front step, face tilted to the sun. Yet again, I had to make a split-second decision. Should I keep on walking and wait until he'd gone back inside, or carry on with my mission, knowing that he'd see me? Figuring that he could be sunning himself for hours, I decided to brazen it out, gaily calling, *'Bonjour!'* to him in my best French accent as I approached the house.

I knocked on the door – three crisp loud knocks as instructed – and waited.

The door opened and a portly gentleman with cheeks as red and shiny as apples greeted me with a beaming smile.

'Antoinette!' he cried, kissing me on both cheeks like I was a long-lost friend. 'You have brought the props! Come, come.' He picked up the case and beckoned me inside. 'Thank you for saving our production!' he continued loudly before shutting the door.

As soon as the door was closed, his smile vanished and his whole demeanour changed. Clearly, he wasn't the only one who threw himself into his roles with vim and vigour.

'Come, come,' he said, leading me along a dark and mercifully cool passageway. 'You must stay for a while, make it look as if we are catching up on our news.'

'Sure thing.'

'You are American?'

I nodded.

'Glad to see some of you are willing to support the war effort.'

'Hey! Don't blame me for my lousy government.'

He looked at me and laughed. 'I must confess, I think I am the one with the lousiest government.' He led me into a kitchen that was so bright and jaunty, it instantly brought a smile to my lips. The walls were painted orange and most of the cupboard doors were adorned with posters, advertising various theatrical productions. A wooden dresser housing plates and cups and bowls in a rainbow of colours formed the centrepiece. The man took two cups from the shelf.

'Coffee?' he asked. 'I have the real thing.'

'Not ersatz?'

He shook his head.

My eyes were on stalks at this development. It had been so long since I'd had normal coffee, this was akin to him offering me King George's crown jewels. 'Yes please! So, I guess you really are a theatre buff then?' I nodded to one of the posters.

'Yes. I am a director. Tell me, have you been to New York?'

'I sure have. I lived there for four years before coming to Paris.'

He clasped his hands together. 'It is my dream to one day bring a play to Broadway.'

'Seriously?'

'Yes, yes!'

I loved the fact that he still had a dream for after the war. The only dreams I'd had in recent months had been to do with keeping Otto alive and defeating Hitler. Talking to this man who I didn't know and would probably never see again lifted my spirits in a way I'd never have imagined possible. The next half an hour passed in a flash as we talked about the joys of performing, without giving away any telling personal details, over the most delicious coffee I have ever tasted. And then it was time to go.

'Thank you,' he said quietly as he prepared to open the front door. 'What you have brought me today will be of such help.' And although I knew he was talking about the mysterious contents of the case, I hoped that he too had benefitted from our life-affirming conversation. I stepped back outside to see that the sunbathing neighbour had gone and there was no one in sight. For a few sweet moments, I allowed myself the luxury of pretending the war had never happened, and that I really had just called in on a theatre-loving friend. It was so lovely to steal a moment of normalcy like this, like capturing a beautiful butterfly inside a jar.

When I recollect this scene now, it brings tears to my eyes. For I now know that in my suitcase that day were two wireless radios. I also now know that over half of the resistance wireless operators in Paris were murdered by the Nazis. I pray that 'Marcel' was not one of those poor souls, and that he one day got to realise his dream on Broadway.

SAGE

March 2018

As the grandfather clock in the hallway struck eleven, Sage stopped reading and looked around the darkened living room. Sam had gone to bed as soon as they'd got back from dinner and she'd been planning on an early night too, given that she had to get up at the crack of dawn to help Hunter, but the compulsion to read more of Florence's story had been too strong. As she sat in her grandmother's rocking chair, she imagined what it must have felt like to have been called a dirty whore, when actually Florence had been risking her life to try and defeat the Nazis. Her blood boiled on her grandmother's behalf. Then she thought of all the names she'd been called online lately. 'Whore' had been used many times, not to mention 'slag', 'slut' and 'bitch'. She'd felt so riddled with shame, especially when that man had sold his story about their night together, but in the light of what she'd just read about Florence, it all seemed so trivial. She'd had sex with someone. She hadn't committed a crime. They'd both been consenting adults. Did she really deserve to be so publicly shamed? Overcome with jet lag, she yawned and turned off the lamp.

As she went upstairs, tiptoeing on the creaking floorboards so as not to wake Sam, she thought of the joy Florence had experienced in talking about her passion for performing with the man code-named Marcel. When Sage had first left university, her heart had been overflowing with dreams, mainly to do with travel and writing. But the travelling and writing she'd ended up doing for work had left her feeling flat and uninspired.

She went over to her bedroom window and peered out into the darkness. With no light pollution for miles, the sky was aglow with stars. As she gazed up at them, Sage experienced a moment of clarity. The pressures had polluted her perspective on everything. By constantly needing to present her life as perfect, she'd become blind to all of the imperfect beauty surrounding her. And she'd become incapable of living in the moment, constantly framing her experiences in terms of whether or not they'd make great content. But since she'd been here, in the wild, rugged beauty of Arkansas, she'd had glimpses of how her life could be, and for the first time in years she felt truly excited. She carefully placed the manuscript on her nightstand and set the alarm on her phone. There was no way she wanted to give Hunter the satisfaction of her not being up in time to help him.

FLORENCE

1941

I arrived home that evening with a spring in my step and a loaf of fresh bread in my bag. In the city, the bakeries were only allowed to sell leftover day-old bread to the locals, as the Germans were the only ones allowed to buy it fresh – but clearly things were a little more lax in the suburbs. As far as I was concerned, this was the second victory I'd had over Hitler that day, and I had the night off from the club. But even better was yet to come.

I found Otto busy drawing at the kitchen table.

'Florence!' he cried. 'How did it go?'

As per the instructions I'd been given from Pennington, I hadn't told him exactly what I was doing or where I was going, but he knew I'd been on resistance business. After the misunderstanding the first time, we'd developed our own special code. I would always say, 'I'm going to see Sylvia,' when I was off on a courier job and he'd always say, 'I'm off for a cycle,' when he was going to see Emil.

'It was great,' I replied, taking off my shoes. My feet had swollen in the heat and were grateful for the release. 'And I have fresh bread! And…' I pulled a small paper bag from my purse and wafted it under his nose.

'Coffee!' he exclaimed.

'Uh-huh.' Marcel had insisted on giving me some to take home with me.

'You are my hero!'

'What have you been working on?' I came to stand behind him. 'Oh my!'

It turned out Otto had been working on a poster, a satire of one of the Nazi propaganda posters that had appeared all around Paris when they'd first begun their occupation. As with the Nazi original, it showed a German soldier surrounded by children. But instead of gazing at the soldier adoringly, the kids were screaming in horror. And for good reason – the soldier's face was that of a monster, complete with blood-red eyes and sharpened fangs. Instead of saying '*Populations abandonnées*' – population abandoned – at the top, it said '*Populations violées*' – population violated. And instead of saying 'trust the German soldier' at the bottom, it said 'defeat the German soldier'.

I felt completely conflicted as I looked at the poster. There was no denying it was a powerful piece of artwork, but the Germans were sentencing people to death for simply defacing one of their posters. What would they do to Otto if they discovered he'd designed such an inflammatory alternative?

'What do you think?' He looked at me excitedly.

'It's excellent, but…'

'But?' His smile faded.

'What are you going to do with it?'

'Give it to Emil, so he can make copies. Then we will put them up all over the city.'

I really didn't want to rain on his parade, but the thought of Otto being caught with one of these posters scared me to my core. But before I could express my reservations, Otto looked at his watch.

'It is almost eight o'clock.' He went over to the radio in the corner and turned it on. The room filled with the sound of jazz. Otto turned down the volume and moved the dial. There was a discordant hiss as he went through the stations, until finally silence and then…

'*Ici Londres,*' a man's voice crackled from the speaker. '*Les Français parlent aux Français!*'

My concern instantly turned to excitement at hearing the words, 'This is London.' Every night at eight o'clock, the Free France movement under the exiled General de Gaulle broadcast to France via the BBC, sending messages of encouragement to the resistance. I only got to hear the broadcasts on my nights off, but Otto listened to them religiously. As the presenter, Franck Bauer, continued to speak, Otto took hold of my hand and gave it a squeeze. Suddenly we were no longer alone in our fight against the Nazis, as tiny and ineffectual as ants waiting to be trodden on; we were part of something far greater.

I pictured the man I'd visited earlier, hunched over his own radio, listening to these same words, and thousands of others like us all over France, all connected via the BBC and the magic of the airwaves. Otto grinned at me, clearly thinking the same thing. Then Bauer announced that Germany's largest battleship, the *Bismarck*, had been destroyed by the British. Otto and I looked at each other, speechless. As soon as the broadcast ended, Otto retuned the radio to a French music station. Then he grabbed my hands and started waltzing me round the kitchen.

'The tide is turning!' he whispered in my ear. 'We are going to beat them!'

We feasted on fresh bread and real coffee. High on caffeine and the news from London, I truly believed Otto might be right, that the end of the war could soon be in sight.

Later, when we got into bed, Otto curled his body behind mine and held me tightly. 'It is only a couple of weeks until the anniversary of us meeting.'

'I can't believe it's been four years,' I murmured, luxuriating in the warmth of his body soaking into mine.

'And two years together,' he replied.

'Well, it sure hasn't been dull!'

He reached for the locket around my neck. 'Do you think we are like the bald eagles? Do you think we will mate for life?'

I gazed into the darkness of the room. The enormity of what he was saying caused my skin to prickle. 'Yes,' I whispered, hoping against hope that by admitting this I wouldn't be tempting some tragic twist of fate.

'I never thought it was possible...' He broke off and sighed.

'What was possible?'

'This. To experience such love in the midst of such evil. It is like when you see a flower growing through concrete.'

I squeezed his arm tighter to me. 'I don't know how I'd cope with this lousy war if I didn't have you.'

'This year, our anniversary is going to be one you will never forget,' Otto murmured, his voice suddenly slackening with sleep.

I kissed his hand and closed my eyes, slowing my breathing to match his.

Our anniversary that year was on a Saturday. On the morning of the Friday before, I was sent on one of my missions, this time to an address in the second arrondissement. My only instruction, delivered to my locker inside a pack of playing cards, was to ask for Madame Bellerose upon arrival at my destination. Even though it had been a year since the Germans had begun their occupation, I still hadn't gotten used to the surreal transformation Paris had undergone. As I made my way through the streets, I missed the hustle and bustle and the honking soundtrack of the automobiles with a pain that felt akin to hunger. I only saw a handful of vehicles on my entire journey. And those people I did encounter, hurrying along the sidewalks or pedalling past on their bicycles, appeared lost in their own private bubbles of quiet despair. It was as if Paris had become a silent movie – drained of all sound and colour, apart from the blood-red blots of the Nazi flags hanging from the buildings.

The road I'd been sent to was in a labyrinth of narrow streets filled with thin, four-storey buildings, tucked behind the bank of the Seine. When I reached the address, I discovered that it was a *maison close*, a brothel, named Lanterne Rouge. I have to admit, this certainly appealed to my sense of adventure, not to mention my nose for a good story. I checked the street both ways, to make sure no one was following me, then rapped on the door.

There was the sound of sliding metal and a little grille in the centre of the door opened.

'*Bonjour?*' a woman's voice said from the other side.

For some reason, the grille set-up made me think of a priest's confessional and I fought the urge to laugh.

'Hello, I'm here to see Madame Bellerose. Please can you tell her it's Antoinette?'

The grille snapped shut again and I heard the sound of bolts being slid open. The door opened a crack.

'*Entrez!*' the woman commanded from the shadows inside. 'I am Madame Bellerose.'

I stepped into a slightly faded but beautiful hallway. The floor was covered in peacock-blue tiles, chipped at the edges, and the walls were decorated with mosaics in red, orange and yellow. The only light came from flickering red lanterns in small arched alcoves. It all had a very Moorish feel. Madame Bellerose stood before me, a scarlet satin robe clinging to her generous curves. Her hair was wrapped in an ornate gold turban embellished with tiny mirrored discs, and her eyes were heavily lined in kohl. Judging from the faint wrinkles fanning from the corners of her eyes, I guessed she was in her late forties.

'Come, follow me,' she said, leading me along a passageway.

She brought me into a small room, decorated in a similar style to the entrance hall, with a green velvet chaise longue positioned along one of the walls.

'Sit,' she commanded, then swept from the room.

I stared after her, confused. Clearly Madame Bellerose was a woman of few words. I sat down and wondered what the next step of this mission would be. Perhaps she would bring me something to take to another address? She reappeared a couple of minutes later, with a man behind her. He was wearing a flat cap, tweed trousers, shirt sleeves and scuffed boots. For an awkward moment I thought there'd been a terrible mix-up, that she thought I'd come to work there and she'd brought me my first client.

'How do you do?' the man said, holding out his hand in greeting. His crisp British accent completely threw me. From his scruffy appearance, he looked more like a French farmhand, which I guessed was the intention.

'Hello,' I replied, shaking his hand.

Madame Bellerose left the room.

'I'm Henry,' he said, 'and you are Antoinette?'

I nodded, assuming that 'Henry' had to be his code name.

'I need you to take me to an address on the other side of Paris.'

'Oh, OK.' So my cargo wasn't to be a piece of paper or an object this time; it was a living, breathing human. A very British human.

'Do you speak any French?' I asked as he showed me a slip of paper with an address. I was familiar with the area, as Bessie and I'd used to go to a market there before the Germans came.

'Yes, although I am not fluent,' he replied in French, but still with a very British accent. 'My story is that I am your long-lost cousin from America,' he continued, in what was a terrible attempt at a Southern drawl. *Lord have mercy.* If I got him across Paris in one piece, it would be a minor miracle.

'Cousin Henry!' I exclaimed, in an attempt to relax him. 'It sure is good to see y'all!'

His mouth remained in a thin, straight line. Clearly this guy didn't do humour at all.

'I was just trying to get into character,' I explained.

'Jolly good. Now, if we get stopped by the Boche, I want you to do all the talking.'

'Trust me, I would be happy to,' I told him.

'And if they ask us where we're going, you're to tell them that we're on our way to see my old college professor, Monsieur Abadie.'

'Monsieur Abadie,' I repeated. 'And what subject did he teach you?'

'Philosophy. He taught me at Yale, ten years ago, but subsequently returned to Paris upon retiring.'

I nodded enthusiastically. It was a great story. I pictured a snowy-haired, bespectacled Frenchman hurrying through the grounds of Yale, a folder tucked under his arm, his tie flapping in the wind.

'When we get to the address, you will come inside for a few moments, before leaving as soon as the coast is clear.'

'You've got it.'

He gave me a withering stare and I could instantly tell he was one of those Brits who thought us Americans were all brash and uncouth. Yeah well, this American was about to save his bacon, so he could keep his haughty stares to himself.

'So, if we're stopped, I'm to use my real identity?' I asked.

'Yes. I understand from Flaubert that you're a journalist?'

'Flaubert' was Pennington's code name.

'That's right.' Now that I was finally writing serious pieces for Otto and Emil's pamphlet, I felt I could finally claim this title with pride.

'Good, good. Make sure you show them your press credentials if we do get stopped.'

'Will do.' I watched as 'Henry' adjusted his shirt collar and rolled down his sleeves. From the beads of sweat now appearing above his British stiff upper lip, I could tell he was nervous. I wondered how he'd ended up in Paris, but knew better than to ask. 'All righty then, cousin, shall we be on our way?'

Once again, I was met with a slightly withering gaze, before he opened the door and we headed out.

It was only when we were on the Métro that the enormity of what I was doing finally hit me. It didn't help that the train was crowded with German soldiers. I deliberately led Henry to an empty seat right in the middle of them. Once again, I was reminded of playing poker with my daddy. *Even if the hand you've been dealt sucks to high heaven, you mustn't let on,* I imagined him whispering in my ear. *Grin like you're the Queen of Sheba.* As we sat down, I treated the soldiers surrounding us to beaming smiles. A couple of them tilted their peaked caps in response. As the train jolted over the track, I felt Henry rigid beside me. It feels perverse to admit this now, but I have to admit feeling a slight thrill at the knowledge that I was getting one over the Nazis yet again. But then I remembered some more sage poker advice from my daddy. *Never get too cocky. Pride comes before a fold.* I placed my hands on my lap and closed my eyes.

We got to our stop without incident and I thought we were home dry as we came up the steps. But as we emerged into the sunshine, I heard a kerfuffle from further along the street: a man yelling and a woman crying. I glanced at Henry. He was staring straight ahead. Two French policemen, in their tall round hats like cake boxes, were standing with guns drawn and aimed at a jewellery store a few yards ahead of us. A man was standing in the doorway of the store, a woman sobbing behind him.

'Come out now!' the police yelled.

I hooked my arm through Henry's and steered him over to the other side of the road.

'Come on, Jew,' one of the policemen yelled.

I felt so sick I could barely swallow. These were the French police, not the Germans. It was as if Nazism had swept through the city like a deadly virus, infecting everyone with its hatred. I could feel Harry tense, as if he wanted to stop and help.

'Keep going,' I muttered. 'Don't even look.' It sickened me to have to say this, but I knew well enough by then that if I was to have any hope of surviving the damn war I had to pick my battles and only engage in those I had some hope of winning. The kerfuffle behind us reached a crescendo – then there was the sharp crack of a gunshot. I glanced over my shoulder to see the man now lying on the floor, blood pooling from his body all over the sidewalk. I quickly looked away. A queue of women outside a *boulangerie* further up the street were all gasping and clamping theirs hands to their mouths in horror. A deathly silence fell, broken only by the sound of Henry's and my footsteps, and the woman's tortured screams.

Thankfully, the rest of my mission passed without any mishaps I delivered Henry safely to his destination then took another route home, avoiding the jewellery store. But all the way home, I felt doubt gnawing at the edges of my mind. With the Nazis *and* the French police against us, what hope did we have of winning? I desperately needed to see Otto, in the hope that he would restore my faith. But I arrived home to find our room empty, the only sign of Otto a note he'd left on the table: *'Please can you see Bessie before work? It's important! See you later,* ma chérie!' Below the note he'd drawn two eagles hooked together. I instinctively felt for the locket around my neck, my anxiety growing. Was Otto taking the poster to Emil to be printed? What if he got caught? And why did Bessie want to see me? In an attempt to stop my fears spiralling out of control, I freshened up, got changed and hurried off to the club.

When I arrived, I knocked on Bessie's office door, praying nothing had gone wrong.

'Come in!' she shrieked.

I went in and a blur of white fur flashed across the floor in front of me.

'Don't just stand there!' Bessie yelled. 'Catch him!'

'What is it?' I cried as I raced after the fur ball, which had disappeared off behind one of the armchairs.

'A rabbit, of course!' Bessie replied, huffing and puffing her way to the other side of the chair. 'Come out, Laurel, you're cornered.'

'Laurel?'

'Yup. Hardy's over there in the cage on my desk.'

I glanced at her desk and sure enough, a brown rabbit was watching us curiously from a cage, its whiskers twitching.

'Gotcha!' Bessie cried, leaping behind the chair and re-emerging with the rabbit held aloft.

I couldn't help laughing at the sight of Bessie decked out in her satin frock and pearls, clutching a wriggling bunny – and boy did it feel good to have something to laugh at! 'What are you doing with a pair of rabbits?'

'Food,' she replied.

I stared at her, horrified. 'You're going to kill them?'

'Well, I was planning on breeding them, but the stupid guy I bought them from got me two boys.' She put Laurel back in the cage with Hardy. 'I guess I'll make a stew with one of 'em and try and find a girl for the other one.'

'Aw.' I went over to the cage and put my finger through the bars. Hardy sniffed at it eagerly. I felt a pang of longing for the animals on my daddy's farm, so strong it nearly floored me. 'They're too cute to eat.'

'It's a dog-eat-dog world, Florence,' Bessie said with a frown. 'Or in this case, chick-eat-rabbit. I'm done queuing for hours just to get the scraps of meat left over by the Germans. Anyways, forget about that, I have news.'

'If it's bad news, can you break it to me gently?' I perched on the edge of her desk. 'I've had a hell of a day.'

Bessie instantly looked concerned. 'Are you OK?'

'Not really. I saw the police shoot someone today, a Jewish guy, out on the street. It really rattled me.'

Bessie sighed. 'I hate this damn war.'

'Me too. So go on then, what's the news?'

'I can't tell you the full story right now, but I need you to stay behind tonight, after we've closed.'

My heart sank. 'What for?' I was already counting the seconds until I could see Otto and make sure he was safe. Today of all days, I really didn't want to get home late.

'We've got a rat infestation, down in the cellar.'

'You're kidding?'

''Fraid not. I need your help moving a few things out before the vermin control guy comes tomorrow.'

'Seriously?' I was so tired, I felt like crying. But Bessie was looking at me so hopefully I had no choice but to agree. And then it dawned on me that maybe this was all a cover for some kind of resistance business. Maybe it was Pennington, not rats, she had down in the cellar. 'OK then.'

'Thanks, dear heart.' She hugged me, and her body felt so warm and comforting it took everything I had not to cling to her and bawl like a baby.

The show passed without incident and the Germans didn't seem to mind when Bessie told them there'd be no after-hours drinking. While I waited for her to lock up, I got out of my costume and into an old pair of trousers and a sweater, just in case she really did want me to help her sort out a rat-infested cellar. I was just about to take off my make-up when Bessie came in.

'Oh no,' she said, looking at my reflection in the mirror. 'Oh no, no, no!'

'What?' I stared back at her.

'You can't look like that.'

'Like what?'

'Like a goddamn hobo!' She marched over to the wardrobe in the corner and pulled out a dress I'd never seen before. It was empire line with a fitted, beaded bodice, flowing out into a full skirt in a beautiful shade of sea green.

'But I don't understand. Why do I need to get all dressed up if we're going to the cellar? Oh…' My stomach knotted as I finally realised what was happening. She must have invited some Germans to stay behind in the bar, and she wanted me to help her extract some information from them. 'I really don't want to do this. I have to get home to Otto.'

'Trust me, honey, you *need* to do this.' I could tell from her steely tone there was no way I was going to be able to wriggle out of this. Clearly, a lot was riding on whatever it was she had planned.

'OK, but I can't stay long.'

'You won't need to. You have my word.'

Feeling slightly reassured, I got changed into the dress. But as soon as I saw my reflection in the mirror, I shuddered. The dress was beautiful and it fit perfectly, but the thought of who I was dressing up for physically repulsed me.

'Oh, honey, you look incredible,' Bessie gushed. She looked so excited. Clearly, she was expecting to get some great intelligence from this soirée. In a desperate attempt to get myself equally geed up, I pictured Churchill in the corner of the dressing room. *Kindle the fire in your heart*, I imagined him saying, just as he'd spoken about the fires Hitler had kindled in British hearts after the Germans launched their bombing blitz on London. If the Brits could stay emboldened in the face of so much carnage, then I could put on a frock and do my bit. As I followed Bessie out of the dressing room and along the corridor to the bar, I thought of the Jewish man I'd seen getting shot, and the woman standing screaming behind him. I had to quit feeling sorry for myself. If

Bessie and I were able to find anything out that might help win freedom from this barbarity, it would all be worthwhile.

'Wait here, I just need to check they're ready,' Bessie said, before slipping inside the bar.

I sighed as I thought of Otto waiting at home for me. It made me sick to think I'd be spending even more of my evening in the company of Nazis rather than him.

'OK, you can come in.' Bessie reappeared with a goofy grin plastered to her face. What the hell was she so excited about? Had she forgotten how dangerous these people could be? She linked her arm through mine and we walked through the door.

'Merciful heaven!' I exclaimed as I looked around. All of the tables had been cleared to the sides, with candles flickering upon them, and sprigs of wild flowers had been laid in two long lines along the floor, forming a floral pathway to the stage.

'What's going on?' I whispered.

But just then, the piano started playing, causing me to almost jump out of my skin. Next, I saw a figure emerge from the shadows beside the stage. A tall, thin figure with tousled hair. 'Is that...? Is it Otto?'

Bessie nodded.

And then I realised that whoever was playing the piano was playing the 'Bridal Chorus'.

'What the...?'

'Isn't it the most romantic thing?' Bessie exclaimed.

'But I don't understand.'

'Come.' Bessie began leading me down the pathway of flowers.

When we reached the stage, Otto was shifting from one foot to the other, like an excited kid. The 'Bridal Chorus' reached a crescendo. I glanced over and saw that Charlie was playing, and just like the others, he was grinning like he'd just had a visit from Santa Claus. The music finished and Otto got down on one knee in front of me.

'Holy smoke!' I gasped.

'Florence,' he said, his voice cracking slightly. 'Will you do me the most wonderful honour of marrying me?'

'Yes!' I cried, falling to my knees, my eyes filling with tears. 'Yes, yes, yes!'

'She said yes!' Otto exclaimed, looking up at Bessie in disbelief.

'Of course she did. The girl's crazy about you,' Bessie laughed.

Otto took hold of both of my hands and helped me back to my feet.

Charlie came out from behind his piano, holding a book, which I realised when he got up close was a Bible.

'Well, ain't this a hoot!' he said, giving one of his baritone chuckles.

I turned to Otto. 'Wait a minute, what's happening? Are we... are we getting married right now?'

Otto's smile faded. 'Are you having second thoughts?'

'No! I just didn't realise I was getting a proposal and a wedding all in one go.'

'I like to save time,' Otto said with a shrug.

'Very enterprising.' I grinned before kissing him on the lips.

'Hey, no hanky-panky, y'all, at least not till I make it official,' Charlie joked. Then he cleared his throat. 'Dearly beloved, we are gathered here today—'

'Hang on a moment,' I interrupted, 'is this actually official? I mean, are you qualified to do this?'

'Yes, ma'am. I was a preacher in Alabama before the Great War.'

'But you're Jewish,' I whispered to Otto.

'I love you,' he replied, as if this was the answer to everything.

'I can't believe you did this.'

'It seemed like the perfect anniversary gift.'

I looked at the clock on the wall. It was a quarter after midnight, fifteen minutes into our anniversary. 'It is,' I whispered.

Charlie cleared his throat and gave me a stern look. 'Any more questions from the bride, or can I do my thing?'

'Please, do your thing!'

Charlie began with a beautiful speech about a marriage being like two flames being brought together to form one, which burns all the more brightly. At this point, Bessie produced two taper candles, one for me and one for Otto, which Charlie instructed us to use to light a larger red candle that had been positioned in front of us on the stage. Then Charlie handed over to Otto, who produced my book of Walt Whitman poems.

'I thought maybe we could say our own vows, inspired by Walt,' he said to me shyly.

I nodded, unable to speak due to the lump now forming in my throat.

He opened the book and read me our poem. When he got to the line: 'Day by day and night by night we were together,' I couldn't stop my tears from spilling onto my face. It was all so beautiful and so perfect.

When it was my turn, I took the book, and repeated that one line back to him: 'Day by day and night by night we were together – all else has long been forgotten by me.'

It said everything that needed to be said about our love. Even after all these years, it still does.

Then Charlie produced two silver wedding bands from his pocket.

'How did you…?' I whispered to Otto.

'Shhh!' he replied with a grin.

With trembling hands, I took the larger ring and placed it on Otto's finger. Then he put the other ring on mine. It was a perfect fit.

'You may now kiss your bride!' Charlie exclaimed, clapping his hands gleefully.

Otto pulled me to him and kissed me.

'I want to kiss her too,' Bessie said, once we'd come up for air. She planted a kiss on my cheek. 'Congratulations, dear heart!'

'Thank you, doll face!'

'And you, Mr Romantic, come here.' She hugged Otto and he almost disappeared into her cushion-like bosom.

'I can't believe we're married,' I said, shaking my head.

'And now for your honeymoon,' Bessie said.

'What? Where?' I looked from her to Otto and back again.

'I've prepared a room for you upstairs, which shall forevermore be known as the Honeymoon Suite,' she chuckled.

'But…'

'But nothing.' She frowned at me. 'It's my gift to you, and anyways, the last thing you newly-weds need is to be caught by the Germans after curfew.'

'True.'

'And I've set up a bed for you in the musicians' dressing room,' Bessie said to Charlie.

'Thank you, ma'am!'

I grabbed him in a hug. 'Thank you, Charlie. I can't think of anyone I'd rather have been married by.'

Otto nodded enthusiastically and shook Charlie's hand.

We followed Bessie up to her living quarters on the top floor of the building. She took us up a narrow staircase at the end of the hall, leading to an attic room. With its steeply sloping ceiling, the room was just big enough for a double bed, covered in a patchwork quilt, and a white nightstand, on top of which was a wash jug and a vase of flowers.

Bessie lit a lamp on the bedside table and I saw that rose petals had been scattered all over the crisp white pillows.

'Can one of you please pinch me?' I said. 'I can't believe this is happening. I can't believe that we're married!' I looked at Otto and started laughing all over again.

'This has been the happiest day of my life already!' Otto exclaimed. 'And it's only been an hour.'

'Yes, well, I'll leave you lovebirds to it.' Bessie beat a hasty retreat to the door.

'Thank you so much for everything,' Otto said.

'No problem. I couldn't be happier for you. You guys make a swell couple.'

Once Bessie had gone, I sat down on the bed, feeling quite giddy from all the excitement.

'I can't believe you are my wife,' Otto said, sitting down beside me. He looked so handsome in his smart suit, yet still managing to look every inch the vagabond artist, with his long, tousled hair spilling over his collar.

'I'm so happy,' I replied softly. Even though the proposal and wedding had been a complete surprise, being Otto's wife felt like the one thing that did make sense in this crazy world of twists and turns we were living in.

I started unbuttoning his shirt and planting a trail of kisses along the side of his neck. He leaned back on the bed and let me undress him.

'Keep your dress on,' he whispered. 'You look like an eagle goddess.'

I slipped off my underwear and climbed on top of him.

'I love you, husband,' I murmured, leaning forwards to kiss him.

'I love you, wife,' he replied, guiding himself inside me. I started to move, but he stopped me. 'Stay still for a moment,' he said, his hands on my waist. 'I want to remember you, exactly like this.'

I gazed down at him, his eyes so full of longing and his hair spilling all over the petal-strewn pillow, and tried to imprint the image on my brain; a mental snapshot to treasure forever. Before I could stop it, a tear had rolled from my eye and landed on his chest.

SAGE

March 2018

Sage looked out of the bedroom window at the pale dawn light creeping over the fields and drew a breath. When she was little, her mother had made a huge point of telling her that fairy tales weren't real and that the last thing she should do was wait around for a Prince Charming to come and save her. Before having Sage, Elizabeth had been married to an English man. She'd uprooted and left her native France to be with him. But the marriage had gone horribly wrong – he'd left her for another woman – and his betrayal had left Elizabeth with a low opinion of men which she'd maintained until her death. She'd been so disillusioned with the opposite sex, she'd elected to have Sage via an anonymous sperm donor.

'Women sacrifice so much when they fall in love,' she'd explained, when Sage had asked her once why she'd chosen to be a single parent. 'We become a supporting role in the man's movie, and any time they like, they can recast our role with someone else.'

It wasn't really any surprise that Sage had inherited her mother's cynicism, which had only been strengthened by her own experience with Tom. She gave a wistful sigh. If only Elizabeth had got to know Florence and learned about her relationship with Otto, it might have restored her faith in love. It was certainly having that effect upon Sage.

She glanced at the time on her phone. It was almost five. Thanks to her jet lag, she'd been wide awake at four, so she'd had a shower and got dressed and done some more reading. She was about to return to the manuscript when she heard the crunch of tyres on gravel and saw Hunter pulling up outside. She put the manuscript down and hurried downstairs.

'Hey,' she said as Hunter got out of his truck. He was wearing a variation on his normal theme of T-shirt, baseball cap and jeans, this time with a sweatshirt tied round his waist.

'Hey!' He looked really surprised to see her.

'Did you forget I was helping you?'

'No, I just didn't think you'd be up.'

'I've actually been up since four.'

'Is that so? Then how come you aren't down there shovelling shit already?'

Sage couldn't help laughing. Hunter was about as different from the sensitive, poetic Otto as it was possible to be.

'What's funny?'

'You. You're such a smooth talker.'

'I'm not really one for talking, period.'

'No kidding!'

After they'd mucked out the stables, a task Sage found strangely therapeutic, Hunter asked her to groom Whisky. As Sage brushed the horse's sleek coat, the thoughts in her mind, which had seemed so chaotic lately, began filing themselves into some kind of order. So what if Tom had cheated on her? He had never been right for her in the first place, and deep down she'd known that way before the break-up. She'd chosen to focus on the version of the story that had cast her as the victim and caused her the most pain. But why?

Whisky gave a happy nicker as she brushed his mane. Sage imagined writing her life story at the age of eighty, just as Florence had done. Surely by that point, Tom would only warrant a couple of paragraphs? Maybe he wouldn't even feature at all. This thought felt strangely empowering. Whisky gave another happy nicker.

'Someone's happy,' Hunter called from the other side of the stable, where he was putting fresh hay in one of the stalls.

'Yeah, I think he likes being brushed.'

'I wasn't talking about him, I was talking about you.'

'But… how do you know?'

'Horses mirror our emotions. The happier you are, the happier he is.'

'Really?' Sage looked at Whisky and the horse nuzzled his head against her shoulder.

'Uh-huh.' Hunter stopped what he was doing and looked at Sage. 'It's good to see.'

'Thank you.'

'Clearly, you were born to shovel shit.' Hunter grinned, causing dimples to form on his cheeks, and just for a moment Sage caught sight of how he must have looked as a boy, happy and playful.

'It is weirdly therapeutic,' she replied.

'Tell me about it.' Hunter came out of the stall, his face glistening with sweat. As he pulled up the bottom of his T-shirt to wipe his brow, Sage noticed a jagged scar snaking up his torso. She guessed he must have got it from his time in the army. Probably from the same incident that had killed his friends. In spite of the heat, she couldn't help shivering. There was something so heartbreaking about the fact that in spite of the horrors that Florence and Otto's generation had experienced, people were still having their lives ruined by war.

Hunter stopped wiping his face and caught Sage staring at him. She quickly looked back at Whisky, but much to her annoyance felt her face starting to flush.

'Well, quit standing around catching flies,' he said, striding past her and out of the stable. 'I've got a barrowful of horse crap I need you to move.'

FLORENCE

1941

Over the next two months, the temperature – and my mood – climbed to boiling point. Hitler's puppet, Pétain, continued dancing to his master's tune, introducing law after law taking France back to the Stone Age. The republican slogan '*Liberté, égalité, fraternité*' – a mighty fine slogan, if you ask me – was replaced with '*Travail, famille, patrie*' – work, family, homeland. '*Famille*' was the part that most infuriated me, as the Vichy government used it to try and turn women into no more than mannequins. We were no longer allowed to wear trousers or have short hair, or even have jobs unless we had to. According to Pétain, a French woman's chief concern should be to be a good wife and mother, and to look pretty for the menfolk – even though most French men had either died fighting or were prisoners of war. But it was when Pétain banned women from being given tobacco rations that I really blew a gasket.

'How can Pétain say that it's morally degenerate for women to smoke?' I fumed to Otto one swelteringly hot August night, as I was trying to write my column. 'He's the degenerate, the way he sucks up to Hitler.' The Vichy government had issued another statute against the Jewish in June and they'd recently had another round-up of Jews in Paris. No one was sure exactly where they'd been sent, but word on the street was that they were being kept in prison camps in suburbs of the city.

'It is OK. I told you already, you can have my tobacco ration,' Otto said, glancing up from his sketchpad.

'That's very kind of you, but it's not the point.' I looked at the sheet of paper in my typewriter. I'd typed '*The Great Tobacco Travesty*' across the top, followed by a rant in which I'd called Pétain just about every name under the sun. It was completely unprintable of course, but at least it had been vaguely therapeutic. I unwound the paper from the typewriter and took it over to the stove, where I set it alight. With the Germans and the French police doing more and more raids, we had to be so careful. Otto had constructed a hiding place inside our mattress for his sketches and my articles before he took them to Emil to be printed, but any rough work we did had to be destroyed immediately. It was very hard not to feel as if a net was closing in on us, and the oppressive heat certainly wasn't helping.

I held the burning paper over the sink, then rinsed away the ashy remains and berated myself for being so wasteful. Paper was getting increasingly hard to come by; I had to stop being so hot-headed. At the very least, I owed it to Otto. I watched him hunched over his pad, his face creased in concentration. His talent for drawing caricatures was growing by the day. Several times, we'd seen his pictures from the pamphlet stuck to walls around Paris – usually on top of the Nazi propaganda posters. Of course, they never lasted long. The Germans tore them down as soon as they saw them, but still. It was a great tonic to think that Parisians were risking their lives to help spread Otto's message.

I went over and placed my hands on his thin shoulders. He was midway through a sketch of an old man – I squinted in the gloom to make sure I wasn't seeing things, but no, it really was an old man wearing a flouncy dress and a ludicrous hat, covered in feathers and jewels. In spite of his crazy appearance he looked strangely familiar.

'Wait, is that Pétain?' I sniggered.

'It certainly is,' he replied. 'I am going to have a speech bubble coming from him saying, "I have a moral responsibility to look chic for my occupiers."'

I hugged him tight and laughed my head off. It's funny now, to think of how often we were able to laugh in those dark days. I guess it was one of the only ways we had to defuse the tension, our laughter like a pressure cooker letting off steam.

A month later however, something happened that was impossible to laugh at. I was on my way to drop off a message at a café in the quartier de l'Opéra, when I saw that a huge banner had been unfurled above the entrance to the Palais Berlitz. The banner was announcing an upcoming exhibition and it was emblazoned with an image of an old man with a hooked nose and claw-like hands grasping a globe. '*LE JUIF ET LA FRANCE*' the stark black lettering above the image read. The Jew and France. I could tell instantly from the grotesque image that this was hardly going to be a favourable exhibition. It sickened me to see yet another building in my beloved Paris infested with the Nazis' hatred and ignorance.

As I drew level, a group of German soldiers clustered outside the door turned to look at me. I arranged my face into an enigmatic smile and sashayed by as if I didn't have a care in the world. But if Otto had been drawing me, I would have had a thought bubble above my head saying, *I hate you! I hate you! I hate you*!

I met with my contact in the café, an American man I'd never seen before, but who for the purposes of our backstory was a contact from the *New York Tribune*. When I got up to go, I left my copy of the paper on the table for him, with a coded message written in pencil in the crossword puzzle. But as I walked away from another successful mission, I didn't experience my normal frisson of pleasure at having got one over the Germans. I still felt too sick at the thought of the exhibition.

I'd been in two minds whether to tell Otto, but when I got home from the club that night, I found him sitting on the bed with one of the posters for the exhibition torn to shreds in front of him.

'Where did you get that?' I asked, staring at the poster in horror, as if it were a bomb about to detonate.

'The railings by the church,' he replied glumly.

'But if the Germans had seen you tearing it down, they could have sentenced you to death.'

'Haven't they sentenced me to that already?' he muttered.

'No! Don't say that!' I ran over and threw my arms around him. 'We will defeat them.'

'How?' He raised his voice. 'They aren't just stealing from us and capturing us and killing us, they are poisoning everyone's minds against us.'

'Shhh!' I glanced nervously at the door. 'The Germans are fighting on two fronts now they're at war with the Russians. You heard what they said on the BBC the other night. This is bound to weaken them. Otto, please.'

He ran his hand through his hair. 'I found out today that my parents have been deported from Austria to Poland.'

'What? Why? How did you find out?'

'I called my father's friend Ernst from Emil's house. That is why they haven't written in all these months. They've been sent away by the Germans.'

'But I don't understand. Why would the Germans send them all the way to Poland?'

Otto's grim stare said everything. I felt sick to my stomach.

He punched the bed in frustration. 'I need to do something more.'

'You're already doing so much. You can't risk doing any more.'

It's an interesting process, this turning one's life into a story. Now that I know what was to happen, I'm able to see the foreshadowing in this scene. Otto hunched on the bed, that terrible poster shredded in front of him, me trying and failing to hug some hope back into him. The first domino to fall, precipitating a terrible outcome.

Otto and I always made such a big deal of the fourteenth of June, the date that had brought us together, but we'd been blissfully unaware of another date that we circled each year and that would come to be just as significant – the fifteenth of November. In 1941, that fateful date fell on a Saturday. I wish I could report that we'd spent the most magical of days together. If this were a work of fiction, I would have given us a morning of hearts and flowers and music and lovemaking, but one thing I've learned the hard way is that the real author of this thing called life has a warped sense of humour.

For a start, I had my period that day and was suffering from the worst cramps, made all the more unbearable by the fact that I had to spend the entire morning queuing for bread. I returned home with a loaf so stale it was more rock than food, in the foulest of moods. Otto was on edge too. He was meeting with Emil later that day to collect some posters, and he always got antsy when he needed to leave the sanctuary of our room. There was one wonderful moment though, a moment I have amplified in my memory, the way one might showcase a prized photograph inside a beautiful frame. It was mid-afternoon and we'd opened the shutters a crack. We were lying on the bed gazing up into the sky, when a tiny robin alighted on the window ledge. It cocked its head and stared in at us, before whistling the sweetest tune.

'Can we make-believe we're in Austria?' I murmured, snuggling up to Otto. We hadn't played our make-believe game for months, so I wasn't sure he'd agree, but he nodded and began to speak.

'We are in the town of Alpbach, high in the Austrian mountains,' he said softly.

I closed my eyes and pictured a mountain range. The robin kept singing.

'The grass and the trees are the most vibrant shades of green you've ever seen,' he continued. 'And so soft, it is as if they are made from velvet. A stream trickles down the side of the mountain, tinkling like a bell as it passes over the rocks.'

My body softened. 'Carry on,' I whispered.

'We are inside a cabin made from logs and a bird is perched on our window ledge, singing sweetly.'

As if joining in our game, the robin outside sang louder, causing me to giggle.

'Yes, he is a very cheery little bird indeed,' Otto laughed. 'But he has good reason to be, because he has a beautiful view too.'

I nodded, picturing the mountains.

'He is looking at a love only rivalled by that of the bald eagles.'

I smiled and opened my eyes.

'A love that will last for eternity,' Otto continued, taking hold of my hand and feeling for my wedding ring.

'I'm so sorry I've been in a lousy mood,' I murmured.

'Me too.' He kissed me gently. 'I was so shocked when I heard about my parents. I didn't know what to do. But think of how much fun we will have once the war is over. Think of the places we will go.'

I pictured a life in which we were free to do and be whatever we wanted, and a scene started playing through my mind. 'OK, it's my turn,' I said. 'Close your eyes.'

Otto curled his body into mine and closed his eyes.

'The war is over and the Nazis have been defeated. Your parents are safe and well and Paris is free once again.'

Otto gave a long, contented sigh.

'You have your easel set up outside in the square, and I am up here, typing away on a serious article that doesn't mention the best way to adorn a hat or apply a lipstick one single time!'

He chuckled. 'That sounds like heaven.'

'Sorry, anyway… I finish my work and I come down to meet you. And you take me in your arms in the middle of the square and we kiss and we hug and all the passers-by cheer to see such love.' Tears burned in my eyes at the thought. 'And then we go to the grocery store and we buy bread that is so fresh, it's still warm!'

'Oh!' Otto moaned longingly.

'And we get cheese and wine – real wine – and we take our feast to the steps in front of the church.'

'Can we get some chocolate, too?'

'Of course. We have so much chocolate we don't know what to do with it!'

'Yes, we do. We eat it!' he exclaimed.

'Will you stop interrupting, please!'

'Sorry.' He hugged me to him. 'Please continue.'

'Thank you. And after we have eaten, you take me behind a cluster of trees.'

'Oh yes?!' He opened his eyes and grinned.

'Shh! Close your eyes.' I waited until he'd done as he was told before I continued. 'And you peel off my dress and make love to me.'

'Oh!' he moaned again.

I looked at the window ledge. The robin had flown away, but he had worked his magic. I kissed Otto on the forehead. 'I'd better get ready for work.'

'I love you,' he called after me, as I headed for the bathroom.

I had a wash, then put on a fresh sanitary pad and belt and a hideous pair of rayon and rubber bloomers, designed to stop leakages. I hated performing when I was on my monthlies, as we called them back then, and part of me considered calling Bessie and asking if I could have the night off sick. But I didn't, and another domino in Otto's and my fate was sent falling.

I applied fresh make-up and put my wedding ring in its safe place beneath the linoleum in the bathroom. I couldn't wear it to the club, for obvious reasons. Then I went back through to Otto and kissed him on the cheek.

'See you later. Stay safe.' As I said our usual parting gambit, I felt a wistful pang for the days when it wouldn't have crossed our mind to say such a thing, when it had been assumed that staying safe was our natural way of being.

I knew something was up the moment I got to Le Flamant Rose and saw a fleet of black Mercedes Cabriolets parked on the street outside the club. My heart sank. The only people who drove these kind of cars – who could afford to drive them these days – were the highest-ranking Nazi officials. Maybe they weren't in the club, I tried to console myself. Maybe they'd just parked there and gone someplace else. But as I walked into the foyer, I heard the clipped bark of a German voice. I looked at Maria, the girl on reception, and raised my eyebrows. She just shrugged and nodded towards the curtains. I peered through into the bar. Bessie was standing in the centre of the dancefloor surrounded by four Nazis, all long black coats and shiny boots. Otto and I had this theory that the shinier the Nazi's boots, the more hateful they were, because only a psychopath would pay so much attention to such things. This thought usually made me smile, but not today. There was something about the curt way the men were talking to Bessie that told me these psychos meant business. I pushed back the curtain and hurried off along the corridor to my dressing room. As I passed the chorus girls' dressing room, I heard their raised voices. Although I couldn't hear what they were saying, I could tell from the way they were talking that it wasn't good. My stomach clenched and I wasn't sure if it was due to my period or fear.

I went into my dressing room and sat down. The show hadn't even started and I was already exhausted. I sat there for a few moments, wondering what to do. I could go ask the other girls what was happening, but since I'd started working for the resistance, I'd carefully cultivated an air of blissful indifference and detachment when I was at the club. I didn't want to seem rattled by the appearance of the German top brass, even though I was. I started putting on my stage make-up, trying to lose myself in the comfort of routine. I was just applying my eyeshadow when Bessie burst in.

'Shit!' she whispered, closing the door behind her. 'Shit! Shit! Shit!'

'What is it? What's happened?' I whispered back.

'We're not allowed to play jazz any more.'

'What? Why not?'

'The Germans don't like it. Apparently it's Jewish and "Negro-fied" music, and it's way too decadent.'

'What the hell?' My fear turned to indignation. 'They've been singing and dancing along to it all year.'

'I know.' Bessie's face was wrought with fury.

'What are we supposed to dance to then, a funeral dirge?' I laughed drily. 'I guess it would be more fitting.'

But Bessie didn't laugh. 'I've been told I've got to let Charlie go.'

'No!'

Bessie nodded grimly. 'Apparently seeing his black skin offends their sensibilities.'

'They can shove their sensibilities up their...' I broke off, so angry I could barely speak. 'What's he going to do?'

'I don't know, but I'm so scared for him.' It was so unusual to see Bessie looking scared, let alone admitting to it. I found it hugely unsettling. 'I feel like it's only a matter of time before they start coming for the black folks the way they've been coming for the Jews.'

'We can't let that happen. We have to protect him.'

'I know, but how?'

'What about Flaubert?'

Bessie nodded. 'I'll ask him the next time he makes contact, but in the meantime, I was thinking I could hide him up in the attic room.'

Before I could reply there was a loud rap on the door. Bessie grabbed a lipstick from the counter and sat down beside me. 'Come in,' she called breezily, as she started applying a coat to my lips.

The door opened to reveal Thérèse, one of the women from the chorus, wearing a peach satin robe over her costume. 'We were just wondering when you would like us to rehearse to the new music,' she said to Bessie.

Bessie looked at her watch. 'Shit, we need to do it now. There's only thirty minutes before the doors open.'

That evening, everything that could go wrong, went wrong. The band were woefully under-prepared for the last-minute change in score, and so much weaker without the presence of their larger-than-life pianist. Bessie had instructed us dancers to do the most basic of routines. If the Germans wanted less 'decadence', then that's exactly what we'd give them. The energy from the audience felt tense, too. There were more braying catcalls from the soldiers, with a definite undercurrent of aggression. Bessie had asked me to come to the bar for drinks after the show, arguing that we needed to show the Germans that we weren't the slightest bit bothered by their ridiculous demands. I knew she was right, but boy was it hard to drag myself back out into that bar to schmooze with the people I detested more than ever.

When I got there, I noticed Klaus sitting at a table by himself in the corner. It was the first time I'd seen him since our meeting on the train. Figuring that of all the Germans in the place he was the least detestable, I made a beeline for his table.

'Howdy, stranger,' I said, in a performance of happy nonchalance that was surely Oscar-worthy.

'Florence.' He smiled up at me, but just like on the train, I saw bags beneath his eyes and his face looked thinner. Clearly, he was the only German in Paris not gorging himself on our meat and cheese. 'Won't you join me?' He gestured at the seat beside him.

'Thank you. Haven't seen you in some time.'

'Yes, I'm only just now back in Paris. How did your friend's play go?'

I looked at him blankly for a moment before figuring out what he was talking about. 'Oh, very well.'

He nodded. Thankfully, he seemed too distracted to have noticed my momentary memory lapse.

'Are you all right?' I asked, gesturing at one of the waitresses to come over.

'Yes. Allow me,' he said as the girl arrived at our table. 'Vodka martini, is it?'

I nodded. Once she'd left with our order, we sat there in silence, the raucous chatter from the other tables clanging like saucepan lids and making my head ache.

'Today is my birthday,' he said quietly. Or at least, that's what I thought he said.

'It's your birthday?' I tried to feign delighted surprise, but he shook his head.

'No, it is my wife's birthday.'

'Oh.'

'She has cancer.'

'What?' I stared at him, shocked.

'Of the breast.'

'I'm sorry.' And just like that moment when we'd first met outside the club and I'd caught him crying, I did feel genuinely sorry. But then I remembered the reality of the situation and my pity faded. If he hadn't helped Hitler to power, he could be home right now with his wife, celebrating her birthday, and nursing her through her illness.

He gave a sad little laugh. 'I do not know why I tell these things to you. It's as if you're my guardian angel, always appearing when I need you.'

Responding to this required all of my acting skills, as the notion of being a Nazi's guardian angel was abhorrent to me. I made myself smile sadly. 'I've never been called a guardian angel before, but I'm glad I've helped.'

We had a drink together, chatting some more about Ancient Egypt, and then I prepared to leave. My stomach was cramping again, my head hurt, and I was longing for Otto and my bed.

'It was real nice to see you again,' I said, getting to my feet.

'And you.' He stood up. 'Would you like me to escort you some of the way home? I'm going to be leaving now, too.'

'Oh, it's all right, you don't have to.'

'But I would like to. Just to the top of the hill again, if you prefer?'

I glanced over at Bessie. She was laughing and chatting with von Fritsch. I guessed there wouldn't be any harm in allowing Klaus to walk me up the hill, and it would certainly help confirm the notion that we were just fine and dandy about the changes the Germans wanted to make to the club.

'OK, thank you,' I replied.

Outside, the street was empty and the cool, crisp air was a welcome relief.

'So, you have had to change the music in the club,' Klaus said quietly.

'Oh yes,' I replied breezily.

'It is a shame.'

Instantly, my skin bristled. Was this some kind of trick? Well, if it was, he'd have to try a hell of a lot harder to catch me out. 'I don't know, I'd gotten kind of bored dancing to the same old music. Change is good.'

'Not always,' he replied, so quietly I wasn't even sure I'd heard him. I decided not to acknowledge it.

We were nearing the top of the hill when the sound of a man shouting in German pierced the silence. Klaus instantly stiffened, stepping in front of me protectively.

'What is it? What's happening?' I whispered as he peered around the corner into a side street.

'Someone is being arrested,' he replied. 'You wait here.' He gestured to the doorway of a corset shop. 'I'll go and make sure everything is OK.'

I was just about to agree when another man's voice rang out – one that was all too familiar to me. Otto's. 'It's… it's OK. I'll come,' I stammered, following him around the corner, dread causing my throat to constrict.

Otto was being pinned to the wall of a café by a German soldier. Another soldier was stalking up and down in front of him, yelling, his gun drawn. I don't think I've ever been as terrified as I was in that minute – so shocked, I let my guard slip.

'What are you doing?' I yelled at them.

Klaus turned and stared at me.

Otto's eyes met mine in the darkness and a spectrum of shock, recognition and then fear passed across his face.

The soldier holding the gun turned to me. Then he saw Klaus and did a weird kind of double-take, followed by a salute.

The soldier rattled something off in German to Klaus, then pointed at the wall. Otto's poster was stuck to it. Again, my guard slipped and I let out a horrified gasp.

'Do you know this man?' the solider asked me.

Before I could reply, Otto began to speak. 'No, she does not,' he snapped. 'I do not associate with filthy whores.'

The soldier holding him pulled back his fist and punched Otto hard on the cheek.

I let out another horrified gasp and my eyes filled with tears. For a moment, I thought Otto was genuinely angry with me for being with Klaus, but then our eyes met again, and he gave a slight shake of his head. I knew then that he was in fact saving my life. I bit down on my lip so hard, I don't know how it didn't start to bleed. Klaus again turned and stared at me. The soldier holding the gun clicked the safety catch, and I prepared to launch myself at him. If he was going to kill Otto, he'd have to kill me first – but then Klaus spoke in German to the soldier. Whatever he said was too fast for me to understand, but the soldier put his gun back into its holster.

I looked at Otto and he looked at me. And for a brief, blissful second, the sound of the Germans talking faded, the horror of what was happening faded, and all I could hear were Walt Whitman's words. I felt for my locket, pulling it out from beneath my coat and holding it tightly. *We were together. I forget the rest.* I stared back at Otto, willing him to be able to see what I was doing. Willing those same words into his mind – and for a split second, a smile played on his lips and he nodded almost imperceptibly. Then the soldier holding him punched him in the gut, causing him to double over in pain. Klaus said something else and the soldiers shoved Otto into the back of their car. Afterwards, the one with the gun came back and fired a couple of rounds into Otto's poster, until it was riddled with bullet holes.

'I need to go with them,' Klaus said to me, placing his hand on my arm.

I nodded numbly. And I watched equally numbly as Klaus marched to the front passenger seat and got in. The engine rattled into life, then the car, and Otto, disappeared off down the hill.

*

Somehow, I made it back to our room. I locked the door behind me and leaned against it, sliding down to the floor. What had happened was too big and too horrific for my brain to begin to compute. The Germans had Otto. They had almost killed Otto. They probably still would. I scrambled to my feet. I couldn't allow it. I had to do something. But what? I marched the length of the room, over to the bed. The covers were still pulled back from when we'd got up, the pillows still hollowed with the imprints of our heads. I grabbed Otto's pillow and hugged it to me, breathing in the scent of him. He couldn't be gone. But he was.

Panic rose up inside of me, burning at the back of my throat. What could I do? I sat down on the bed, trying to tame my racing thoughts. The Germans had caught Otto putting up one of his posters. Why had he been putting up one of his posters so close to home?

His words from earlier echoed back at me: 'I need to do something more...'

The punishment for defacing a poster was death. What would they do to him for putting up his own? But Klaus had stopped the soldiers from shooting him. Why had he done that? My heart sank as I realised it was probably only to protect me from witnessing an execution. If only Klaus knew the truth of what he'd protected me from. My throat constricted. What if he'd figured out the truth? Why had he stared at me so intently? Had he seen the tears in my eyes? But surely if he'd suspected anything, he'd have arrested me too?

I stood up, sat down and stood up again. Then I remembered what Charles Pennington had said about not telling anyone about my missions – because if they were captured and tortured, it would put the whole circuit at risk. I ran to the bathroom and threw up in the toilet, the taste of stale martini filling my mouth. The Germans were going to torture Otto. They were bound to. They would want to know if he was working with anyone else. They would want to know where he lived.

I went back out into the room and looked around. The place that had been our safe haven for so long now felt as dangerous and exposed as an open battleground. I pulled my case from the closet. I had to go, but where? I had only one answer to that question – Bessie – but I didn't know if it was the right thing to do. If I went to her, I could be putting her at risk. But I had to let her know what had happened.

I could feel myself start to spiral again, so I went and fetched my case. I needed to clear the room of anything incriminating. I lifted the mattress and felt around for the slit in the seam. My fingers found paper and I pulled out Otto's sketchpad. I took it over to the kitchen and lit the lamp. As I opened the pad, I swallowed hard, praying the pages would be blank. It would kill me to have to destroy any of Otto's work. At first I thought I was in luck, but as I flicked through the pages, I found a drawing towards the back. It wasn't about the Nazis, though. It was a drawing of me, in my wedding dress.

The enormity of what had happened slammed into me, sucking the oxygen from my lungs. I had to stop the Germans from killing Otto – but how? Again, Bessie's name came to me. If anyone knew what to do, it would be her. I tore the picture from the pad and folded it until it was small enough to tuck inside my bra. Then I packed my case with clothes, shoes, identity papers and passport, the painting of the Place du Tertre and the wooden bird Otto had given me, my wedding ring and my Walt Whitman book. I looked around the room one last time, trying to console myself that it might not be the last time I saw it. And then, as he so often did in my times of need, my daddy came to me in a memory. It was from the day I had left Arkansas to go to New York. I'd told him I'd probably only be gone a few weeks, but I think we both knew that I needed way longer than that to sate my restless spirit. I'd gone to hug him, and even though he always made out that he hated shows of affection, he hadn't flinched like he normally would. When we'd finally parted, he'd given me a gentle nudge.

'I'll be seeing ya, then,' he'd said, his grey-blue eyes awash with tears.

'Yeah, I'll be seein' ya,' I'd replied, grateful for the first time in my life that he wasn't big on ceremony.

I looked around my beloved room now and whispered, 'I'll be seein' ya.' Then I hurried out the door.

I took the narrowest backstreets back to Le Flamant Rose, skulking in the shadows. I had no story prepared if the Germans did catch me out with a suitcase. My brain was too befuddled from shock to be capable of being creative. But thankfully, I didn't encounter another soul. I slipped down the passageway beside the club and tried the side door. Of course, it was locked. The only other option was the cellar. There was a hatch further down the passageway for deliveries. I put down my case and tried prising it open with my hands, but succeeded only in tearing a fingernail.

'Damn it!' I hissed, close to tears. I looked up at the side of the building. The only window overlooking the passageway was in Bessie's office. I searched in the darkness for a stone and threw it up. It hit the glass with a loud crack, amplified by the silence. I pressed myself against the wall and waited. Nothing. I picked the stone up and threw it again. Again, it made contact, but there was no sign of life from the blacked-out window. I slid down the wall, fighting the urge to sob. Then suddenly, there was a sound, and the side door opened a fraction. I was about to hurry over when I saw the barrel of a gun protruding from the door. I took a step back, a sound that again seemed so much louder in the silence. The gun had to belong to a German, which meant that at least one of them was still in the club. My panic mounted. What was I going to tell them? What was I going to say?

More of the gun's barrel appeared and then, 'Who's there?' Bessie's voice hissed.

'Bessie! It's me!' I exclaimed.

'Florence?' The door opened wider and there was Bessie, outlined against flickering lamplight. 'What the hell are you doing out there? Quick, come in.'

I picked up my suitcase and hurried inside. As Bessie bolted the door behind us, my legs almost buckled. I leaned against the wall to steady myself. 'What's with the gun?' I stammered. 'You scared the hell out of me.'

'Ditto!' Bessie exclaimed. 'I got it from Flaubert, in case things ever get hairy. What's happened? You look as if you've seen a ghost.'

'They've got Otto,' was all I was able to say.

'Who?' Bessie's mouth fell open. 'Oh, no. How?'

'They caught him putting up one of his posters, here in Montmartre.'

'Come, let's go upstairs.'

I followed Bessie up to her office, where the remains of a fire were smouldering in the grate.

'You're shivering; go sit by the heat.' Bessie guided me towards the fire, then went over to the drinks cabinet and fetched a bottle of Scotch and two glasses. 'How did you find out? Are you sure they've got him?'

'I saw it happen.' I sank onto my knees in front of the fire.

'What!' Bessie clapped her hand to her mouth.

'On the way home from here. He was in the side street by the corset shop.' In spite of the fire's welcome heat, I couldn't stop shivering. It all felt so surreal, as if I was recounting a nightmare rather than reality.

'Oh, honey. What did you do?'

'What could I do? I was with Klaus. He'd offered to walk me home.' My teeth started chattering as I replayed the scene in my mind. 'Oh, Bessie. They were going to kill him.'

She handed me a Scotch and sat down on the floor beside me. 'Who was? Tell me exactly what happened.'

I recounted the whole terrible story, in between sobs and sips of whisky.

'So, Klaus told the soldier not to shoot him,' Bessie said once I'd finished.

I nodded. 'But I'm certain it's only because I was there and he didn't want me to see it. What if they've taken him somewhere else and killed him? What if he's dead already?'

Bessie shook her head. 'They'll probably try him first – because of the poster. They'll want to make an example of him. Damn it. Damn those fucking Germans.' She looked at my case. 'Are you worried he'll tell them where he lives?'

I nodded. 'Only… only if they torture him.' I fought the urge to retch. 'And there's something else. It's probably nothing, but…'

'Go on.'

'I think Klaus may have figured out that I know Otto.'

'How?'

'When I saw those brutes manhandling him, I couldn't help crying out. One of the soldiers asked me if I knew him, and Otto did a real good job of telling them otherwise, but I don't know. Klaus kept looking at me.'

'But surely if he suspected you, he'd have arrested you too?'

'I know, but I thought I should tell you just in case. I don't want to put you in danger, but I didn't know where to go.'

Bessie looked thoughtful for a moment. 'We need to get word to Flaubert.'

'But how?'

'Leave it to me.'

'And in the meantime?'

'I say you act like nothing has happened.'

'But what if… what if they torture Otto?'

'Are you crazy? That man would never denounce you.'

'I wouldn't care if he did,' I muttered. 'If they're going to kill him, they might as well kill me.'

'Enough of that talk!' Bessie shot me one of her steely glares. Then she stood up. 'Wait there.'

I stared into the dying flames of the fire and felt for the locket around my neck. I'd always known that this moment might come, but nothing could have prepared me for the soul-shattering loss I was now experiencing.

After a couple of minutes, Bessie returned, holding an envelope. 'For you,' she said, passing it to me. I saw my name in Otto's writing on the front and my pulse quickened.

'He gave it to me, to give to you if anything like this should happen,' Bessie explained, topping up my whisky.

I opened the envelope with trembling hands and began to read.

'My dearest Florence,

If you are reading this, then the worst has happened and I am so truly sorry. I know you didn't want me to put my life in danger, but I couldn't do nothing in the face of such evil. As your hero Walt Whitman advises, we should "Resist much, obey little." I know he wrote that for you Americans, but I think it is true for all humans. If we blindly obey or hide away in the face of hatred and evil, it will triumph. I hope that you can forgive me for whatever I did to have brought this letter into your hands, and I hope that some small part of you is able to feel proud of me and the fact that I resisted until the very end. It is so hard for me to write these words, because it feels as if I am writing my own death sentence, but if I am to die before this cursed war ends and the Germans are defeated, I want you to know that in spite of it all, I feel blessed. To paraphrase your honorary grandfather, Walt: I came to Paris in 1937 to immerse myself in the architecture and the art and dreams of my future, but all I remembered was you. All that mattered was you. And you made me the happiest man on earth when you agreed to be my wife. So, wife, do not let sorrow conquer you. Do not let evil win. Keep resisting. All that matters is that we were together, and our souls shall always be together, spiralling through the sky like fearless eagles. This I truly believe.

All my love always,
Otto'

I pressed the letter to my heart and I began to sob.

SAGE

March 2018

'No!' Sage slammed the manuscript down beside her on the porch swing and burst into tears. At first, she was crying for the pain and loss Florence had experienced in seeing Otto captured, but then her tears started coming from a deeper, more personal place. Her mind filled with a memory she'd been trying to block out for almost a year. Her mother in a hospital bed, Sage by her side, lacing her fingers through her mother's and squeezing tight, trying to stop her from leaving. But she had gone – right in front of Sage's eyes, she'd slipped from her body and vanished into the ether.

Sage sobbed and sobbed, as the pain from that moment finally found an outlet.

'Sage! What happened?' Sam came hurrying out onto the porch.

But now Sage had finally started crying for her mother, she couldn't stop.

Sam sat down beside her. 'Here.' He pulled a handkerchief from his jeans pocket and handed it to her.

'Thank you.' She wiped her tears. 'I just read the bit about Otto being captured and… and…'

Sam nodded gravely. 'That was a terrible business, all right.'

'I… I don't understand,' Sage stammered. 'All Otto had done was put up a poster. Why did they have to take him? Why do people have to be so hateful?'

'People are complicated,' Sam replied after a pause. 'They can be hateful, but they can be brave and strong and loving too. You'll see that, once you've read some more. Don't worry, the story isn't over yet.' He nodded at the yellowing manuscript on the swing between them. 'But right now, I think you could do with a break, so I'm gonna take you out to our finest nightspot, Fat Louie's.'

'Oh, I'm not sure if I'm in the right mood to go out.' All Sage wanted to do was crawl into bed and pull the covers over her head.

'I'd say that's exactly when you should go out. Anyways, the place I'm taking you is guaranteed to bring a smile to your face. They do the best ribs in all of Arkansas.'

'OK.' As Sage passed the handkerchief back to Sam, it reminded her of Klaus and Florence. What if the one German Florence had formed some kind of bond with had ended up killing Otto? It didn't bear thinking about.

Sage had a quick shower, with the water on fast and cool to try and rinse the sorrow from her body. That day in the hospital, watching her mother die, she'd felt something inside of her close up like a drawbridge. The enormity of what had happened was too huge for her to process, so she hadn't processed it at all. She'd carried on living her life online as if everything was perfect, and at night she'd numbed the pain by drinking herself into oblivion. But now there was no escape. She'd burned her pretend perfect life down to the ground.

She went back into the bedroom. *How did you cope?* she imagined asking her grandmother. *How did you cope when you lost Otto?*

She looked at the manuscript waiting for her on the night-stand. Maybe it would contain some answers to help her, but they would have to wait.

*

Fat Louie's turned out to be a bar and diner with a blues theme. As soon as Sage stepped inside, she was glad Sam had persuaded her to come. The music, chatter and laughter that wrapped itself around her like a warm blanket was a much-needed reminder that life wasn't all pain and sorrow.

'Hey, Sam!' A young waitress hurried over and greeted him with a hug.

'Hey, Gina. This is my niece, Sage. She's come all the way from London, England to visit.'

'Wow!' Gina gave Sage a welcoming smile. 'It sure is nice to see you. I hope you're enjoying Arkansas.' She looked back at Sam. 'Normal table?'

'Please.'

Gina led them over to a booth next to a huge old-style jukebox in the corner. She handed them menus and filled their glasses with iced water. 'I'll come get your order in a couple of minutes,' she said, before heading over to the bar.

'The ribs in this place are something else,' Sam said, looking at his menu.

'Let's make it ribs all round then.' Sage grinned.

He looked at her and laughed. 'You have my mom's smile, too. It's the strangest thing.'

'I know. You really remind me of my mum.'

'I do?' His eyes lit up.

'Yeah, you have the same nose, and jawline. And when you talk, you have the same mannerisms. It's really strange – but in a good way. I wish she could have got to meet you. It's… it's the anniversary of her death tomorrow.'

Sam's smile faded. 'Oh, I'm sorry. You know, I always wished I had a brother or sister.'

'When did you find out that you did?'

'Not until I read my momma's story.'

'But that wasn't until she was eighty!' Sage exclaimed. 'I can't believe she didn't tell you sooner.'

'She didn't even tell me then.' Sam sighed. 'She only showed me the story when she was on her death bed.'

'But I don't understand...'

'Oh, you will,' Sam replied enigmatically.

FLORENCE

1941

The following day passed in a stunned haze. I'd spent the night on a makeshift bed in Bessie's office, barely able to get a wink of sleep. Then, after a breakfast I could hardly swallow, I went through the motions of rehearsing our new routines to music deemed suitable by the Germans. That evening, I somehow managed to dance in the show. The only thing that stopped me vomiting at the thought that I was now entertaining Otto's captors, was my determination not to do anything that might arouse suspicion and put Bessie in danger. As soon as the show ended and I got to my dressing room, I collapsed in a chair from the effort. But before I could lose it completely, Bessie appeared in the doorway, ashen-faced.

'Klaus is in the bar. He's asking for you.'

'Right.' I went over to her and hugged her tightly. 'I will never, ever betray you,' I whispered.

'I know.' She kissed me on the cheek, then wiped off the lipstick print with her fingertips. 'I love you, dear heart.'

'I love you, doll face.'

I changed out of my costume and headed back into the bar. My nerves were so ragged and I was so exhausted, I could barely see straight. I found Klaus sitting at his normal table in the corner. He was with another man, also dressed in a smart black suit rather than a military uniform. I took a deep breath and remembered Otto's words from his letter. *Keep resisting.*

'Good evening,' I said, in my best attempt at cheerfulness. Both men got to their feet to greet me. This was something at least; they hadn't leapt up to arrest me.

'Ah, Florence,' Klaus said. 'Please, join me.'

'I shall leave you in peace,' the other man said to Klaus, with what looked like a knowing grin.

'I just wanted to make sure you were all right, after what happened last night?' Klaus said once the other guy had gone, offering me a cigarette.

I took the smoke and studied his face for any sign that this was a trap. If it was, he was as good at playing poker as I was. All I could detect in his expression was concern.

'Oh yes, I'm fine,' I replied. *Keep resisting…*

'It must have been quite traumatic,' he continued.

The hairs on my skin stood on end. Why was he saying that?

I forced myself to shrug. 'You see people getting arrested on the streets all the time these days. I guess I've gotten used to it.'

He nodded. 'I thought you might like to know that the offender has been dealt with.'

'Dealt with?' My mouth went dry.

'Yes. He has been taken to an internment camp in Drancy.'

'Oh. OK. Good.' Otto wasn't dead, *yet* at least. Now it took everything I had to contain my joy. I so badly wanted to ask what would happen to Otto, and if he was going to be executed, but I couldn't risk showing my hand.

'Tomorrow, I shall be going away,' Klaus said quietly, leaning closer to light my cigarette.

'Oh.' I could barely focus on what he was saying; all I could think was that Otto wasn't dead. He was a few miles away, in Drancy, living and breathing.

'It's a funny thing, isn't it?' Klaus said. 'Love.'

Now he had my full attention. 'What do you mean?'

'Men say that love is weak, but really it is the strongest thing.'

'I guess,' I replied noncommittally. Why the heck was he getting all poetic on me?

He stood up and cleared his throat. 'It has been very nice to know you, Florence.'

'Oh… uh…' I quickly stood up, too. 'You, too. Does this mean…? Will I see you again?'

He glanced around furtively, then shook his head. He held out his hand. As I took it, he pulled me closer, as if in embrace. 'I spared him from execution,' he whispered in my ear. Then he stepped back from me, bolt upright, as if standing to attention. 'Goodbye, Florence,' he said, his eyes shiny.

And in that moment, I realised that he hadn't been playing poker at all, and that I was in fact looking at the unlikeliest of guardian angels.

Later that night, once the club had shut, I mulled things over with Bessie, trying to get what had happened straight in my head. Otto was still alive. Klaus had saved his life – or spared him execution at least – but how? And why? And why was Klaus going away, and where? And were the two things connected? For the first time since the occupation had begun, I allowed myself to consider the previously unthinkable. Could it be that some Germans didn't actually agree with Hitler – or couldn't bring themselves to commit acts of evil in his name? It had always baffled me, how so many people could have been so easily convinced to do Hitler's bidding. What had happened with Klaus had restored my faith in humanity slightly. But more importantly, it had given me hope that I could somehow save Otto.

Bessie, being Bessie, was more circumspect.

'I think you may need to lay low for a while,' she said. 'Even if Klaus is for real, what if the others find out he saved Otto? What if they discover he was looking out for you?'

Much as I didn't want to agree, I knew she was right, and my new-found hope became tainted with fear.

'What should I do, then? Where should I go?'

'Lanterne Rouge,' Bessie replied. 'Flaubert will get word to you there about what to do next.'

'I can't leave Paris. I can't leave you. And what if Otto somehow manages to escape? What if he comes looking for me?'

'I'll still be here, and I can let him know what's happened. You'll be of no use to either of us if those bastards get you.'

I knew that what she was saying was right, and that by going to ground I would be protecting her safety as well as my own, but it didn't make the prospect any more palatable.

Bessie lit two cigarettes and passed one to me. It was something she'd done a thousand times before, and it cast me back to the days when we'd first become friends, when life had revolved solely around music and dance, and New York City had felt like one big playground.

'How the hell did we get here, doll face?' I smiled at her, but I could feel tears building.

She gave a wry laugh. 'I'll be damned if I know.'

'Do you ever wish you'd never come to Paris?'

I was expecting her to say 'Hell yeah!' but to my surprise, she shook her head.

'I don't. I mean, obviously I could do without Hitler pissing all over my parade, but…' She broke off and took a smoke. 'This is going to sound kind of crazy…'

'When's that ever stopped you?' I quipped.

'But for the first time in my life, I feel like I mean something.'

'Of course you mean something. You've always meant something.'

'No, no I haven't. I've never really stood for anything before – other than having a good time, which I'll obviously always stand for.' She gave one of her throaty chuckles. 'But now, doing what

I'm doing, you know, to help Flaubert and the resistance, I feel
as if my life has meant something. If I were to die tomorrow—'
    'Don't say that!'
    'But if I were, at least I could die knowing that I fought for
freedom. And so can you.' She looked at me and her eyes were
glassy with tears, which of course set me off.
    'Damn it, doll face, quit getting so mushy on me.' I leaned
into her and we both started half-laughing, half-crying. 'I'll be
back,' I said. 'You can count on it.'
    'Oh, I know,' she replied with utter conviction.

The next morning, I set off just after sunrise for Lanterne Rouge.
Bessie helped me to concoct a backstory about needing to go home
to see my folks in case I got stopped and questioned about my
case, but I got to the brothel without incident. When I knocked
on the door, I had to go through the same routine as before with
Madame Bellerose and the metal grille, but finally she let me in.
    'You need to wait here,' she told me, taking me to a pantry
at the back of the building and down some stone steps to a
cellar. Thankfully, it was slightly more homely than the cellar
at Le Flamant Rose. There was even a small bed tucked away
in the corner. 'Do not come upstairs at any time, and do not
make a noise,' Madame Bellerose continued. 'I will bring you
food and water, and you have this.' She pointed to a chamber
pot in the corner.
    'Thanks.' I sat on the bed and watched her ample hips sway
back up the steps. Then the door at the top of the stairs closed
and I was left in darkness. I lay down and stared up at the ceiling,
feeling for the locket around my neck.
    'Can you hear me?' I whispered into the dark, trying to
connect to Otto somehow. I thought of the day we had been
reunited on the steps by Sacré-Coeur, and how he'd told me he'd

picture me looking at the tree whenever he wanted to connect to me. I wondered if he was doing something similar now. Although there was no way on God's green earth he'd be picturing me in the cellar of a brothel. Once again, I found myself wondering how it had all come to this, how our magical love story had turned into something so tragic. Then I remembered what Bessie had said about finally finding meaning and purpose. The truth was, those days we'd shared in New York might have been fun, but there had been no real substance to our lives back then. Maybe that was why I'd ended up leaving. Maybe this was what I'd spent my whole life running to, without realising it: a life with meaning. But surely without Otto, my life was meaningless.

'I'm going to find you,' I whispered, closing my eyes and conjuring the memory of Otto lying beneath me on our wedding night. 'I'm going to save you.' And in that moment, I realised that saving Otto was the best possible purpose I could give to my life.

It was almost twenty-four hours before someone came for me. Madame Bellerose had been true to her word, bringing me bread and cheese and water at regular intervals. At some point, I'd succumbed to exhaustion and fallen into a deep sleep. I woke with a start at the sound of footsteps coming down the stone steps and saw a man's frame silhouetted against the shaft of light behind him. I leapt off the bed, adopting a fighter's stance, but then I saw that the man wasn't wearing a uniform; he was wearing a flat cap, tweed trousers and a scruffy overcoat.

'Antoinette?' he asked, and I could tell instantly from his accent that he was French.

I nodded.

'I have a message for you, from Flaubert.'

'Go ahead.'

'He wants you to meet with him in London.'

'Say what?' I'd been expecting to be sent out of Paris for a while, but not out of France – and certainly not to England!

'You're to pretend that you're travelling back to America, to see a relative who is dying.'

'But—'

'I have a train ticket for you, to Marseilles. There, you will see the American consulate, who will arrange the visa for your passage.'

'To London?'

He nodded.

'In England?'

He looked at me as if I was an imbecile. 'Yes, in England.'

'But I don't want to leave France.'

'It will only be temporary. You will be coming back to France.'

I sat down on the bed, trying to take it all in.

'But why do I have to go to England?' I really didn't want to sound like a whiny brat, but all I could think of was Otto. The thought of being in a different country to him was horrifying.

The man shrugged. 'I'm sure Flaubert will explain it all to you.'

I sighed.

'He told me to tell you that Churchill needs you.'

That sure got my attention. It was as if Flaubert knew the one thing that would make me consider leaving Paris. If I could help Churchill defeat the Germans, I would also be helping save Otto.

The man felt in his pocket and pulled out a scrap of paper. 'This is the address you are to go to when you get to London. You're to ask for Mr Jones. I want you to memorise the address, then I must destroy it. And remember, if you are questioned, you are travelling to England to get the boat home to America.'

'To see a dying relative. Yes, got it.' I unfolded the piece of paper and focused all of my attention on memorising the address: 64 Baker Street.

SAGE

March 2018

Sage settled back on the porch swing and breathed a sigh of relief. Maybe hope wasn't lost for Florence and Otto after all. She took a sip of her tea and looked out over the fields. The sun had set and the sky had turned inky blue. After she and Sam had feasted on ribs, followed by the most delicious apple pie Sage had ever tasted, they'd come back to the farm and Sam had turned in for the night. He'd said he was tired, but Sage had a feeling he was allowing her to get back to Florence – and that's how reading her grandmother's story felt now. It was no longer words on a page, it was her grandmother talking to her. She imagined Florence coming out onto the porch, as she must have done thousands of times before, and sitting down beside her, ready to share the next instalment of her life with her granddaughter.

She'd been so brave, deciding to try and save Otto, rather than crumple in defeat. But had she managed to save him? And why had she been asked to go to England?

Sage tingled with excitement at the thought of her grandmother travelling to her own home city. It formed another thread of connection between them. She turned the page on the manuscript and continued to read.

FLORENCE

1941

I'd always been aware that having a vivid imagination was a bless-
ing. Imagining that I could talk to trees, and daydreaming my
days away as a pirate or acrobat or circus performer had certainly
saved my sanity during the lonely years of my childhood. It was
no different on that trip to England. The only way I could bring
myself to leave the same country as Otto was by creating a story
in my mind in which everything I was doing was to bring about
our reunion. I was going to London to do whatever Pennington
wanted me to, so that I could return to France and help defeat
Hitler and free Otto. This kind of thinking might seem deluded
to some, but one thing I've learned over the years is that the stories
we tell ourselves go a long way to creating our reality.

All the way to England, I kept up a regular communication
with Otto inside my head, as a way of keeping him with me. It
was only when I arrived on British soil that the strength of my
imagination almost faltered. Suddenly being surrounded by fellow
English speakers really brought it home to me that I was now in
a country that hadn't fallen to the Nazis. This should have felt
reassuring, but all it did was make me feel disloyal to Otto, that
I should be in relative safety, while he was being held captive.
But every time I felt my resolve begin to waver, I retold myself
the story that this was all a vital step in saving his life.

It helped that I'd been told to go to Baker Street. I'd loved reading about the adventures of Sherlock Holmes when I was a kid – although *The Hound of the Baskervilles* sure made me jittery around dogs for a while. I obviously knew that Holmes was a fictional character and I wasn't going to see him strolling around in his deerstalker hat, puffing on his pipe, but the literary connection somehow gave weight to my own mission.

Although number 64 was a bit of an anticlimax, if I'm completely honest. A blank stone façade with rows of plain rectangular windows, and none of the pretty flourishes of Parisian architecture. A wall of sandbags had been piled up around the door, reminding me that I might be safe from Nazi occupation for now, but no one was safe from their bombs. I went into a small reception area, as blank and unforgiving as the exterior of the building.

'I'm here to see Mr Jones,' I told the doorman.

'Fourth floor, madam,' he instructed, with a tilt of his cap.

I took the elevator to the fourth floor, emerging into a door-lined corridor ringing with the clickety-clack of typewriters and hum of voices. I went over to a man sitting behind a small reception desk and introduced myself.

'Take a seat,' he said, gesturing to a row of wooden chairs that were exactly as uncomfortable as they looked. He disappeared off along the corridor, returning a couple of minutes later, asking me to come with him.

He took me to a room, and there, behind the desk, sat Charles Pennington – or Flaubert, as he'd now become known to me – dressed in a military uniform. It was such a relief to see someone familiar. Even though we'd only met a couple of times before, and even though he had that buttoned-up, stiff-upper-lipped British way about him, I had to fight the urge to hug him.

'Florence!' he said, standing up.

We shook hands. His was comfortingly warm.

'How are you?' he asked. 'Can I get you something to drink? A coffee, perhaps?'

'Is it real coffee, or that chicory travesty?'

He smiled. 'It's real.' He picked up the phone on his desk and ordered some drinks. 'So, I understand things got a little hairy back in Paris?'

I nodded. 'My husband was arrested.'

'Your husband?' He glanced at my ring finger.

'Yes. He was caught putting up a poster he'd designed, denouncing the Nazis.'

'I see. And how much did your husband know about the work you were doing?'

'For you?'

He nodded.

'Nothing. I mean, he knew about my newspaper column and he knew I was helping the resistance, but I never told him any details about the... *errands* I ran for you.'

'Good, good.' He picked up a wooden box on his desk and flipped it open. 'Cigarette?'

It had been three long days since I'd had a smoke. I eagerly took one.

'We've been very pleased with the work you've been doing for us, very pleased indeed.'

'Thank you.'

'I've brought you here because we would like you to utilise you and your skills further, for the war effort, in occupied France.'

I breathed a sigh of relief. Ever since I'd left France, I'd been fighting the nagging fear that I wouldn't be allowed to return. 'Of course. What would you like me to do?'

'We would like you to undergo some training for an organisation called the Special Operations Executive.'

'Special Operations Executive?' I echoed.

'Yes, or as I like to refer to it – Churchill's secret army.'

I decided on the spot that this was exactly how I liked to refer to it, too. 'And what would this training entail?'

'All manner of things. We need people over there to liaise on our behalf with the French, and to distribute supplies and suchlike.'

'What kind of supplies?'

'Information, weapons, explosives.'

'Explosives?' My pulse quickened.

'Yes. We need to make sure the French are organised and ready to rise up and join us in the fight against Hitler when the time comes. We think you would be perfectly placed to undertake such work.' He cleared his throat. 'I have to warn you, though, it would be very dangerous work. Far more dangerous than anything you've done for us before.'

I didn't care. I would risk anything to try and free Otto. 'I danced in Harlem,' I quipped. 'I can handle dangerous.'

Pennington cracked another smile. 'That's the spirit. Well then, in that case, I would like to introduce you to someone.' He picked up the phone and dialled a number. 'We're ready for you,' he said, then put the phone down.

'Have you had word from Bessie?' I asked. 'Is she OK?'

He nodded and I sighed with relief. There was a knock on the door and a woman with neatly set hair and an imperious expression came in.

'Florence?' She held her hand out in greeting. 'I'm Vera Atkins. How do you do?' Her accent sounded Eastern European.

'Very well, thank you.'

She looked me up and down as if appraising me. 'So, I hear you're a dancer?'

I nodded.

'Good, good. You'll be very physically fit, then.'

'I guess so, yes.'

'And Mr Pennington tells me that you've been working as a courier for the war effort in Paris.'

'I sure have.' Being questioned by this woman was a strange experience, like being at an interview for a job I hadn't actually applied for and knew nothing about.

'Are you able to speak French?'

'*Oui!*' I replied.

She didn't smile. 'How good is your French?'

'Fluent. I've been living in Paris for four years. I can speak some German too.'

Now she did look impressed. 'Excellent. And would you say that your role as a performer would make it easy for you to take on assumed identities?'

'For sure. It already has.'

She looked at me questioningly.

'When I had to pretend to be friendly to the Germans who came to the club where I danced, the only way I was able to stomach it was by pretending I was playing a role.'

'Good.' She looked at Pennington and nodded. 'Well, in that case, I would like to invite you to come with me for the first stage of your training.'

'Sure. How long will this training last?'

'A couple of months.'

'Months!' I'd been hoping for a couple of weeks, maximum.

'Yes.' She must have detected my disappointment, because she quickly added, 'Of course, it could be sooner, given your experience.'

I had no choice but to nod along. *This is your only hope of helping Otto*, I reassured myself.

After a hasty coffee, I bid farewell to Pennington, and Vera accompanied me outside, where a car was waiting for us. As I settled into the back seat beside her, I felt a weird sense of relief. The rootless feeling I'd experienced since leaving Paris disappeared, as I realised I was now back on course to France and Otto. I only hoped that it wouldn't take too long.

I leaned my head against the window and drank in the scenes of London. Seeing the black taxicabs and red buses, and the policemen with their funny, bell-shaped helmets, gave me a wistful pang. If only I could have been here under happier circumstances. Every so often, we'd drive past a huge crater in the street, as ugly as a missing tooth, and I'd remember all over again that I wasn't only doing this to save Otto.

We drove until the jagged edges of London softened into open fields. Vera didn't say much; she was too busy reading a bunch of files on her lap. But that suited me just fine. The effort of all this travelling was catching up with me, and that, combined with the rhythm of the car's engine, was almost soothing me to sleep. Finally, our driver pulled onto a bumpy dirt track and we emerged in front of one of the grandest houses I'd ever seen. I gave a low whistle under my breath as I took in the sprawling red brick pile with its huge sloping roofs.

'This will be your home for the next few weeks,' Vera informed me. 'It is where you shall complete your basic training.'

We went into a grand entrance hall, tiled in black and white like a huge chequerboard, but dirtied with muddy footprints. A chandelier sparkled above us, still looking magnificent in spite of not being lit. I wasn't sure what I'd been expecting from my trip to England, but it surely wasn't this. Vera introduced me to a woman called Davina, who issued me with some regulation pants and sweaters. They were hardly what you would deem chic, but I was so happy to be reunited with pants again, I didn't give a hoot.

Next, I was taken up to a room in the eaves of the house. It contained three single beds in a row, each with a nightstand beside it.

'The others are out on exercise,' Davina told me. 'You can stay here and rest until dinner.'

One of the beds had a French novel on the pillow, so I went over to an unoccupied bed by the window. Dusk was falling and I could hear the birds beginning their final song of the day. I gazed into the darkening sky and thought of Otto.

'You won't believe where I am now,' I whispered into the ether. 'But it's all to help free you, so you'd better not get yourself killed in the meantime, you hear?'

I heard the sound of someone coughing and turned to see a slight, dark-haired woman in the doorway. She was wearing one of the uniforms I'd just been issued with and was smiling at me wryly, no doubt wondering why I was talking to myself.

'Hello, I am Paulette,' she said, holding out her hand. Although she was speaking in English, she had a strong French accent.

'I'm Florence.' I shook her hand.

'You are American?'

I nodded. 'But I've been living in Paris for the past four years.'

She immediately frowned. 'Do not say any more. We are not supposed to tell each other about our lives outside of here.'

'Ah, OK.'

'It is good to see another woman here at last.'

'Wait, are we the only women here?'

'Doing the training, yes,' she replied. 'And I am afraid that a lot of the men think we do not have what it takes.'

'Huh! What do they know?'

She smiled. 'Come, it is time for dinner. I'll take you to the mess.'

The mess turned out to be what I guessed was once the dining hall of the house. It was a grand affair, with a huge fireplace and ornate light fittings. A long table ran the length of the room, populated by men who were eating and chatting avidly. Paulette led me over to another table at the end of the room, housing two large pots with steam curling from them. They smelled delicious, and my poor empty stomach let out an appreciative grumble. As

I ladled some chicken stew into a bowl, I couldn't help feeling guilty. It had been so long since we'd been able to get chicken in Paris. I thought of poor old Bessie, being forced to breed rabbits.

'It is good, *non?*' Paulette said once we'd sat down and I'd begun shovelling forkfuls into my mouth.

I nodded. A blonde guy with a thin moustache came and sat down beside me.

'Oh great, another female,' he said loudly, in that pompous accent belonging to the crème de la crème of the Brits. A couple of the other guys sitting nearby looked at me and smirked. 'I don't know what Churchill was thinking of, letting you lot join us,' the blonde guy continued. 'You couldn't fight your way out of a paper bag.'

I glared at him. Who the hell did this jackass think he was talking to? Maybe if I hadn't been so darned tired and worried about Otto, I'd have let it pass, but I couldn't help biting back.

'What's got your goat?' I asked, turning to stare at him. 'Did Mommy take away your favourite toy?'

More people laughed this time.

'Ha, Braithwaite,' a red-haired man called from the other side of the table. 'Looks like she's got you bang to rights.'

'I beg your pardon?' the blonde man spluttered at me.

I knew that was toffee-nosed Brit speak for 'how dare you', but I pretended to interpret it literally. 'That's OK, just don't let it happen again.'

His pale face flushed an angry red. 'I look forward to seeing you tomorrow in training.'

Again, I knew he meant this as some kind of threat, but again, I pretended to take it literally. 'Thank you. I look forward to seeing you, too.'

More laughter rippled along the table. It was only when we were back in our room that Paulette told me Braithwaite was in charge of teaching us combat skills.

'*Ooh la la,*' she said theatrically as she got into bed. 'I think he might kill you.'

I'd like to see him try, I thought to myself as I slipped under the covers and rolled onto my side. After everything I'd been through, it would take way more than a stuck-up Brit to scare me.

Paulette had warned me that we'd be woken early to start training, and she wasn't kidding. At 5 a.m. we were rudely awoken by a man yelling and a bell clanging. I stumbled from bed and followed Paulette's lead, getting changed into trousers, a sweater, thick socks and boots. Apparently, every day of basic training began with a run across the fields surrounding the house. It was still dark when we got outside, and the air was so cold it felt like inhaling tiny daggers. I hadn't run any great distance since I'd left my daddy's farm, but thankfully my years of dancing had kept me in pretty good shape. After the first thirty minutes or so, I found my rhythm. Boy, did it feel good to be running freely in so much open space. I pretended I was a gazelle as my feet pounded over the frozen ground. As time progressed, I found myself overtaking several of the men. I thought of the asshole I'd encountered at the dinner table the night before. If only I could overtake him, too, but he was nowhere to be seen. As we reached a valley and began circling back to the house, the sun started rising over the horizon, highlighting a line of trees, skeletal and black, like a charcoal sketch. Their stark beauty soothed my soul.

I'm coming to save you, I said to Otto in my mind. *I'm coming to save you.* I repeated it over and over, in time with the rhythm of my feet. I overtook another man, and another. By the time we got back to the house, there were only a couple in front of me. Braithwaite was standing by the door. As soon as he saw me, he frowned.

'How are you back so early? Did you do the full circuit?' he barked.

'She did, sir,' another guy panted as he came running in behind me. 'I've been tailing her the whole way.'

'Maybe that's why Churchill wants us females,' I said as I went past Braithwaite. ''Cos we can run circles around you guys.'

The man behind me laughed, catching up with me and extending a hand. 'Pleased to meet you. I'm Johnny.'

'Good to meet you, too. I'm Florence.'

'Good luck later, in combat training.' He nodded back at Braithwaite. 'I'd say you're going to need it.'

'We'll see.'

After breakfast, we had a lesson in map-reading. Then it was time for firearms training. As I was issued with my revolver, I realised that Pennington hadn't been kidding when he'd said the work would be very dangerous. Feeling slightly nervous, I followed the teacher's instructions and loaded bullets into the chamber, but as soon as we were taken out to a range in one of the gardens, I felt something closer to excitement kicking in. It wasn't as if I'd never seen a gun before. My daddy had a cabinet of hunting rifles at the farm. When I was about twelve, he'd shown me how to shoot, practising on targets placed on top of old grain barrels. Now I had cardboard cut-outs of what I assumed were supposed to be German soldiers to practise on. The figures were on a pulley system, and we had to try and shoot to kill as soon as one came lumbering into view. My co-ordination was a little off at first, but I kept imagining that the juddering figure was one of Otto's captors and that every fatal shot would secure his release. This was all the motivation I needed.

After a lunch of bread rolls and cauliflower soup, it was time for the infamous combat training. I could tell from the way Paulette went deathly quiet and ashen-faced that this was not the highlight of her day. The training took place on the grass in front of the house, next to a large, freshly dug vegetable garden. Some mats had been laid out for us, the kind you would find in a gymnasium. There were a couple of instructors present, but of course, as soon as he saw me, Braithwaite told me to join his group.

'Today, I'm going to teach you the correct way to fall without injuring yourself,' he said. He pointed to me. 'Will you help me to demonstrate, please?'

'Sure.' I strode over to meet him on the mat. A drizzly rain had started to fall, the kind that gets into your eyes and coats your skin like a film.

'I want you to pay close attention,' Braithwaite said, turning his back to me to address the group. Then, without warning, he spun around, grabbed me and threw me over his shoulder. I landed hard on my back, my head spinning. For a moment, I saw stars.

'Whoa!' I heard someone calling, and a couple of the others laughed.

'You didn't warn me!' I yelled.

'And do you think the Nazis will warn you?' Braithwaite loomed over me with a sneer. 'Do you think they'll say, "Excuse me, madam, would you mind terribly if I attack you now?"'

There were more sniggers from the others, which got me burning with rage. I scrambled to my feet and stood so close to him, our faces were just a couple of inches apart. 'What the hell do you know about Nazis, tucked away here in your palace, playing at fighting? I've been living amongst them, risking my life every day for over a year. I know people who've been captured by them. I've seen people killed by them. People with more courage than you've probably got in your pinkie.' A terrible silence fell, broken only by the distant cawing of crows.

'Everything all right over there?' the other instructor called.

'Yes, everything's fine,' Braithwaite snapped. He turned back to me. 'You do know we're not supposed to talk about our lives outside of here?'

Well, quit being an asshole then, I felt like saying, but somehow I managed to zip my lip.

'Can I have another volunteer, please?' Braithwaite turned away from me and beckoned Johnny onto the mat.

I went back to stand by Paulette, still smarting from the humiliation of having been thrown to the floor. Much as I hated to admit it, Braithwaite was right. Of course the Germans wouldn't send a calling card ahead of any attack. I had to be better prepared. *I'm sorry*, I whispered in my mind to Otto. *I promise next time I'll get it right.*

Paulette moved closer to me and for a split second I felt her icy cold hand brushing against mine. I looked at her and she smiled at me. A smile of solidarity.

Over the next couple of weeks, my days took on a strict regime of running, assault courses, rifle practice and, of course, combat training. I actually found the routine strangely reassuring. I had hardly any time to fret about Otto, and when it was finally time to go to bed, I was so bone-tired I fell into a deep sleep.

We were midway through dinner one evening in early December when one of the officers came marching into the mess.

'The Japanese have attacked America,' he announced gravely.

'What? How?' I called.

'They've bombed a naval base at Pearl Harbour in Hawaii,' he replied.

To my surprise, a couple of the men began to cheer.

'Maybe now they'll finally join us in fighting Hitler,' Braithwaite said, with a side glance at me. Relations between us had been tense but civil since our altercation on the mat. But I couldn't help sharing his sentiment. For so long, I'd longed for Roosevelt to join with the Allies in the fight against Hitler.

'Reports say that thousands of souls have perished,' the officer continued.

A silence fell on the mess as we all tried to digest this news.

Later that night, I lay in bed, gazing up into the darkness, thinking of Otto. *America might be joining the war,* I tried telling him, telepathically. *If that happens, we'll have you out of that camp in no time.*

But what if we didn't? What if we never found him? What if he was…? I closed my eyes tightly and forced myself to stop thinking such things.

In spite of being exhausted, that night, sleep didn't come easily to me.

The following day, the United States declared war against the Empire of Japan, and not even a class on how to pick locks, given to us by a bona fide former burglar called Raymond from a place called Essex, could lift my spirits. If America were focusing all of their efforts on fighting Japan, Hitler would be free to continue his conquest of Europe. Even though the Nazis hadn't reached Britain yet, my time in Paris had taught me that they were waiting and ready to pounce right on the doorstep. Then three days later, something wonderful happened – well, wonderful in the context of a world war at least – Hitler declared war on America. The news was greeted with rapturous disbelief that night in the mess.

'He'll never have the capability to take on the Russians and the Americans,' Braithwaite said.

And much as I hated to agree with him on anything, I wished with my heart and soul that he was correct. That night, a lot of celebratory beer was consumed.

The following day, I had another reason to celebrate, when Paulette and I were pulled from breakfast for a meeting with Vera Atkins.

'I've been reading your notes from your instructors,' she said, gesturing at some files on her desk, 'and you've both had glowing reports.' She smiled at me. 'I understand you're something of a long-distance runner, not to mention a crack shot.'

'Yeah, well, I've got my daddy to thank for that. Growing up on his farm.'

'You grew up on a farm?' She stared at me intently.

'Sure did. So if you ever need me to milk cows for the resistance…'

But instead of laughing at my joke, she wrote something in one of the files and said, 'Very good.' Then she shuffled the files so they were just so, and straightened her tie. 'I want you both to go and pack up your things. Tomorrow morning you will be leaving for Scotland.'

'Scotland!' Paulette and I said in unison.

'Yes. For the next stage of your training.' She stood up, signalling that the meeting was over.

'And then will we be going back to France?' I asked.

'If you complete your training to a satisfactory standard, yes.'

I took a deep breath. There was no way I'd be doing anything less.

We travelled to Scotland by train, a journey which took all day and most of the evening. Our destination, Arisaig House, was high on the west coast. A car picked us up from the nearest station and we were issued with passes, which we had to show at a road block that was heavily guarded by soldiers. Then we travelled down a twisting, bumpy country lane, until finally, we reached our destination.

It was dark when we arrived, and obviously the house was blacked out, but a silvery half moon highlighted its silhouette, looming in front of us like a haunted house, all chimney stacks, turrets and eaves. Paulette and I were shown upstairs to a dormitory containing five beds. There were sleeping figures in two of them, and it heartened me to see that there were other women training to join the SOE.

We were woken early the next day to go for a run. Any tiredness I felt soon disappeared when I saw the landscape in the pale dawn light. The grey stone house was surrounded by towering pine trees, and beyond those, a dark, craggy mountain range. A huge lake shimmered at the bottom of a hill beside the house.

'Holy cow!' I whispered under my breath, as we began running through the trees towards the water. It all reminded me of Arkansas, and I got a pang of homesickness so strong it almost floored me. I'd been so focused on Otto and seeing him again, it hadn't occurred to me that I might never see my daddy again. What if Hitler achieved his plans of world domination and conquered America? Telling myself off for being so foolish, I focused on my running, increasing my pace until my lungs burned and I'd pushed all the fears from my mind.

The rest of that first morning in Scotland was taken up with combat training, with the focus on how to kill someone silently with our bare hands. The implications of this were instantly sobering, and a reminder that no matter how beautiful the surroundings, we weren't here on vacation. After lunch, we had training in grenades and explosives.

'When you return to France, you may be called upon to undertake acts of sabotage,' our instructor told us, showing us how to attach a stick of dynamite to a bridge – or in this case, a pretend bridge made of plywood.

That night, in my imaginary conversation with Otto, I updated him on these latest developments. *By the time I've finished here, I reckon I'll be able to take on Hitler single-handed*, I joked. I pictured him treating me to one of those grins of his, then pulling me into his lap. I hugged myself and closed my eyes. Sometime later, when I'd fallen into a deep sleep, I was rudely awoken by the sound of a man yelling. I'd been having a nightmare about the

Germans turning up at the club to arrest me, so for one horrible moment, I thought I was back in Paris.

'Get up!' the man yelled at me again, grabbing my arm and pulling me from the bed. Although he was speaking in English, he had a strong European accent that I couldn't quite place. Was he German? Had the Germans invaded while I was asleep? Was I about to die? All of these questions echoed around my head as I stumbled to my feet. In the bed next to mine, Paulette sat bolt upright.

'What's happening?' she mumbled.

To my surprise, my captor completely ignored her and dragged me from the room. Another man was waiting in the hallway outside, and as I came to my senses I realised that they were wearing grey uniforms with black jackboots. Seeing that uniform again chilled me to the core. The men bundled me downstairs. I looked around for any signs of the others, but the place was deserted. They took me into a small room off the main hall, furnished only with a desk and two chairs.

'Sit!' one of them barked at me.

I sat.

'What is your name?' the other one said.

'Antoinette.' I had no clue what was going on, but I knew that whatever was happening, I needed to say my code name.

'And how long have you lived in France?' the first man said, sitting down in the chair opposite me.

I stared at him for a moment, confused. We were in Scotland. And then the penny dropped. This was some kind of test. My imagination whirred into life. 'I have lived here for five years,' I replied in French. 'Since marrying my husband.'

'And who is your husband?' the other guy barked, coming to stand right over me.

I sat bolt upright, as if to show I wouldn't be intimidated. 'Pierre Hermet,' I replied, Bessie's Pierre being the first French man who sprang to mind.

'And where is he now?'

'I don't know. He never returned from the front.'

The questioning continued for hours, in which time I'd concocted a fake life for myself so colourful and detailed, I'd almost begun believing it myself.

I clearly wasn't the only one enjoying getting into character. My interrogators seemed to be revelling in their position of power over me. At one point, one of them even hit my arm with a metal rule. I almost reacted with violence, but then I realised that if this was for real and Nazis were interrogating me, fighting back would probably get me killed. So I relied on my mind instead, summoning up the same powers that helped me refuse to believe that Otto was dead. I wasn't going to let these suckers get one over on me. I also realised that this would be one of the tests I'd have to pass before being allowed back to France. So even when they tied me to a chair and left me, I didn't falter.

The men returned at dawn.

'Well done,' one of them said, undoing my ties.

'You're a very convincing liar,' said the other, with a half grin.

'Thank you… I guess.' I rubbed my aching wrists.

The first guy offered me a cigarette, which I eagerly accepted. 'We wanted to see how you would handle the element of a surprise.'

'Yeah, I figured.' I only hoped that I'd never need the practice.

Christmas arrived and I hit my lowest point since leaving France. Thinking back on my previous Christmas with Otto, and wondering where he was spending this one, broke my heart. Worse news was to come in early January, when Vera Atkins paid us a visit and asked to see me.

'We will need to extend your training,' she informed me.

'What? Why?'

'Now America is officially at war with the Germans, you won't be able to travel back by boat.'

My heart sank.

'How will I get back there, then? I have to get back there.'

'By parachute. You will leave here in the morning for your parachute training in Manchester.'

What choice did I have but to agree? At least I'd be getting back to France and Otto.

I'd been so focused on returning to Otto that it was only when I arrived in Manchester that it hit me that I'd now have to jump out of a plane in order to do so. Much as I was a daredevil, this prospect really did give me the heebie-jeebies. Paulette, on the other hand, was beside herself with excitement.

'I always wanted to fly a plane,' she confided, as we got ourselves settled in our new digs, one of several pre-fabricated huts in the middle of a field. 'This will be the next best thing.'

Apart from the fact that a pilot never gets thrown out of the plane mid-flight, I felt like saying, but I didn't want to dampen Paulette's spirits. She'd struggled with the combat training, so it was good to see her looking forward to something.

Our parachute training was led by a retired member of the RAF named Wing Commander Reynolds. He had mottled reddish-purple cheeks like beets, and a white handlebar moustache oiled and curled to perfection.

'There's a lot more to parachuting than leaping out of a plane,' he barked at the start of our first class. 'And contrary to popular belief, it's not about courage, it's all about technique. Master the correct technique and you'll have nothing to be scared of.'

I breathed a sigh of relief. As a dancer, I was more than used to learning techniques.

'A good jumper is a skilled jumper,' Reynolds continued. 'And a skilled jumper is essential because he lands in one piece, and is therefore able to carry out the mission he's been sent on.'

I coughed pointedly, to remind him that he wasn't just addressing a crowd of 'he's.

Reynolds looked at me and frowned. 'Do you have something to say, miss?'

I was about to remind him that there were two women present, but then I remembered how I'd gotten off on the wrong footing with Braithwaite. Seeing as this guy was probably going to push me out of a plane at some point, I thought maybe I ought to keep my mouth shut. I shook my head.

'Right then,' he said, straightening up. 'Time to get started on your physical training. And let me tell you, this will separate the men from the boys.' He looked straight at me when he said this, but I didn't bite. If keeping this guy happy and jumping out of a plane was going to help me defeat Hitler, then by God, I was going to do it.

The physical training was different to what we'd done in our previous two training camps, as it was geared specifically to making us strong enough to control a parachute. There were a lot of squats and push-ups. Once again, I was mighty glad for my dance training. And I could tell I'd even won Wing Commander Reynolds' grudging respect when I was able to match most of the men in rope climbing.

Then we went on to practise our landings, which it turned out was a critical part of parachuting, as land the wrong way, and you could end up with a busted ankle – or worse. Thanks to my dance training, I perfected the art of a forward tumble from a beam straight away.

After a week of physical training, we moved on to the practicalities of putting on a parachute harness and preparing to jump, practising in the mock fuselage of a plane. Once again, it was all about the correct posture and technique, and once again, my dance training came in real handy as I practised pivoting my leg, chin up, back and arms dead straight.

Finally, the time came to practise for real, jumping out of a plane. It's funny to think that the very first time I ever went in a plane, I also jumped out of it – that's something even Lucky Lindy didn't do. This thought didn't exactly reassure me though, as we soared over the British countryside. The noise of the plane was deafening, and there was a rattling sound that made me worry the whole thing was going to fall apart at any second. Even Paulette looked kind of ashen-faced.

'You OK?' I asked her as we banked suddenly.

'Of course,' she replied defiantly, but I could tell from the way she was chewing on her lip that she wasn't exactly fine and dandy.

Just when I thought I might pass out from the fear, Reynolds shouted, 'OK, chaps, stand by for action!'

We all stood in a line, and did a final inspection of each other's chutes.

'Action stations!' Reynolds yelled.

A flap in the bottom of the plane opened, and suddenly I could see the fields way down below, laid out like a patchwork quilt in different shades of brown and green.

'And go!' Reynolds yelled.

We'd all been assigned a number upon boarding the plane. I was number one, which I would find out later was a deliberate ploy by Reynolds. If a woman jumped first, he thought the men would feel compelled to follow her lead as a matter of pride. I took my position by the opening, pivoting so that my left foot was three inches out of the plane. It was at this point that I truly believed I was going to vomit.

'One!' Reynolds yelled.

I thought of Otto as I swung my right leg out and then suddenly, I was falling. It was such a rush, I almost forgot to count the three seconds before opening my chute. I brought my legs together, facing the plane's tail, counting, *one thousand, two thousand, three thousand,* in my head, then I tugged on the parachute cord. I heard a great flutter above me and glanced up to see my chute opening. It was OK. I was going to be OK. I couldn't help letting out a whoop of relief. And then the most incredible thing happened. As I swooped through the air, I realised that I was experiencing what it was like to be a bird. I brought Otto into my mind, picturing us holding hands like two bald eagles, talons locked. It was uncanny; I was sure I could hear him whooping and laughing too. I was so lost in the magic of the moment, I almost forgot to prepare for landing. I remembered just in time and turned to face the direction of the drift. Then I grabbed the risers and pressed my feet together, toes pointing downwards so I'd land on the balls of my feet. I'd left it a little late, so I came in faster and heavier than was ideal, but I managed to perform a forward roll. It wasn't exactly a textbook landing, but I was down and nothing was broken, and more importantly, I now knew what it was like to swoop through the sky like a bald eagle.

We did a few more practice jumps over the coming week and then it was time for the very last stage of training, where we were issued with everything we would need for our return to France – including our new personas. Now that America had entered the war, it was no longer safe for me to return under my true identity, so I was to become Madeleine Fortin, a French widow whose husband had been killed fighting on the front.

'You are going to be dropped in Forest Fontainebleau outside of Paris,' Vera Atkins explained. 'The contact who meets you there will take you to the farm where you are to be based.'

'A farm?' I looked at her and raised my eyebrows.

She nodded. 'You said you had farming experience.'

'I do, but…'

'It will come in very useful for what you will be doing, especially as you will be able to grow your own food.'

'But what about my dancing and my writing?'

'It is becoming far too dangerous for Americans to be in Paris.'

My heart thudded as I thought of Bessie. I'd assumed that, as the Germans were so fond of Le Flamant Rose and she'd done such a good job of convincing them that she was a colluder, she'd be safe. But what if she wasn't? 'Will I go back to Paris at all?'

To my relief, Vera nodded. 'I'm sure there will be occasion for you to visit, but it will obviously be far more dangerous for you than it was before. So you must not just pretend to be a different person up here in your mind.' She tapped her head. 'You have to embody her, also.'

'What do you mean?'

'I mean, you need to change your entire demeanour. You are no longer a dancer, so maybe you could, I don't know, slouch a little? And you need to change your laugh.'

'What's up with my laugh?'

'It's too loud.'

'Gee, thanks.'

'You need to get rid of anything that is reminiscent of the old you, so that none of the Germans who might have seen you before at the club will recognise you.'

'Of course.' I understood what she was saying, and truthfully, this all appealed to the performer in me.

That night, I practised walking with a slouch in the dorm, hamming it up for effect to make Paulette laugh.

'Why are you laughing? I am no longer a gay gal about town. I am a grieving widow with the weight of the world on my shoulders.' As I said it, I felt a chill. What if I actually was a widow? No, I couldn't be. I'd felt Otto's presence so strongly that day of my first parachute jump. He was alive, I knew it.

'Well, Madeleine,' Paulette replied, 'I think you might need to see someone for deportment lessons.'

We laughed – me making sure to tone mine down to a dainty, nondescript tinkle. Then we fell silent.

'Do you think we will make it out of this alive?' Paulette asked quietly.

'Of course,' I replied, with way more bravado than I felt. 'We've jumped out of a plane. We can do anything, including defeat Hitler.'

She nodded. 'You know, I really am a widow.'

'Shoot! I'm sorry. I hope my kidding around didn't cause offence.'

She shook her head. 'Not at all. I'm going to miss you making me laugh.'

'I'm going to miss you, too.' *Damn this stupid war,* I thought to myself. It was always tearing you apart from people just as you became close.

'What was his name – your husband?' I knew we weren't supposed to tell each other anything about our lives before, but I wondered if Paulette might like to talk about him.

'His name was Raphael,' she said with a sad smile.

'Great name.'

'He was a great man. He is why I am doing all of this.'

'Really?'

She nodded. 'After he was killed, I truly didn't want to live. But then I thought, if I want to die, I might as well die doing something useful, and so I agreed to come here.' She smiled. 'It is funny because coming here has made me want to live again.'

I laughed. 'That sure is ironic.' I clasped her hand in mine. 'I came here because of my husband, too.'

'You are married?' Her eyes widened.

'Why so surprised?'

'I don't know, you seem so free-spirited.'

'Yeah well, I met my kindred free spirit.'

'Did the Germans kill him?'

'No. But they've captured him. That's why I'm here, to help save him.'

She nodded. 'I shall fight for him also.'

'Thank you.' I swallowed hard, trying to get rid of the lump forming in my throat. I wondered if I'd ever see Paulette again. I knew she was being dropped into the Vichy area of France, where she was from, so there was a high chance our paths would never cross again, even if we did make it out alive. That prospect felt so painful, I had to shut the thought down, just like I'd trained myself to shut down my fears over Otto.

A week later I was called to see Vera Atkins and was told I was being dropped back into France that evening.

'The cloud cover we'd been anticipating seems to have gone,' she told me, 'so the moonlight should be bright enough.'

I had to dye my hair black, then I was issued with a Colt revolver and a phial of tiny round pills.

'Cyanide,' the issuing officer told me. 'For if you're captured. If you swallow one whole, you'll get symptoms resembling typhoid, which could help you escape if you're sent to a hospital. If you chew one, you'll be dead within forty-five seconds.'

'Efficient,' I quipped, trying to ignore my churning stomach.

'You're to take it if you're being tortured and you think you might crack,' he continued.

'Right.'

'There are secret compartments in the heels of your shoes. You can store them there.'

'Got it, thank you.'

I got changed into an outfit that had been carefully made to pass as appropriate for a French widow: a sensible blouse, tweed skirt and matching jacket. As I put on the clothes, I pictured Bessie shuddering at their plainness, although I was pretty sure she'd be impressed by the secret compartments in the shoes.

I had a final test on my new life as Madeleine Fortin, which I passed with flying colours, and then a recap of my training in how to land in a forest. Apparently, keeping one's legs closed was the key to staying out of trouble. I resisted the urge to make the obvious wisecrack. Finally, I was given a box of belongings for my new life in France – French clothing and cosmetics, hair dye, photos of my dead husband, an ID card, a ration card and a certificate of non-belonging to the Jewish race, which I had to fight the urge to burn.

I wasn't allowed to take any of my personal effects that might link me to my old life, so I left my wedding band, the wooden bird, my Whitman poems and Otto's pictures with Vera, with strict instructions to mail them to my daddy. I couldn't bear to be parted from my locket, though, so on a trip to the restroom, I managed to hide it in the heel of my shoe.

When the car arrived to take me to the airfield, Paulette and Vera saw me off.

'I shall never forget you,' Paulette whispered as we embraced. 'And everything I do shall be to free your husband, too.'

'Don't make me cry,' I replied. 'I spent a long time perfecting this look.'

She burst out laughing. My 'look' was odd to say the least. I had to wear my flight suit over my tweed French widow apparel, so that I could get into character as soon as I landed. As a result, I bore more than a passing resemblance to an apple barrel.

'Bon voyage,' Vera said crisply, shaking my hand. 'Thank you for everything, and very best of luck.' She looked away swiftly, but I could have sworn her eyes were glassy with tears.

*

The driver who took me to the airfield wasn't the talkative type, but that suited me just fine; I needed a moment to gather my thoughts. It felt a little like the first night of a show, with different variations on what could go wrong playing on a loop in my mind. But of course, no show on earth involved the possibility of getting shot out of the sky by German gunners or breaking your neck by landing awkwardly in a tree, so it was impossible to quiet my mind. When we reached the airfield I was ushered over to a hangar, where four men were sitting on a bench waiting, looking as apprehensive as I felt.

'Evening, chaps,' I greeted them. 'Is this the queue for the night plane to Paris?'

Thankfully my quip raised a few grins.

'I say, are you the air hostess?' one of them replied with a chortle.

'Nah, I'm here to show you guys how parachuting is supposed to be done.'

There were more chortles, and then one of them offered me a battered metal hip flask. 'Fancy a nip of brandy?'

'Don't mind if I do.' The brandy was instantly warming and I passed it back with a grateful smile.

'Are you really going to be jumping too?' a wide-eyed guy asked. He looked no older than eighteen.

'Sure am,' I replied with a flush of pride as I sat down beside him.

'Good for you, old girl,' another of the guys said, in an accent so prim and proper he sounded like the King of England.

'Why thank you, old bean,' I replied, mimicking him. 'You might want to lose that accent before we land, though.'

He laughed and replied, '*Mais oui, bien sûr!*'

An officer appeared and we were given our chutes to put on and assigned a number for jumping. I was number one, *quelle surprise*. It turned out the others were all going to be dropped in a different location. We put on our harnesses and a plane came lumbering across the ground towards us, front propellers whirring.

As we walked over to the plane, it felt as if my stomach had dropped right down to my feet. I'd never felt fear like it. Climbing up the steps, I glanced at the bright full moon and said a quick prayer, asking her to watch over us. Once on board, we were greeted by a crewman and the pilot. In training, the routine of standing in a line to check each other's chutes had seemed so straightforward, mundane even – but not now. As I checked the parachute of the fellow in front of me and felt the guy behind checking mine, the enormity of the situation hit me all over again. If any of us missed something, it could mean certain death.

'Your eyesight better be good,' I said over my shoulder.

'Who said that?' he joked, and I have to admit, having something to laugh about was a welcome release.

'OK, chaps, prepare for take-off,' the pilot called.

We sat down on the floor of the plane and strapped ourselves in. The engine began to rattle and roar, and we started moving down the runway. It was about the tenth time I'd flown by this point. I wondered if I'd live long enough to take a flight where I didn't get chucked out mid-air. The flask of brandy got passed along the line, and after a while someone suggested a sing-song. I can't remember what we sang; I was so numb with fear and adrenalin, it's all a little hazy. Finally, we made it across the Channel and over France.

'Hold tight, chaps,' the crewman called. 'Things may get a little hairy.'

I didn't need any further explanation. I knew from my days in Paris and the beaming searchlights that swept across the night sky that we could now be targeted by German gunners. The thought made my palms sweat. After almost three months of relative freedom, I was back in occupied territory – or over it, at least. But I was closer to Otto and Bessie, I consoled myself, thinking of them somewhere in the darkness beneath me. Thankfully, we didn't encounter any enemy fire, and after a nerve-wracking wait, the co-pilot called, 'First drop zone coming up. Number one, stand by for action.'

I stood up and checked my emergency chute, attached to the front of my harness. The crewman picked up my box of belongings, attached to its own chute. 'Good luck,' he whispered. I nodded my thanks. *Left leg out, right leg pivot*, I said over and over in my head, as if rehearsing lines. *Then count three seconds and pull the chute open.*

'Action stations!' the crew member called.

'Good luck,' the posh guy called.

The hatch in the plane opened, sending an icy wind billowing inside.

'Go!' the co-pilot yelled.

The crew member dropped my box through the hatch. 'Number one!' he yelled.

I knew I had to jump straight after the box or we'd land too far apart, so there was no time for last-minute nerves.

'Number one!' I called, pivoting and dropping. *One thousand, two thousand, three thousand.* I pulled hard on the cord and heard the sweet sound of my parachute fluttering open above me. Dropping at night was a whole other ball game to jumping in the daylight, but it didn't make it any less beautiful. Once I'd turned in the direction of the drift and checked my position, I gazed out around me. The sky was shimmering with stars. I whispered 'thank you' to the moon and breathed a sigh of relief. So far, so good. *Oh, Otto, if only you could see this too!* As I sent the thought out to him, I felt a shiver of excitement. 'I'm coming to get you,' I whispered into the cool breeze rushing past me. I pictured it carrying my message straight to Otto, landing inside his heart.

It was only once I started approaching the ground that the reality of landing in a forest hit home. I scanned the darkness for some kind of clearing I could guide myself into, but the place was dense with trees. I clamped my legs together and said a little prayer. *Dear trees, I've always been one of your biggest fans, please don't kill me.* And then all of a sudden, branches were rushing up to meet me. I came down just to the side of a pine tree so I didn't make full impact with it, but my chute got tangled in one of the branches, leaving me dangling about twenty feet above the ground. We'd had training in what to do if this happened, so I released my back-up chute, so that the cord would form a rope to the ground, then I attempted to work myself free from my harness. When I'd practised this at the base, I'd had no trouble wriggling my way out of the straps, thanks to the agility years of dancing had given me. But my fear at being a sitting duck for any Germans who might be taking a late-night stroll through the forest got me all hot under the collar, and before I knew it, I was caught up in a tangle upside down. I heard footsteps hurrying towards me on the ground below and I froze. *Please don't let me die upside down in a tree*, I thought to myself. *Please let me die with a little dignity.*

'Well, well, what a delightful flower we have growing on this tree,' a man said in French, laughing quietly. He was tall and broad and had black curly hair poking out from beneath his flat cap.

I breathed a sigh of relief. He must be the contact sent to greet me. 'Don't give me any of your French schmooze bullshit, just get me down,' I replied, trying but failing to wriggle myself upright.

'All right, all right, I was only trying to be friendly.' He laughed again. 'And also, I am Polish, not French.'

'I don't care if you're the King of China, just get me down.'

'China has never had a king, and its last emperor had to abdicate in 1912.'

I stared at him, upside down, through the branches. Was this guy for real, giving me a history lesson? I made one last desperate bid to right myself, and it worked. I slipped out of my harness and shimmied down the cord to the ground.

'Madeleine?' he said, still grinning, as I quickly slipped out of my flight suit.

'Yes.'

'I am Claude. I have been sent to accompany you to your accommodation. Come, let's get your chute and find your box and get out of here.'

Claude climbed up the tree and retrieved my tangled chute, then we found my box, also dangling from a nearby tree. Thanks to some acrobatics involving my standing on Claude's shoulders, we managed to cut it free. Then we started half-running, half-walking through the forest.

'We have quite a long way to go,' Claude said. 'I hope you will be OK.'

'Of course I'll be OK,' I retorted.

After what was probably only an hour but felt like a lot longer, we emerged from the forest. The moon had now been swallowed by cloud, so it was hard to see much, but I could make out the outline of a house at the bottom of a sloping field. 'Almost there,' Claude whispered.

We followed a track through the field, the earth beneath our feet frozen solid, until we reached the house. Claude produced a huge iron key from his pocket and unlocked the front door. I followed him inside. The door opened onto a kitchen with a large but sadly unlit hearth. Next to the hearth loomed a dresser, its shelves displaying an array of plates and cups, glowing white in the darkness. There was a big wooden table in the centre of the room, with a couple of bench seats either side of it. My first impression of my new home was how bone-chillingly cold it was. Iciness seemed to radiate from the stone walls and floor.

'Are you hungry?' Claude asked. 'There is some cheese and bread.'

I shook my head. I was still too hyped-up to think about eating. We both sat down at the table.

'So, this farm belonged to a gentleman named Max Fortin,' Claude said. 'He was conscripted to go and fight in the war and he was killed at the front. He was actually a bachelor, but you have now officially become his widow.'

'Right. But won't the Germans find out I'm a phoney if they check the records?'

Claude shook his head. 'We have a friend in the nearest town, Barbizon, who works for the local authority. Let's just say the records have been *lost*.'

'OK. So, what am I supposed to do here, exactly? Apart from play the part of the merry widow?'

'This will become a safe house, for you to hide people in.'

'What kind of people?'

'People we need to protect from the Germans. Raul, our network organiser, will come to see you tomorrow. He will give you more information.'

'Right.'

'Are you sure I cannot get you anything?'

I shook my head.

'Would you like me to show you to your room?'

'Gee, it's just like staying at the Ritz.' Before I could remember to censor myself, I'd spoken in my native tongue.

'You are American?' he asked.

I nodded and reverted back to French. 'I'm sorry. I forgot.'

'It is OK. I never would have guessed. Your French is very good.'

'Well, that's reassuring to know.'

I picked up the box containing my belongings and followed him down a couple of steps into a living room. There were some blankets and pillows in a heap on the sofa.

'I have been staying here the past couple of days and shall stay here tonight too,' he explained.

'Sure.'

I followed him out of the living room and up a winding set of steep stone steps.

'There are three bedrooms up here, but I think this one is the best,' Claude said, unlatching one of the wooden doors leading from the landing. It was hard to make much out in the dark, but I saw a bed. The urge to lie down was suddenly overwhelming.

'Is this OK?' he asked.

'Absolutely.'

'Right, well, good night then.'

'Good night, and thank you.'

Claude left, shutting the door behind him. I got into bed, fully clothed, and pulled the blankets right up to my chin. Although my body was exhausted, my mind was still racing. I took my locket from my shoe and put it back around my neck. 'I'm back,' I whispered into the darkness to Otto. 'I'm back,' I kept on whispering, until finally I fell into a fitful sleep.

I was woken the next morning by a cockerel crowing. For one crazy moment, I thought I was back on the farm in Arkansas. Then I lifted the blankets and saw that I was wearing a blouse and tweed suit.

'Toto, I have a feeling we're not in Kansas any more,' I laughed, quoting from *The Wizard of Oz*. I got out of bed and made my way over to the window. Pulling back the heavy drapes, I couldn't help but gasp. The landscape before me was as stunning as a painting in the Louvre. A carpet of frost glimmered on the field in front of the house, and on the horizon, the pine trees of the forest pointed arrow-like into the pale blue sky. I heard the sound of a door opening below me and Claude came out, tightly wrapped in an overcoat, hat and scarf, his breath forming a misty trail in the cold air behind him. He headed across the yard to a shed. As I watched him, I was struck yet again by the strangeness of war and how it pulled random people together, just like the moon pulled the tides. After a couple of minutes, Claude re-emerged from the shed holding a large wooden bowl. As he got closer, I saw that the bowl contained a handful of eggs. I was so excited by this development, I raced from the room and downstairs.

'Good morning,' Claude said, as I entered the kitchen. 'Are you hungry? Would you like some breakfast?'

'Yes, please.'

A fire was crackling away in the hearth and a cast-iron pot was suspended over it, with water bubbling merrily inside.

'Say, how far is Drancy from here?' I asked nonchalantly, as Claude plopped a couple of eggs into the boiling water.

'Drancy? It is about forty, maybe forty-five miles. Why?'

I breathed a sigh of relief. Just knowing that I could reach Otto in a couple of hours – if I had an automobile, at least – felt strangely reassuring. 'I know someone who is there. I was just wondering.'

'Are they in the internment camp?'

I nodded.

Claude's expression grew grave. 'I hear they are keeping thousands of people prisoner there. It was originally supposed to be a housing project and was only built for seven hundred. It hadn't even finished being built when they started bringing people there. The windows and doors haven't even been fitted. They must be so cold.'

It broke my heart to think of Otto living in those conditions. It was cold enough in the farmhouse, with its windows and doors.

'Try not to worry,' Claude said, clearly detecting my gathering gloom. 'We will soon beat the Germans and then we will liberate all those they've taken captive.'

It's painful to recall now, but I actually agreed with him. The war had been raging for almost two and a half years by that point. Surely, I thought, it would be over soon.

SAGE

March 2018

'What's up, ain't you got a bed to sleep in?'

Sage started at the sound of Hunter's voice. She opened her eyes and blinked in the early morning sunlight. For some strange reason, she was lying on the porch swing – she'd been *asleep* on the porch swing. Hunter was standing on the grass in front of the porch, looking up at her with a bemused grin.

'I fell asleep.'

'I can see that. I thought Sam had got a pig up there, from the sound of your snoring.'

'I don't snore!'

'Hmm, maybe it was thunder.' Hunter looked up at the pale blue sky. 'Don't see any storm clouds brewing, though.'

'I was out here reading last night; the jet lag must have hit me.' Sage sat up and rubbed her eyes. 'What time is it?'

'A little after five. You wanna go for a ride? There's someplace I'd like to show you.'

'What, now?'

'Uh-huh. Unless y'all have something better to do? Meet me at the stables.' And with that, he turned and strode away.

'Who made you the boss of me?' Sage muttered as she got to her feet. But after a quick glass of water and a freshen-up, she decided to join him. Not only was she was interested in what

Hunter wanted to show her, she wanted to show him that she wasn't some kind of lightweight.

She got to the stables to discover that he'd already saddled up Whisky and a black horse named Colt.

'Here,' he said, handing her Whisky's reins.

As they trotted out towards the woods, Hunter and Colt started picking up speed and Whisky followed suit. Sage felt a little apprehensive at first, but then she remembered what Hunter had said about horses mirroring humans. She tried to relax her body and settle into the rhythm. As the wind blew through her hair and Whisky broke into a canter, she felt an exhilarating sense of freedom. She thought of what Florence had written about her mother, Sage's great-grandmother, riding like the wind, the day she was killed. That was another thing she shared with Florence – they'd both lost their mothers too soon. And then she remembered what day it was. She'd been dreading the anniversary of Elizabeth's passing, but that had been when she was on her own, back in London. Now she was in Arkansas, she felt the presence of the women who'd gone before her so keenly, their lives fitting around hers like a set of Russian dolls, it was impossible to feel alone.

When they reached the woods, Hunter slowed Colt to a trot and Sage followed him along a trail. The trees formed a canopy above them and the fresh morning air smelled of warm earth. She felt herself relax even more.

'Whoa,' Hunter called, slowing Colt to a halt as they arrived in a clearing. Up ahead of them stood the oldest-looking tree Sage had ever seen. It was so gnarled and characterful, it was like something from a children's fairy tale. She half-expected it to start waving its branches and begin talking.

'This was your grandma's favourite tree,' Hunter said, dismounting. 'Do you need a hand?'

'It's OK.' Sage clambered off Whisky, landing slightly awkwardly.

They walked over to the tree. Its thick roots protruded from the ground like outstretched arms, forming welcoming nooks against the trunk, perfect for sitting in.

Hunter cleared his throat. 'When I first came to work at the farm, Florence brought me to this tree and... and she told me to talk to it.'

'Really?' Sage tried not to smile at the thought of the gruff, monosyllabic Hunter being told to talk to a tree.

He scuffed the toe of his boot on the ground. 'I don't know if Sam's told you anything, but when I first came here I was in a bit of a bad way.'

'He said you'd been in the army, and that you'd seen some of your friends killed,' Sage said quietly.

He nodded. 'It messed with my head. Had me raging at the world. I didn't think anyone understood what I was going through, but somehow your grandma did.' He laughed. 'At first I thought she was crazy, telling me to talk to a tree, but you know what, it worked.' He went over to the tree and placed his hand on the trunk. 'This tree knows all of my darkest secrets. Reckon it knows most of your grandma's, too.'

Sage's skin tingled as she thought of Florence standing in the same spot, pouring her heart out to the tree. She pictured her words etched into the bark and woven into the leaves.

Hunter glanced at Sage. 'I was thinking maybe you could use a little time with him, too.'

'How do you know it's a he?'

Hunter shrugged. 'He, she, it's all the same to me. What do you reckon? Do you want to spend a little time here? I could leave Whisky with you and take old Colt for a ride around the woods.'

'That would be great, thank you.'

Hunter tied Whisky to a nearby tree, then took off on Colt, heading deeper into the woods.

Sage went over to the tree and placed her hand on the trunk. 'Hello, Mister Tree,' she whispered, feeling slightly ridiculous. But then she imagined Florence standing next to her.

'I've messed everything up,' she whispered, but it wasn't the tree she was talking to, it was her grandmother. 'I've made so many wrong choices. I wish I was more like you.' She closed her eyes and leaned against the trunk. The tree was so tall and strong, it felt as if she was being held. *You are like me*, she imagined her grandmother whispering in response, but of course it was just the sound of the wind rustling through the leaves. She got a flashback from Florence's book, to the part where she spoke of her frustration at having to write about trivial things for her newspaper column. It had taken a world war for Florence to find meaning in her life, but that had been in large part down to the time she was living in. Women had fewer options back then. But they didn't now. Sage opened her eyes and looked around the clearing. Whisky was grazing happily and the birds above were singing. Maybe that was the answer to her problems: maybe Sage needed to find a deeper purpose to her life, too.

FLORENCE

1942

Raul, the leader of our circuit, arrived later that morning. He was a serious-looking Frenchman, with small round glasses and thick black hair cut in the shape of a bowl.

'I understand you have experience working on a farm?' he said, as we sat down at the kitchen table with Claude and my dreaded nemesis, a pot of insipid chicory coffee.

'I do.' I couldn't help smiling inside at the irony of my going to such lengths to escape farm life in Arkansas, only to have apparently come full circle.

'That's very good.' Raul nodded approvingly. 'We will need you to work the farm, planting vegetables and taking care of the livestock.'

It turned out that as well as the shed full of chooks, I was now the proud caretaker of a cow and a couple of pigs, that were to be reared for breeding.

'It will be very physical work. Are you sure you will be fit enough?' Raul looked me up and down.

'Of course I will. In my former life, I was a dancer.' I broke off, remembering that I wasn't supposed to tell them anything about my true identity.

'You were a dancer?' Claude asked, annoyingly drawing attention to my faux pas.

'Yes, and what of it?' I snapped.

'Nothing, but that explains it.'

'Explains what?' I frowned.

'How you were able to wriggle your way free from your harness last night.'

'Good job I was too, or I'd still be upside down and you'd still be giving me a history lesson about China!'

As Claude laughed, Raul shrugged his shoulders. 'I think I'm better off not knowing.'

After our foul pretend coffee, Raul gave me a tour of the place, and showed me a bicycle leaning against the back wall that was mine to use to cycle into town.

'The bookstore in town will be your letter box,' Raul told me. 'This is where you will receive instructions for your missions. When you go into the store, you are to give your name and ask if the book that you ordered has been delivered. If there is a job for you, the store owner will give you a book, and the details will be inside. If there is no job, he will tell you that the book hasn't arrived yet and when to come back.'

'OK.'

'It is really important when you go into town to be as inconspicuous as possible,' Raul said, as we went back into the house. 'You never know when the Gestapo might pay a visit, and you have no idea who might be a collaborator.'

'Your new motto should be, trust no one,' Claude said.

'That's always been my motto,' I replied. I was only half-kidding.

The guys left mid-afternoon.

'It has been most entertaining to get to know you,' Claude said, shaking my hand, his green eyes twinkling. 'Don't go getting stuck in any trees while I'm gone.'

'Well, if I do, I'll know not to call on you,' I retorted. Then our smiles faded.

'Good luck,' he said quietly.

'You too. With my lousy luck, I'm sure I'll see you again.'

He laughed. 'I hope so.'

'Good luck, Madeleine,' Raul said, shaking my hand.

'And you.'

And then they were gone.

I sat at the kitchen table for a while, staring into the glowing embers of the fire. For the first time in years, I was living in the middle of nowhere. And for the first time ever, I was completely on my own. I thought of the forest stretching out on the other side of the field, and how anyone could emerge from the trees and find me here. I went upstairs and fetched my revolver and placed it under the sink. Then I decided I needed to do something to keep the heebie-jeebies at bay, so I went and milked the cow, who I'd decided to name Vera, in homage to my formidable SOE recruiter. By the time I'd fed the chooks and pigs and had fetched more firewood, I felt a little more settled into my new life. There was a comforting familiarity about it that made me appreciate my roots like never before. I thought of my daddy, all those thousands of miles away on his farm. *If only you could see me now*, I thought. I had a feeling he'd find it all highly amusing.

The following day, after consulting with the map Claude had left me, I cycled into town to get some groceries. Barbizon was beautiful, all ivy-clad grey stone cottages, cobbled streets and pretty stores. It was nice to see a part of France that wasn't so obviously affected by the German occupation, although I did catch sight of a couple of swastikas fluttering on flags atop the town hall. As soon as I got off my bicycle, I got into character, stooping slightly and bowing my head as I shuffled my way to the *boulangerie* to queue for some bread. I'd gotten so used to turning heads wherever I went, it was strange to suddenly feel so invisible. But I have to say, I kind of liked it, as it made me feel a whole lot safer. Once I'd bought some bread, I located the bookstore. A bell above the door jangled loudly as I went inside. I found an old man with a bushy white beard to rival Walt Whitman's standing behind the counter.

'*Bonjour!*' he called, looking at me curiously.

'*Bonjour.*' I glanced around to check the store was empty. 'My name is Madeleine Fortin. I was just wondering if you had the book I ordered?'

He looked at me, and for a split second, I had the awful thought that he might be a collaborator and it could all be a trap. I pictured German soldiers hiding upstairs waiting to arrest me.

But: 'Yes, I do,' he replied, reaching under the counter and producing a book in a brown paper bag.

'Thank you very much.'

'No, thank you,' he replied.

I took out my purse and paid him, my heart pounding. Then, much as I wanted to race out of there, I forced myself to meander, even stopping to take a look at the stand full of copies of *Gone With the Wind* by the door.

It wasn't until I was cycling along the dirt track back to the farmhouse that my pulse rate returned to normal. It had been so long since I'd had to do a job for real, rather than in training. I leaned the bike against the wall and checked the front doorstep for any sign that the earth I'd sprinkled there before I left had been disturbed. This was a trick I'd been taught in England, so I'd be able to know if there'd been an intruder. I was relieved to see that it was just as I'd left it.

I went into the kitchen and took the book from the bag. It was a copy of *The Great Gatsby*. I couldn't help feeling wistful for the carefree days of the Roaring Twenties. As a young girl back then, I'd assumed that the thirties and forties would be one long party, too. Pushing my longing from my mind, I searched the book for a message. It turned out to be written in code via pencilled notes and underlined words. It was actually quite good fun trying to decipher it. And I felt even happier when I discovered my mission. I was to go to Paris, to a store in Montmartre, for a quarter after eleven the following morning. I felt beside myself with excitement. The store was right by La Flamant Rose, and more importantly, Bessie.

The next morning I was woken at the crack of dawn by Claude the cockerel – I'd named him this as they were both equally annoying. After I tended to the livestock and fetched the morning's freshly laid eggs, I began working on my disguise. While I was in England, I'd been trained in how to dramatically change my appearance using stage make-up, a wig and padding. I put on the grey wig and padded corset I'd been given. Then I applied my make-up to make it look as if I had wrinkles. Finally, I got changed into one of my tweed ensembles and inserted some padding into the sides of my mouth to fill out my cheeks.

'Oh, Bessie, if you could see me now,' I said to myself as I looked in the mirror. The thought I'd been trying to ignore since the day before loomed large in my mind. What if Bessie *could* see me like this? What if I paid her a visit before going to my destination? It was practically next door, after all. I knew it would be wrong to put myself at extra risk but the thought of being so close to Bessie and not going to see her seemed unthinkable. I decided to compromise. I would walk past Le Flamant Rose, and if it was fated to happen, I would somehow see my beloved friend.

To get to Paris, I had to cycle for forty minutes to the nearest station, where I caught a train to Gare de Lyon. I then caught the Métro a few stops before getting out to walk the rest. The first thing I noticed when I got to Paris was how much more drab it seemed. It could have been the leaden sky and biting wind, but even the people seemed to be faded, somehow. The women I passed all looked frayed at the seams. A lot of them, I noticed, had stained their bare legs brown and drawn a line up the back to make it look as if they were wearing stockings. There was something so poignant about this, the writer in me ached to begin composing a column. But of course, I was no longer a writer; I was a farmer's widow. I shuffled along the street, clasping my string shopping basket, head stooped, and just like the day before, it was as if I'd become invisible.

When I got to Montmartre, my heart was pounding so loud I could barely hear myself think. I couldn't bring myself to go near Sacré-Coeur or the Place du Tertre for fear of the painful memories of Otto they would trigger, so I approached Le Flamant Rose from a different direction. When I reached the passageway alongside the club, I saw that the side door was open for a delivery. Taking this as a sign from fate, I slipped in behind the delivery man and glanced up and down the corridor. The coast was clear, so I made my way to Bessie's office. I was just about to knock when the door opened – and there she was – my wonderful best friend. It was all I could do not to grab her in a hug, but it was good job I didn't as there, right behind her, was Officer von Fritsch!

'Can I help you?' Bessie asked. She seemed really distracted and showed no sign of recognition.

For a moment my mind went completely blank, then thankfully I found inspiration.

'I have come to be interviewed for the cleaning job,' I said, deepening my voice.

'What cleaning job?'

Officer von Fritsch stepped out from behind her and gave me the once-over. As he moved past me, I winked at Bessie.

'The one you advertised.' I stared at her intently, praying she would figure out it was me.

'Holy cow!' she exclaimed, clamping her hand to her mouth.

My heart almost stopped beating as I thought she was going to give the game away.

'I can't believe I had forgotten the interviews,' she said quickly, ushering me into her office. 'Please, wait in here. I'll only be a minute.'

I went inside and hovered by her desk, my throat tight with fear. Had von Fritsch suspected anything? I looked around the office. It was a whole lot messier than usual. A bunch of files were scattered over the desk, along with dirty glasses imprinted with Bessie's scarlet lipstick. The ashtray was overflowing. There was no sign of the rabbits.

Come on, come on, I silently urged, looking at the door. I started mentally rehearsing all I'd learned in combat training about how to kill a man with my bare hands, just in case von Fritsch came back in to arrest me. Finally, the door opened and in came Bessie, mercifully unaccompanied.

'Florence,' she hissed after shutting the door. 'Is that you?'

I nodded, suddenly too overcome with emotion to speak.

'Dear heart! I'd given up hope I'd ever see you again!' She grabbed me in an embrace, but instead of smelling of her signature Chanel, she smelled of stale cigarettes and sweat.

'I know, I'm sorry. I got delayed after America entered the war as I wasn't able to travel back by boat.'

'How did you get back?' Bessie whispered, wide-eyed.

'Parachute.'

'Well, I'll be…' It gave me a thrill to see her look so impressed. But then her expression of awe turned to horror as she stepped back and looked me up and down. 'What's with the grandma couture? And what the heck's happened to your cheekbones?'

'I have padding inside my mouth. I have to wear a disguise when I come into Paris.'

'Come into? So you're not living back here?'

I shook my head.

Thankfully, she knew not to ask any more questions.

'I can't stay long, but I couldn't come by without trying to see you. It is so good to see you!'

'And you!' We hugged again.

'I'm so glad you're OK. I was worried for your safety now that America's at war with the Germans.'

'I know. Things sure are getting tricky. They've already started rounding up American men. I'm hoping my friendship with von Fritsch will protect me, but who knows.' Bessie glanced over to one of the armchairs. I followed her gaze and saw a black satin bra draped over the back, as if it had been flung there in a fit of passion.

'Just how friendly are things getting with von Fritsch?' I'd meant it as a joke, but she didn't laugh. She didn't even smile. She just looked at the floor sheepishly. 'Bessie?' I stared at her. There were dark rings beneath her eyes that even her make-up wasn't able to conceal, and the roots of her hair were greasy. 'What's going on?'

'Nothing. I just want this war to be over already.'

I frowned. She seemed so different to the Bessie I had left, waxing lyrical about finding her purpose.

'Has something happened to you?'

She looked as if she was going to say something, but then she shook her head. 'Nothing I can't handle, dear heart.'

'I don't suppose you've heard anything about Otto, or Drancy?'

Again, she shook her head. 'I heard that Klaus deserted, though.'

'What?'

'Uh-huh. Von Fritsch let it slip.'

'Holy cow.'

'Do you think it's to do with him saving Otto?' Bessie asked.

'I'm not sure. He told me his wife was sick with cancer. I think maybe he left to be with her.'

Bessie gave a tight little smile. 'Well, it's good to know they're not all psychopaths.'

Again, I studied her face. Something had clearly happened. 'What is it, Bessie? Have they done something to you?'

'Of course not.' She looked away. 'Ain't you got work to do?'

'Yes, but…'

'You were risking a lot coming here.'

'I know, but…'

'You'd better get going, then.'

'Oh, OK.'

She opened the door and checked the corridor, then bustled me out. 'Well, thank you very much for coming for the interview,' she said loudly.

'No problem,' I replied, but she'd already shut the door in my face.

I arrived at my destination – a nondescript apartment above a carpet merchant's – to be greeted by a nervous-looking woman named Agnes, or code-named Agnes, anyways. She introduced me to a middle-aged man, who I was told was named Leonard. He was quiet and studious, and like Agnes, had a real nervous air about him. I tried to put him at ease with a few wisecracks, which sadly fell upon unappreciative ears, then we got clear on our backstory, in case we were stopped by the police or the Germans. Leonard was my cousin, and he was coming to stay with me awhile. Thankfully, we made it through the checkpoints we encountered on the way back to the farm without issue. Another benefit of my new invisible woman persona was that I no longer turned the heads of the Germans.

Winter eased into spring and I eased into my new routine, the adrenalin rush of each new job soothed by the dependable rhythm of farm life. Much as I hated to admit it, and would never admit it to my daddy, there was something reassuring about feeding the pigs and chooks and milking Vera. And anytime fear or stress got too much, I'd spend a couple of hours digging and planting, folding my troubles into the ground.

There was one issue that no amount of digging could help with, though: my growing concern for Otto and my frustration that although I was only forty miles away from Drancy, he might as well be in another world. If indeed, he was still at Drancy. These were the thoughts that would drive me crazy at night when I was unable to sleep. One night, I had a terrible nightmare, in which Otto was crying out for me. I'm not sure if I was going slightly crazy from spending so much time on my own and having too much time to think, but as the fourteenth of June approached, the compulsion to go to Drancy became overwhelming. I hadn't gone completely doolally. I knew that I couldn't exactly waltz into an internment camp and demand Otto's release, or even to see him, but the internal tug to be under the same patch of sky as him, if only for a few minutes, was intense. And so, at the crack of dawn on the fourteenth of June 1942, I set off to be closer to Otto.

I went in my disguise, with a string bag of tomatoes hanging from my handlebars: just a humble French widow, out for a cycle with some groceries. I also had my revolver hidden inside my purse at the bottom of the bag, and my cyanide capsules in the heel of my shoe. It was a cloudy day so I didn't find the cycling too exhausting. All the way there I felt a growing excitement; finally, I was doing something to bring me closer to Otto.

I arrived in Drancy four hours later, saddle-sore and with legs like jello. I padlocked my bicycle to some railings and strolled along the drab streets until the camp finally loomed into view. It was easy to spot, as it included some of the very first high-rise apartment blocks to have been built in Paris. Of course, it hadn't been built to be an internment camp; it was supposed to have been a ground-breaking residential project, named La Cité de la Muette – the City of the Silent – which now seemed full of sinister irony. The prisoners were kept in a large three-storey, U-shaped complex in the shadow of the blocks, surrounded by watchtowers and barbed wire fences. As I walked along a side street parallel to the camp, it made me sick to my stomach that something like this could exist on the outskirts of my beloved Paris. To make matters even worse, it wasn't Nazis guarding the complex, but French police. *What is wrong with you?* I wanted to yell at the gendarmes standing at the entrance. *How can you do this in your own country – to your country?* But I kept my cool and remembered to stoop instead of stride, glancing to my right every so often.

As I drew level with the entrance, I could see that it opened onto a large courtyard. Some people were shuffling around inside. Could one of them be Otto? I felt sick from dread and fear. I knew I that I mustn't do anything to draw attention to myself, so I kept walking, trying to calm my racing mind. I found a café a couple of blocks away and went in to order a coffee. It felt strange, going into an unknown café without actually having to meet a contact, or deliver or collect a message – although it could be said that I was on a mission of my own. But how could I possibly reach Otto? If I approached the guards and asked after him, I risked blowing my cover and being arrested by association. And how could I ask after him, anyway? I had no idea which identity he'd given to the Nazis. I shuddered as I thought of the awful night I'd seen him arrested. That couldn't be the last time I ever saw Otto; I wouldn't allow it. I downed my coffee and ordered another. I knew I'd have to move on soon; I didn't want to arouse suspicion by staying there too long, but I couldn't leave Drancy without some kind of plan. I drank my second coffee, then left.

While I'd been inside, the sky had filled with banks of grey cloud. It was starting to rain. I strolled back the way I'd come. This time, when I drew level with the entrance to the camp, I saw that the rain had caused the gendarmes to take shelter in a hut-like structure by the gate. I bent down and pretended to lace my shoe, glancing into the courtyard. I could see a couple of men standing talking inside. They were painfully thin, and I noticed yellow badges on the fronts of their shabby jackets that gave me goose bumps. The previous year, after phoning his parents from the safe house where Emil was staying, Otto had told me that Jews in Austria were being made to wear yellow stars on their clothing. Now it was happening in France. Again, I felt a surge of anger at the French police guarding the camp, who were allowing this to happen. *Shame on them.*

I had just finished pretending to tie my lace, when one of the guards came out of his shelter and called over to me. I pretended not to hear and continued on my way. But he shouted 'Halt!' again.

I slowly turned and he beckoned me over.

'What are you doing here?' the guard asked. He was stocky and sour-faced, and his breath smelled of garlic.

'I've just met my friend for coffee, sir,' I replied meekly, fully immersed in my widow role – on the surface, at least. Inside my head, I was calculating how long it would take me to retrieve my pistol.

'Papers, please,' he barked.

'Of course,' I replied calmly, my heart pounding. I opened my purse and pulled out my papers, my fingers brushing against the cool metal of the revolver.

As he inspected my papers, I looked back at the men in the courtyard. *Otto, if you are here, please see me,* I silently willed.

After what felt like an eternity, the guard handed me back my papers. 'And what is in your bag?'

'Just some tomatoes, sir.'

He glared at me. 'Where did you get these from?'

'I grew them, sir.'

'And what are you doing with them?'

'I am taking them to a friend.'

'Hmm.' He stared at me. 'Are you selling them on the black market?'

'No, of course not.'

'I do not believe you. I shall have to confiscate them.'

I handed the tomatoes over, a hatred for him and everything he stood for pumping through my veins.

'Go on then, be on your way,' he snapped.

'Thank you.' *And to hell with you,* I thought, as I carried on up the street. As I reached the end of the block, I glanced along the side of the building at the rows and rows of glassless windows, and I remembered what Claude had said about the building still being incomplete. If I yelled Otto's name now, there would be a chance that he'd hear me. But there was an even bigger chance the gendarme would come after me. About halfway along the building, on the second floor, I spotted someone leaning out of the window, gazing up at the sky. Could it be? My heart began to pound. *Please, please, please, be you,* I willed. But I had to keep on walking. And when I glanced back again, the figure had disappeared.

*

I was so distracted by my thoughts and the driving rain on the cycle home, I ended up going the wrong way twice and didn't get back to the farm until dusk. I was in such a state, I even forgot to check the step for any disturbance to the soil I'd sprinkled there, and came into the kitchen to find a man standing by the hearth.

'Who are you? What do you want?' I cried, gripping my purse, ready to retrieve my gun.

'Where the hell have you been?' The man turned to face me and I saw that it was Claude.

'Out,' I replied, placing my purse on the table.

'Out where?'

'It's none of your business.' I snapped back, in no mood for an inquisition.

'Of course it's my business. We have a job to do and you had disappeared.' His eyes sparked with anger.

'What job?' I asked numbly.

'There's a drop-off this evening and I need you to come with me.'

I felt like telling him to stick his job where the sun didn't shine, but of course, I couldn't.

'I can't believe you would go off like that. You're supposed to stay here at all times.'

There was something so infuriating about him talking to me like this, that I'm afraid I saw red and all of my training went out of the window.

'You don't tell me what to do!' I slammed my hand down on the table. 'If I want to go and see someone, I'll go and see them.'

'Great.' Claude scowled. 'So while we're trying to win a war, you've been off socialising with your girlfriends.'

'I haven't been socialising with my girlfriends; I was trying to see my husband!'

A terrible silence fell upon the kitchen. I sank down onto one of the bench seats.

'Your husband?'

'Yes.'

'Where is he?'

'At Drancy.'

'He's the person you know in the camp there?'

'Yes.'

'Oh.' He sat down opposite me.

I knew I could get in a whole heap of trouble for giving away my personal story, not to mention going to Drancy without being told to, but I no longer cared. I was too exhausted, physically and emotionally.

'I'm sorry.' Claude finally broke the silence. 'But surely you were not able to see him?'

'No. It was a total waste of time. It's just that – today is an important date for us. It's the anniversary of us meeting.'

'June the fourteenth?'

I nodded. 'I had this crazy notion that somehow I'd see him if I went there today. It was foolish. I'm sorry.'

'No, it wasn't foolish. It wasn't foolish at all.' He smiled softly. 'Why don't you go and get changed into some dry clothes? Then we need to leave for the drop-off.'

'OK.' I got up to go upstairs, then stopped in the doorway. 'Thank you.'

The drop-off that Claude and I had been sent to meet turned out to be another woman, parachuted in by the SOE. She stayed the night at the farm, before Claude took her on the next leg of her journey. It was only once they'd gone that the full sorrow over my futile visit to Drancy hit me. Ever since I'd been parted from Otto, I'd clung on to the dream of me saving him, but now I could see it for what it was: a total fantasy. I'd lost my life's purpose, and depression rushed in to fill the void. I'd never been a melancholic person before. Whenever life had knocked me down, I'd been able to pick myself up and dust off my britches. But not this time. This time, I felt as if my spirit had been well and truly broken.

I carried on going through the motions of my life – feeding the animals, picking and planting vegetables, going into town to visit the bookstore for messages – with all the passion and zest of a used dishcloth. I had no hope of saving Otto, and I was out of my mind with concern for Bessie, too. One week in August, I paid a visit to the bookstore to be told that the book I'd ordered wasn't yet in stock. I was about to leave when I spied a couple of notebooks on the counter and on an impulse, I bought one of them, along with an ink pen.

That night, I sat at the kitchen table and poured my heart onto the paper, writing to Otto as if I was writing him a letter. Releasing all of my pent-up thoughts and feelings felt like lancing a boil. Then, when there were no more words left inside of me, I tore the pages from the book and dropped them onto the fire, picturing my thoughts drifting up on the smoke through the chimney, up and away, all the way to Drancy.

The following night, once all of my chores were done, I sat down and wrote again. And so, day by day, page by page, writing restored my link to Otto, and indeed, to my very soul.

SAGE

March 2018

Sage put the manuscript down on her bed, went over to her bag and pulled out a notebook and pen. Ever since her mother had died, it had been as if the invisible umbilical cord that had always connected them had been severed in the most brutal way imaginable. She felt the loss of their usual daily check-ins acutely. It had never occurred to her that she could write to Elizabeth, until she'd read about Florence writing to Otto. She opened the notebook and took the top from her pen:

> 'Dear Mum,
>
> So, it's been a whole year now since you left. The worst year of my life. I honestly wasn't sure if I'd be able to make it without you. Seriously, things went from bad to worse to catastrophic! But then the most incredible thing happened...'

Sage paused. It felt so weird, writing to her mother, knowing that she'd never read the letter. But Florence had known that Otto wasn't going to read her letters to him, and she'd said it helped. Sage carried on writing:

> 'I've finally solved the mystery of your birth mother, and it turns out she was the most incredible woman. I only wish

you could have found this out too; I feel like it would have made such a difference. Do you remember that night you took me out for dinner to celebrate my graduation from uni, and I thanked you for being the best mum and friend in the world? You replied that you wondered if you'd have been able to say the same about your own mum, if you'd had the chance to get to know her. Then you said you were certain you wouldn't have been able to, because if she'd wanted to be your best mum and friend, she wouldn't have abandoned you. I'd never realised how much it had hurt you until that night. You were usually so matter of fact about what happened, but I guess that was you putting on a brave face. The saddest thing is, she wasn't a horrible person at all. I don't know why she left you in that church yet, but I'm sure there's a very good reason, and it's not anything to do with her not caring about you.

It turns out you have a brother, too – or a half-brother at least – and he's the sweetest, kindest man. You would love him. He lives on a farm in Arkansas in America, the same farm your birth mum grew up on. Sometimes, when I look at him, I see you. Not just in how he looks, but his mannerisms too, which is the weirdest thing, given that you never met each other! Anyway, it's been so lovely getting to know him, and my grandmother through him – it's as if they're reconnecting me to you. I love you, Mum, and I miss you so much. If there is such a thing as the spirit world, I hope you're here with me…'

A tear rolled down Sage's face, landing on the page and blurring the ink. She felt a definite sense of release. It was as if a valve had been opened on her bottled-up grief. She looked back at the manuscript. It had been horrible, reading about Florence hitting rock-bottom. All through the scene in Drancy, Sage had been biting her lip, hoping for some kind of miracle, that Florence and Otto would be reunited. But of course, she wasn't reading a novel, and real life wasn't nearly so convenient. Real life was full of loss and disappointment. It was weird, but reading about Florence's despair had made Sage feel slightly better about her own recent meltdown. Maybe she wasn't a terrible and stupid person. Maybe messing up was all a part of being human. And so was rising up and overcoming.

She flicked through the notebook. Apart from her letter to her mother, the pages were blank. Ever since Sage had graduated uni, she'd never left home without a notebook, just in case inspiration struck. And it had struck a lot, back in those days, especially when she'd been out and about in London. Interesting characters, striking street art, overheard snatches of conversation, unusual outfits, hairstyles or tattoos – all were grist to her creative mill. But somewhere along the way, the outside world had lost its fascination to her, and her notebooks had remained empty. But why? She turned to a fresh page, and wrote:

'*Because none of it was coming from my soul.*
Because it all became about making money.
Because I no longer had full creative control.
Because I could no longer tell the truth.
Because I was so worried that I might lose followers.'

She put down her pen and sighed. She wondered what Florence would have made of the world of social media. Something told her she would have snubbed it completely, too busy living her life to the fullest, seeking out adventure and talking to trees. Sage thought back to her ride with Hunter. He'd returned to the tree after about half an hour, cautiously entering the clearing as if he didn't want to disturb her.

'You OK, or do you need some more time?' he'd asked softly.

'I'm OK,' she'd replied.

And the truth was, she'd felt way better than OK. Tuning in to her grandmother via the tree had brought her the greatest feeling of acceptance and peace. They'd ridden back to the stables in silence, and then, as they'd unbridled the horses, Sage had thanked him.

'No problem,' he'd replied gruffly. As she'd been about to set off for the house, he'd turned to her. 'Your grandma once told me we'd all be a whole lot happier if we lived like trees.'

'What did she mean?' Sage had asked.

Hunter had grinned. 'That's exactly what I said when she told me. She told me to go figure it out for myself.'

'And did you?'

'Uh-huh.'

'And?'

He'd chuckled. 'Go figure it out for yourself.'

Sage went over to the window now and gazed out across the fields to the woods. What had Florence meant? She looked back at the manuscript. There wasn't much left to read now, but maybe she'd find the answer inside.

FLORENCE

1942

After a couple of months of going through the motions, carrying out jobs, tending to the farm and writing to Otto, in September 1942 I received an instruction via my bookstore letterbox to go to a church in a village to the north-east of Paris.

It was one of those beautiful fall days when the crisp air smelled of bonfires and the leaves were just beginning to turn, painting brush strokes of gold among the green. The village I'd been sent to was a small affair, made up of a short row of shops and a cluster of houses around a green. It was easy to locate the church, its spire reaching into the blue sky at the top of a hill. A bicycle was leaning against the grey stone wall of the church. I left mine next to it and went inside, the old wooden door emitting a loud creak as I pushed it open. It was so dark inside, it took a moment for my eyes to adjust. As I did every time I arrived at one of these jobs, I wondered if it was all a trap, and if this was the occasion when I'd finally fall victim to a collaborator. I guessed that even men of the cloth wouldn't be above betrayal for self-preservation.

I'd been told to wait inside the church, so I sat in a pew about three rows from the front and bowed my head, as if in prayer. And I'm not sure if it was the lingering fragrant aroma of incense or the utter stillness, but my pulse began to slow, and I felt the same sensation I'd experienced that day in Sacré-Coeur with Otto.

Only this time it was silence rather than music that was moving through me, softening me. *Please keep him safe*, I prayed, to a God I wasn't sure I really believed in.

I started at the sound of footsteps on the stone floor behind me, but kept my head bowed. I mentally rehearsed my cover story. *I was just passing through the village on a cycle ride; I thought I'd stop to pray.* The footsteps stopped and I heard someone slipping into the pew behind me. The hairs on my skin prickled. What if it was a trap? What if I was about to be arrested, or shot? I took a deep breath.

Behind me, a man cleared his throat. 'Excuse me, but are you Madeleine?'

I sat as still as the statue of Jesus nailed to his cross on the wall in front of me. It couldn't be. I had to be imagining things.

'Yes.' My reply came out in a squeak.

'I am Frank,' the voice whispered. *His* voice whispered.

Barely able to breathe, I slowly turned and stared at the figure behind me, taking in the shaven head, large brown eyes – made even larger by the hollowed cheeks – and the jawline shaded with stubble.

My breath returned, but in short, sharp judders. It couldn't be…

'I understand you are here to—' He broke off, his mouth falling open. 'Florence!' he gasped.

'Otto!'

Somehow, I managed to regain my composure. My head was filling with questions, but overriding them all was the burning desire to get him to safety.

'Did they give you a bicycle?' I whispered.

He nodded. 'It is just outside the door. Is this… Am I dreaming?'

'Well, if you are, we're both having the same dream.' I fought the urge to throw my arms around him. 'We have about an hour's ride ahead of us. If we're stopped, we're to say that you're my brother, come to pay me a visit. Did they give you false papers?'

He nodded.

'OK, good.' I stood up and he followed suit. He was so thin, his stomach curved in. 'There's something else you need to know,' I whispered.

'What?'

I leaned in closer to him. 'It's taking everything I've got not to kiss you.'

His thin, pale face broke into a grin, and there was my old Otto again. 'I guess that wouldn't look too good, given that I'm now your brother.'

'Exactly. Come.' I led him out of the church, and as we got our bicycles, a priest in his robes came out of the house beside the church and gave us a furtive smile.

'Bon courage,' he muttered under his breath as he passed by.

'Merci,' Otto whispered back.

As the reality of what had happened began to sink in, I felt drunk on a cocktail of shock, fear and excitement. How had this happened? How had we both ended up here? Had I wished for it so hard, I'd triggered some kind of weird magical manifestation? Had God answered my prayer? But that was ridiculous. I'd made my prayer seconds before Otto appeared. God might be able to move mountains, as my daddy used to say, but he couldn't make a grown man appear out of thin air.

We mounted our bikes and cycled from the village in silence, Otto following me, coughing intermittently. Once we got onto the twisting, turning country road, covered on both sides by a wall of trees, I slowed down so that our bikes were level.

'I can't believe you're here.'

Otto smiled, but I could tell he was struggling for breath.

'Are you OK?'

He nodded. 'I'm… just… not… as… strong… as… I… was,' he puffed.

'Don't worry. Save your energy. We can talk at the farm. I have a farm. I mean, obviously it's not mine, but it's where I've been staying.' I wittered on like this for a while and then we fell into a companionable silence, broken only by the rasp of Otto's breath.

After what seemed like an eternity, we arrived at the farm.

'Take a seat… please,' I said, leading him into the kitchen. I felt suddenly shy in his presence. So much had happened in the ten months we'd been apart. For both of us. And for a horrible moment, I thought that maybe we'd forgotten how to be with each other.

But instead of sitting down, he came over to me. 'Oh, Florence.' He hugged me, and even though his arms were now as thin as sticks, he held me with an urgency that took my breath away. As I pressed my head to his chest, I could hear his heart beating, and this just about undid me. For so long, I'd spent so much energy convincing myself he was still alive, but all the while, beneath my bravado, had bubbled the fear that he might be dead. Tears poured from my eyes, soaking his shirt. Otto took my face in his hands and began kissing the tears from my cheeks. 'I love you,' he whispered between each kiss, until finally, my lips found his. I'll never forget that kiss, and how it was a balm to so many months of longing, fear and pain.

'I never gave up,' I sobbed when we finally broke free. 'I thought about you every day, even when I was in England. I kept talking to you, in my mind. I kept trying to send you messages with my mind.'

'You were in England?'

'Yes.'

'But how? Why?' He took a step back and swayed slightly.

'Sit.' I forced him into a chair. 'Let me get you something to eat and drink.'

I poured him a glass of milk, fresh from Vera that morning, and cut him a chunk of bread.

'Thank you.' He drank the milk thirstily. 'Why were you in England?'

'I was asked to go there, after you were arrested, to have some training so that I could help with the resistance. Then they dropped me back here – by parachute! Oh, Otto, it was just like being an eagle. You'd have loved it.'

He laughed, but now I was able to get a proper look at him, I noticed a grey pallor to his skin that instantly worried me.

'How did you get here? I'd heard that you were in Drancy.'

'I was. I escaped.' He took hold of my hand. 'Come here. Please.'

I perched lightly on his lap. He felt so frail, I was afraid I might break him.

'How did you escape? The camp is so well-guarded.'

He frowned. 'How do you know? Have you been?'

'Yes. I went there on our anniversary. I had this crazy notion that if I walked around outside, I might see you.'

He sighed. 'I was lying on the floor thinking about you that day, and it felt as if you were next to me. I thought I was delirious from hunger, but maybe I could actually sense you outside.'

'Why were you lying on the floor? Did you not have a bed?'

He gave a dry laugh. 'Of course we didn't have beds. We are Jews, dirty kikes. We had to sleep on straw like animals.'

I gulped. 'Oh, Otto.' I stroked his shaven head. He might have still been my beloved, but he was changed. How could he not be? 'How did you escape?'

'The resistance had been passing messages into the camp. A couple of the gendarmes who work there are sympathetic – or easily bought by the promise of tobacco, at least.'

I thought of the guard I'd encountered the day of my visit. Something told me he wasn't one of them.

'You remember my friend, Emil?' Otto asked.

'Yes.'

'Well, he got a message to me a couple of months ago, to let me know that the Germans were starting to deport prisoners to camps in Poland, where they were being murdered. He told me that if I got put on a train to one of those camps, I should do whatever I could to escape. And then last week, I was one of those rounded up.'

'What happened?' I asked, dread growing in the pit of my stomach.

'They put about a thousand of us onto a convoy of trucks and old buses, and we were taken to the station.'

The thought of all those people being driven through the drab streets of Drancy, being driven to possible death, caused my heart to splinter. What if it had happened the day I was there? What if I'd seen those trucks filled with people pass by me?

'Then, when we got to the station, we were herded onto cattle trucks,' Otto continued, his face etched with sorrow. 'There were children on their own, crying for their parents. Old people, barely able to walk. Newborn babies in cardboard boxes.'

My eyes filled with tears and I had to look away. How could this be happening in France? How could people be letting this happen?

'Once we were all crammed into the box cars, we were left there, at the station. We stayed there all night without moving, with just one bucket in our car for all of us to relieve ourselves in.' He stopped talking and took hold of my hand. 'Do you want to hear this?'

'Yes.' The truth was, I didn't *want* to hear it but I knew that he needed me to.

'Pretty soon the bucket was overflowing, so we had no choice but to use the floor. Our degradation was complete. And the stench...' He shuddered. 'I can still smell it now. It's as if it's trapped inside of my nose forever.'

I squeezed his hand tightly.

'Anyway, while I was standing there in my corner of the carriage, I felt this... this fury building inside of me. That we should be treated in this way. That we should be made to suffer so. There were women there who had just given birth. Old men in their suits...' His voice broke. 'In their suits. As if dressing up smartly would somehow save them. And I vowed... I vowed that whatever happened, I was going to get off that train, or I was going to die trying.'

Now I was crying, too. 'I'm so sorry,' was all I could say, but it felt so useless. What could I ever do or say to make amends for what Otto had been through?

'Then finally, as dawn broke, we heard the soldiers outside and the train started moving.'

I couldn't begin to imagine the terror the people on the train must have felt by this point.

'I saw a young couple close to me start to embrace and it made me think of you, and I grew even more determined.' He stopped talking and coughed.

'Can I get you some water? Do you need to take a break?'

He shook his head.

'So how did you do it? How did you escape?'

'I came up with a plan with a man called Josef who I'd befriended at the camp. We decided to use our sweaters to bend the bars on the window.'

'Your sweaters? Were they strong enough?'

'Not when they were dry, but if you make a fabric wet and then wring the liquid from it, it becomes strong, like a tourniquet. So we made them wet.'

'How?'

He looked away. 'We used the bucket – and the floor.'

My stomach contracted as I realised what he was saying. 'Then what happened?'

'We kept twisting and twisting the sweaters round the bars, and finally, they started to move. It took hours, but finally we bent them enough to make a gap big enough to jump through.'

My eyes widened. 'You jumped from the train while it was moving?'

'Yes, it had slowed as we were going through a ravine, so we decided to take our chance.'

'But, what happened to your friend? Why was he not there with you today?'

'He landed badly and broke his leg. I managed to get him to safety in another village. Then I was moved on to the church where you found me.'

'I still can't believe I found you.'

'I can,' he said softly, looking at my locket.

'Oh, Otto.' I hugged him tightly. 'Thank you for not giving up on me.'

He frowned at me. 'Why would I give up on you?'

'I don't know. I just thought… after the last time I saw you.' I stared down at the floor.

'With the German?'

I nodded, still unable to look at him.

'He saved my life. He told those two animals who'd arrested me that he would take care of things. He made it sound as if he was going to kill me, but instead he took me to Drancy. I have no idea why, but he chose to save me.'

'He was the man I told you about at the club. The one who stopped me from being attacked. I think he figured out that I knew you – that I was in love with you.'

'Was?' He gave me one of his grins.

'Am. I *am* in love with you,' I declared, hugging him to me.

Otto looked so tired and frail, I insisted he go to bed straight after he'd eaten, and I went and tended to the animals. Normally, when I had my 'guests' staying, they would sleep in the barn, out of sight, but there was no way I was doing that to Otto, especially after he'd told me what he'd been made to sleep on in Drancy. As I mucked out the pigs while he slept, I silently fumed. How could the Germans – and the French gendarmes for that matter – treat other humans like livestock? What had happened to make them be able to behave in that way? All afternoon, as I mucked out, fed and milked the animals, I pondered this question. The only answer I could come up with was ignorance and fear. I remembered what Klaus had said to me, when we were saying goodbye, about love being stronger than anything. I truly believed he was right – hadn't the strength of our love pulled Otto and I back together? But fear was strong too, and it could spread like a plague.

I returned to the house with a fresh jug of milk and some eggs, and went to check on Otto. I found him still asleep, his face slick with sweat.

'Otto,' I whispered, stroking his arm. 'Otto?' I put my hand to his forehead. It was burning up. 'Otto,' I said again, louder.

He moaned and opened his eyes, starting to cough.

'Let me get you some water.'

When I returned, he was sitting up in bed and there was blood all over his chin and the palm of his hand.

'What happened?' I cried.

'It was when I coughed. I'm sorry.'

'It's OK. Hold on…' I fetched a damp cloth and cleaned him up, then I passed him a cup of water.

'I'm sorry,' he said again, taking a sip.

'You don't need to apologise.' I plumped up his pillow. 'You need to rest.'

That evening, while Otto continued to sleep, I sat in front of the fire in the kitchen, trying to ignore my growing sense of dread. Otto probably just had a chill. After everything he'd been through, it was to be expected. *But you don't cough up blood when you have a chill,* my inner voice so kindly reminded me. There was a doctor in the town, but I could hardly ask him to pay a house visit. And there was no way I could risk taking Otto into Barbizon, even if he was physically able. I would have to wait until I received contact from my circuit. Someone would be here to collect Otto soon; that was the usual form. No one ever stayed at the farm longer than a few days. The thought of Otto leaving was awful, but if he needed medical attention, I would willingly let him go. Round and round my thoughts spiralled, until I couldn't take it any more. I put out the fire and went back upstairs, making myself a makeshift bed on the floor in his room. I'd just managed to drop off to sleep when I heard Otto call my name. I opened my eyes and saw him looking down at me.

'What are you doing down there?' he whispered.

'Watching over you,' I replied.

'Come here.' He shifted up and made a space for me.

I climbed into the bed and into his arms.

'I love you, my wild eagle,' he whispered into my hair.

There was no real improvement in Otto the next day. He spent most of it sleeping. That evening, as I was making some potato soup, Raul arrived.

'Did you collect your contact?' he asked.

'Yes. He's upstairs.'

'In the house?' He frowned.

'He's ill.' I'd decided not to tell anyone in the circuit that I actually knew Otto. I didn't want them to think that I'd be compromised in any way.

'How ill? I was hoping to move him on today.'

'He hasn't been out of bed. He has a fever and a really bad cough. He's been coughing up blood.'

'Oh, no.' Raul sat down at the table.

'What is it?'

'It could be tuberculosis.'

I shivered as he spoke aloud my deepest fear. 'Can we get him medical help?'

'We don't have a doctor anywhere near here – not one who is on our side, at least. He will have to stay here a while longer, and you will have to take care of him.'

Needless to say, my happiness at this development was heavily tainted with fear.

And so I come to the moment I've been dreading from the day I first sat down to write this story. But it's also the very reason for me writing this, so I must continue. I've never been able to speak of what happened over the next few days at the farm, or indeed the next few years. But I have lived with the memory playing on a loop in my brain every day since. Maybe writing it all down will provide some kind of release.

As Otto's body grew weaker, his spirit seemed reborn. It was the strangest thing. The sorrow he'd arrived with lifted, and his joy returned, like sunshine burning through a dawn mist. Every morning I would do my chores, then bring breakfast up to him. Tea, a slice of bread, a boiled egg. Some days he was able to keep it down, others it would prompt a coughing fit that could last for hours. For the rest of the day we talked, we slept, we reminisced. We dreamed out loud about returning to Montmartre once the Germans were gone – although I'm not sure if either of us believed they ever would be gone, by this point. Every day he would ask me to recite some Walt Whitman to him. Sometimes, while I did this, he would hold my locket to his lips.

'We are always together, you know,' he whispered one day, after I'd recited our own special poem. 'Even when we're not.'

I knew exactly what he meant. All of the months we'd been apart, I'd felt him with me. Maybe this was what it meant to meet your kindred spirit. It was an act of remembrance, because on some level your spirits had always been spiralling through the air together, and they always would be, dancing together for eternity.

After about a week, Otto seemed to improve slightly.

'I want to go outside,' he whispered breathlessly after breakfast. 'I want to see the birds and the trees.'

I wrapped a blanket round his shoulders and helped him out into the sunshine. I'd planned on staying right by the house, but Otto insisted on sitting beneath a tree.

'I want to hear the leaves,' he told me.

As we settled beneath a tree on the edge of the forest, I asked him if he remembered quoting from Walt's poem about the oak tree the first time we met.

'*It grew there uttering joyous leaves of dark green*,' he replied with a smile.

'That was the moment I knew you were my kindred spirit,' I said, as I nestled into the crook of his arm.

'I knew the minute I saw you stop and ask that old man for directions.'

I frowned. 'But I asked for directions long before I got to Sacré-Coeur. Were you following me?'

He laughed and his pale face flushed. 'Yes, but not intentionally. I mean to say, I was going to Montmartre anyway, but when I realised you were going that way too, I thought I would keep an eye on you, to make sure you didn't lose your way.'

'Holy cow!' I grinned. 'Next thing, you'll be telling me you made my case fall open so you'd have a reason to talk to me.'

'Maybe I did.' He chuckled. 'Let's just say I was wishing so hard for an excuse to talk to you, and then, all of a sudden, your belongings were all over the steps!'

'Well, I'll be darned.' I wrapped my arm around him and held him tight.

'I will always be right by you, you know, watching over you.'

I felt a lump rise in my throat. 'I know you will. Do you think I'm going to let you out of my sight again?'

'Florence,' he whispered, a little later.

'Yes.'

'I think I am dying.'

'Don't say that!' I sat up straight and glared at him, but he just smiled back sweetly. His hair had grown back a little, and he looked so handsome it took my breath away.

'It is OK,' he whispered. 'But I need to ask you something. It's really important.'

'Of course.' I could barely speak for the sob building in my throat.

'That day, on the train, before I escaped…'

'Yes?'

'A lot of the other passengers were telling us not to try and bend the bars.'

'Why?'

'Some of them thought it was pointless. Others were worried that if we succeeded and the guards found out, they would all be punished on our behalf. Some of them had fallen for the lies the guards at Drancy had told us about our journey simply being a resettlement.'

I shuddered at the thought of those innocent people being led like lambs to their own slaughter.

'But then, when they'd all said their piece, an old man spoke.'

'What did he say?'

'He said that if we escaped, we'd be able to tell our story; we'd be able to let the world know about the horrors we'd experienced, to try and stop it from ever happening again.' He took hold of my hand and squeezed it tightly. 'I need you to tell our story.'

'To who?'

'Everyone. Write it. Let people know. Please.' He closed his eyes.

'Of course.' Everything went blurry as my eyes swam with tears.

'I love you, my wild eagle,' he whispered.

And I forget the rest.

SAGE

March 2018

Sage gulped as she looked across the dining table and pictured Florence sitting there, hunched over her typewriter, finally telling the story of herself and Otto after so many years of keeping it pent up inside. She had barely been able to breathe as she'd read about Otto's experiences on the train. She didn't know whether she felt more furious or heartbroken. She'd known about the atrocities of the holocaust, about the millions of people slaughtered, but there was something about the enormity of the numbers that had stopped it from feeling real, somehow. But now she'd read the details in Otto's account – the newborn babies in cardboard boxes, the bucket for the toilet, the old men in their suits – it felt all too real, and all too horrific. She felt a burning inside of her. A desire to do something – but what?

'Howdy, Sage.' Sam came into the room and placed a brown paper bag of groceries on the table.

'Oh, hey.' Sage was so affected by what she'd just read, it took a moment to come back into the present.

'You OK?'

She nodded. But then to her embarrassment, she started to cry. 'I'm sorry, it's just so sad.'

'Did you get to the part about Otto?' Sam came over and placed a hand on her shoulder.

'Yes. I can't believe she kept all of that bottled up inside for all those years.'

He nodded. 'I sure wish she'd told me sooner. When she did finally give me the story, she said she couldn't bear the thought of having to recount what had happened to other people. She said she'd only be happy for it to be shared once she was dead. I guess back then, they didn't have the kind of support people have nowadays. The war ended and they were supposed to just get on with it, no matter what trauma they'd been through. And she was traumatised. Why else would she have left your momma the way she did?'

'But why did she leave her? And who was the father? Who was my grandfather? It can't have been Otto. He… he died too soon.' Sage's eyes filled with fresh tears.

Sam patted her on the back. 'I think I'll let her tell you that.'

Sage watched as he picked up the groceries and left the room. Then, with a pounding heart, she picked up the final pages of Florence's story and began to read again.

FLORENCE

1945

I never recovered from Otto's death, and it took me a mighty long time to realise that we're not supposed to recover from the loss of a kindred spirit. To try and return to the person you were before you met, loved and lost them is an impossible feat. I've since learned to live with the hollow his loss carved into my heart, but for the rest of my days in France, I was submerged in a fog of grief.

Raul came to the farm the day Otto died, and when he found out what had happened, he summoned Claude. Together, they dug a grave beneath the tree where Otto had drawn his last breath. Even though I wasn't able to tell them what Otto had meant to me, Claude seemed to sense it, and suggested I give some kind of eulogy. I recited our poem, and at one point, I saw Claude brush away a tear. It was yet another reminder that when it came to war, our losses were both personal and universal.

I stayed at the farm for the remainder of the war. Strangely, in spite of my pain, Otto's death made me even more efficient in my work for the resistance. My desire for revenge made me laser-focused, and my feeling of having nothing left to lose gave me a courage that bordered on arrogance. Our circuit suffered some losses; two of our radio operators were killed, and Claude was captured en route to sabotaging a munitions factory. He didn't have the explosives on his person, but he was out after curfew and the police figured out his papers were false, so he was arrested and sent to an internment camp. But I kept doing what I was doing, playing the role of the simple farmer's widow and providing a safe haven for fugitives at the farm, and thankfully the Germans never discovered me. Perhaps this was Otto, keeping his promise to watch over me.

And then, all of a sudden, it was over. Finally, the Germans were beaten in Europe. Finally, they'd been driven from France. The circuit was disbanded and the farm requisitioned by the French authorities, and in June 1945, I returned to Paris. The first place I headed was Le Flamant Rose – only to find it boarded up and closed. Someone had written 'NAZI WHORES' in red paint on the wooden boards nailed over the door. I stood gazing up at the faded flamingo sign, my stomach churning with dread as I contemplated what might have happened to Bessie. I turned and walked swiftly up the hill to the Place du Tertre. The artists were back at their easels and the cafés were open. Trying not to notice all the memories of Otto that hovered around the square like ghosts, I made my way to La Crémaillère. And there, standing behind the bar as if nothing had happened, was François. He glanced at me, looked back at the glass he was polishing, then did a double-take.

'Florence!'

I threw my case on the floor and went running over. He hugged me tightly and kissed me on both cheeks. Like the rest of us, and indeed like the city itself, François appeared faded and worn, but his beaming smile was still the same.

'I am so happy to see you!' he exclaimed. 'Coffee?'

'Please.' I sat on a bar stool and undid my jacket.

'So, it is all over,' he said.

I nodded. But I think we both knew that what we'd been through would never be over, not really.

'Are you back for good?' he asked, placing a small cup of black coffee on the bar in front of me. 'Your room, it is still available. I have been using it to store things in.'

I wasn't sure moving back into my old room with all of its memories was such a great idea, but it would be easier than trudging around trying to find someplace new. 'I'm not sure how long I'm staying, but if I could have it for tonight, that would be great.'

'Of course.' He fetched some keys from beneath the counter and handed them to me, and I was struck by a strange feeling of déjà vu.

'I just went looking for Bessie.'

His face fell, causing the hairs on my arms to prickle with fear.

'The club was closed. Do you know what happened?' I held my breath, preparing for the worst.

'After the liberation of Paris, she was denounced for *collaboration horizontale*.'

I stared at him blankly.

'For betraying France by sleeping with a German officer.'

I wanted to protest that Bessie had risked her life for France, not betrayed it, but my training in saying nothing kicked in. 'What happened to her?'

'She and other dancers from the club were brought out into the street and their hair was shaved off.'

'What?' The thought of Bessie losing her beautiful auburn tresses to a baying mob made me sick to my stomach.

'It was terrible,' François continued. 'People spat at them, slapped them, tore off their clothes.'

My sickness turned to a cold fury. 'Do you know where she is now?'

He shook his head. 'No. I'm sorry.'

I finished my coffee and checked my watch. It was coming up to eleven. 'I have to go but I'll be back later. Thank you for the coffee, and the room.'

'You are welcome.' As he walked me to the door, he touched me softly on the arm. 'Can I ask, what has happened to Otto?'

'He… he passed away.'

'I'm so sorry. He was a very good man.'

'Yes. Yes he was.' Feeling choked up, I forced a smile. 'Gotta go.'

As I made my way across the square, I felt I'd made a huge mistake returning to the city. I'd been hoping it would be emboldening to see Paris free from the Germans, but all it did was sting like salt in a wound. Yes, the Germans had gone, but they'd forever left their mark on all who'd suffered through their occupation, scarring us all with their cruelty.

I followed the cobbled street round to the front of Sacré-Coeur and gazed up at its milky white domes. As the clock struck eleven, I sat down on the stone steps and thought of Otto. Obviously, I knew that he wouldn't be showing up for our special date, but I hoped that if he was watching over me, I'd sense him there, somehow. I gazed out over Paris, and thought back to the day I'd first arrived, fresh off the boat from New York. Meeting Otto had felt like the beginning of a fairy tale. I'd had no idea of the pain and horror to come.

'I love you,' I whispered, gazing up at a wisp of cloud in the forget-me-not blue sky.

'Florence?'

I jumped at the sound of the man's voice behind me, and for a split second I thought I was actually hearing Otto's spirit talking to me. But no, it couldn't be. I turned around.

'Claude?'

He was standing a couple of steps behind me, his curly black hair longer than before and a thin scar running down his cheek. I scrambled to my feet. And then I realised that he hadn't called me Madeleine. 'Wait? How do you know my real name?'

'Otto told me,' he said with a sad smile.

'Otto? But…'

'He told me that this was the place where you first met, and where you were reunited, and how this date was so special to you. I thought that if you were still in France, maybe you would come here today, and here you are.'

'But I don't understand.' My mind raced, trying to catch up with what he was saying. Had Claude known Otto's identity when he came to the farm? But the only time they'd been together at the farm was after Otto had died, when Claude had helped Raul bury him. 'How do you know these things?'

He smiled shyly. 'My real name is Emil. Otto and I used to work together in the store. He might have mentioned me?'

'You're Emil?' My eyes pretty much burst out of my head. 'You were the one who started the pamphlet that Otto illustrated?'

He nodded.

'I wrote things for you!'

'I know, and thank you. You are an excellent writer.'

'But you… You're…' I mentally revisited all of my encounters with Claude, now seeing them through the lens that he was Emil – one of Otto's closest friends.

'Did you know who I was from the start?'

'What, when I found you hanging upside down from a tree?'

I grimaced. 'Please, don't remind me!'

'No, it was when you said something later, in an American accent, and then you let it slip that you were a dancer. Otto had told me about you dancing in the club. And he was always sketching pictures of you on his lunchbreak when we worked at the store. So, even though your hair was a different colour, I recognised your face and put the pieces together.'

'Wow.'

Claude, or rather Emil, must have realised I was a little light-headed from the shock and he took hold of my arm. 'Would you like to go somewhere and get a coffee?'

'I think I need more than coffee!'

We adjourned to a nearby bar on the Place du Tertre, and over a bottle of wine, we continued putting the pieces of the jigsaw together.

'I'd never known what had happened to Otto,' Emil said. 'He just disappeared. I'd been imagining the worst for months. Then you told me that your husband was in Drancy.'

'I should never have let my guard slip.'

'I'm so happy you did. By doing that, you saved him.' He offered me a cigarette and I took it gladly.

'What do you mean?'

'As soon as I knew he was in Drancy, I was able to get a message to him.'

'Yes! He told me! But I never thought for one moment that it was you – Claude.' I laughed and shook my head.

'I told him that if he got the chance to escape, he should take it.'

'Yes, and he did, on the train.'

Emil nodded. 'I received word through the network that a couple of men had escaped from a train out of Drancy. I sent one of my contacts to see them and he let me know that one of them was Otto. That's when I made arrangements for him to be collected by you.'

'That was your doing?' I stared at him in disbelief, then I started to laugh. 'I thought it was the power of my prayers.'

'Well, maybe in an indirect way it was,' Emil replied with a grin. Then his smile faded. 'I'm so sorry that you lost him.'

'I'm so grateful that I found him,' I replied, and then another piece of the puzzle fell into place. 'So when Raul asked you to come to the farm to help bury him, you knew it was Otto?'

He nodded.

'And that's why you suggested I give a eulogy, and why you cried when I read the poem.'

'I tried so hard not to. I didn't want to give the game away, but...'
He broke off and cleared his throat. 'He meant so much to me.'

I placed my hand on top of his. 'You and me both.'

Emil and I spent the rest of the day drinking wine and reminiscing about Otto. He told me all about the fun they'd had working together in the store before the war, and the daring deeds they'd gotten up to once the Germans arrived, working together on the pamphlet. And once again, I realised that in a weird way, my prayer had been answered. I might not have conjured up Otto's spirit, but I'd appeared to do the next best thing, conjuring his presence through the power of our memories.

By the time the evening rolled around, we were both drunk and emotional. As we finally left the restaurant, Emil revealed that he was heading back to Poland the following morning, to try to find what was left of his family. Despite Europe now being at peace, everything still felt so transient and fragile.

'Do you feel kind of strange now that it's all over?' I asked, as we made our way around the square.

'What do you mean?'

'Well, the war was so terrible and all-encompassing, we couldn't think about anything else, but now...'

'Now we don't know what to think?' he offered.

'Yes. And I have absolutely no idea what I should do or where I should go, or where I even belong.' To my horror, my eyes filled with tears.

'You're the kind of person who will belong wherever you go,' he answered softly. And maybe it was the poetic nature of what he said reminding me of Otto, or maybe I was just so damned tired and drunk and desperate to be held, but suddenly his finger was tracing my cheek and wiping away my tears, and suddenly our lips were touching. And maybe it was because it was the gentlest of embraces, filled with such tenderness, but within moments we were kissing with the urgency of the drowning gasping for air.

'I have a room,' I whispered.

'OK,' he replied.

And then, there I was, unlocking that old familiar door, and walking into that cool dark hallway, up those endless steps and into a room crammed so full of memories I didn't dare look. And there in the darkness, I closed my eyes and I pretended Emil was Otto. I don't know what was going through his mind, or who or what he was thinking of, but before I knew it, we were on the bed and we were naked. And maybe it was because he touched me with such compassion, stroking my skin and kissing my hair, but before I knew it he was inside me. I wrapped my legs around him, my eyes still tightly closed, trying desperately to conjure images of Otto.

But, of course, he wasn't Otto. And as he began to moan with pleasure, I was brought to my senses.

'No!' I cried.

But it was too late. He'd finished. And everything collapsed in that instant. I felt myself sinking further and further, shrinking smaller and smaller. Emil lifted himself up and out of me, and horror swept in on his wake. I'd meant today to be a memorial for Otto, but I'd betrayed him in the worst possible way. The guilt was instant and overwhelming.

'Are you all right?' Emil whispered.

But I couldn't speak. I rolled onto my side and curled into a ball and began to cry.

'I'm sorry,' he said. 'I thought you wanted—'

'I want you to go,' I gasped.

'But—'

'Please!'

I heard him get up and get dressed. Then he came back over to the bed.

'I'm really sorry,' he whispered.

And then he left.

Of course, looking back on this now, with the benefit of so many years of hindsight, all I see in that room are two people traumatised by war and loss, clinging to each other, trying desperately to breathe some kind of comfort into each other. But back then, all I could see was a traitor. I was the one who deserved to have 'WHORE' painted on my door. Not only had I betrayed Otto, but I'd betrayed him with his friend.

Again, the healing power of hindsight makes me feel that Otto would have understood. He loved us both so much, and he knew the horrors of war better than anyone. But this is now and that was then, and of course, it was impossible to shake off the shame of what I'd done – because I'd fallen pregnant.

SAGE

March 2018

Sage stopped reading and took a breath. Elizabeth's father was Emil. Her grandfather was Emil. She quickly skimmed back through the manuscript, searching out mentions of his name, and of course, the name Claude. This revelation felt just as good to her as if it had been Otto. Emil had been so brave. He'd done so much for the resistance. *And this is who you are from*, she imagined Florence whispering to her across the table. The granddaughter of two courageous freedom fighters. Sage gulped as the full enormity of this fact sank in. For so long, she'd felt so ashamed and so confused about who she really was. Her whole life seemed to have become a sham – but that was just her online persona. Her true self shared the same genes as Florence and Emil.

Her heart broke as she thought of how ashamed Florence had felt at supposedly betraying Otto. When Sage had read the account of how Elizabeth was conceived, all she'd felt was love for Florence and Emil. But what had happened next? How and why had Florence abandoned her baby? She turned the page on the manuscript and continued reading.

FLORENCE

1945

The morning after my fateful encounter with Emil, I felt so low, I genuinely feared for my sanity. Instead of comforting me with memories, as I'd hoped it might, Paris seemed to be taunting me, tainted by my betrayal and crammed with reminders that I'd lost the two people I'd cared about the most – Otto and Bessie. Thankfully, a deeper instinct for self-preservation kicked in and I decided to go in search of Sylvia. Shakespeare and Company had been shut down by the Germans in 1941 after Sylvia had refused to sell a German officer her personal copy of *Finnegan's Wake*, but perhaps it would now be open again.

When I got to rue de l'Odéon, my heart sank. The Shakespeare and Company sign had been painted over and the store was empty. I stood there for a moment, unsure what to do. Sylvia had owned an apartment on the fourth floor above the shop. Perhaps she still lived there. After a moment's hesitation, I rang the bell. Nothing happened. I tried one more time and was about to leave, when the door opened a crack.

'*Bonjour,*' came a voice from inside. It didn't sound like Sylvia.

'Hello. I'm looking for Sylvia Beach,' I replied, peering through the crack of the door into the darkness.

'Who is it?' the voice muttered.

'Florence. Florence Thornton. We used to know each other. Before the war.'

'Florence!' The voice grew considerably louder, and no longer sounded French. It sounded American. 'Dear heart, is it you?'

The door flew open and there stood Bessie. Or a version of Bessie, anyways. She was so much thinner, her trademark bosom shrunk and her hair cut into a short sharp bob.

'What the hell?' was all I was able to say.

She grabbed my arm and pulled me through the doorway. 'I thought you were dead,' she gasped.

And finally, all the pain I'd been carrying since Otto's death came spilling out of me. I collapsed into her arms and let out a cry that sounded more like the keening of an animal.

It turned out that after Bessie had been set upon in the street, she'd sought refuge with Sylvia, who'd provided her with a safe haven in her apartment. Although it felt wonderful to be reunited with my dearest friend, it didn't take long for me to realise that my old friend was gone. Whatever Bessie had been through at the hands of von Fritsch and then the French, she was never able to speak of it. Just as I wasn't able to talk about how I'd betrayed Otto. It was as if the spark that made Bessie who she was had been well and truly snuffed out.

We huddled together in my room on Place du Tertre for weeks, barely going out. Talking only about the old days in New York, as if our time at Le Flamant Rose had never happened.

And then the sickness and missed periods began. At first, I tried to deny what was happening, but my body kept showing me proof, in increasingly unsubtle ways. Then one day, when Bessie caught me hurling my guts up in the bathroom yet again, she figured out the truth. I told her it had happened from a one-night stand with a stranger. Somehow, this felt less shameful to me.

Bessie was excited at the news. 'It's a new life. It's new hope,' she said, rubbing my back as I retched. But all through my pregnancy, my dread and shame grew. When I imagined holding the baby, I knew that all I'd see was evidence of my betrayal gazing back at me. I was terrified of what this would do to both of us. And in my traumatised state, I truly believed that the baby would be better off with adoptive parents, a mother *and* father who'd be able to love it without complication.

I didn't seek any medical assistance during the pregnancy. I wasn't afraid of something going wrong. I was so desperate, I would have welcomed it. But the pregnancy continued without incident. And in March 1946, I went into labour in my room on the Place du Tertre, with my fairy godmother Bessie by my side to deliver the baby. Bessie had been so sure that once I saw the baby, I'd feel differently. But looking into that tiny innocent face for the first time and seeing Emil staring back at me, practically broke my heart in two.

'I can't keep her,' I cried, overcome with exhaustion and sorrow.

And so we cooked up a plan to leave her in Sacré-Coeur, as I knew the nuns would take good care of her. I took her there first thing in the morning, swaddled in a towel inside a hat box. Before I left her, I took off my locket. I'd been planning on leaving the whole thing with her as some kind of protection, but I couldn't bear the thought of having nothing left of it to remind me of Otto, so I snapped off the back and put it in my pocket. Then I put what remained of the locket around my baby's neck. I also placed a scrap of paper in the box beside her, with the name 'Elizabeth' written on it. I'm sure that whoever ended up adopting the baby would have given her a name of their own choosing, but in my mind, she has always been Elizabeth, named after my truest friend, Bessie. If she ended up with half the courage and kind-heartedness of her namesake, she will have been OK.

*

Bessie and I returned to America as soon as I was fit enough to travel. I left her in New York and made my way back home to Arkansas. I'll never forget my daddy's face the day I walked through the door.

'Florence!' he cried, his eyes filling with tears. 'You're home.'

He was a man of few words, but he always said the right ones. Returning home had such a bittersweet effect on me. As the woods and mountains healed me, my regret at leaving my baby grew. So, when I sought solace in the arms of an old school friend and fell pregnant again, I saw it as a chance to make amends. I poured everything I could into being a good mother to Sam, trying not to think about the fact that he had a sister out there somewhere. The only way I could cope was by filing that chapter of my life away, pretending it had never happened, the same way I'd dealt with the loss of my own mother as a kid. But then my eightieth birthday came lumbering over the horizon like a storm cloud.

Eighty. Holy cow, does that sound old! Now I feel death's presence at my shoulder again, but this time, I'm not afraid or fighting it. I'm excited at the thought of finally being reunited with Otto. And now I have nothing left to lose, I want to tell his story. Our story. Maybe I've left it too late. Maybe no one will want to know what we went through. The world has moved on. But I see through Hunter and the folks he helps with his horses here at the farm, that war still wounds in ways that might be invisible to the naked eye, but scar a person to their very core. My daddy once told me that he believed trees were the wisest creations on God's green earth because they grow close enough to give each other shelter but far enough apart to allow each other to thrive. He said that he wished us humans could live like trees. I wish that, too. And I hope that my story encourages people to do so, allowing each other the space to grow in their own unique ways, but supporting each other, always.

SAGE

14th June 2018

Sage began climbing the steep stone steps, her gaze fixed on the beauty of Sacré-Coeur up ahead. Finally, she was here, walking in her grandmother's footsteps. It was a very strange sensation to actually be in the place she'd read so much about, the place that had prompted the chain of events that had ultimately led to her very existence. She wondered which of the steps Florence's suitcase had come undone on. She'd read that scene so many times now, she could practically see the hot and flustered Florence, in her trouser suit and fedora, right in front of her. She could also see Otto with his floppy hair and irresistible grin, picking up Florence's stockings and handing them to her.

Not for the first time since learning of her grandmother's story, Sage thought about the magic of serendipity, and how on any day and at any time, you could meet someone, or discover something, that would transform your life forever. In the three months since she'd gone to Arkansas, Sage's life had changed beyond all recognition. And now here she was, in the place it had begun, completing the circle. She reached the top of the steps and gazed up at the basilica. It really was breathtaking. Elizabeth had never wanted to go back there. To her, it had always represented the scene of her abandonment. If only she'd known the truth, Sage was sure she would have felt differently.

Taking the small cobbled street that wound around to the left, Sage made her way towards the Place du Tertre. Just as Florence had experienced all those years before, she smelled the sweet aroma of the crêpes before she arrived. She took a moment and gazed around. The square was exactly as she had pictured it. There were the bustling restaurants, there were the people sitting at tables outside, laughing and chatting, and there were the artists at their easels. As Sage made her way around the square, her heart began to pound, thinking of Florence's feet treading that very same path, time and again over the years. She thought of the night Florence and Emil had walked this same way, on their way to the moment that would ultimately bring about Elizabeth's birth. It was a very strange and powerful feeling.

And then she saw it: La Crémaillère. She'd already looked the restaurant up online, so she knew it was still there, but nothing had prepared her for the flood of emotions she experienced as she took in the restaurant front and the nondescript door at its side, leading to the apartments above. She gazed up to the windows at the very top of the building. One of the shutters was open, and for the briefest of moments Sage imagined she saw Florence gazing out at the tree. And there was a tree, right outside the restaurant, stretching up to the window. It must have been planted there after the war. Something about this fact filled Sage with hope.

She checked the time on her phone. It was a few minutes before eleven. She hurried back around the cobbled square, this time picturing Florence doing the same, with baby Elizabeth swaddled inside a hat box. If only Florence had realised she had nothing to be ashamed of. If only she'd kept Elizabeth. But then the path of Elizabeth's life would have been so different, and Sage would never have been born.

When she got to the front of Sacré-Coeur, Sage sat on one of the steps and pictured Florence doing the same, the night she thought Otto had forgotten her, the night they were reunited.

She imagined a man's voice calling, 'Florence!' and then she thought of her grandfather doing the same, the year the war ended. Three lives, crossing on these steps and creating their own piece of history.

Sage swallowed hard and felt for her locket. Now that it was whole again, it felt like an even stronger link to Florence and Elizabeth, and indeed to Otto. As the church clock began striking eleven, she thought of her own part in their shared history. She'd had the idea to try and get Florence's story published as a book as soon as she'd finished reading it. Her desire to do something, coupled with her grandmother and Otto's wishes for their story to be told, made it seem so obvious. She'd hurried through to Sam and told him of her plan and he'd been over the moon.

When she'd started reaching out to literary agents, they'd all been excited to hear from her – no doubt seeing pound signs at the prospect of a shamed influencer's confessional. But when she'd told them it was her grandmother's story she wanted to tell, they'd been less enthusiastic. So Sage had pitched a revised idea, one that wove the story of her own fall from grace into the synopsis. The irony was, her story hadn't turned out to be a fall from grace at all. At least, not as far as Sage was concerned. As she'd sat at the dining room table in Arkansas, typing Florence's words into her laptop, then writing her own responses, she'd realised that what was actually happening was more like a rebirth. Just as a caterpillar has to dissolve into a pool of liquid inside the cocoon before it can become a butterfly, the old, online version of herself had to die in order for her true self to emerge. And getting to know her grandmother had helped her learn exactly who that true self was.

As the clock finished striking eleven, she stood up, just as Florence had stood up all those years before, to greet Otto and then Emil. She felt so happy, she could barely breathe.

'Sage?'

The sound of a man's voice broke her reverie. She turned and saw Hunter striding up the steps towards her, holding two cups of coffee, a beaming smile on his face.

'Wow,' he exclaimed as he handed her a drink and took in the panorama of Paris spread out beneath them. 'This place is something else.'

Sage nodded, and as Hunter put his arm around her shoulders and pulled her close, she pictured Florence, Otto, Emil and Elizabeth spiralling above them in the air like wild eagles. Kindred spirits, bound together forever.

A LETTER FROM SIOBHAN

Dear Reader,

Thank you so much for choosing to read *An American in Paris*. If you enjoyed it, and want to keep up to date with all my latest releases, just sign up at the following link. Your email address will never be shared and you can unsubscribe at any time.

www.bookouture.com/siobhan-curham

Although I've been a published author for twenty years now, *An American in Paris* is my first historical novel. Researching the Second World War in such depth was fascinating and deeply moving, and I can honestly say that I've never been more affected by writing a book. The whole process was made all the more powerful by the fact that I wrote it during the pandemic while the UK was on lockdown, and immersing myself in the characters and their story provided a welcome escape. While I was writing I had the following quote from the American poet Robert Frost pinned to my desk: '*No tears in the writer, no tears in the reader. No surprise in the writer, no surprise in the reader*', which I used as a motto to work by. It ended up being a very emotional experience! I hope that reading *An American in Paris* surprised and moved you, and if you did enjoy it, it would mean the world to me if you would write a review. I'd love to hear what you think, and it will make such a difference when it comes to

helping new readers discover the book, which is critical for me
as a brand new historical novelist!

I always love hearing from my readers so please feel free to get
in touch via my Facebook page, Twitter, Goodreads, Instagram
or my website.

Thanks so much,
Siobhan

Siobhan Curham Author

@SiobhanCurham

@SiobhanCurham

www.siobhancurham.com

ACKNOWLEDGEMENTS

First and foremost, I want to thank my lovely editor, Cara Chimirri, for asking me if I'd like to write a novel set during the Second World War, which in turn has led to the most rewarding creative experience of my writing career. Thank you so much, Cara, for this wonderful opportunity and for being such a sensitive and astute editor. Huge thanks also to Kim Nash, Peta Nightingale and the rest of the Bookouture team for being so proactive, caring and supportive of their authors – signing with you is a real dream come true. Much love and thanks to Jane Willis at United Agents for being such a fantastic agent. I've said it before and I'll say it again: knowing I have you by my side makes such a positive difference to my writing career and I'm so grateful for all you do.

Researching for this novel was a painstaking process and there are two books in particular that I'm indebted to: *Les Parisiennes* by Anne Sebba, which helped so much when it came to the background details of life in occupied Paris, and *Leap Into Darkness* by Leo Bretholz and Michael Olesker, which inspired the scene on the train from Drancy. I really hope I did that scene justice and helped keep the story of what happened to Bretholz and the other people on that train bound for the concentration camp alive. I'm also full of gratitude and awe for all of the brave women and men who sacrificed so much working for the SOE and the French Resistance. Reading their stories was breathtaking and humbling and again, I hope I've done their bravery justice.

Huge thanks to my UK family for all of the love, support and fun times: Jack, Michael, Anne, Bea, Luke, Alice, Katie, Mark aka Treasure, Beardy Danno and John – I love you. And much love and gratitude to my American family for inspiring so much of Sage's story once she gets to Arkansas – not to mention solving the riddle of 'biscuits and gravy'! Marybelle Ervin, Sam Delaney, Charles (Chuck) Delaney, David Ervin, Gina Caperton Ervin, Justin Snowden, Lauren Hardin, Lacey Ervin Jennen, Rachel Kelley, Mitch Freeman and Amy Fawcett, to name but a few!

I'm eternally grateful to the following friends for always being so encouraging and supportive of my writing: Tina McKenzie, Sara Starbuck, Linda Lloyd, Sammie (and Edi) Venn, Pearl Bates, Stuart Berry, Charlotte Baldwin, Steve O'Toole, Lexie Bebbington, Marie Hermet, Coline Pagoda, Mara Bergman, Jennifer Merritt, and Thea Bennett. I can't tell you how much your support means to me. Ditto Abe Gibson, Paul 'Ebbsy' Ebbs, Nick Tomlinson, Mary Esther, K-Ci, Victoria Connelly, Nicole Regelous, Nessie Mason, Celine Vial, Jessica Huie, Donna Hay, Kate Taylor, Sarah Leonard, Jonny Leighton, Reg Always Wright, Stephanie Lam, Tony Bell and Nathan Parker. Huge thanks also to the wonderful writing community I've amassed over the years through my writing workshops: Tony Leonard, Michelle Porter, Liz Brooks, Miriam Thundercliffe, Dave Moonwood, Rachel Swabey, Jim Clammer, Ade Bott, Paul Gallagher, Meriel Rose and the rest of The Snowdroppers. Jan Silverman, Patricia Jacobs, Mike Davidson, Mavis Pachter, Phil Lawder, Julia Buckley, Gabriela Harding, David Stroud, Barbara Towell, Mike Deller, Pete 'Esso' Haynes, Lorna Read and the rest of the Harrow and Uxbridge Writers. Big love to Lara Kingsman, Lesley and John Strick, Pete Barber, 'Captain' Iain Scarlett, Anita, Gill, Gillian, Claire Gee-Gee, Karen Edlin, Rebecca George, Graham and Shirley and the rest of the Nower Hill crew. And thank you to Kayhan for making me laugh till I snort (in a very attractive way of course) and showing me that men like Otto really do exist.